NO PLACE FOR A LADY

NO PLACE FOR A LADY

ANN HARRIES

BLOOMSBURY

First published 2005
This paperback edition published 2007

Bloomsbury Publishing Plc, 36 Soho Square, London W1D 3QY

A CIP catalogue record for this book
is available from the British Library

ISBN 0 7475 7896 6
ISBN 13-9780747578963

1 2 3 4 5 6 7 8 9 10

Typeset by Hewer Text Ltd, Edinburgh
Printed by Clays Ltd, St Ives plc

www.bloomsbury.com/annharries

AUTHOR'S NOTE

Not being very fond of novels about war, I was surprised to find myself writing one. I blame this aberration on my last novel, *Manly Pursuits*, for which I researched into the Jameson Raid and grew increasingly fascinated by the chaos created by army discipline during wartime. This was most terrifyingly realised in the contradictory behaviour of General Lord Horatio Kitchener, also known as K of Chaos. When it became apparent to me that the racist system of apartheid in South Africa was to a large extent founded on the outcomes of the Anglo-Boer War, I took up residence in various war museums in order to find out more.

To work in these spaces dedicated to instruments of death turned into an unlikely pleasure – mainly because of the friendly, helpful librarians, too numerous to mention by name, who often made inspired contributions to my research. I would like to record my heartfelt thanks to all of them, in particular the staff of the South African Museum of Military History in Johannesburg; the Anglo-Boer War Museum in Bloemfontein; and the National Army Museum in Chelsea for their interest and encouragement. Equally, my eyes were opened by vivid tours of battlefields and black and Boer concentration camps given by Elria Wessels in the Bloemfontein and Paardeberg areas, and further north round Pretoria and Belfast by Rykie Pretorius.

Among the many histories of the Boer War which I read, Sir Arthur Conan Doyle's account was particularly riveting, as was, of course, Thomas Pakenham's. But the book I found most revealing was the collection of Emily Hobhouse's letters, immaculately edited by Rykie van Reenen, which inspired the evolution of a central theme of the novel. A visit to the Wellcome Trust library in London provided me with information about lepers on Robben Island at the turn of the nineteenth century, and I found interesting details about the regulations for the Army Nursing Service Reserve in the Red Cross archives, again with the help of staff.

Extracts from the telegrams and correspondence of Milner, Roberts, Kitchener, Chamberlain, and other non-fictional figures, are taken from the archives. All the Hobhouse letters are actual transcripts from Rykie van Reenen's *Boer War Letters of Emily Hobhouse* (Human & Rousseau, 1984).

I owe a special debt of gratitude to my loyal and inspired editors, Rosemary Davidson and Marion McCarthy, and to my ever-patient agent, Maggie Noach. I am also forever grateful to the eagle eyes and discerning taste of my well-informed copy editor, Robyn Karney.

Thanks also to the many academics who promptly answered sudden e-mailed queries, and even sent me extremely interesting and often unpublished material. Their interest and enthusiasm was invaluable, as was that of friends and family who lent me useful books and introduced me to knowledgeable people.

I gratefully acknowledge financial support from Southern Arts, and the Society of Authors in London.

Finally, a note of apology for the repeated use of 'kaffir'. This now derogatory and racist word was in commonly accepted usage during the period of the novel's events, and for purposes of historical authenticity I could not avoid using it.

Ann Harries
Overberg, South Africa
March 2005

One

Cape Town, 17 March 1899

One morning Patrick Donnelly strolled down the steep streets of the District, enjoying the appreciative glances of women and kicking idly at the occasional rat. Behind him the mountain reared up like a great stony wave about to break, with all the houses of the District clinging to its lower slopes like specks of foam; beyond lay the harbour, fluttering with the sails of tall ships. And further out, in the blue eye of the bay, the leper island bulged. Already the smell of blood rose from the slaughterhouse below.

There was something fluid in the young man's movements that distinguished him from other pedestrians: a swing in the shoulders, a suppleness in the hips, a buoyancy of footwork: he could have been sauntering in time to a tune in his head. He was jauntily dressed in blazer and boater, though a glance at his trousers and boots revealed them as well worn, even shabby. His boater was tilted at an angle so that his dark, well-oiled hair was at least partially visible. A green ribbon fluttered on the breast pocket of his blazer, which itself was striped in a variety of shades of that verdant hue. Yet nowhere was this colour more intensely concentrated than in the young man's eyes which flickered emerald every time a pretty girl swayed past.

Although Patrick Donnelly had an appointment to keep in the city's great harbour, it was not his style to hurry, and he paused on the busy Parade to practise his new grin in a stall of window-glass and mirrors. He arranged the left side of his mouth into a careless half-smile, and narrowed the eye above it suggestively. A dozen smirks blossomed back at him: he was satisfied.

'And a happy St Patrick's day to ye, young Patch!' cried Mr O'Brien, the coal heaver, on his way back from a night shift at the docks, and similarly adorned with bright green ribbon. 'And may the snakes never get ye!'

'Oh, don't you worry, it's the snakes who's afraid of *me*!' retorted Patch, undoing his smile quickly. He had indeed chased a cobra out of his landlady Mrs Witbooi's kitchen on the slopes of the Mountain – or rather, the snake had slowly coiled and uncoiled its way out, hooded head erect and forked tongue fluttering so fast it seemed to belong to some other creature in the cobra's body. Never mind that it had taken a couple of hours for his pounding heart to beat normally and his hands to stop shaking; no one had seen *that*.

It was Mrs Witbooi who had put him on to the morning's mission. Two days ago she'd said, 'There's a job waiting for you at the harbour. All you have to do is turn up at the Gateway for the interview, nine o'clock Thursday morning. Ask for Dr Simmonds.' It so happened that Patch was at that moment suddenly unemployed and in urgent need of cash, so this was good news – until she added, looking up from the chillies and ginger she was chopping, 'You like lepers, don't you?' and refused to be drawn any further.

Now a young woman called to him from behind terraced buckets of cut flowers: lilies, roses, dahlias, marigolds, all turned their faces to him with an accusing air. His heart sank, for when Mrs Witbooi's daughter Fancy was angry she was dangerous as any snake. Her dark face blazed with passion. 'I waited till ten o'clock last night!' she yelled from a thicket of hostile sunflowers. 'Where were you?' Her gaze swung wildly round her stall as if looking for something to throw at him, a stone jug, perhaps, or a bucket full of thorned roses.

Patch ducked in advance. Fancy had a surprisingly accurate

aim. She had once knocked him out with a hurtling chamber pot in mid-argument. Dammit, he'd meant to avoid the flower market. 'Well, top of the mornin' to ye, Fancy!' It came naturally to him, when charm was needed, to adopt the Irish brogue he'd learnt from the nuns. 'Sure, did anyone ever tell you that you're the most beautiful girl in the District? In Cape Town? In the Colony?' As his knowledge of geography did not extend much beyond these boundaries he added, with dramatic emphasis: '*In the whole wide world!*'

This eulogy did not appear to achieve the desired effect. 'Don't try that fake accent out on me!' Fancy shook her head scornfully, but her gaze softened as it settled on his self-deprecating half-smile. 'It's actions, not words I want.'

The unconscious thrust of her body roused him but he was not going to be distracted from his plans. 'Sure, I must be off now,' he cried, raising his boater in mock-politeness. 'I'll celebrate St Patrick with ye tonight instead, ye'll see if I won't!'

He skipped along the broad avenue lined with palm trees that led to the docks. Fancy's image tumbled through his head in all its brilliant colours: her black hair gleaming with blue lights; her teeth whiter than the sprig of jasmine behind her ear; her brilliant red skirts; her blue blouse checked with lemon yellow; and beneath it her warm brown breasts. But Fancy must never find out his intentions, not till he was safely out of the way. He wasn't ready for wedding bells, not yet, but she was persistent. He slowed down to his former lazy saunter.

He was passing the orphanage convent of Our Lady of Mercy where he had spent his entire childhood and early adolescence, till three years ago. Perhaps he should slip into the little church to ask his plaster parents on either side of the altar for advice on his future. His mother, azure-eyed Mary, brushed back the folds of her powder-blue cloak to reveal the seven swords of sorrow stabbing right into her heart, with blood spilling all the way down her long white frock, while his father, poor old St Joseph, held Baby Jesus out of danger, away from all those dripping blades. In spite of her wounded heart (and each sword represented a terrible sin of mankind) she gazed sweetly at Patch every time he came to visit her. There was sadness in that gaze, for Patch was a wayward son. The reason why he was unemployed was that he'd just lost his job as salesman in Mr Feinstein's shoe stall on the pavement of Dover Street, high up in the District. Who'd have thought the old man would have noticed he'd borrowed three pairs of patent leathers for the night, when competing in the Tivoli Talent Contest with the Trusty Trio. The Trio was made up of Fancy's brother Johan; the limey Cartwright, recently arrived from England and hoping to make his fortune on the gold-fields in Jo'burg but unable to wrench himself from the District; and of course himself. Johan, famous for his hair-dressing innovations, had plastered their coifs into the three mountains of Cape Town: Patch had Devil's Peak with its open-mouthed profile; Cartwright had Lion's Head over one ear and Signal Hill over the other, which made him look as if a dog was sleeping on his head; Johan had the great flat-topped Table Mountain perched above his forehead, so that he somewhat resembled Frankenstein's square-headed monster.

One of the nuns stared at him coolly as he entered the church, resisting his hopeful smile. Strange how they still held his childhood behaviour against him when he'd left the orphanage so long ago. Why had they never allowed him to be an altar boy and swing the incense up and down the aisle all over the congregation, and ring the four-tongued bell at the consecration of the host into Jesus' flesh-and-blood body? He still felt an ache of disappointment about this, but now he could see Mary with her outstretched hands, already welcoming him into the dim interior of the church.

Q56 *Is the Blessed Virgin our Mother also?*
A 56 *The Blessed Virgin is our mother also because, being the brethren of Jesus, we are the Children of Mary.*

It was just as well Mary had taken on these maternal responsibilities in spite of being a virgin, as his own flesh and blood mother had dumped him with the Sisters of Mercy eighteen years ago when he was a few days old, with a mother-of-pearl rosary wrapped round his hand to show he was Roman Catholic. 'Sure, you came without the invitation,' said scornful Sister Madeleine, as if he should have got permission to be born. 'You could have been put in a shoe box and thrown into the sea, like many an unwanted baby.' He still had bad dreams about this: the cardboard box came bobbing towards him on the slithery oceans of the night, inside it a lifeless boy-child curled up, his tiny hand fisted against his chin.

The nuns believed in getting permission. If you asked, please, sister, may I wet the bed? they'd have said, yes, my child, but if you just went ahead and wet it without asking, they whipped out the bamboo stick, specially cut from the thicket by Jonas the gardener, and beat your bottom, leaving thin red stripes criss-crossed all over it, and a trace of blood. If Sister Madeleine was really angry with you she'd make you sit in a tub of water and then beat your wet bottom, till it felt it might burst into flames. It was as if the nuns wanted to thrash his spirit into a shape of their own, and turn him into someone quite different from Patch Donnelly. Well, they hadn't suc-ceeded, had they, but he didn't hold it against them, though he'd have liked a little kindness sometimes.

The air in the church was still heavy with incense from the early morning Mass, the altar rails festooned in green satin ribbons to celebrate the saint's day. He felt a surge of pleasure, as if this display were there to celebrate his own name. He dipped his fingers into the bowl of holy water in the porch but just as he was halfway through the sign of the cross, a bugle call and a drum roll sent a thrill through his body. 'Sorry, mother,' he whispered to the patient statue, and sped out into the brightness of the day to watch the Tommies march past. The regiment was newly disembarked to judge from their grey skins but they marched with a brisk precision, a boyish bugler leading the way. He felt a twinge of envy. How much smarter *he* would have looked at the head of this pith-helmeted, khaki-clad parade – why, that little bugler could be no more than fourteen years old, a mere child, look at his smooth, smug face!

He at last reached the harbour. Cape Town was now the busiest seaport in the world, it was said, something to do with the gold and diamond fields up north and all the merchants and mining men hurrying there to get rich – not to mention all the Tommies arriving, now that war over the gold seemed likely. In fact, merely to walk into the dockland was to find yourself in another country, for the whole place was seething with foreign sailors who shouted to each other in strange languages – and within the arms of the harbour a whole city of tall ships rocked and shuddered with the sweep of the tides and the flurry of the wind, a city of masts and riggings and ropes and ladders that rose from the decks of a hundred different sailing vessels: three-masted frigates, four-masted barques, square-rigged schooners, tea-clippers, yachts – all with their sails furled and their flags a-flutter and their hulls creaking impatiently. A Dutch sailor who spoke perfect English had told the incredulous Patch that every single rope had its own name and that each rope was attached to a different sail, each sail also having its own name. Not being of a maritime disposition, the only sail Patch could remember the name of was the mizzen topgallant which the Dutchman called *grietje*, being the last sail visible to poor sad Mar-*grietje* standing on the *dijks* of Holland and waving to her sweetheart as he sailed off over the horizon. The steamers, lacking the glory of sails, had a different appeal as their funnels slid over the far edge of the bay, one by one, leaving a ghostly trail of smoke after the boats themselves had disappeared.

Now he pushed his way among the already drunk seafaring men until he arrived at last at the door of the Gateway to Africa tavern. Gusts of tobacco smoke and raucous laughter burst out of the gloomy inn, entwined with the thin wail of a sailor's hornpipe. In a sudden fit of nervousness Patch fingered the miraculous medallion which hung round his neck.

'Oh Mary, Mother of us, send me a sign. Tell me if I can work among the lepers. For I am afraid.' He could feel the small raised image of Mary, long beams of light radiating from her hands. The beams heated up beneath his touch till they nearly burnt his fingertips. Already he felt bolder.

But once he was inside, so thick was the smoke and so crowded was the interior with Jack Tars from all over the world regaining their land-legs with rum and brandy, that he could not see anyone who might be his new employer. He pushed his way to the bar counter. 'Know someone Sinning here?' he asked Isabella whom he knew well. 'I'd say just about everyone here's sinning, me dear,' she grinned, pouring a large tot of Cape Smoke into a glass. 'But if it's Doctor Simmonds you want, he's under the stairs.'

In the depths of the tavern, beside a rickety flight of steps, a solitary man sat at a table. A sign bearing the legend INTER-VIEWS leaned against a pewter mug. So gloomy was the position the interviewer had chosen that Patch could not decipher his features until he hovered at the table's edge, uncertain how to proceed. The man, whose lower face was shrouded in an unfashionably cut black beard, glanced up at him with sharp eyes. 'You Patrick Donnelly?'

'I am, sir,' said Patch in a voice drenched in humility. He removed his boater and smoothed his hair.

The interviewer stared hard at him for a few moments, as if gauging his very essence. For several minutes, it seemed, he continued with his fierce exploration of the young man's face, until Patch was obliged to rearrange his features into a more ingratiating composition. 'Sit down,' said the interviewer, finally; then leaned over and narrowed his eyes. 'Do you have a hard heart, boy?' he asked, in sepulchral tones.

Patch looked down at the left side of his chest. He thought of Fancy, from whom he was fleeing; of Sister Madeleine's beatings; of his own abandonment; and a shadow passed over his tender young features. 'Yes, sir,' he declared. 'Hard as nails.' He curled his long limbs into the small chair and tapped the mug hopefully. 'Or as hard as this tankard.'

The doctor raised his thick eyebrows in mock amazement. His teeth shone in his beard. 'The name's Jack Simmonds. I'm the doctor at the leper hospital on the Island.' He looked deep into the green gaze of the young man. 'You're not afraid to separate husbands from wives or parents from children, should they try to come together? By force, if necessary? According to the Leprosy Repression Act.'

Patch swallowed, though his mouth was dry. 'N-no, sir.' He had not thought of this. Oh Mary, Mother of God, come to my assistance. He had thought only of getting away from the District to that cowpat of an island dropped into the dead centre of the glittering bay, an island inhabited by convicts, lepers and loonies, the outcasts of society, where he could feel at home and earn a bit of money.

'You're not afraid of catching leprosy?'

'A leper lived among us in the District,' murmured Patch. 'Not one of us caught the disease.'

'You are right,' said the doctor. 'Yet leprosy is spreading. Amongst both white and coloured classes. We have wealthy Dutch farmers on the Island as afflicted as the most wretched Hottentot or Kaffir. And a considerable number are closely concealed on the mainland, carefully hidden by their friends and family.' He paused for a moment, frowning. 'We still know little about the causes of leprosy. Some believe it is contagious or at least communicable by means of a cut or sore; others that it is inherited; yet others that the bacterium is present in saliva and snot. Also in more intimate bodily discharges.' He looked meaningfully at the young man. 'The guard's job is to keep husbands and wives apart. And to make sure they don't try to escape to the mainland in their flimsy home-made boats.'

'Is there no cure?' Patch slid his eyes towards the empty tankard.

'In certain ways the disease may be temporarily arrested. But as a rule it goes steadily from bad to worse, until death removes the patient from a life that is almost worse than death.' The doctor's voice was dreary; then, noting how the colour had drained from the young man's eyes, he added: 'But on a more positive note, the system sometimes throws off the disease – it cures itself. I call such cases "self-cured". I know of several such cases. The extremities may be lost, but the ulceration heals. The disease never returns, even though perforating ulcers may re-occur on the body due to the continued presence of the diseased bones. In my view such ulcers are not the *symptom* of leprosy but the *result*.' He could see Patch growing restless. 'You can start on Monday. Seven pounds a month. Every third weekend off.' As Patch did not reply he added, 'It's not all doom and gloom, you know. We even have a sea-water swimming pool. And some of the women have done wonders with their gardens.' He looked to see if this meant anything to Patch; paused a minute; then said, 'Come across to the Island with me now on the *Tiger* and you can see for yourself. Don't take any notice of the lunatics and convicts on board. They won't be your responsibility.'

There was something weird about the Island, as if it was inhabited by a desolate spirit which welled invisibly out of the sea and infected the sharp heat. Black crocodile's-teeth rocks fringed its ragged shores waiting to bite into passing boats. Dr Simmonds wasn't affected by it. He showed Patch round the lazaretto with some pride. 'Six pavilions for the men, five for the women. Whites, kaffirs, coloured folk all in separate pavilions. And here's the sea-water swimming pool.' A few malformed kaffirs splashed about in the pool with a nun looking on. 'And a church.' They walked along a gravel road which led away from the sea. He pointed to a neat white-washed building surmounted by a cross. 'Designed by the same young architect who built Cecil Rhodes' house. Herbert Baker. Rhodes recently donated a bath chair for white female lepers.' The doctor shot a look at Patch's blank face. 'Let's go inside.' It was a sin for Catholics to enter non-Catholic churches but Patch didn't want to seem lily-livered. No stained-glass windows or statues with bleeding hearts in Herbert Baker's church. No smell of incense. No tabernacle with a red light burning to show Jesus was in there. Also no pews. 'Where do they sit?' whispered Patch. He touched the medal under his shirt.

'They don't.' The doctor cleared his throat vigorously, a sign, Patch would later learn, that there was a quotation coming. '*They also serve, who only stand and wait*. Or *lie* and wait.'

Patch ignored this. They were walking towards a male pavilion now. A fearful stench filled the salty air. 'Kelp,' said the doctor quickly. 'Rotting seaweed.'

The kelp looked alright to Patch, swirling near the rocks like the tangled brown hair of some prehistoric monster.

'There's also the women's huts for those who seem to be self-cured. You'll see some fine vegetables growing out of this sea sand. Carrots, cauliflowers, and the like. Even an English country garden or two.' He glanced at the young man as if waiting for a response; then lapsed into silence. They walked past the evil-smelling hospital. Next came the lunatic asylum. A couple of men were digging out potatoes in the grounds of the building. 'They all suffer from delusions. Either they're the Tsar of Russia, or someone is out to kill them. I know little about madness. It's not my field.'

It was a relief to get back to the coastline and scramble along a rough path. A flock of black cormorants rose gracefully from the rusting hull of a shipwreck. In the far distance you could see Cape Town, pale and shrunken beneath its towering trio of mountains. The sea that lay between the Island and the mainland looked so calm you'd think you could easily swim the distance. If you could swim, that is.

The air began to thicken and cool and a mist descended swiftly, seeping into their clothes, blotting out the bushes just ahead. A foghorn started to howl. The doctor began to declaim. '*Fog everywhere. Fog up the river, where it flowed among the green aits and meadows; fog down the river, where*

12

it rolls defiled among tiers of shipping and the waterside pollutions of a great and dirty city. Read any Dickens, Mr Donnelly?'

'What's *aits*?' enquired Patch cleverly.

'An ait is a small island in a river or a marsh. You find them in the mouth of the River Thames.' Doctor Simmonds stopped walking. 'We won't see much in this Dickensian smog. Let's get back to the jetty. Watch out for snakes.'

Snakes? Should he tell his cobra story?

'Mole snakes mostly,' continued the doctor. 'They live underground most of the time but they like stealing seabirds' eggs. You sometimes see them sunbathing on the beaches. Their venom won't kill you.'

The mist was melting as suddenly as it had arrived. 'Look at that!' exclaimed the doctor, pointing at a turbulence in the sea.

The air above the movement of waves was suddenly alive with flying creatures: gulls spiralled above a ring of exultant dolphins who soared and dipped around a hump of barnacle-encrusted rock, which now heaved itself upward before plunging deep below the water's surface. A gigantic forked tail emerged, twitched, then plunged as well. In the minutes that passed a small black shape surfaced, new and shining. The dolphins leapt higher. Patch's sharp eyes could see their grinning snouts, and he could hear their high-pitched song, borne on the chill wind.

'Protecting the whale while she's calving. Scaring off the great white sharks.' The doctor was whispering. 'You don't see that often.'

Patch stared at the circle of celebration, all foam and frenzy and flight. For a hot moment he felt he might grow wings himself and join the mother and child.

'I'll take the job,' he said hoarsely. The Blessed Virgin had signalled.

Lord Ramsay's Country House, England, August 1899

'And then he lifted the finger bowl to his thick, purple lips, and drained it to its dregs!' announced Lady Mary Fenwick.

'*Quel horreur!*' Louise screamed, half-covering her eyes with her monogrammed table napkin and glancing hopefully at the young captain beside her. Further down the table Sarah sat polite and still among her startled neighbours.

'And how did Her Majesty respond?' If his daughter's screech had caused a flicker of impatience across his features, Lord Ramsay spoke in his usual measured tones from the head of the table, his expression impassive.

'Just as you would expect.' Lady Mary raised her fingers to her lips and swallowed an imaginary liquid, her face even more expressionless than that of her host. In fact, Lord Ramsay had heard this story many times but never, as it were, from the horse's mouth: Lady Mary had actually been present at the infamous dinner at Buckingham Palace where the Boer president, Paul Kruger, had gulped down the water in his finger bowl, eschewing the champagne (Veuve Cliquot 1860) which bubbled in the crystal glass at his right hand.

'And how did the table react, my dear?' prompted Lady Ramsay, hoping that this would not bring on another shriek from her intemperate daughter. Oh, if only Louise could be more like calm, angelic Sarah. What a shame that none of Sarah's seriousness – to say nothing of her quiet beauty – had rubbed off on Louise, whose face was now red with hilarity as she prepared for Lady Mary's reply. And just look at that *décolletage*! Louise's plumpness was flagrantly exposed in the plunge of her neckline, where her large, powdered breasts seemed likely to break their banks at any moment. Whereas Sarah . . . A pale gauze shimmered at her bosom as if a cloud had floated down from heaven and settled round the ivory shoulders of this gentle creature who smiled wanly as the entire company, imitating Lady Mary, lifted imaginary finger-bowls to their lips and swallowed in unison. Louise's high-pitched giggle soared above the wheezy chuckles and snickers that broke out across the table.

'To the shape of the earth!' called out some wag, for the Boer president was known to believe the planet to be not only round as a cake but also flat as a pancake. This sally was greeted with yet further mirth, and raised glasses.

'I should not make fun of my fellow countrymen,' murmured the elderly representative from the Dutch embassy to Sarah, whose melancholy expression suggested disapproval.

'Oh, is Mr Kruger a Dutchman?' There was no hint of censure in the young woman's face. What lovely eyes she had, dark and brimming as the canals of Amsterdam, though much purer. And in their depths, some unfathomable sorrow which made him want to crush her to his chest, to comfort her.

'I believe his ancestry is German.' The under-secretary sighed. 'But these Boers all speak some sort of ancient Dutch now. Most of them are the descendants of gardeners who settled in the Cape over two centuries ago. They have become a savage race, like plants grown wild. How different from our sober Dutch burghers.'

'I lived in Holland as a child,' ventured the quiet young woman. 'My father is a botanist with a special interest in tulips.'

'His name?'

'Robert Palmer,' said Sarah modestly.

'Mr Palmer! I am a great admirer of your father's scientific papers. I believe he is writing an exciting new book about the history of our tulips.'

'Yes, indeed, he is halfway through it.'

Mynheer de Haas smiled. He could sense that this young lady would not care to engage in botanical discourse but, being reluctant to end the conversation, he enquired with a fatherly interest, 'And do you speak Dutch, Miss Palmer?'

'*Ik kan een beetje onthoun.*'

'Well I never! That is very impressive. You must speak Nederlands every day!'

Sarah blushed at the extravagant compliment. 'I learnt to speak it when I was three years old. Or rather, I heard it, then spoke it – like any child.

The arrival at Lord Ramsay's side of the white-gloved butler holding a silver tray upon which lay a telegram distracted Mynheer de Haas, though he very much wished to continue this discussion about the early acquisition of linguistic skills with this charming young lady. Lord Ramsay opened the missive then muttered something that could not be heard, though the word 'war' slithered down the table. '*Sham!*' roared several Members of Parliament simultaneously; others bellowed '*shame!*' and, within seconds, the dignified dinner table was transformed into a replica of the House of Commons, with several of the younger gentlemen leaping to their feet and shaking their fists, while every male person seemed to speak or shout simultaneously. For their part, the ladies began planning war-time meals and arranging knitting circles to provide spare socks for the poor Tommies, even though it was by no means clear that war had actually been declared. Foremost among the women was Louise, excitedly offering her services to nurse the wounded in South Africa, and calling upon Sarah to join her: '*And we'll insist on a field hospital, won't we, darling?*'

Sarah very much wanted to tell Louise that one of her pads was visible beneath the yellow hair which her maid had struggled in vain to twist, curl and pin in such a way that the innate thinness of the strands was disguised. But a couple of pads – or *rats*, as Louise called them – were necessary to give the coiffure extra volume so that it bulked out fashionably all round the head, the upward sweep of the hair culminating in a hidden knot. Sarah patted the back of her thick dark hair, twisted into a simple chignon, in an effort to mime the warning message, but Louise had already turned her attention to the military gentleman at her side.

'So – it is war with South Africa then?' Sarah could make no sense of the gabble all round.

No, in fact, war had not been declared, but that wily old Kruger, he of the purple lips, had conceded a five-year franchise and ten seats in his parliament to the British immigrants on his goldfields: the very concessions the High Commissioner, Sir Alfred Milner, had been demanding from Kruger three months earlier at the Bloemfontein conference! Sarah was puzzled. Surely everyone should be delighted? But no. It seemed that Kruger was not to be believed, he would bluff up till the cannon's mouth. What about the unfair tax and tariffs? Milner and Chamberlain must show their strength; fifty thousand Boer troops equipped with the most modern artillery and ammunition were gathering in the Natal colony with the intention of capturing the ill-defended port of Durban; ten times that number of British troops must be sent immediately; there were no end of reasons why this gesture of conciliation, this step-down, must be dismissed out of hand.

Thank heaven it was now time for the ladies to leave the table and allow the men to drink port, smoke cigars, and pronounce on how the war could be won before Christmas. How much better everything would be if *they*, the house guests, rather than Chamberlain and Milner, were running things, thought Sarah as she slipped her hand into Louise's; their opinions seemed founded in rock, and their abilities almost godlike. Yet (the disloyal thought lurked in her head), as the mines actually belonged to the Boers, surely they could do what they liked about franchises and taxes and dynamite monopolies and all those topics which had been discussed *ad nauseam* all through dinner? But who could answer this question without making her feel absurd? Sarah could think of no one; Louise had only contempt for Boers, though knowing absolutely nothing about them other than that they drank from their finger bowls and believed the world was flat.

Once the women were together, they fell to discussing more immediately relevant matters such as upcoming weddings, outrageous legacies, disappointing children, ridiculous Paris fashions, plans to landscape the garden or sack the gardener, or buy a second town house. It was with some relief that Sarah accepted Louise's suggestion that they slip out on to the balcony which led from the drawing room. The night air was deliciously cool and scented with jasmine.

But something had happened to Louise. All her vigour and excitement had vanished. Instead, large tears rolled down her cheeks, carving a trail blackened by kohl through the powder.

'Darling, what is it?' Sarah blotted her friend's face with the edge of the silk shawl she had sensibly thrown round her shoulders.

'He ignored me! He scarcely looked at me!'

'Who? Captain Marshall?'

'All he could talk about was blooming old South Africa. I tried and tried to attract his attention, joking and teasing and so on, but no, that fat old baggy-eyed president was far more interesting.' She wrenched the 'rat' from her head and allowed her hair to sag about her face. 'As for this wretched thing – why can't my hair stay up neatly like yours? I do believe that not even a hurricane would ruffle a single hair on your head.' But she pressed Sarah's hand warmly, and managed a sniffly smile.

'But what about your plans to go to South Africa if war breaks out?' Sarah was skilful at diverting negative thoughts. 'It's a wonderful idea. You're just the right sort of nurse for the wounded soldiers – the life and soul of the ward. Anyway, Captain Marshall looked very dull to me.'

'He kept staring at you, didn't you notice?' Louise gulped.

'I was too busy trying to speak Dutch to the old man next to me.' Sarah put her arm round her friend's hot shoulders. 'You looked lovely tonight, you really did. He's just a boring old officer. Let's walk in the garden for a while.'

'I was serious about going to South Africa,' said Louise as they strolled through the shrubbery together. She was calmer now, and ready to plunge into some new excitement. 'If only to escape from Ma and Pa and their never-ending nagging. But you must come with me, dearest, or I shan't go.'

'Let's wait for war to be declared first,' suggested Sarah, experiencing a tremor of alarm. What if Louise really did leave the country? She had become dependent on her friend's madcap temperament to shake her out of her lethargy; she basked in the warmth of her vivacity, and felt her own mysterious melancholy evaporate in her company. The two young women had known and loved each other since Sarah's return from Holland, when they attended the same school for young ladies. Then, a few years ago, thinking that hospital wards were inhabited by eligible young physicians, Louise had decided to train to become a nurse. Sarah, who had no idea of what she wanted to do with her life, rather lamely followed suit. Though her inclinations tended towards poetry and dreaminess, she felt the need to be useful without becoming a 'do-gooder' – the type of bossy woman much despised by her family. Now the two friends nursed in the same London hospital, and Sarah felt her deficiencies even more keenly. Although patient and capable at her work, she knew she lacked flair. Nurses should be jolly and try to cheer their patients up, and Louise's laughter could be heard from one end of the ward to the other; she could rush down the long aisles between the beds like a hurtling bullet; she had already been promoted to ward sister, her talent and energy having been recognised very early. She seemed so sure of what she wanted, and *who* she wanted, and – perhaps more importantly – who she was. If only Sarah had a tenth of Louise's exuberance . . . but try as she might, she could not infuse her own spirit with enthusiasm. Yet Louise, for her part, would gladly exchange her hearty laugh and social confidence for her friend's doe eyes and slight figure upon which even a nurse's uniform draped itself elegantly. How painful it was when the apprentice surgeon or the junior physician sought out Louise just so that he might find favour with Sarah. It was maddening that Sarah felt nothing for these attractive young gentlemen, whose interest Louise tried vivaciously but unsuccessfully to divert to herself. Perhaps a war *was* the answer: going abroad to an exotic foreign land under such dramatic circumstances would surely offer opportunities rich in romance.

Extract from Telegram: Sir Alfred Milner to Mr Chamberlain, Colonial Secretary
30/9/99 I would urge sending out troops themselves as fast as possible, even if on first arrival they cannot move far for want of transport. Every reason to think we shall be fighting in Natal in a couple of days, and at considerable disadvantage at first in respect of numbers

Chamberlain to Milner
5/10/99 Every provision for the Army Corps is now going on as rapidly as possible. The real sticking point of the whole business was the necessity for purchasing an enormous number of mules. Of course the animals will have to be raked up in all parts of the world. It is unfortunate that our troops, unlike the Boers, cannot mobilise with a piece of biltong and a belt of ammunition, but require such enormous quantities of transport and impediments. I hope your health continues to bear the strain well.

Milner to Lord Selborne
11/10/99 War dates from today, I suppose. We have a bad time before us, and the Empire is about to support the greatest strain put upon it since the Mutiny.

London, November 1899

Three weeks after Boer forces invaded Natal, a newly qualified young nurse arrived on Sarah's ward. Sophie Harris was of a Quakerish disposition and considered to have an unhealthy interest in politics, but her connections with Liberal grandees ensured that her position in the hospital was secure. Besides, she was dedicated to her work with an almost religious intensity. Other nurses were efficient, reliable, kind, clever, considerate, but Nurse Harris was devoted to duty and overflowing with love. She raced up and down the ward aisles with her patients' bedpans as if she were bearing gifts of frankincense and myrrh; she bathed old women and soothed them sweetly as she cleaned their smeared buttocks; with a bright smile she pushed fallen wombs and bladders back into tired bodies. In fact, so much did she seem to take delight in these scatological and gynaecological tasks that nurses on her ward contrived to leave such operations to her as often as possible while they washed the patients' upper torsos or administered medicine or bandages or meals.

Louise disliked Nurse Harris intensely, partly because she did not laugh sycophantically at her jokes or ward banter, but also because the new nurse made no effort to disguise the plainness of her features; surely she could dab a splash of colour to those sallow cheeks, and pluck away the excesses of her ferocious eyebrows? On top of everything she was known to be pro-Boer, which meant her instincts were treacherous. How annoying that she was so blameless in her work and actually enjoyed the tasks which Louise as her superior would have given her in revenge. Sarah, on the other hand, began to take an interest in young Sophie Harris, whose purpose in life was so clearly defined but who apparently still had time to hold strong opinions about the war – no doubt very different from the ones she had heard at Lord Ramsay's dinner table two months earlier. How enviable to hold a strong opinion; Sarah's head was awash with indecisions, queries, doubts and riddles which were unable to resolve themselves into the relief of certainty.

One morning, while she and Nurse Harris were making beds together, tucking the starched sheets tightly into each corner of the mattress so that not a crease or a wrinkle was visible, she found herself murmuring, 'I wish I could understand why we are at war with a handful of farmers.' This conundrum had not left her, and as she and Sophie folded blankets, smoothed coverlets, and plumped pillows until each bed reached the point of packaged perfection required by Louise, she felt that this young nurse might be able to help her.

Sophie briskly pushed a pillow into its case. 'So you understand?' Her words were scarcely audible as she shook the pillow until it doubled in size.

'No, not at all,' said Sarah hurriedly. 'But I am confused.'

Sophie appeared to be ironing the bedspread with her strong hand. Ripples of Egyptian cotton (for this was the ward for the lower classes where linen was not permitted) fell into place. 'It so happens I am attending a private meeting on Thursday night. These issues will be discussed. Your attendance would be welcome.'

A flicker of danger set Sarah's heart beating fast for a minute. It was an unexpectedly pleasant feeling.

'May I come with you?' she whispered. 'I am not on duty that night.'

Sarah's Diary

4 November 1899

This evening I did something which Father and Mama – to say nothing of Louise – must never know about. I attended a meeting of the South African Conciliation Committee, a newly-founded organisation which many see as having Boer sympathies. My parents are totally anti-Boer now that war has actually broken out, in spite of having had some early sympathy because of their fondness for the Dutch nation.

On the face of it, my journey to Bruton Street with Sophie seemed innocent enough. We discussed the possibility of nursing in South Africa and she surprised me by saying she would like to join the Army Nursing Service Reserve but had already discovered that three years nursing experience are necessary before one can be sent out. I told her that I was seriously thinking of offering my services as well. I did not mention that Louise had already volunteered and had been accepted, though no date is set for her departure.

Once we arrived at our destination in the heart of Mayfair we were courteously received by an elderly butler and directed into a drawing room filled with an equal number of men and women, many of whom were Quakers. Both Lord and Lady Hobhouse, our Liberal hosts, were present; though elderly and a little frail they spoke with a vigorous commitment that strangely excited me. It turns out that Sophie is distantly related to the Hobhouses. They enquired after my parents' health after Sophie had introduced me (like so many, Lord Hobhouse too admires

Father's botanical studies and is looking forward to his new book on the tulip history.)

A number of extra chairs had been brought into the drawing room on the seats of which were displayed pamphlets with titles like *Shall I Slay My Brother Boer?*, *Sir Alfred Milner's War*, *Olive Schreiner's Appeal*, all for sixpence each. I paged through them as we awaited the speakers, and was much struck by the passion expressed in these slender volumes.

When we had all taken our seats, three members of our gathering positioned themselves behind a table laden with books and pamphlets. Two of them were women: one, who was small, dark and quick, led in a twinkling gentleman in a bright blue waistcoat who was clearly blind; the other was a tall woman with a strong, sympathetic face. Her honey-coloured hair was drawn simply beneath a large hat, laden with autumn fruits and leaves, and her slightly melancholy grey eyes regarded us with intelligent interest as Lady Hobhouse introduced the trio. The blind gentleman was Leonard Courtney, Member of Parliament for Liskeard, Cornwall, a world expert on South African affairs and the president of the South African Conciliation Committee. The small woman beside Mr Courtney was his wife, Kate, chairman of the Women's Industrial Committee (Sophie whispered to me that she is sister of the notorious Socialist, Mrs Sidney Webb), and the lady in the autumnal hat was Lady Hobhouse's niece, Emily.

I have to say that I was momentarily intimidated by the self-assurance and natural power of these women who clearly regarded themselves as in every way equal to their men; I felt pretty sure that they must be involved in the battle for women's suffrage as well. It was another world: men and women communicating with each other on equal terms – but a world that required the woman to be a serious creature who was not afraid to say what she thought, vigorously and in public.

Mr Courtney rose to speak, Emily Hobhouse made no effort to disguise the reverence she felt, her eyes filling with admiration as she turned her face towards him. He immediately disabused me of my pro-Boer expectations. The purpose of the committee, he said, was to establish *goodwill* between the British and Dutch races in South Africa, and to convince the British public of the urgent need for Conciliation in that country. He spoke with fine authority and a deep, resonant voice, and assured us that the committee took no sides in the South African dispute, but longed only for a peaceful solution. It would be unrealistic to call for an end to war while Boer forces were still on British colonial territory: the aim of the Conciliation committee was to educate the public into understanding the true situation in South Africa and correct the many misrepresentations in British newspapers. Facts received from the best and most reliable sources of information were now being disseminated by ardent workers who enlightened their audiences at meetings in village halls and drawing rooms throughout the country. The keynote was calmness and control with no suggestion of temper or exaggeration. Miss Emily Hobhouse was just such a campaigner. Already she had experienced jingoistic fury when speaking in public, and had remained unruffled. Courage was needed to persuade the British people to see the situation in perspective and Miss Hobhouse did not flinch from her crusade, even when insulted or abused by those whose patriotism clouded their judgement.

I suppose my parents and Louise's family would consider Emily Hobhouse to be one of those ridiculous do-gooders who spend their time defending and supporting the underdog instead of looking after their own families, yet when she rose to speak I sensed something powerful in her presence and was instantly captivated. An immense energy enlivened her words, which brimmed with good sense instead of the hysterical ranting I had half-expected. She admitted that she had only recently taken an interest in South African matters, being moved to do so because of her horror at the injustice of war between Britain and the Boers. She had spent many long hours in the British Library learning of the history of the Boer people, and had also had the privilege of being educated in

26

this respect by Mr Courtney. There was a strange irony in the South African demography, she told us. In the early part of the century many Boers had trekked into the harsh interior of South Africa to avoid British rule which went against their culture; those who remained in the Cape were known as the 'loyal Afrikaners'. Now, with the flood of British immigrants to the gold-rich Witwatersrand, there were actually more British than Boers in the Republic of the Transvaal, while there were more loyal Afrikaners in the British Cape Colony! Now the might of British imperial power was trying to bring down Kruger, led by that arch-imperialist, Sir Alfred Milner. Every government in Europe except Turkey opposed Britain's entry into such an unequal war with a simple, pre-industrial society. 'I am a British patriot,' she said simply. 'I am primarily concerned about my own country and whether or not she is acting on the highest principles of justice and humanity.'

A storm of questions followed her speech, not all of them as sympathetic as I might have expected. One of the questions was addressed by a small handsome woman, plainly dressed, whose manner I found quite frighteningly aggressive as she spoke at top speed, demanding to know how the greatest source of wealth in the world could be run successfully by a few primitive farmers with no experience whatever of the complexities of mining, banking, investing etcetera. There was plainly no alternative but for the capitalist forces of Europe to be given full political rights on the Boer parliament. And was Miss Hobhouse aware that as a result of the Jameson Raid the Boer forces, far from being a defenceless pre-industrial society were now armed with the most modern guns and rifles: each of the fifty thousand fighting burghers of the two republics was now equipped with at least two rifles, one of which was the new small-bore magazine German Mauser. Mr Courtney replied that there would soon be three or four times that number of fighting British. He pointed out that Kruger was offering a quarter of the Boer parliamentary seats to the 'uitlanders'. (I made notes, having no head for figures.) Sophie whispered to me that the handsome outspoken woman was

Beatrice Webb herself, a founder of the Fabian Society with her husband Sidney.

Another question (which turned into a rather lengthy speech) from an elderly gentleman reminded us that the Boers and the British were not the only races in South Africa; that there was a large indigenous population who by far outnumbered the colonists, and on whose labour the mines, being exceedingly deep, were entirely dependent; and how did Miss Hobhouse feel about the abusive way the Boers in their republics treated these indigenous folk, known as 'kaffirs'? It was well known that Boers, believing kaffirs to be an inferior race, pushed them off pavements, treated them like slaves, whipped them mercilessly, and forced them to carry documents which prevented them from moving about the country freely. One article of faith was shared by all Boers: to deny political rights to anyone whose skin wasn't white. Mr Courtney skilfully replied that the British mine-owners and Randlords treated these kaffirs far worse by exploiting them even more than the Boers: they locked the miners up in compounds and split up families; they subjected them to terrible dangers in the deep level mines with little or no compensation for death or injury, and more iniquities that I failed to note, my hand having grown tired of scribbling.

'Yes, but the Cape has a franchise for all civilised men regardless of skin colour!' shouted Beatrice Webb. 'And if Britain wins the war that franchise will be extended to the whole of South Africa.' She sat down with an air of finality, as if her observation settled the matter.

'I'd like to see that in writing, signed by Her Majesty the Queen,' replied Mr Courtney, not a little sorrowfully.

I left the meeting with a handful of pamphlets, my head spinning but much stimulated, even though not all my questions had been answered (I would never dare actually to ask a question from the floor, much as I might rehearse it, being too afraid to make a fool of myself). I now feel that I will definitely volunteer to nurse in the war. Somehow South Africa seems to beckon. What a fascinating country, riven by such different problems from those we have here.

The image of Miss Hobhouse has remained with me today: her mournful eyes as she spoke of injustice; her determination to educate the public. Sophie told me a little about her earlier life. Apparently she is recovering from a broken heart (and Sophie's private opinion is that much of the sadness in her gaze originates from this unfortunate condition). After living with her clergyman father for over thirty years in a remote Cornwall village, she took flight to America upon his death. There she ran a temperance campaign among alcohol-addicted expatriate Cornish miners in Minnesota; then, to the horror of her family (who, though Liberal, are just as snobbish as any Tory, according to Sophie), fell in love with a grocer, or was it a butcher? She bought a ranch in Mexico, expecting to marry him, and squandered her small legacy on his escapades. Then something went wrong and she returned to England, still a spinster but determined to start a new life. Until recently she had been working for the Women's Industrial Committee, of which Kate Courtney had been chairwoman till her husband became blind.

I felt very affected by this story and not a little envious that Miss Hobhouse's heart could be so moved by romance.

My own heart is yet unmoved. I have read many romantic novels and lovesick poetry in an attempt to stir it into action, but in vain. I can feel pleasure or pain for *other* people, but, left to myself, I feel nothing. I envy Miss Christina Rossetti when she cries triumphantly *My heart is like a singing bird whose nest is in a watered shoot*. How hard I have tried to coax my heart to sing when the apprentice surgeon or the junior physician declares his love for me. I whisper to myself Miss Rossetti's surging rhythms and melodic metaphors but, alas, there is only a dreary thud in response: my songbird has yet to be awakened.

Robben Island, December 1899

You'd think the bleeding war was happening in Cape Town, what with khaki drill and pith helmets jamming up the streets and pavements, and Tommies setting up camp on lawns meant for leisure. Patch had spent his day off swaggering along the beachfront in his new cream flannels, boater and verdantly striped blazer, Johan at his side sporting a new hairdo which resembled a small palm tree similar to those which lined the main road; Fancy leaning on his arm. Patch had bought her an ice cream and slipped his hand up her skirt while they sat on the rocks and watched whole regiments of Tommies erecting rows of bell tents along the Green Point lawns, and sweating in the heat.

It was getting difficult for the launch to weave its way back to the Island now that a forest of foreign ships had sprung up right across the bay. Patch and Dr Simmonds had had to struggle through the crowds of Tommies who'd taken over the docks and were already engaged in the purchase of cheap liquor and making appointments with local whores.

'Hospital ship from the motherland,' snorted Dr Simmonds as the *Tiger* nearly crashed into a great grey vessel with a red cross painted on its side. 'Must be filling up pretty fast.'

The Island's foghorn let out a groan as mist gathered and ballooned out towards the ships; a lunatic in the custody of a warder began to croon a melancholy response. The two men were leaning on the starboard rails, watching Table Mountain and Devil's Peak recede, all blue and dreamy, untouched by the Island's fog, with white buildings the size of crumbs spilt down the slopes and into the sea. Fancy had promised she'd wave her red skirt from the balcony of the Witbooi house, and Patch was straining his eyes to locate it when Dr Simmonds gave a great sigh. 'They won't even get a chance to stretch their legs when they go ashore, poor beasts.' The launch was nosing between two ships whose forward decks were crammed with horses. 'They'll get loaded straight on to railway trucks and get taken to the remount centre in Stellenbosch.' Although he received no reaction to these gloomy observations, the doctor nevertheless continued. 'Well, the penny's finally dropped. Britain has noticed that every Boer has six legs. I feel sorry for the poor buggers in the infantry who're going to have to learn how to ride that lot.'

Patch, having discovered a tiny flash of red up the District slopes, smiled with satisfaction. Perhaps when he turned twenty-one he might consider settling down with her . . . who knows? At least living on the Island, so lacking in temptation, meant he had saved up quite a bit for whatever might lie ahead.

That Methodist missionary man, Fish, leaned on the rails further down, keeping his distance. He came every week to tell the lepers Jesus loved them and would be waiting for them at the Pearly Gates if they converted. He had varying degrees of success: the Mohammedans preferred their own version of Paradise, and the Christians preferred to stay Anglican, Catholic or Baptist. The kaffirs fell for it every time and joined the Methodist church just before they died, thinking how lucky they were to have a lovely white-man's heaven, scrubbed clean and shining and ready for them to enjoy for ever and ever amen.

Now that the launch was getting nearer the Island, the temperature began to drop and that shadowy phantom seemed to well out of the rocks together with the mist, darkening the atmosphere, and causing the two men to shiver. 'Friend of mine's joined up,' said Patch, to keep away the desolation. The limey Cartwright had surprised them all by volunteering, and had been sent almost immediately to Natal (one way of going north for free, observed Johan) where things weren't going too well for the British. *We're sorting out them Boers*, said the postcard he sent to Johan. *We'll relieve Ladysmith, don't you worry*. This seemed optimistic as repulses, reversals and outright defeats were the order of the day as Buller struggled to cross the Tugela River and reach the besieged little town.

'Bloody fool,' muttered the Doctor. 'I wouldn't follow that chap Buller out of the garden gate.'

'You won't catch me joining up,' Patch reassured him. That morning Johan had mentioned volunteering, inspired by Cartwright's postcard. But there was a rumour in the District that this was to be a white man's war; no kaffirs, coloureds, Malays, Chinamen etc to participate in the fighting. Then Fancy had made them both swear they would never, ever join up, whatever colour you had to be to fight. In any case, Patch had a secret fear of horses. Even the ships loaded with those dispirited looking creatures made him feel nervous. So there was no way he'd volunteer and end up a mounted infantryman.

The launch cast anchor in the bay of the Island. Though a jetty was being built it was still necessary to be rowed by convicts in small boats to the shore. From there the men got carried to dry land on the backs of the convicts, clad and numbered in penal garb; the women were carried in chairs. Patch never felt entirely happy about clasping a murderer's back like an infant but the arrangement kept his feet dry, and he had just bought a pair of gleaming new boots with his last month's pay so he swallowed his pride once again.

Once on *terra firma* he and the doctor made their way past the wards of the lunatic asylum and the pretty whitewashed church. The mist made it difficult to see where they were going but both men knew the way well. Doctor Simmonds turned left towards the new wards for females in an advanced state of decay. *Oh that this too too solid flesh would melt* he murmured as they parted company. By now Patch knew that this was Shakespeare. The doctor sometimes invited him to tea in his little sitting room filled with books. 'Dickens, Milton and Shakespeare,' said the doctor. 'That's all you need.'

Doctor Simmonds was an Englishman who had been on the Island for twenty years. A reclusive man, the place suited him perfectly, its bleakness chiming in with his view of life. Of real life, that is. The life inside the covers of books was what he retreated to every evening, a glass of whisky at his side. He told Patch that opening a book was like opening a door to a house of many rooms leading into each other, each filled with strangers who became friends. You could leave by the door if you didn't get on with the company or the architecture. Patch liked Dr Simmonds, gruff and reserved as he was. Although the doctor made no effort to talk about personal matters, he had the feeling that his own slippery nature was completely understood by this man. Often he would leave with a slim volume under his arm. He enjoyed what he read, for the doctor had chosen accurately: Sherlock Holmes; some Kipling stories; a selection of poetry. At the orphanage the children had been allowed to read only the Bible, religious tracts, or the lives of saints; all works of fiction were regarded as sinful lies which would lead you into evil ways.

After a couple of months Dr Simmonds looked at him long and hard and said, 'Here's a lengthier book which might interest you.' The book was *Oliver Twist*. The door opened with a description of Oliver's birth, and Patch entered a world that reminded him of the District in its turbulence and lawlessness, with gangsters like Bill Sikes and Fagin skulking in dark doorways, knives in their back pockets. He felt a sudden wave of homesickness for the overcrowded homes, the noisy taverns, the pavements cluttered with hawkers, foreigners, kaffir workers, musicians, drunks, rats, pigs, cats and dogs chasing each other or being chased by outraged women or laughing children . . . and the Witbooi family, of course, who had taken him in when he'd fled from the orphanage. Mrs W treated him like a son from the start, no questions asked. He'd shared a room with Johan and two cousins who worked in the slaughterhouse by the Castle. How had motherly Mrs Witbooi come to know of this job on the Island? He'd asked her several times for her source of information but her lips were sealed on the subject and he'd stopped asking her to tell him.

So why did he remain? Was it just for the money? No, he was growing to enjoy the space and privacy of the Island. In the District you were lucky if there were just three or four of you to a room, coming and going at all times of the night. Here he had an entire bedroom to himself – which made him feel lonely sometimes, but which was also a luxury he'd never dreamed of. There were other leper guards but most of them preferred their own company. He was proud of his uniform (they'd had to lengthen the trousers). The Anglican nuns who worked in the leper hospital were more human than the Sisters of Mercy. Three meals a day were provided. He saw Fancy and Johan every three weeks and continued to sing duets with Johan in the Transvaal Tavern though the Trusty Trio was a thing of the past now with Cartwright gone. And he came back to his bedroom every night to find a cocaine-addicted detective, a maddened highwayman, and a traumatised orphan boy awaiting his return, for they could not resume their busy lives till he released them from their pages.

By the time Patch had changed into his uniform the mist had melted away. Glad to stretch his legs (unlike those poor horses), he set off on his evening tour of the Island, hurrying past the old ward devoted to male lepers in an advanced stage of the disease. A nauseating odour emanated from the ward, the evil effluvia of decaying bodies, but something else was floating from the ward – an unearthly whistling, as if the lepers inside were trying to blow into flutes made of bamboo or pipes of straw; the sound made Patch uneasy. Though he knew it was caused by tubes inserted into their throats to help them breathe, it made him think of ghosts and ghouls talking to each other about the afterlife, planning to drag him off with them into their weird spirit world which most probably was

Purgatory, the intermediate detention place, almost as bad as Hell except people could pray for your soul and get indulgences for you. He quickened his step.

It was a relief to get to the jagged shores and look at the waves endlessly rolling in, mere ripples at the moment, as if a giant pebble had been thrown into the centre of the ocean causing lazy circles to undulate all round the Island. At low tide, like now, they sighed placidly, hardly bothering to unfurl, but Patch knew that, in a few hours' time when the tide came in, they would transform into tigers with bared teeth and claws, thundering on to the shores as if straining to submerge the whole of the Island. Often the wind would join in, shrieking like a pack of demons through the cracks in windows and doors, trying to blow down trees and buildings, vying with the ocean for destruction. It seemed a miracle that everything was still standing the next day.

Patch's patrol took him right round the Island. He always liked to start with the view of Cape Town and the mountains, then walk on the sandy path to the other side where there was only infinite ocean. Dr Simmonds had shown him a map of the world where he could see that the same Atlantic Ocean that washed the shores of Cape Town washed also the shores of Ireland. That was a comforting thought. He liked to stand on the rocks and move his gaze over the horizon, trying to guess where Ireland was if you drew a straight line north. No matter that this view pointed west, as the setting sun now reminded him. The colours in the sky were turning violent mauve and pink and orange, as if God had daubed the favoured flamboyant colours of the Cape Mohammedans on the horizon with his heavenly paintbrush.

It seems the whole of mankind feels compelled to construct a simile when viewing a spectacular sunset, and Patch was no exception. Grinning at the image which had occurred to him, he continued his patrol along the beaches. He shouldn't spend so long gazing out to sea; his job was to look out for lepers. What about convicts or madmen though? He wouldn't fancy bumping into one of them at this time of day. He felt cold at the thought, then realised that the wind had suddenly risen and was slicing through his uniform.

He moved on. A lump of something dark and large lay on the wet sea sand that blazed purple and pink from the sunset. As he walked towards it – could be a drowned man – a husky Irish voice addressed him.

'Just take a look at that, will ye.'

He spun round. Sitting on a rock close to the sea was a leper woman with wild grey hair flying about in the wind. Even in the twilight he could see wet pustules and patches all over her skin. There wasn't much left of her nose.

'Look!' she commanded, waving the stump of her forearm in the direction of the dark shape. This woman shouldn't be here, but with his curiosity overcoming his sense of duty he obeyed her barked instruction. Then exclaimed in astonishment.

The lump was a large shark which fishermen must have caught earlier in the day. Alongside it were six full-sized seals, taken out of its stomach.

'You'd think that shark had given birth to those seals, from the look of it,' said the woman, not moving from her position on the rock.

'Strange shark that gives birth to seals,' mumbled Patch.

The woman put her head on one side and looked at him sardonically. '*I* gave birth to six seal pups, would you believe it?'

Spare me this, thought Patch. 'No, I would not,' he said.

'All boys,' she mused. 'Each one as different from me as seals from a shark.'

'You shouldn't be here,' said Patch sternly. 'You're not allowed beyond the fence.'

'Sure, d'ye think I'm going to try to escape? Build myself a wee boat like those others?' she sneered. 'I'll be off then, officer. Ye won't catch me breakin' the law.' She scuffled off towards her hut and he sniffed the air to see if she stank.

Patch followed her home, to make sure. He didn't go near the women's huts as a rule: the inner Island wasn't on his beat.

36

Her garden, which he'd seen briefly over the high hedge on his first visit with Dr Simmonds, took him by surprise: a little spot of woman-made beauty in the midst of all this desolation. Resolving to visit it the next day, he bade goodbye to the woman and finished his tour of duty as darkness fell.

But that night the wind howled itself into a frenzied storm and a fishing vessel splintered on the rocks and Patch was called to help rescue the crew. The next day, with the storm still raging and a search party out for two missing sailors, he was too busy to sneak off to view country gardens.

It was nearly a week later, on an innocently pleasant day, that Patch got to the garden. A little pebbled path wound its way through a mass of flowers, all shapes and sizes, as if Fancy's stall in all its brilliant colour and variety had been transplanted to that desolate hillock. You'd think some of the plants would've been flattened by the storm but they seemed untouched by the gale. Perhaps that's why she'd grown the hedge all round. He stood by the little wooden gate and feasted his eyes. She was picking the dead heads off one of her bright purple flowers with a remaining forefinger and thumb. 'Good garden.' He nodded condescendingly, as a patrol guard should. But in his heart he was excited; he drank in the fragrance that hovered, as seductive as the perfume of a woman.

'Come in and have a look,' she offered, wiping a strand of grey hair from her face.

The gate meowed as he opened it and he looked round for the cat.

'That ole gate needs oilin',' she said as she straightened herself.

He could see she was once beautiful, but had coarsened under the scabs and pustules. He could not think what to say. 'Your grass is green,' he muttered.

' 'Twould be a lot better if I had a proper lawn. You can see this kikuyu grass isn't taking. What I need is some good grass seed, sure I do.'

The concept of gardens was new to Patch. The District didn't have room in its crowded streets for gardens, though Mrs Witbooi tried to grow some nasturtiums in an old sink in her backyard. But this arrangement of path, riotous floral borders, grass, vegetables at the back, pleased him. It settled his mind.

He said, 'I can get you some grass seed when I next go to Cape Town.'

Her blue eyes gleamed. 'That'll be mighty kind of yer. There used to be an officer brought me seed for the hollyhocks and pansies. Now they seed theirselves.' Some butterflies were floating about on waves of honeysuckle scent. 'One thing's good come out of bein' here and that's this.' She nodded at the garden. 'I wasn't thinkin' about flowers and the like on the mainland. Too many other things to think about.'

'I must get on,' said Patch, in case she started to tell him about those other things.

He returned to his patrol round the edge of the Island. In spite of all the warnings three leper men had made a secret boat out of old tins and boxes. He was glad he hadn't been the one who'd discovered them; he might have let them get on with it. Mind, it would be even more difficult to get to the shores of the mainland now that there were so many ships in the bay, weaving towards the docks to deliver men, horses, ammunition, hay; or anchored at sea, waiting their turn. Patch enjoyed watching the schooners zigzag out of the harbour and across the bay. You could see the young boys working on the topsails, hanging from the rope ladders and clinging to the masts, the whole crew tacking, luffing, and generally out-witting the gusts of wind that wanted to blow the vessel back into the harbour. Then finally, sail by triumphant sail, the ship would slip beneath the rim of the ocean, sometimes into the setting sun. Would he ever get away on one of them? Ireland was where he wanted to go, to prove he was an Irishman. Perhaps he should save his wages to buy a fare . . .

As he leapt across rock pools and scrunched over the sea sand in his new boots, he was surprised to find himself thinking about the leper woman. He wanted to visit her garden again and learn how to make plants grow. What did she do to the thin soil to make them flourish?

When he got back to the hospital office he looked up her surname in the register of lepers. When he saw it was the same as his own he was startled. He clutched the rosary in his pocket, then the Miraculous Medal: *Help me, Mother of us all.*

That night he dreamt he was little Oliver sleeping among the coffins. He awoke, his body clenched into a question mark, and aching. A rash seemed to have broken out all over his skin but when he looked it was smooth and tanned as ever. Yet all day he itched and scratched.

The next day he visited the woman again. He stood at her gate in silence. She looked up from her cabbages and cauliflowers on the side of her hut as if she had been expecting him. A bitter wind swept between them. 'You forgot to tell me what sort of grass seed. I'm going to Cape Town on Saturday.'

With her forearm she brushed back a hank of greying hair blown loose by the wind. 'Buffalo is best. If you can get it.'

He paused. 'How long?' he said. 'How long since you've been here?'

She thought. 'Must be twenty years. They say they'll let me out when these have cleared up.' She tilted her head. 'But they'll never go. They're here for good.'

He could scarcely bring himself to speak. 'Do you see your family? Do they visit you?'

She laughed coarsely. 'I've six sons blown to the four corners of the earth. Priests, all of them, except the youngest. They wouldn't visit a leper mother if you paid them.'

'What's happened to the youngest then?' Patch fiddled with the loop of wire round the gate.

'Never met him. Except when he popped out of course!' She gave that harsh laugh again.

He looked at her in sudden disgust. She had laid aside her trowel and was rolling some tobacco into a crude paper tube.

'You couldn't bring me a mite o' baccy, could ye? They've clean run out at the hospital shop.' Her eyes were cunning, trying not to show her hope. She knew she was taking advantage of him. She hazarded an asymmetrical smile.

'I'll try,' said Patch shortly, and turned away before she'd ask for brandy as well. He touched the medal round his neck. The Blessed Virgin would guide him.

Sarah's Diary

23 December 1899

Here I sit curled up in my deck chair in the wind and rain, covered in wraps, as the *Dunottar Castle* heaves across the Channel. I think and hope I am at last entering into a new, brighter phase of my life. Already I feel the stir of anticipation, but not of course the wild excitement which Louise is experiencing. She has brought a huge wardrobe of extraordinary clothes, as well as Dolly, her lady's maid. I wonder when she expects to wear those outrageous creations, mostly from Paris. There is one evening dress made entirely out of khaki serge with gold fringes and ostrich feather trim, as khaki has become all the rage in the world of fashion. Only Louise could bring herself actually to wear such a garment.

My decision to apply to nurse in South Africa was taken in some trepidation, after several changes of mind. War is such an extraordinary development in my quiet life that I was not sure if I was strong enough to cope with the vicissitudes it must entail. I have to say the appearance in the *Daily Mail* of verses by Mr Kipling helped me to make up my mind. This great poet has written *The Absent-Minded Beggar* to raise funds for indigent families left behind by volunteers and reservists, and Sir Arthur Sullivan turned the verses to a thumping march:

> Duke's son – cook's son – son of a hundred kings—
>   (50,000 horse and foot going to Table Bay!)

Each of 'em doing his country's work (and who's to look after their things?)
Pass the hat for your credit's sake, and – pay! pay! pay!

And goodness me, the public *are* paying – I believe £340,000 has already been raised for the Soldiers' Family Fund. Now you can go nowhere without hearing the stirring sounds – from organ grinders to music halls, from street corner musicians to patriotic drawing-room concerts – and thousands have joined up as a result, for it is a recruiting song as well as a fund-raiser. Someone has etched the image of a bloodstained, bandaged Tommy pointing his bayonet at an (invisible) cringing Boer; we see this picture everywhere, on cigarette cases, tea towels, ashtrays, ladies' purses and so on. I was strangely moved by this heroic trooper, even though I feel my sympathies drifting towards the high aspirations of the Conciliation Committee and have actually attended several of their meetings. When dear Aunt Harriet presented me with a trinket box bearing this stirring image on its lid, I finally capitulated, and made my application to the Army Nursing Service Reserve. Within days I was called up – and so was Louise, who had been put on their lists some time back. We were of course delighted to find that we'd be sailing to Cape Town on the same steamer.

I feel sorry for Sophie as she would love to go to South Africa to see how things really are there. As she has not been nursing long enough to qualify for the Army Reserve Service, she has instead offered her services during her free time to the Conciliation Committee and is busy educating herself about South African history so that she too can address the public across the length and breadth of the country in an effort to educate the British people and promote peace as soon as possible. Brave, high-minded Sophie! She has even rehearsed some of her speeches with me, peeking only a few times at her notes, so I am unusually well-informed about the history and politics of South Africa. I have promised to send her detailed accounts of my experiences in the military hospitals – we have no idea where we will be sent.

I must say that our departure from Southampton this morning was quite extraordinary and made me feel I was indeed participating in a great moment of history. I think my parents were proud of me as we enjoyed a final cup of tea among uniformed officers and nurses in the first class dining saloon. We watched the huge mass of well-wishers who had crowded excitedly into the Southampton docks to wave goodbye to the *Dunottar*; they seemed to have covered every available space – some had settled on to the lattice work of dockside cranes, others perched on railway carriages, all waving flags and breaking into song (the Absent-Minded Beggar was a favourite); wives and children clung to sallow, khaki-clad Tommies who then poured in endless streams into the bowels of the ship, blanket rolls and rucksacks on their backs. And never have I ever seen so many varieties of *horse* in one small area! Filing up the high gangway to the forward deck where their stalls awaited them were horses of all shapes and sizes: pure Arabs, heavy drays and mules normally seen pulling omnibuses or waste carts, light hansom ponies, race horses – all jumbled together in a sudden democracy that must have amazed them as much as it did me. And the mailbags! There must have been a dozen letters for every soldier in South Africa coming up yet another gangway in a great torrent of leather bags. 'It seems the working classes have suddenly become literate,' remarked my father, who finds it hard to believe that his gardener or chimney sweep might be able to read, let alone write.

A sudden hush fell over the crowd as a train steamed up to the quayside. Out of it emerged a group of sombre-looking gentlemen, all clad in black. As they made their way towards the first-class gangway everyone's interest was focussed on a tiny, white-haired old man in frock coat and high hat, a mourning band around his right sleeve. The little man's sunburnt face and vigorous body suggested a disciplined, outdoor life, but his features bore the mark of suffering, which moved the crowd into voluntary cheers: *Hooray for Bobs! Hip hip . . .*

Father recognised the old man immediately as General Roberts, who has lived in India most of his life and won many battles. He has been appointed Commander-in-Chief, to replace Buller, who is making a hash of things in Natal. Apparently Roberts' only son was killed in action under Buller just last week. I have to say that General Roberts (or 'Bobs', as the Tommies call him) looks far too old for battle – Father says he is at least sixty-seven – but it is clear that he has kept himself very fit. Mother wondered if he'd brought his charger Volonel, awarded medals in Afghanistan for bravery along with his master.

I tried to look interested in my parents' chatter as we moved from the dining saloon to the upper deck rails where passengers were waving and throwing streamers to the crowd below. Dear Sophie had come to say farewell, but now, out of delicacy, had left me alone with my parents. I'm afraid that my mind was on the voyage to come, when the chill December wind at present tormenting my cheeks will become a warm breeze, scented with the spice of Africa . . . I could see Louise a little further down the deck, rolling her eyes at me as she tried to comfort her anxious mother who fears the worst. All around us more young women of high birth were bidding farewell to – or, more accurately, I think, escaping from – their families in order to tend the wounded and sick and lead a life of freedom. The excitement among them rivalled that of the crowds below but for different reasons: already they were glancing over their furs at handsome officers and laughing a little too hard.

Fortunately, a sharp little bell rang for the visitors to clear just as my parents began arguing about the amount of champagne Buller is reckoned to consume per day, and, after brief hugs and kisses, off they scuttled down the very gangway Roberts had climbed. Louise, having said goodbye to *her* parents, came to join me and press my hand. She and I will share a cabin for the duration of the voyage. I fear she, like the other females, is set on capturing the heart of an officer and nothing else will do.

Then the funnels began to trumpet like cows in agony; the crowds erupted into a sea of handkerchiefs; the band played some patriotic songs; Sophie and I clung to each end of a streamer which stretched to breaking point as the tugboats pushed and pulled until they had us the right way round; all streamers snapped and the great steamship began to hum and throb its way out of the harbour, with a flock of cormorants in its wake.

As I write this, I feel more than ever that my life is about to change fundamentally. It is an awesome sensation, inspiring me with both terror and hope. Would I have volunteered had the war been waging in some dark, European country? Is it sunshine and warmth that is attracting me rather than patriotism? Whatever the reason, I am prepared to risk my life for change.

Louise's Diary

25 December 1899

Sarah is spending Christmas Day scribbling in her diary so I am going to do the same, as everyone worth speaking to has gone to sleep. Mother gave me this very beautiful book in which to record my impressions of South Africa, but I shall use it instead to write about my adventures, my dreams, my anxieties, which of course I hide from everyone except Sarah.

The first of these concerns Sarah herself. It is indeed galling for me to watch the eyes of men light up as graceful Sarah drifts past. She does not cast them a second look, which seems to add to her allure. Perhaps if I lost some of my weight I would have more success in capturing the hearts of men. Already I am twenty-five, and not one offer of marriage. So unfair!

Well, now that that's off my not inconsiderable chest I shall write about last night's Grand Christmas Eve Dinner. The officers appeared in full uniform (which *does* have the effect of transforming frogs into princes) and we nurses could abandon our red and white. I wore my favourite salmon pink tulle and taffeta, and Dolly spent a whole hour attending to my hair with curling tongs and irons. At the end she sighed, 'Well, that's the best I can do!' and I felt like smacking her. I thought I looked rather fine, like one of those larger-than-life goddesses who loll on sofas or river banks in the paintings that hang on the walls of the galleries at home. Dolly was not sure about the jewelled band with the crimson ostrich feather I insisted on wearing round my head (partly to hold the wretched 'rats' in place) and murmured something about cowboys and Indians, but I was determined. The flair of feather gives one a certain brio that distinguishes one from unplumed rivals. Needless to say, Sarah agreed that it looked wonderful even though, as usual, it was *she* who looked effortlessly beautiful – in her simple white silk evening gown, with elbow-length satin gloves, and a diamond choker at her throat. I could weep. Why are women made so differently?

An impatient bugle call summoned us to dinner (it had already sounded three times, but if one is not ready one cannot appear!) and off we set at last, arm in arm, to have some fun. Everyone looked at us appreciatively as we entered the dining saloon, and I like to think the appreciation was not directed at Sarah alone. It was quite astonishing to witness how all the drab nurses had become beautifully dressed, jewelled and perfumed young ladies, their hair, previously hidden by stark white veils, now piled mountainously on their proud heads. We were given pride of place at the Captain's table, while the crowds of silly girls fluttered and giggled in the outer circles. A seasick little band, attempting gamely to render a few music-hall favourites for our entertainment, contributed to the festive atmosphere. I found myself seated between an old whiskered Colonel and a smoothly shaven young(ish) Captain; Sarah had similar neighbours on her side of the table. The Colonel at once tried to monopolise me, informing me gleefully (as if expecting me to faint in response) that the *Dunottar* carries thousands of tons of lyddite (a form of dynamite, apparently) in her hold, as well as a huge range of artillery guns – navals and howitzers, whatever they are. I told him that I very much hoped to be sent to a field hospital on the front. 'Out of the question!' he snapped. 'The battlefield is no place for young ladies. There are plenty of male orderlies there to attend to the wounded.' He looked at me accusingly. 'The role of women is to comfort, merely.' What a geriatric crowd these Colonels and Generals seem to be!

At this, Lady Weatherby, who sat opposite us, said that she was not a nurse, but had nevertheless come to help nurses and comfort the men. In her loud penetrating voice she assured us that she would do what she is told. Above all, she says, she can hold her tongue. I wonder. In addition to these skills, she and her maid are engaged in the task of knitting five hundred balaclavas for the wounded. I wondered what use they would be in the height of summer, but I too can hold my tongue – sometimes.

At the mention of balaclavas the Colonel swelled up. 'These voluntary offers are of no use at all unless there is an organisation capable of dealing with such offers, an organisation capable of efficient distribution!' he thundered.

Lady Weatherby cast him a withering look. 'I believe a lady in India has contributed sixty thousand handkerchiefs and one dozen walking sticks to the war effort,' she replied. 'But she has had the wisdom to present them to the Good Hope Red Cross Society – which is where my balaclavas will go, I can assure you, Colonel Summers.'

At last the officer at my side, feeling no doubt it was time the subject was lifted on to a loftier plane, spoke up. 'They say Mafeking should be relieved by the time we arrive in Cape Town. I had the good fortune to serve under Colonel Baden-Powell in India.'

Seizing my chance, I cried out in jest, 'B-P seems to be turning Mafeking into quite a desirable residence, wouldn't you say, what with Saturday night Gilbert and Sullivan and Sunday cricket! I imagine there must be many who quite envy the residents!'

I could see at once that this had not been received in the spirit I had intended. Oh, why do so few people have a sense of humour? I hurriedly added, 'Of course, I am only teasing. Colonel Baden-Powell is a great hero, and the residents of Mafeking are suffering terribly.' And then, quite against my will, I heard myself snigger, 'But it's quite astonishing how he can wear pantomime wig and skirts as Widow Twanky while thousands of Boers rain shells upon the city!'

'I fear you have your facts quite wrong,' said the Captain stiffly. 'First of all, Mafeking is no city but a mere railway siding in a desert. Secondly, though Colonel Baden-Powell may lift the spirits of Mafeking with theatrical entertainments, he will instantly resume his role of commanding officer in the event of a raid.'

I was plainly making no progress here, specially as the men at the table now launched into an interminable discussion about how at least the raid was drawing off the Boer leader General Cronje and the seven thousand Boer soldiers who completely encircled the town – I mean, railway siding – and kept up a steady bombardment on the good citizens of Mafeking. To my utter astonishment Sarah made a contribution. 'I am told that the kaffirs of Mafeking have been armed. I had thought this was a white man's war.' Her voice shook with nervousness as she spoke. How on earth does she know about such things? This sweetly delivered observation evoked a torrent of denials or excuses from the male company, who then speedily moved on to the other sieges in South Africa – I had not even realised that Ladysmith and Kimberley (where my diamonds come from, I'm told) were under siege. It does sound as if Britain is in need of the little man with the funny white beard, who has declined to join our celebration meal.

Later, as the champagne and good wines did their good work, the Captain began to mellow and applauded me for my courage in leaving home for the dangers of war. Just when I thought I was beginning to make my mark he leaned close to me, smelling rather strongly of claret by now, and murmured, 'And who, may I ask, is that well-informed young lady across the table? I saw you come in together, and had hoped she might be seated beside me.'

I was about to respond with a sarcastic remark when the ship began to lurch fearfully and several glasses and plates flew through the air in spite of the frames designed to fix them to the table. It was impossible to remain seated, and in any case most of us felt our heavy dinners rise out of our bellies and we rushed to the deck to 'pay tribute to Neptune' as our jolly, whiskered Captain calls our agonised vomiting into the ocean.

Sarah's Diary

27 December 1899

This morning, two days after Christmas, the *Dunottar* dropped anchor unexpectedly at Gibraltar. I was somewhat annoyed, or disappointed I suppose, at this mysterious diversion because Louise and I had planned a day out together on the island of Madeira, an excursion which I feared would now be spoilt by the delay in getting there. Still, it was rather exciting to be poised in the rugged crack between Africa and Europe, and while the other passengers gathered on the decks to admire the Rock, I preferred to stand alone on the other side of the boat and stare at the northernmost tip of Africa. I was lost in imagining the spice-laden smells of the markets in Morocco and the vast, shifting sands of the Sahara beyond, when Louise broke into my reverie. She tugged at my hand and begged me to move to the other side of the ship where the crowds were murmuring excitedly, although in some restraint. 'Come, dear, you must watch this!' Louise urged. She was quite determined and so, albeit reluctantly, I followed her.

At first it seemed a gigantic ironclad sea monster had risen from the Strait. Then the lofty control tower and heavy armaments of a great warship revealed themselves, silhouetted against a trail of glittering sunshine. I clutched Louise's warm hand for, in truth, a warship is a hideous thing, designed to strike terror into the hearts of all who observe her. Its massive guns were pointed straight at the *Dunottar*.

A launch bobbed beside the monster. From the bowels of the warship a long-legged figure came into view and climbed briskly down a gangway into the waiting vessel. The figure in the launch who approached our waiting steamship seemed himself to be forged from metal: his cold eyes staring scornfully ahead, the medals and decorations pinned to his chest flashing as if from his body itself. 'Oh my God! Isn't he gorgeous!' gasped Louise.

'The Lord of Chilled Steel!' exclaimed Lady Weatherby, who had put aside her knitting for the moment. 'I remember,' she went on, 'how he came to visit my dear deceased husband on some matter of state. Kitchener is so ill-at-ease in the company of women that Lord Weatherby requested the females to go out that evening, to save him the embarrassment that we would cause.'

I, too, found myself marvelling at Kitchener's appearance. 'Just look at that moustache!' I commented. 'How on earth does he manage to eat?' 'And he's not even married!' squealed Louise, ignoring my query.

The shaky little band struck up a curious rendering of *Rule, Britannia!* and Lord Roberts, in full military splendour with a plume of sportive ostrich feathers in his helmet (which raised his height by at least a foot) and a large sword on his hip, marched forward to greet his Chief of Staff. The jovial captain stood proudly by. But within minutes the two military men had disappeared into the bowels of the ship, followed by their uniformed staff. They kept away from the other passengers for the rest of the day and took their meals in their cabins where, apparently, they held endless councils of war.

1 January 1900

On this the first day of the new century I can already feel a lightening of my spirit, perhaps because we have just spent two glorious days in Madeira. What an exquisite island – *C'est le Paradis*! It is bathed in a light such as I have never before beheld. For it is not only the blaze of sunshine which drives away the mists in my mind and body, it is the clarity of the light – every leaf and petal glows separately, each demanding one's attention – and the sharpness and denseness of the shadows which one feels might permanently stain the land upon which they lie! The white houses everywhere have green jalousies and green verandahs, and little balconies from every window, with here a great pot of flowers, and there an overhanging creeper. The tiles are red, and many of the houses, overhanging the narrow streets, are five and six storeys high. In the market square is a tree of scarlet poinsettia in full bloom; and hanging over the courtyard of the old church, a brilliant, bell-like orange flower the name of which no one could tell me. As we moved among the cobbled streets we wondered at the overhead trellis-work curtained with flowers. Such flowers! Here a scarlet geranium in the niche of a castellated wall, there a mass of blue plumbago tumbling over the front of a house; azaleas, wildly extravagant and, most glorious of all, the bougainvillea in every shade of colour, purple over the rocks, flame-colour on one side of the street, and deep magenta on that trellised roof overhead. Glimpses of quaint interiors as we walk up, and of the terraces intersecting the houses. Mules and bullocks pulled sleigh-like carts made of basket work and canopied in cotton tapestries . . . can Cape Town possibly be as picturesque as this? I fear I am spoilt forever by the beauty of this little island.

All this is lost on Louise who has dedicated herself to trying to entrap Kitchener. Sometimes he is to be seen stretching his long legs on the deck with Bobs, but mostly they are locked in their cabins with their staff. Yesterday, however, as we were watching the whales near the ship spurting spray into the air, Kitchener suddenly appeared on deck and made the mistake of leaning over the rails to get a better view of these extraordinary creatures. Louise could scarcely believe her good luck, and immediately made a point of lurching up against the poor man with such vigour that he was obliged to shift his gaze from the performing whales and fasten it upon my friend's cheerfully apologetic smile. Words fail me as I try to describe the expression on Kitchener's face: *dread* perhaps gets closest to it. And then, before my very eyes, as Louise rattled off her false apologies for stumbling against him, I saw his dread turn into abject terror – clearly he would have preferred a thousand charging Arabs with scimitars drawn than have to exchange one word with a flirtatious woman. Babbling an incoherent excuse he rushed back into his cabin and left Louise still trilling her contrition . . . She has no shame. 'I shall try a different approach next time,' declares she. 'I shall ask him whether Mafeking has been relieved yet. He will not be able to resist giving me a lecture, whether it has or not.' I very much doubt that there will be a next time and told her so. She gave me a rather poisonous look and accused me of being a killjoy. 'Just enjoy yourself for once,' she hissed, before running off to join a game of deck-quoits.

I do not care for deck-quoits, but am otherwise enjoying myself very much in the brightness of the African sunshine, thank you very much, Louise.

Louise's Diary

3 January 1900

Well, Sarah, how wrong you were! In spite of all your predictions, I have at last gained a smile from Horatio – even though his lips are totally hidden beneath his massive moustache. But the giant handlebars suddenly stretched apart, like curtains, as it were, and somewhere in its depths I detected a row of quite normal teeth, quite protuberant, in fact, not the line of sharpened canines, ready to bite if angry, as one has been encouraged to expect.

This momentous achievement occurred last night as I was taking a solitary stroll (or *patrol*, if I were honest) on the lower deck before retiring. To my astonishment I came across the shadowy hulk of a tall man, cradling some small creature in his hands. He seemed to be grief-stricken. I at once recognised the figure, and without thinking twice I strode towards him to offer my assistance. I was wearing my nurse's pelisse and white uniform which must somehow have cancelled out my femaleness, for, instead of shrieking in terror and running for his life, Kitchener raised an agitated face and said, 'Nurse, can we save its life?' He stretched out the cup of his hands. Inside it wriggled a little flying fish which had leapt on board, attracted by the lights. 'Well, we could throw it back into the ocean,' I suggested gently. 'Oh no, nurse,' exclaimed he, 'I should love to have it in my cabin – is there not some container we could use?' 'Just a minute!' I cried, my brain racing. I rushed into the dining room and wrenched a bouquet of exotic blooms from a crystal vase which I then filled with seawater stored in barrels in case of fire. This I presented to the sensitive Lord, who deposited the gasping fish into its new home with shaking hands. 'Thank you, thank you, nurse,' he murmured, and then turned to me and bared his teeth as described above. 'You see,' he added in a choked voice, 'this little fish has flown far higher than all the others – it has reached the upper deck which no other fish can do. Does it deserve death for flying so high?' His red-rimmed ice-blue eyes roved wildly round the deck as he spoke, reminding me of a demented patient who spent some time in my ward before being confined to the local Bedlam.

Strangely, after this midnight rendezvous, as I like to think of it, I now feel no desire to proceed further with my plans to capture his heart. The poor man was quite unable to establish eye contact with me – one of his eyes has a caste of some sort – but I could see from the range of agonised emotions that flitted across his face that he has no place in his heart for the softness of a woman, unless she happens to be covered in fur, feathers, or fins!

In fact, I think I shall not tell this story of triumph to Sarah. She will listen politely, then give me her sweet smile and say something really irritating like, 'But surely the fish will fly out of its vase?' That's not the point, Sarah! Let's have a good laugh!

Sarah's Diary

12 January 1900

After Madeira, the Fairest Cape could only be an anti-climax. Our boat steamed into Table Bay just as the sun was rising, and everyone rushed to the decks to gawp at Table Mountain – but there was nothing to see above the little scattered city but a screen of grey mist which reached from the foothills of the three mountains (which we were assured do exist) to high up in a cloudy sky. Four decks of passengers groaned in disappointment. How vexing that the mountains should veil themselves today.

We had to manoeuvre our way among ship after ship bringing in yet more horses and troops, to say nothing of hideous instruments of death. After a lot of bureaucracy on board about landing, we disembarked by means of a number of small boats that came to fetch us, the pretty young ladies squealing in excitement as they climbed down the ladders, and were told where we nurses were going. Louise and I had hoped to sail further north to Durban, which is near the great battlefields, but we were told in very peremptory tones by officious military men that we were to be posted to the general hospitals in grey, dreary Cape Town. To our horror we learnt that we were to be separated – Louise to the number two hospital in a suburb called Wynberg, while I was to go to number three. Louise tried to make a fuss about our separation but was very quickly put in her place by an impatient lieutenant who reminded her she had not come here on holiday but to obey the orders of the army.

Off we set in our open-ended Cape carts to our different hospitals, feeling bitterly disappointed and suddenly apprehensive. I was taken to the leafy suburb of Rondebosch and dropped off at a large rambling bungalow filled with brisk Australian nurses. Frangipani Villa is to be my home until I am posted north, if that ever happens.

As I stepped out of my open-air cart and my luggage was balanced (to my astonishment) on the head of the black driver, a wonderful thing occurred. Although the sky had been overcast throughout the journey from the Cape Town docks to Rondebosch, the sun suddenly broke through the cloud and lit up Frangipani Villa as if with a spotlight. All at once the bougainvillea and hibiscus in the garden flamed in welcome and the house seemed to catch fire as all kinds of colourful bushes and creepers blazed in the sunlight. At the same time the front door was flung open and two young coloured girls ran out to greet me and help with the luggage. In their quaint, musical accents they introduced themselves – Rushda and Saleema – and informed me that they had been hired at twelve shillings a week to wash, iron, cook and clean for us. By the time I had entered the cool, clean villa I felt strangely at home; every room had a familiar and welcoming air to it. I could smell a faint aroma of cloves and nutmeg in my bedroom, which I was to share with one of the Australian nurses.

My pleasure was further enhanced by an introductory visit to the nearby 'Number 3', as it is called. It is almost embarrassing to admit that this must be one of the most exquisitely located and cared for hospitals in the world. Seventy-three double marquees, fitted with wooden floors and each holding up to seven beds, are situated beside beautiful pine woods, which emit a warm, nutty perfume and sigh and sway in a rather strong wind, to which I believe Cape Town is prone. Large pots of flowers are placed beside the tents, and easy chairs are scattered beneath the trees.

I have not yet met the men I shall be nursing. Hard work

starts tomorrow, but now Louise and I plan to meet up in Cape Town – there is an excellent rail service – to explore the shops and streets and admire the frontal view of Table Mountain, unveiled!

Robben Island, January 1900

The decision to leave the island had come slowly. When he handed the grass seed over to the leper woman he averted his eyes from her grateful, suppurating face. The demon of the Island had entered his breast: it possessed him and made his head ache, his heart beat hot and fast. Was *she* the demon? In fact, was she the demon mother? He had lied to Dr Simmonds: his heart was not hard. It was soft as Our Lady's, stabbed with all those swords.

Unable to resist, he paid her a final visit. She was scattering the grass seed into the runnels she had dug. Her remaining fingers were quick and supple. He leaned over the gate, watching her. Finally she noticed him, and nodded. He pushed the gate open with uncertain hands. It mewed plaintively; he should have brought oil. A surge of emotion drowned his better instincts. 'And what has happened to your sixth son?' he cried. A flock of seagulls, after the seeds, nearly drowned his words with their tangled yelps. She had stood up straight; leaned against the nearby spade. 'He's the split image of his father.' Her hair fell over her misshapen, beautiful face. 'Long since dead now.' He had swung away on his heel, unable to speak.

That evening in early January Dr Simmonds heard an urgent knock on the front door of his cottage. Expecting to find an orderly on his doorstep with some hospital emergency to report, he was surprised but pleased to find the young leper guard, Patrick Donnelly. Though the two men had spent several evenings together over the past few months, often without uttering many words, the invitation had always come from the doctor, when he had felt the need for the young man's company, or an impulse to educate. In silence he opened his bottle of Jameson's whisky, and poured two glasses of the lovely golden brown liquid.

'Those perforating ulcers,' the boy had begun as soon as he was settled in the doctor's second armchair. 'They don't mean leprosy, do they? Not if you've had them for eighteen years?'

'You're talking of the self-cured lepers?' The doctor did not look surprised at the question. Nevertheless, he could not resist an opportunity to lecture. 'Well, in most self-cured cases the perforation clears up never to return. But sometimes the ulcers remain long after the disease has been cured because the bones have become necrosed – they die – through a defect in their nerve supply. They become virtually foreign bodies.'

The boy was listening intently, the muscles of his face rearranged in an expression of acute seriousness which the doctor, having witnessed previous unsuccessful attempts at solemnity, could see was genuine. 'So, if the dead bone is removed, the ulcers will clear up?'

Dr Simmonds swirled his whisky between his cheeks, then sipped thoughtfully. 'If the patient wishes to prove him or herself to be finally free of leprosy, this would be the course to take. Because even in the cases of self-cured ex-lepers whose ulcers have long disappeared, some medical men consider that the ulceration is only *arrested*, and if you wait long enough, it will start afresh. But surely there is a limit to everything. Why be Micawbers in dealing with lepers? Why keep the patients languishing in a lazaretto until death removes them from your expectant eye, waiting for something to turn up – waiting for the ulceration to recur? And speaking of Micawber, I have a new book for you to read.' He reached out for a volume on the sideboard next to his armchair. '*David Copperfield*. Another maltreated orphan: the story of Dickens' own difficult child-hood.'

The young man glanced indifferently at the offering; then

asked, in agitated tones, 'Have you ever carried out this operation – on the dead bones?'

'Yes. Several times.' The doctor was silent for a moment. 'Are you thinking of a particular leper?' He searched Patch's eyes but could discover only *a green thought in a green shade*; the line that always insinuated itself into his head when he looked at the boy.

'No!' The word was spat out. 'I'm interested, that's all.' Patch swallowed the liquid trembling in his glass. The warmth of it calmed him. His face slipped back into the old familiar half-smile as he looked at the book on his lap. 'You'll make a bookworm of me yet.' He flicked the pages, already cut in preparation. 'I've had more education from you than I ever had at the convent.' There was a valedictory cadence to these words which the doctor noted with a pang of regret.

On returning to his bedroom, he opened the book called *David Copperfield* and read the opening sentence. *Whether I shall turn out to be the hero of my own life, or whether that station will be held by anyone else, these pages must show.* The words entered his very being. He was unable to read further. That Charles Dickens had put his finger on his own dilemma. Was Patrick Donnelly the hero of his own life, or was someone else? The chilling truth was that there was no heroism whatsoever about his life. The Catholic church did not provide heroic opportunities to become a man as did, for instance, the religion of the Xhosa people he had met in the District. How he had secretly envied the young men of his age as they prepared themselves for initiation into manhood in the bush round Cape Town. What challenges to their courage lay before them: their foreskins sliced off, their bodies naked and smeared with clay; fasting for days on end; rituals of manliness. They always came back different, their boyhood gone. *They* would always be the heroes of their own lives.

The next day, while gazing at the flotilla in the bay, he knew what to do.

The doctor was not surprised when Patch (who had considered slipping away on the ferry without saying goodbye) told him of his new plans. He refrained from reminding the young man of his vow never to join up and instead offered some advice. 'Make sure you always have a billycan of clean water,' he said. 'And you'll find Mr Dickens very good company.'

Patch left the island the next day. Dr Simmonds had run up to the jetty waving a book wrapped in brown paper just as he was mounting a giant convict's back. 'Part two,' he panted. 'Keep David ready for emergencies.' And stood watching the departure of the young man, who himself felt a certain forlornness as the ferry made its way through the anchored ships in the bay.

General Hospital Number 3, January 1900

He dropped his suitcase off at the Witbooi's and paid a surprise visit to Johan's hairdressing salon. Here he learnt to his astonishment that Cartwright was in the Rondebosch military hospital after being wounded in one of those disastrous battles in Natal. He'd come down from Durban on a hospital train donated by a princess. Johan had been to visit and told Patch how to get there, while applying Vaseline and straightening irons to his client's tightly curled hair, which gradually assumed the shape of a miniature warship, with six portholes. He recommended taking a bottle of Cape Smoke. 'Cartwright is very furious because some say he was running away when he got shot.' A funnel emerged beneath his expert fingers. 'He says they was wrong, he isn't a coward. Yes, sir, I can give you a puff of smoke as well.'

On his way to the railway station, Patch bought a bottle of cheap Cape brandy and a block of tobacco, to keep things cheerful. He'd never been to Rondebosch before, it being inhabited exclusively by toffs, but, once he got there, those snobbish women in their posh clothes still looked at him appreciatively as he sauntered down their roads in his leisurely fashion, his shoulders swaying in time to the melody in his head. Now he peered behind the hedges, where great lawns and floral borders unrolled like carpets to whitewashed houses, each with different kinds of windows, some latticed, through which you could see heavy curtains and framed pictures on the walls. Tomorrow he would sign up to one of those colonial volunteer forces, the same one that Cartwright belonged to. Two weeks training would turn him into a soldier. At least he wouldn't have to wear one of those stupid pith helmets; the colonials wore slouch hats like the Boers, which gave them a daredevil air suggesting effortless bravery and a physical toughness gained from a lifetime in the open veldt. But you need more than a flattering hat to prove your manliness; perhaps a wound was essential, even if gained while fleeing.

It was almost like being in church in this quiet, salubrious suburb, and he was relieved to reach the site of the hospital, which was all laid out neatly too. Snow-white tents and marquees ran in straight lines under the pine trees with pots of plants in between them, and nurses running about in their white dresses and veils with little red cloaks draped over their shoulders. After enquiring, he found Cartwright's tent.

'Hullo, my friend!'

Well, Cartwright seemed fit enough, not even in bed, striding towards him with one arm in a sling, the other raised in sardonic welcome. A Mauser bullet had gone clean through him; you could see the scars on either side of his chest, one between the right ribs and the other somewhere under his shoulder blade. Though the wounds had healed rapidly, a second bullet had smashed his elbow, hence the sling. Cartwright displayed these badges of apparent valour almost immediately, at the same time trying to get the attention of the nurses with his flashy smile. Patch, remembering Johan's warning, made no comment. All around in rows of metal beds lay men or, rather, parts of men, for some had their faces missing, you could see their teeth all bared with the cheek blown away, and some had lost their legs but still screamed in agony at the gangrene that was no longer there. It was a relief to get outside and sit under the pine trees drinking brandy and smoking and listening to Cartwright's stories about the uselessness of the British Army's commanding officers.

His battle stories were a little short on detail. It seemed that his volunteer brigade was part of Buller's attempt to cross the

Tugela River so as to relieve Ladysmith, but unfortunately there were rather a lot of well-armed Boers dug into trenches all around, and the Tugela twisted and looped in such a way that, unless you knew the terrain, you could end up crossing it two or three times. The thing was to find the bridges or fords across it, but the scouts gave the wrong information, and the troops ended up milling about chaotically, cannon fodder for the sharpshooting Boers hidden in the ground. The worst of it was that you couldn't even tell where their sharp shooting was coming from on account of the smokeless gunpowder. Cartwright's face twisted in contempt as he spoke; if *he* had been in charge, Ladysmith would have been relieved weeks ago no question, was the underlying message.

Patch's thoughts drifted as he listened to his friend's catalogue of complaints and criticisms. He was thinking about heroism again. He was frightened by the appearance of the mutilated men in the tents; he was discouraged by Cartwright's accounts of British leadership; yet wasn't this what heroism was about: to plunge forward in the face of disaster? To risk everything – not for your country but for your own manhood. Patriotism didn't come into it at all. He felt no particular allegiance to Britain – the nuns hadn't tried to hide their antagonism towards England, though he'd never understood why. And he certainly had no truck with the Boers up north, savages with long beards, unable even to speak English, the language of civilisation (though he had to admit that the Loyal Afrikaners he'd come across in Cape Town, or, more precisely, whose boots he had polished as a sideline in Feinstein's shoe store, had seemed cultured and hygienic, and the nose of a shoeshine boy had the advantage over other noses in these matters).

'So Long abandons his field guns, doesn't he, you should've seen them horses trying to escape but still harnessed to the artillery, talk about panic, then Buller sends in three officers to rescue the guns and one of them's Freddie Roberts, son of you-know-who, and next thing he's lying dead with a bullet through his stomach, and Buller orders a retreat. Meantime

I'm lying in a heap of bodies, some dead, some alive, some with their guts hanging out like sausages you see in the butchers . . . let's have another swig of that brandy, eh, Patch?'

Patch had a swig himself to steady his nerves; then, just as he passed the bottle to Cartwright, he saw a vision from heaven.

She was dressed like most of the nurses, with a little red cloak round her shoulders and her hair hidden under her veil, but for a moment he thought she must be Our Lady visiting the hospital in disguise. Like Mary, the young nurse smiled sadly to herself, her eyes downcast, her face perfectly oval and pale as ivory. For all the world, she looked like the statue of Our Lady in the church, climbed down from her niche beside the altar. On her breast a great cross blazed, red as Mary's blood.

'You should've seen John Smith's head explode off his shoulders when he stood up to pee,' Cartwright was saying. 'Bits of his brain whopped into my eye, and him only eighteen.'

Patch fingered his Miraculous Medal. This was the closest he'd got to an Apparition, like Our Lady of Fatima. But an orderly was running up to the Madonna-nurse, gesticulating angrily in Cartwright's direction. She followed his gaze with patient eyes. Patch's heart beat violently. He adjusted the angle of his boater and brushed invisible dust from the sleeve of his green blazer, for now she was advancing towards them with an effortless movement that suggested a cluster of cherubs was bearing the weight of her little feet. He could see that her eyes, no longer gazing downwards, were, unexpectedly, dark brown and flashing, unlike Mary's powder-blue orbs. If she should gaze in his direction he felt he might faint with pleasure. Instead, she was looking reproachfully at his babbling friend.

'Private Cartwright!' The mere intonation of these four syllables was enough to tell Patch that the Virgin was a Lady. A lady from England, upper crust for sure. She spoke, in fact, just how you'd imagine Our Lady would speak; low, musical, posh. She pronounced all her t's with sharp authority.

The two men struggled up. In an effort to draw attention to himself, Patch vigorously waved away the cloud of smoke they'd produced. He wished he could burst into song, so that she could hear his fine tenor voice. He would sing *Sweet Rosie O'Grady*, establishing meaningful eye contact on the words *how happy we'll be*. But she had eyes only for Cartwright; eyes now radiating scorn, he was relieved to note. Cartwright, flushed by Cape Smoke and his own manhood, attempted flirtation.

'Yes, Sister Palmer?' He could do wonders with his eyebrows when necessary. 'What can I do for you?'

Sister Palmer froze his eyebrows with an icy stare. 'Private Jenkins complains you have taken his baccy. I don't need to tell you Private Jenkins is dying.' She inhaled deep into her body and her fine bust rose beneath the red cross. 'It is inconceivable to me that a trooper can steal from a man who will be dead tomorrow. Kindly return the tobacco to me and I will put it by his bedside.'

'Lord, Sister, he ain't got no mouf, hardly,' exclaimed Cartwright, his origins south of the River Thames surfacing suddenly, as if to convince Sister Palmer that a Cockney trooper understood death better than she ever could. 'What's the use of his baccy now?'

The nurse's face contracted in disgust. 'Please hand over what you have stolen.' Her toff's voice shook.

'Well, Sister, I ain't got none!' And Cartwright pulled out his pockets to confirm their emptiness.

Patch watched the ice in the young woman's eyes suddenly crack apart as her anger blazed out. He wondered if she might start to yell and scream like Fancy, when similarly indignant. He held his breath. But she stood silent as her cheeks flooded with sudden, violent colour.

In his own pockets lay the block of baccy he had bought at Cape Town station. He closed his fingers round the pouch.

'Sure, I've got some to spare, Sister.' In his best Irish brogue, smooth, brimming with sympathy. He withdrew the pouch and offered it to the startled nurse.

She seemed deprived of speech, but her face returned to its ivory pallor. Her brown eyes stared at him in apparent panic. 'Th-thank you,' she stuttered. 'How kind.'

'Take the bag as well,' said Patch generously. 'Baccy's no good without a bag.' What on earth made him say that? Now what was he going to do for a baccy pouch?

'You are too kind,' whispered the nurse. Then, confronting Cartwright again, she blurted, 'Perhaps you can learn something from your friend!' And, nodding briefly at Patch – and was that straightening of the rosy lips the beginning of a smile? – she turned back towards the marquee, a billow of nutty pine aroma rising in her wake.

'Eh, mate, what's got into you?' smirked Cartwright. 'Got the hots for the ice queen? Want to get into her frillies?' He narrowed his eyes and winked. 'And trying to impress her with your Irish brogue, eh? District accent not good enough for you?'

The last rose of summer . . . crooned Patch in reply. His heart was so full he had to sing. Cartwright joined in and even shuffled his feet about expertly. 'Pity old Johan's not here,' he said as they finished their performance, which Patch hoped the nurse might have heard through the marquee canvas.

And as he made his way to Rondebosch station, he found himself experiencing a sense of excitement at the thought of her soft white hands holding his leathery pouch. Her gaze lingered in his memory. That brilliance in her eyes kept flashing through his head, a bit like the revolving beacon of the Island lighthouse pulsing out its magnified beam into the fog, over and over.

Back at the Witboois' house he found Fancy alone, having returned from her day in the flower market earlier than the rest of her family. He crept behind her and folded her against his body. 'I'm joining up tomorrow,' he whispered down into her ear. 'Don't go crazy, sweetheart.' He began to undo the buttons of her blouse from behind, nuzzling her ear at the same time in the way she liked. 'When I get back we'll get married.' This was cowardly, but he couldn't think of any other way of quelling her anger.

'You promised me you wouldn't go to war. And you needn't think I'm going to write to you.' Though her voice was sulky he could tell the mention of marriage had done the trick. She turned round to face him, her face triumphant. 'Let's go to the bedroom, soldier boy. Maybe we can quickly make a baby while everyone's out.'

Sarah's Diary

18 January 1900

Though the weather and the surroundings are even more glorious than I had hoped for, I am strangely disappointed in my work. It is so very different from what I had expected. Because no great battles have been fought recently we find ourselves nursing those soldiers who are recovering from older wounds or a range of diseases. In fact, the diseases far outnumber the wounds. Though there are some distressing cases of torn and mutilated bodies, most of the Tommies I nurse are suffering from debility, frail circulation and chronic rheumatism. It amazes me that so many of them passed their medical examinations. On top of this many of them have incurred fearful sunstroke and heat apoplexy. A particular problem is the back of the Highlanders' knees: a kilt is not the best uniform to wear in temperatures of over a hundred degrees.

When I am not administering medicine, changing bandages, moistening dry lips, or helping the orderlies make beds etc – there is an awkwardness between the male orderlies, who are really troopers with a little medical training, and the nurses whom they often resent – I sit by the bedsides and listen to the wounded Tommies' stories, which they are always anxious to tell and which I find extremely interesting and educational. For instance, there is much bitterness about Magersfontein, a battle fought near Kimberley last month, where a courageous Highland Brigade was ordered to march shoulder to shoulder in the darkness of the night into what turned out to be a trap set by the Boers, hidden in their thousands in well-disguised trenches. As if this wasn't bad enough, when the Black Watch heroically charged into the line of Boer fire, their bayonets drawn, they found themselves rushing straight into yards of barbed wire fencing used to hold in the vast flocks of sheep that evidently graze for miles across the veldt (of which there is no sign in Cape Town.) This instantly halted their pointlessly brave charge, and hundreds of them were shot as they tried to disentangle themselves. Why had the scouts not detected and reported the wire fences? On the other hand, there is no way that the scouts on the ground can detect the invisible trenches; the war balloon should have been sent ahead to spy out these lethal underground lines of battle. Over nine hundred are dead or wounded, some of the latter recovering in 'my' hospital, and muttering angrily about the management of the battle. It does seem extraordinary that men trained for so many years to plan battles could make such elementary mistakes. I suppose this is why Bobs and K of K have been brought over.

It came as a surprise to me to hear the Tommy occasionally speak well of the Boer. For instance, one young man described to me how, lying wounded, his lips swollen black with thirst in the blazing heat of the veldt while bullets from both sides whined above, a Boer crawled over to him, at considerable danger to himself, with a water bottle. Lifting the astonished Tommy's head, and allowing him to drink the bottle dry, the Boer jovially remarked in perfect though guttural English, 'Sorry I haven't got the whisky to go with it!' Later, the young man was actually saddened to find the body of his saviour stretched out further up the hill (which the British were attempting unsuccessfully to capture), his arm thrown above his head, a neat hole drilled through his forehead. I too am saddened by the story of the Thoughtful Boer, though there are of course many instances when the Boer has been the very opposite of thoughtful. I am told he has a tendency to hang out white flags and then, as our men move in, to shoot them dead.

Though I am surrounded by sadness I find that the bright sunshine and the beautiful surroundings make the tragedies on the ward easier to bear. Just to see the trees and marquees bathed in brilliant light makes something brighten inside me, just as it did in Madeira. It is this continual stimulation of the senses, I think, that helps arouse me from the twilight of my earlier life. In addition to the glorious exotic smell and taste of our little servants' cooking in our villa, there is the blue presence of the mountains and the sweet calls of birds quite new to me – some with long fluttering tails such as I have previously observed only on the brims of ladies hats.

It is as if I have till now seen the world only in soft, misty hues: greys, pinks, creams. Africa has changed all that. The landscape is a blaze of primary colours which demand your attention – I wonder how the Old Dutch artists would have dealt with it? Somehow I have always known that sunshine is the chief ingredient of happiness, and this is the land of sunshine and flowers. What a tragedy that the monstrous engines of war are dragged over it merely to satisfy man's greed for gold and territory. I have sent Sophie a postcard which expresses these thoughts. I think of her often and wonder how she would react to the situation here.

Louise and I send each other notes and plan to meet again in Cape Town at the wonderful Dix's Café. It seems her hospital is not as well run as this one. On the other hand she seems already to have fallen in love with one of the doctors. Oh dear, I hope she will not break her heart once again.

19 January

Something extraordinary happened today. A really slimy limey, as Louise would say, called Cartwright was sent down here with other wounded men after a failed attempt by Buller to cross the Tugela River in Natal, and he has done nothing but steal other Tommies' possessions and try to flirt with the nurses, not perceiving how repulsive we all find him. This afternoon a rather flashily dressed friend of his came to visit him, and while they were drinking brandy in the pine forest Orderly Jones informed me that Cartwright had stolen poor Private Jenkins' tobacco as he lay on his deathbed. Private Jenkins had actually managed to ask Mr Jones to roll him a cigarette (though he is incapable of inhaling smoke at this stage) when the discovery was made. I immediately ordered Cartwright to return the stolen property, but he claimed not to have any tobacco in his possession. To my astonishment his friend then offered to give me his own baccy, pouch and all. He spoke with an unusual Irish brogue, which immediately endeared him to me. (Why is the Irish accent, north or south, so irresistibly attractive?) When I turned my stern gaze to meet his, I have to confess that a miracle happened: without any warning the silent bird in my heart burst into song. There is no other way to put it. I had no need to murmur Miss Rossetti's lines as I stared into his eyes, and felt as if I were rushing down a tunnel of greenery, where leaves, moss, ferns, grass, stems, and all manner of undergrowth gleam in different shades, beckoned me to go yet further into the foliage. It was with some difficulty that I was able to reply courteously to his offer.

Now, several hours later, the bird yet sings . . . how very unexpected. I suppose I have never before met anyone quite like this Irishman, clad in the colours of his homeland. There was something about the tilt of his head, the disposition of his limbs, the asymmetry of his smile that . . . that what?

If coals could burn green, they would burn the colour of his eyes.

20 January

Today some colonels' wives distributed the Queen's chocolate round the encampment. Great excitement! A few men are eating the chocolate but most are keeping it or sending it home. The box will be treasured forever, of course. The Queen would be pleased if she knew how much they care for it.

31 January

The tranquil atmosphere is utterly changed now that the wounded men from Spion Kop are pouring into our marquees, carried down from Natal on the hospital trains. What a shameful defeat! Fifteen hundred of our men killed, wounded or captured. Buller is being blamed and everyone waits for Bobs to bring victory at last. Now trainloads of wounded men are starting to arrive, but we as female nurses are not allowed to attend to their wounds or bandage them as this is considered too indelicate a task for ladies. There is also the fear that the wounded men may grow soft under the tender care of we women!

The dreadful Cartwright has been returned to his regiment as his arm is now quite healed. Although I was glad to see the back of him, I was sorry there would be no further opportunity to see his Irish friend again. After poor Private Jenkins had died, I gave the tobacco pouch to Cartwright and asked him to return it to his friend. With a smirk he informed me that Patch – that seems to be the young man's curious name – had joined up and was now busy training to become a mounted infantryman. As an afterthought he sneered, 'Thought he might catch leprosy, you see. On the Island.' As I did not want to enter into conversation with him, I refrained from informing him that leprosy is no longer thought to be contagious. However, I am curious to know what 'Patch' was doing on the leper island, which we see glimmering in the bay when I sit on the veranda of Dix's Café with Louise, eating strawberries and ice cream.

The nightingale in my heart still sings as full-throatedly as Keats' ever did, but there is little chance that I will ever lay eyes on the reason for this ecstatic song. I shall merely enjoy it while it lasts.

More excitement yesterday when the creator of *The Absent-Minded Beggar*, Mr Rudyard Kipling, who of course also wrote *The Jungle Book* and the *Barrack Room Ballads* which my men love so much, arrived at our hospital in the woods. He handed out cigarettes and magazines, and chatted to the men so naturally. They hung upon his every word. 'God bless him! He's the soldiers' friend!' they whispered in awed gratitude once he'd left.

Louise's Diary

1 February

I have never in my life met so many busybodies poking their noses into the running of the hospital – busybodies with no knowledge whatsoever of medical matters and no technical training. First we have the 'lady amateurs' (several of whom I recognise as those giggling co-travellers on the *Dunottar*) who are young women of means and leisure shipped over from England, wearing fancy dress caps and aprons over their fine silk gowns, pretending at being nurses. For the life of me I can't imagine how they got into this hospital when I think of the stringent rules of the SAVC: Sarah actually had to *lie* about her age as she is a year younger than the minimum twenty-five years. These masquerade nurses are scarcely out of their teens, and get in everyone's way. Never mind that some of them are not bad looking with soft flutey voices, attracting the attention of the medical officers here; the sick Tommies are tired of being spoilt and petted by them. I heard one of them ask a poor wounded soldier, 'What can I do for you, my poor man? Shall I wash your face?' 'Thank you kindly,' the man replied, 'but I have already promised fourteen ladies that they shall wash my face.' Another Tommy informed a gushing lady amateur that he was too sick to be nursed by her. I half expect to see Lady Weatherby distributing her five hundred balaclavas.

Then you get the grand ladies who think they can 'boss' the real nurses about because of their position in society. A case in point is Mrs Chamberlain, sister-in-law to the British Colonial

Minister, who spends all her time and money in the officer's ward where she hosts extravagant parties. Dr Prescott claims she is responsible for the deaths of two enteric patients whom she invited to a tea-party when they were recovering, and fed them on *currant buns* when they are supposed to be on a strictly liquid diet! At last the Chief Medical Officer has made a move to restrict the flow of ladies into the military hospitals because they do more harm than good.

But busybody men can be just as exasperating as the ladies. Just because you happen to be a famous writer and poet does not mean you can run a hospital as well. I know Number 2 is shamefully short of bandages, but that is no excuse for Mr Kipling to turn up at the hospital with a consignment of bandages which he'd bought himself. I happened to be standing outside the central marquee (smoking a surreptitious cigarette, if the truth be known) when he arrived, bursting with importance. He looked at me disapprovingly (ugly little toad with a walrus moustache and bottle-glass spectacles) and asked to see the Superintendent Sister. When I enquired why he wished to disturb her, he informed me of the presence of the bandages in a Cape cart outside the hospital awaiting delivery; he wished the sister in charge to arrange for some orderlies to carry them in. I duly did what I was told (with rather bad grace, I'll admit) and called Sister Hopkins, who very patiently explained to the great man that only bandages purchased by the Regular Army Medical Services could be used on the wards. At this the little toad flew into a fearful rage and shouted, 'Well, then, I shall dump the bandages on the pavement and the orderlies can clear up the litter. Perhaps *that* will get the bandages into the hospital without tearing any Red Tape, I hope!' Off he stormed, never to be seen again. I can understand his impatience with hospital bureaucracy, but I do not like being spoken to in that officious manner.

At the same time, I have to say it is an absolute scandal the way this hospital is run. Everyone blames everyone else when things go wrong. In particular, the medical officers blame Roberts for the deficiency of hospital equipment, saying hospital needs are put at the bottom of the army pecking order – well below the consignments of officers' champagne, for instance – with the result that *they* are blamed for not having bandages when the hospital consignments haven't even left England! It's a mystery to me therefore how Sarah's hospital, the Number 3, is so well equipped – in fact, the model hospital in every way.

But almost the worst aspect of the hospital is the orderlies. These men are simply rank and file Tommies who've taken a first aid course and consider themselves to be fully fledged nurses. Their fingernails are long and filthy, a condition I draw to their attention every day, with nothing but a glare in response; their uniforms need washing, and their breath stinks of beer. They're half asleep most of the day as they start their day at five a.m. with an inspection parade, then they engage in menial tasks such as washing the patients' private parts (we nurses may only wash hands and faces, it being considered that soldiers will get too excited if women wash their genitals!); arranging breakfasts, washing up, cleaning the ward, scrubbing the floor, changing the bed linen, fetching meals. They hate being told what to do by us female nurses, in spite of our years of training and experience, and accuse us of having airs and graces. What a nerve!

The senior medical officer, Dr James, has invited me to dinner at the very grand Mount Nelson Hotel where the officers are billeted, poor things!! It should be great fun! I think I am falling in love with him and he with me. Well! There is one young lady I shall NOT be introducing him to for the moment . . .

Two

Flank March, February 1900

A giant wave of dust is breaking over the South African veldt. It floods across the broad and barren plain, surging among the stony hillocks that erupt occasionally from the flat red landscape. The herds of springbok in its path scatter neatly; one after another they rise and fall in soundless ripples: then freeze at a distance, as if posing for a photograph. The great tide sweeps on. Like surf upon faraway shingle, it rumbles: a deep, primeval roar that amazes watching Boer and beast alike. For this is no ordinary dust-storm which spins red across the veldt without warning and blinds the eyes, carpets the floors, coats the bedclothes, covers the milk and is the curse of every Boer housewife in this desolate Boer Republic: this is the dust of the British Army sweeping over Africa; this is the thunder of thousands of hooves, the beat of marching boots, the rumble of horse-drawn field guns and howitzers; the whole force of cavalry, infantry, light horse of all descriptions, horse-gunners, field-gunners, two great bullock-drawn naval five-inch cannons, followed by miles and miles of mules and wagons, ambulance carts, teams of oxen whipped by four thousand hooting kaffir drivers.

There is no gleam of arms, nor glamour of scarlet and gold, though when the tips of the six-foot-long spears of the Lancer brigades pierce through the dust cloud, their metal points and fluttering pennants suggest something of long-lost medieval romance. Over the rolling veldt heave the mighty columns, pouring over ridge after ridge, tramping through the short tufty grass or along the fine veldt roads, marching in perfect unison. As they reach the foot of a ridge of *kopjes*, each troop in turn gets the order 'Sub-sections, left!' and they wheel smartly in fours and file through a road cut into the rocks. And up there in front on his black charger is the wiry little figure with the bronzed face, the white whiskers and the straight back in whom the hope of Great Britain resides. A mourning band still encircles Bobs' khaki-clad arm; the handle of the sword of Kandahar protrudes from his hip. Behind him rides a turbaned sepoy, his personal valet from India. And there's the red-eyed Lord Kitchener, the Sirdar himself, also known as Lord of Chilled Steel, or King of Chaos, trotting austerely beside his chief, not even a medal on his broad chest to flash out their location, but for all the world looking as if he's the one who's in charge.

What makes anyone want to live here, that's the mystery. What made those Boers trek out of the lushness of the purple-mountained Cape to set up home in this dust bowl? The two-mile front of dragoons, hussars and lancers must be the most thrilling thing that's happened here since time began. Not that it's particularly thrilling for the troopers who've eaten nothing but a biscuit and some mielie-pap in the last twenty-four hours, the Boer general, De Wet having ambushed the stores at Waterval Drift. 'Put 'em on half rations. *They'll do it for me*,' smirks Bobs when he hears that two hundred wagons, nearly a third of the transport, were stranded with their kaffir drivers beside the Riet River, surrounded by cheering Boers. Vast supplies of biscuit and bully beef, medicine and bandages, all meant to last for weeks – all abandoned to De Wet. Now there's so much dust in his throat Patch doubts he could swallow anything anyway. It coats his face and trickles down his neck and mingles with the sweat and vermin beneath his khaki tunic. His water bottle is empty: half water rations don't last long when the temperature is over a hundred.

He can just see Cartwright in the same regiment further down the line. Cartwright recovered in time to rejoin for this manoeuvre – a swift recovery which Patch rather regretted as he'd been looking forward to another visit to that hospital. The pale little nurse occasionally flits through his mind, fixing him with her dark stare, but she'll be sailing back to England soon as the war's over, back to her toffee-nosed family, so forget her, mate.

Who'd have thought he'd end up riding a bleeding horse? And getting fond of the melancholy old girl, at that. He'd never had much time for animals before, and in his childhood had done some vile things to Dominic, the convent cat, just to show who was boss. The nuns never did find out where Dominic disappeared to, not surprising. But now he thinks of the nag Olga as a sort of friend, with her heavy-lidded eyes and gentle movements, not meant for war, not at all. When he'd volunteered he'd signed up as an infantryman, a foot-soldier, hoping he wouldn't have to ride a horse, but Bobs wants to mount at least half of the forty thousand troopers he's taking up north, just as Dr Simmonds had predicted. Trouble is the Boers know how to ride, they can ride their little Basuto ponies before they can walk, it's said. As if there could ever be any comparison with these pale shrunken Tommies who tumbled off their nags the moment trotting started. Well, finally Patch had got the hang of lifting up his bum and pushing down into the stirrups, but not before he'd taken a fall or two.

Bobs is certainly changing things; changing the whole way the British Army goes to battle because, even though this is meant to be a white gentleman's war, the enemy don't fight like gentlemen, taking pot-shots from behind a rock or from inside their trenches, then riding home to a slap-up meal on their farms while Tommy chews his biscuit . . . Now it's horses, horses, horses, coming in from all over the bleeding world: Argentina, wherever that may be, Russia, Britain, Australia, you name it. The harbour's stuffed with boats full of nags, fillies, mules, ponies, whatever you want to call them. The whole of the South Arm is given over to army stores, armaments and forage from Argentina, which seems to have an endless supply of hay. Next, the poor nags have to get used to the thunder of firearms. They have to get shot at (blanks, of course) day after day till they can advance into volleys of rifle fire with absolute fearlessness. They have to lose their instinct to run away at the sound of explosions; to believe that whistling bullets, screaming shells and thundering cannon have no connection whatsoever with the shattered and lifeless bodies of men and horses that lie all around them. After a few weeks they know every bugle call and obey their messages every time.

But now, on this great flank march, the horses are suffering. At least Patch has a nosebag for Olga with a little grain in it, but nosebags are in short supply. Also in short supply is what goes inside them. The horses need a minimum of fifteen pounds of grain a day to keep themselves in reasonable condition, but they're down to half that, and a little hay (in spite of the vast stores on the South Arm). The gunhorses are falling in their traces from pure exhaustion, and so are the mules who pulled the ambulance carts, not that there are many of them after Bobs and K of Chaos decided to cut back eighty percent. The newly Mounted Infantry aren't doing much better as the monstrous weight of saddle gear takes its toll on their horses. You can see birds of prey circling in and out of the dust overhead. Patrick feels Olga stumble again. She was never made for battle: the regimental breastplate, with its lower straps passed between her front legs, gives her a warlike air but no one's fooled. Patch makes a sudden decision and slides off Olga's back and walks beside her. His sacrifice seems to have made no difference. Her neck still droops. She can scarcely lift her hooves.

Patch unstraps the wallet fastened to the front arch of the saddle. Contained in the wallet is Olga's grooming brush, some cutlery, a change of underclothes, a post for tethering horses, and as much tobacco as he has been able to squeeze in. Not fair to expect the old girl to carry all this as well as everything else. She raises her head a little.

He unstraps the rolled blanket and carries it under his arm. Her neck straightens.

Then he remembers *David Copperfield*. 'Must weigh a bleeding ton, you poor old thing.' He dives into the rucksack attached to the saddle and pulls out the two volumes wrapped in brown paper. His instinct is to throw them away into the thorn bushes, but remembers Dr Simmonds' advice about emergencies. He hesitates; then tucks one under each arm, cursing their weight. Olga slides him a look of relief and begins to trot again. He has to jog alongside her, loaded with all that gear, but never mind, he's less exhausted than she is. And to think the Boer on his pony carries nothing but his gun, his bandolier, and his umbrella!

> *Boots, boots, boots, boots*
> *Marchin' over Africa . . .*

That came out of the poetry book Doctor Simmonds had given him. Funny how verses come into your head when you're out on the veldt for days on end, with an empty belly and a dry, swelling tongue, and a ton of equipment on your back if you're infantry. Maybe he got it right, that poet called Kipper or something like, that's why he's famous. And overhead that bleeding balloon is floating up in the gigantic blue sky, looking out for Boer snipers crouched behind those hills with their Mausers. You can see a man in the balloon basket peering down through field glasses. Probably there's bottles of champagne up there, and roast chicken and smoked salmon. Oi, guv, chuck us down a bone or two!

The sun beats down so hard you wonder how these grey-skinned Tommies can stand it. Their precision marching is impressive but they're dropping like flies now on this forced march; they haven't the stamina to carry a rifle and a hundred and fifty rounds of ammunition, to say nothing of what was in their haversacks. Cartwright says most of them are rotten with syphilis. But when it rains it's worse. The sky curdles with sudden black clouds, then cracks open and releases the deluge. It can thrash down for hours, with thunder exploding above your head as if the artillery's got lost in the sky. Then it's pitiful to see each man's face turned towards the sky, mouth open to catch the drops of rain that fall.

Yesterday, when they rose at dawn the air seemed full of snowflakes. But these flakes had gauzy wings which, fluttering in the early morning sunlight, produced the exact effect of windblown snow. Or so Cartwright told him, Patch never having experienced that wintry phenomenon. The locusts whirred past in their millions, leaving the troops alone, but baffled. 'Bloomin' 'eck, even the bleedin' butterflies are khaki-coloured!' cried one trooper.

Young Colonel Hannay's in charge of Patch's division. It's good to see an officer you can admire. He's out there in the front, leading the MIs and making them feel all right even though they've only just learnt to ride. The officers aren't wearing their swords in case they flash in the sun and get mistaken for heliographs. Everyone's straining their eyes for a strip of green on the horizon. The Tiger Scouts with those stupid wildcat skins on their hats are up ahead, supposed to be leading the men to the Modder River, and they'd better know where they're going. The Modder River. Even Patch, with his shaky grasp of Dutch, knows that Modder means mud. Still, when your water bottle's been empty for hours and your mouth's full of dust, even mud sounds thirst-quenching.

But what if the river's lined with Boers and their killer-rifles? Patch tries to do his trick of thinking of pussy to divert this speculation. He hasn't seen real action yet and doesn't know if he's a man yet, or not. He's got plenty of swagger, specially in his slouch hat pinned up stylishly on one side, which attracts the girls (he knows that), but right now he'd gladly turn back home, wherever that is, for a glass of cold beer and a shower and a clean shirt. Back to pussy now: that lovely wetness between Fancy's legs he had slipped into before he left, tonguing her ear and gripping her shoulders, but what about those Mausers, they can pick off a man a mile away and the cartridges don't have to be reloaded every time like the Lee Enfields.

Maybe a prayer would be a good idea. A prayer to the Virgin Mary. That virgin nurse. Seems like a sin to think about her fanny. Nevertheless Patch distracts himself for a few minutes by undressing the virgin nurse, who turns out to look like the statue of Mary, stripped, her eyes downcast, her hands chastely covering her bush. What about the other hair, the hair beneath her veil? What does that look like? As a child, Patch tried to see under the wimples of the Sisters of Mercy to ascertain whether hair grew in so tightly confined a space. Once Sister Theckla's wimple had slipped a fraction and to his horror he could see only bristles beyond her forehead! His young stomach had lurched at the thought of a female shaven head.

Best move on from the Virgin. Perhaps it'd be safer to address the Son of God directly.

O sacred heart of Jesus I place my trust in thee.

Sarah's Diary

13 February 1900

Our little villa has taken in three new nurses from Australia, all very highly organised and efficient though somewhat overbearing. Middle-aged and bespectacled, lean and energetic, they have only one object in life: to work, and work they do with a vengeance. The little graces of womanhood and the feminine pleasures and varieties are not for these women of steel. They come to Africa with nothing but a tiny tin trunk the size of a biscuit box, and a kit-bag. But for the sick and wounded they brought a whole cargo! Packing case after packing case of shirts, Nightingale scarves, linen, Vi-cocoa, dressings, and I don't know what besides. Most estimable women.

Sameela and Rushda are worth their weight in gold! Not only do they do all our cleaning etc for us, they also cook us glorious meals very cheaply (and food is so expensive here, and meat hard to come by). But the girls seem to have private access to a 'Halaal' butcher because they are Mohammedans. They present us with all sorts of very spicy meals with curious combinations and rice, sometimes dyed yellow, always accompanies what they cook. In our sweet-smelling pantry there is a circular box divided into eight segments, each one filled with a different type of spice: clove, coriander, nutmeg, cinnamon (I don't know the names of the others), which the girls grind up with a pestle and mortar, perfuming the whole house.

14 February

This is a letter dictated to me by one of my favourite patients, George Tomkins, as one of my jobs is amanuensis to those who cannot write through illiteracy or wounds or general weakness:

> Dear Mary,
> Just a note to let you know I am getting on famous and hope to be home soon. I was hit by a bullet in the right forearm, and the surgeon had to take it off below the elbow. They have made a famous job of it. I have no pain and I am eating heartily. It will be quite easy to strap a hand on to the stump. You must *not* worry about me as I am really alright. I am lying in bed smoking a cigar. Our baby is due any day now, please get someone to write as soon as she arrives (I know it will be a little woman, cute as her mother).
> With much love I am your devoted Husband
> George

This is typical of all the men – they are determined not to let their families know the true level of their suffering. George does not mention the gangrene that has set in despite the removal of his forearm; nor the infection in his wounded leg which we fear will become gangrenous as well. He lay too long on the battlefield before being delivered to the hospital train. He is actually a very sick man, and the doctor here is worried about his chances of survival. Yet in all his pain he cracks jokes, teases and flirts, and blues the air with his swearing, though they all try not to curse in front of us.

15 February

The Australian nurses and I got the fright of our lives this morning when Rushda and Sameela turned up for work clutching blood-stained cloths to their lips. On removing the cloths they revealed the cause of the bloodshed: both have had their beautiful front teeth removed! I didn't like to ask the reason why but Sister Talbot had no such compunction – Australians are very forthright, I am learning – and demanded to know why they had performed this ghastly act upon their gums. At this the girls became very coy, nudging each other knowingly, but refusing to offer an explanation. Once they had left the room, another rather plain nurse from 'down under', whose own teeth could have done with some attention, said in a severe voice 'I believe it is done for sexual pleasure.' I found myself blushing violently at this untrammelled language, and a sudden silence fell as we all tried to imagine what she meant by her remark.

Today Louise and I made the long trip to Simonstown, Cape Town's naval base. (I decided not to tell her about the missing teeth as she is liable to explode with lewd laughter at the mention of the word 'sexual'.) We were astounded by the beauty of the coastline. Simonstown itself nestles within its natural harbour which is filled with ships of every description. Incarcerated on several of them are Boer prisoners-of-war. They are also held in large compounds. The sick and wounded Boers are attended to at a Barracks hospital called 'The Palace' – in jest, for it is anything but palatial. Apparently the fit prisoners are being exiled to the British colonies of St Helena, Bermuda and Ceylon as there is not enough room for them in the camps here. One cannot help feeling sorry for these men; they are so attached to their land here and now they are being shipped off to such terribly foreign parts. We saw them wander about their compounds: they look like any other white man, many of them with kind, sensitive faces.

16 February

Kimberley is relieved and we have won a battle. It seems scarcely credible. All Roberts' doing, of course. The Australian sisters in our villa were suddenly sent to the Front and

Louise and I are envious. We love the beauty of Cape Town but feel guilty that we are not in the thick of war, binding the wounds of heroic soldiers . . . Though Louise wants to go to the Front, she is very much in love with Dr James, the chief medical officer of her hospital. This is absurd as he is a married man. Nevertheless, she contrived to get herself invited to a dinner at the very grand Mount Nelson Hotel where apparently there is much glitter and entertainment and wine flowing. Some officers are still stationed there for the time being, while the Tommies who haven't been sent up North camp on open land in and around Cape Town. Because Louise is so animated she received a great deal of attention and could talk about nothing else when we met for ices and strawberries and cream on the veranda of Dix's Café.

We greet, rather coolly, the young ladies from the *Dunottar* who cluster round Dix's tables and relate their adventures in breathy, high-pitched voices. Louise darts furious glances in their direction because some of them are invited to the 'Nellie' as well, and try to steal her thunder – or this is how I interpret the state of things. I could hear them bewailing the disappearance of so many eligible bachelors up North.

I must say the streets of Cape Town seem quite empty now that the bulk of the army has moved on.

Dear Sarah,

By now you will have arrived in Cape Town. How sad I felt as I watched the *Dunottar* steam out of S'Hampton – though at least we were able to keep contact till our streamer finally snapped. I wonder so much whether you will have continued your voyage to Natal to nurse closer to the war front (nothing but bad news there), or if you have been allocated to a military hospital in Cape Town itself. Do let me know when you have a minute.

I'm pleased to say there has been a good response to the public statement of the Conciliation Committee's aims – some four hundred letters from sympathisers, which is very encouraging. The wonderful news is that Miss Hobhouse has agreed to be secretary of the women's branch of the SACC, which means I am in close contact with her at least once a week. What an inspiration she is! And what unbounded energy, which puts us younger women to shame. You should see her hurtle up the steps of Rossetti Mansions, throw herself into her flat on the third floor – drawing disapproving stares from neighbours who consider her to be pro-Boer and therefore as bad as the enemy – and immediately get to work on the immense correspondence and piles of pamphlets that cover her dining room table. We helpers stuff envelopes and write addresses and listen enthralled as she tells us news of the war. Our main task now, as you know, is to disseminate accurate information about the war, as most of the rabble-rousing jingoism in our newspapers and journals cannot be believed. Miss Hobhouse's brother Leonard is political correspondent for the Manchester Guardian, which is one of our sources of accurate information. Sometimes he rushes in on his long spidery legs as well, running his fingers through the wild bush of his hair, and talking twenty to the dozen about everything – not only the war but his theories of plant evolution and sociology in such an amusing and entertaining fashion that all our heads begin to spin and we have to hold our sides which ache from too much laughter.

There is great excitement here over the three sieges, in particular that of Mafeking, though Leonard's opinion is that the siege is entirely due to B-P's failure of judgement. I myself find it rather tasteless to be adding up the number of siege days as if a game of cricket were being played – which I believe it is, anyway, on Sundays in Mafeking.

I wonder if you have heard about the scandal over the Queen's chocolate. Her Majesty wanted to give every trooper a bar of chocolate to mark the arrival of the twentieth century, and placed an order with the Quaker chocolate makers for some fifty thousand bars – only to be told firmly that Quakers are pacifists and do not support warmongering. Even though I am a Quaker myself I have to say I don't see that giving a Tommy a bar of chocolate from his Queen is actively support-ing the war effort. Her Majesty had to beseech them to change their minds about this and eventually they rather grudgingly agreed. One can only admire the high principles of these chocolate makers who would rather lose an enormous order than betray their own beliefs.

I long to hear from you and, if I may, will pass on your news about the hospitals and the wounded soldiers to Miss Hobhouse as she takes a great interest in the war work of the Red Cross.

Yours affectionately, dear, brave Sarah,

Sophie

Dear Sophie,

I was so delighted to receive your letter today. I think of you often, and soon after my arrival sent you a postcard of Table Mountain which I hope arrived safely. It was good to hear your news about the work of the Conciliation Committee; I enjoyed your description of Miss Hobhouse bounding up the stairs of her block of flats and annoying the neighbours. How wonderful that she is now in a position of responsibility in the women's branch. Her strong, compassionate face remains with me, but I fear she will be disappointed in my hospital news: Cape Town is definitely not Scutari.

On the other hand I have to say that I have been so overpowered by my new challenges and experiences that the whole concept of conciliation seems very far from the day-to-day life in the military hospitals. Cape Town is so far removed from the Boer Republics that it is difficult to be aware of the presence of the 'enemy' other than in the wounds of my patients, and the stories they tell me about the 'Boors'. (I have enclosed a few extracts from my diary which speak of these wounds and stories in more detail and will, I think, be of interest to you.) Knowing what I do about the Boer history – largely through attending meetings and listening to you rehearse your speeches – it is almost impossible for me to think of this 'enemy' as something wicked. Even the Tommies have a certain respect for their plucky opponents who occasionally behave like gentlemen and have the same skin colour, unlike the men they have fought in previous wars. As for the Tommies, it is a disgrace that they should be sacrificed at the altar of Mammon, for this war is about greed and gold, and the rank and file are cannon fodder, merely.

By the way, I have to say that the delight which the Queen's chocolate brought to these same Tommies would have melted the hearts of those stern Quakers who reluctantly made the chocolate when Her Majesty went down on her knees (hard to imagine, even metaphorically). Most of them are keeping the pretty boxes as treasures to take home. They are hesitant about eating the chocolate itself but I don't think they will hold out for long.

I look forward so much to hearing all your news.

Yours very affectionately,

Sarah

Paardeberg, February 1900

Patch is confused. He is in the middle of a battle, yet no one seems to know what's going on, least of all the men in charge. Where is the enemy? Where, for that matter, is Bobs? You can see Cronje's laager of covered wagons extending for miles on the river banks on the other side of the Modder, looking for all the world to the starving Tommies like gigantic loaves of newly baked bread, but of the Boer commando there is no sign. Except, of course, for the showers of bullets and shells that seem to be bursting out of the ground before the river and slaughtering the British Army.

The river is as muddy as Patch imagined, with carcasses of horses and oxen floating in its brew for good measure. Its banks are fringed with karee trees and green willows whose leaves trail picturesquely in the khaki water, inviting picnics and lovers and messing about with boats. Behind the line of wagons, where black scouts and servants scurry about with horses, dogs, firewood, three-legged pots, and other objects which Patch can't identify, are the caves. You can just see the shapes of women and children crouched in these caves, beyond the reach of British shells and bullets. Fancy bringing your entire household with you into battle – no wonder Cronje's commando got trapped here when trying to escape from Roberts' mighty advance. In the stench of battle, there is the smell of cooking – something sweet and spicy blending with the aroma of burnt wood.

The units are staggering with fatigue after the long march,

but now that maniac Kitchener is galloping among the men screaming out orders for the mounted infantry to storm Cronje's laager: now from here, now there, now stop, now start again over there. It's quite obvious to even the most inexperienced trooper that you're wasting your bravery against well-hidden rifles: far better to bombard the laager into submission with lyddite. Kitchener seems to be making it up on the spot; he's panicking. Don't these people have to draw up battle plans; isn't that what they learn to do at army school? One brigade slithers behind anthills as sleet of bullets whistles out of the trenches. Another is making little rushes to the river bed, with men falling all the time. They shoot into nothing: you can't aim at men hidden in the ground.

Why is Kitchener in charge? Isn't Bobs supposed to be plotting the battle in a cool calm way, ensuring the support and admiration of his troops? Patch is waiting for the command for his unit to plunge forward into sure death. He feels his knees turn to water, and realises that he is not yet a man, worthy of adult respect. In the midst of his fear he also feels rage, indignation that in obeying Kitchener's orders he is to die so pointlessly. Clearly the professional troopers don't feel anything as lily-livered as this. Look how, further on, long dotted rows of Tommies advance, lie down, rise and advance again in perfect unison, regardless of the shells which burst and shriek all round them. Not one of these men pauses or checks his advance as the deadly shower ploughs up the ground at his feet, or tears and mauls at the flesh of his neighbour with jagged splinters. Can these be the same puny creatures who, off the battlefield, steal, fart, swear, get drunk, and display not a jot of this useless discipline and courage that Patch, astonished, now witnesses.

Someone says that little Bobs *with a smile round both his ears* – Patch has read the poem – has caught a cold and is spending the day in bed.

Is K of Chaos enjoying this bloodbath? Perhaps he would be ashamed of a bloodless battle. Here he comes, shouting again from his charger, waving his sabre in the air, his red-rimmed eyes blazing like machine guns, and next thing Patch hears the bugle command and finds himself charging on Olga towards the Boer trenches on the side of the river; swarms of bullets fly out of the ground and every man around him gets shot and a hundred horses gallop riderless to the river and get shot too. Now Patch's head is pumping with the fusillade of battle, the song of the bullet, the thunder of Olga's hooves, the great belching yellow flames of shells exploding in the laager, and he gallops faster through the bullets, shooting all the while at the cloud of smoke that pours across the laager, then Olga gets hit and buckles under and he's done for. He flings himself to the ground and prepares for death. But for some reason the Boers stop firing for a while, maybe they're reading the Bible or praying to the Lord to be their sword and shield as of old or maybe they've just plain run out of bullets.

Olga is dying before his eyes, along with all the other horseflesh around him, and he looks away, angry. Should he shoot her through the head to end it quickly for her? She gives a groaning spasm; he turns round and her eyes are filming over, but still have that sweet look which breaks his heart. The signal to retire sounds and he crawls back, his body unwounded, but his brain shattered and strange from the noise and the smell and his astonishment at his own brief burst of bravery. Somewhere in this cocktail of adrenaline he feels the ache of sorrow for Olga, as if she was his sister or sweetheart or something weird like that, gone forever. But better for her to die that way, nobly; better than starve or sicken to death like all those other nags. And there's Cartwright also crawling, also lost his horse, his face sallow with exhaustion, though probably, knowing Cartwright, he's thinking of some girl's breasts and fanny even in the jaws of death, and the thought of this makes Patch think along the same lines and he begins to feel a bit normal again.

But who's won that battle? The enemy are still in their trenches, and the British are re-forming – if that's what you can call the muddle of men tottering about now, their eyes staring crazily through the soot and filth on their faces. He supposes he must look the same. Now the captain tells them they can eat and drink and rest for a while. There's only a biscuit and that's dinner, and water from the river afloat with carcasses. They're supposed to boil the water first but there isn't time for such refinements. Thank God he's got good strong teeth, not like most of the Tommies who have to soak their biscuits on account of rotting teeth and gums. Then, just as he settles down, the order comes: *Renew the assault!! Ford the river and rush the position*! The captain is white-faced, he's worn out, same as the men. False alarm! There's not enough horses to make up a mounted infantry so it's back to the biscuit for the moment anyway.

While he munches he watches the Canadians and the Cornwalls charge the laager in a magnificent surge from the other side of the river, undaunted by the falling men. The artillery behind them are bombarding the covered wagons from all directions and you can't help feeling queasy about the women and children inside it when you hear the shriek and scream of shells; when you see the yellow-green fumes as they explode; when you smell the stink of sulphur. But the bullets are flying out from the Boer trenches at the charging troopers, and Cronje's pom-pom canon is sending forth shells with its seven-fold cough as fast as the Maxims send forth shot. The ground shudders and throws up great geysers of red earth when the shells explode, and the men shudder too, in mortal fear, when they hear that *how-how-how-how!* Now the regiments of Stephenson's brigade are rushing at smoke with fixed bayonets and the Highland Brigade have found a safe crossing for reinforcements. Stretcher carriers are stumbling about picking up the wounded, some of the mission people among them, taking the chance to pray over dying men and help them into heaven.

But what's that down on the north river bed? Who's that solitary horseman charging the laager, straight into the line of vicious Mauser fire bursting in volleys out of the ground? *What madman gave this crazy command?* That's some of the men who arrived earlier coming up a way behind him, hesitant, no wonder, it's suicide, they've spent all morning fighting off Boer reinforcements, they're utterly spent, and they are falling already. But who is that in front?

It can't be, but it is: Colonel Hannay, the prince among men, charging his horse into the firing squad, firing from the shoulder himself. Then his horse is struck and crumples and Hannay gets flung and the force of a Boer bullet flings him again and he throws out a hand and then is still. In all the rage of battle, a song drifts through Patch's head: *Oh Hannay boy* . . . There, is K. satisfied now? It seems the suicidal dash has saved the brigade from certain slaughter; the charge is called off because K can at last see it's useless.

As Patch rests, enjoying the inexplicable surge of elation that has overtaken him, he wonders if surviving this battle means he has officially achieved manhood, like the Xhosa boys or the boys further north who have to kill a lion before they can be recognised as men. Also, the witnessing of Hannay's superhuman bravery was in some mysterious way a privilege; it has been absorbed into his own frailer system; he is the better for it. Perhaps it's true that men are made on the battlefield, even when the battle is a cock-up. He half-smiles (it comes naturally now), and begins to fall asleep, like so many troopers around him.

He hears a harp playing. The sound floats out from behind him, silvering the sordid air. In a flash he understands everything: he has died in battle and an angel is coming to fetch his soul. He is excited, though apprehensive. This is the moment all those catechism lessons in the orphanage have been preparing him for, and the act of contrition leaps to his lips for the second time that day: *O my God I am heartily sorry and beg pardon for all my sins* . . . But even as he mutters the words that will automatically open the gates of heaven for him he begins to recognise the tune the harp is playing. It is a ditty he and Johan have often sung together and it's not a hymn. It seems unlikely that an angel would be playing a music-hall favourite to usher him into paradise.

It is almost disappointing to think that maybe he is alive after all. He experiments with turning his head – it still works – and can see only a pile of rocks among the bushes at the foot of a little hill, no radiant heavenly gates, no plump beckoning cherubs. The music is pouring out from behind the thorn bushes. He looks around; no one else seems to be hearing it – too busy chewing or chattering or just plain snoring. Cronje's men are shooting shells from the laager spasmodically – *pom-pom-pom* – but not in this direction. He rises to his blood-stained feet.

A small figure with carrot-coloured hair is hunched beneath a blue gum tree. His helmet and rolled blanket lie on the ground beside him. The music appears to be coming out of his trousers. There is no sign of a harp. The trooper's back faces Patch, the head dropped as if in sleep. The familiar melody streams out from his lap, and the little man's shoulders convulse. Cautiously Patch approaches. The music is stirring him as well. Partly because the unsung words touch on his raw nerve. There is no *home sweet home* for Patrick Donnelly, never has been. He clears his throat extravagantly and the trooper swings round in alarm.

'That's nice music,' says Patch. At which point the plangent sounds stop in mid-stream.

'Needs windin' oop.' The man's voice is snivelly.

'What does?'

The man holds up what looks like a silver cigarette case. 'Music box.'

Patch is astounded. 'I thought music boxes were . . . big chappies.'

The trooper smiles and Patch can see half his teeth are missing. He extends the box to Patch. 'Snuff?' Or, more like, 'snoof'.

The two men sniff up the lovely spicy powder and indulge in a bout of sneezing and nose-blowing. 'The name's Bill,' snuffles the Tommy. 'Bill Patterson. From Belfast. Me home sweet home, see.'

Belfast! Patch feels his heart jump with a terror more profound than anything he felt on the battlefield. *Belfast* means Presbyterians trying to prevent Home Rule in Ireland; *Belfast*, the enemy of Dublin and the Vatican; *Belfast* North, Dublin South. The only geography he had ever learnt at the orphanage. How many times every day had the Sisters of Mercy not tiraded against Belfast, than which there can be no more evil place? He stares deep into Bill Patterson's pinkish, friendly eyes.

'Patrick Donnelly,' he says. And adds, benignly, 'Call me Patch,' though his instinct is to shout *Get thee behind me, Satan!*

'It's leaving the kids behind is worst,' Bill says. 'A boy and a girl. And a wife, of course.'

Now comes the moment that Patch always dreads: the photograph. But Bill has a surprise for him – not photographs but pen and ink drawings. Someone has made a pretty good picture of a smiling woman's face with a boy's face on one side and a girl's on the other.

'Very nice,' says Patch politely. 'Who's the artist?'

'I've always been good at likenesses,' says Bill. 'You married, then?' He begins winding the box.

'Me? Nah!' Patch snorts. 'Not ready for that yet.' (He ignores Fancy's outraged screech.)

The music suddenly bursts out of the little box. The volume is astonishing. Patch clears his throat – and begins to sing without thinking. He does not look at Bill's face for fear of tears:

> 'Mid pleasures and Palaces though we may roam
> Be it ever so humble, there's no place like home!

He has a clear tenor voice and holds one hand up to his chest. Halfway through, Bill joins in:

> Home! Home! Sweet sweet Home!
> There's no place like home!

Bill's singing voice is a melting baritone, utterly different from the pinched voice he speaks with. He harmonises with Patch, a third below to begin with, but then he meanders about in a strong counterpoint which enriches the tenor voice. The sweet mournful tones entwine with the chimes of the music box and envelop them in a protective cocoon, or so it feels. The shelling from the Boer pom-poms seems to have stopped.

'Sure, there's nothing like a good song to set the heart right,' says Bill after a while.

The sun is setting now, doing its trick of bleeding into the sky so you half expect to see Jesus hanging up there on his cross and a choir of angels bursting through the heavens. 'Mmmm,' agrees Patch, enjoying the surge of warmth brought on by the music box, the sunset, Bill's words. Bill is telling him the story of his life in Belfast. The word is suddenly drained of its previous poison, and reverts to being a city in the north of Ireland. Patch sits down and listens. He likes the way the little man speaks, twisting the words up into an unfamiliar shape with his tongue, then sliding them out through his nose.

It turns out that Bill is an orphan too, though at least he had known his parents for a while. An aunt took over the young family. Patch finds it easy to tell him how he was dumped at the Sisters of Mercy orphanage, and to talk about the pain of this, which he has discussed with no one else before, not even Johan (though Dr Simmonds seemed to understand without being told). Bill looks at him mischievously and grins: 'You a Papist then?'

'I am,' says Patch with sinking heart.

Bill laughs, a surprising baritone wobble, and says, 'That makes us enemies then for I come from an Orange family.'

'How d'you mean?' asks Patch, briefly conjuring up mother, father and children all stained carroty-colour, like Bill's hair.

'Sure, man, have you never heard of the Orange Order?' Patch has not. This had not been mentioned by the nuns. 'The marchin'? The sashes?' Bill is incredulous. 'The fife and drum? The glorious twelfth? King Billy on his white charger?'

Patch looks blank.

Bill is beginning to brighten. 'The arches! The banners! The sashes! King Billy walking hand in hand with Queen Mary!' He has entirely shed his melancholy. 'The bonfires the night before, man, high as a steeple!' He glances slyly at Patch. 'The kick-the-Pope bands.'

Patch is enjoying this monologue, though he can't understand a word of it. He chuckles.

Bill is disappointed. 'What kind of a Papist are you then?'

'I'm a Papist alright,' growls Patch. 'Being Irish,' he unwisely adds.

'Irish, are ye?' cries Bill. 'And you haven't heard of the Orange Order? Where've you been living, man? There's more Presbyterians in Ulster than Papists I can tell ye.'

Patch can feel himself blushing under the soot. 'I'm an Irish Catholic but not born in Ireland,' he mumbles. 'It's my mother who is Irish.'

Bill is not bothered. He has moved on to other things. 'The strange thing is that them Boers we're fighting are Orangemen as well. They even call this Boer republic The Orange Free State, did you know that? We're all descendants of the House of Orange in Holland, from two hundred years back. Yet they certainly aren't loyal to Her Majesty like us, it's a puzzle. More snuff?'

As he holds out the snuff music box a strange thing happens to Bill. He seems to be changing into a giant frog, he gathers his limbs together and leaps, his arms and legs splayed out, everything moves quickly and slowly at the same time, he lands on Patch who is surprised at the hardness, the power, of the little man's body, and knocks him over not just sideways but skittering along the stony earth for a few yards. At the same time an ear-splitting explosion and a burst of yellow smoke rise from the spot where Patch had been sitting. The smell of rotten eggs permeates the already foetid air. Patch's brain feels blown to a thousand pieces. He wonders if he has gone deaf.

A missionary runs over, he sees they are both alive and not in need of last rites. 'That was close!' he says to Patch in a jolly voice. 'Lucky your friend was there to save you.'

Bill is looking for the music box. He finds it still tinkling under a pile of hot earth, miraculously undamaged. He offers it to Patch. 'Snuff?'

Patch is shaking too much to accept. He finds that nip of brandy in his pocket and takes a swig, then passes it to Bill. 'I'd be dead now,' he reflects, 'if you hadn't done that.'

'Sure, we'd both be in heaven,' grins Bill.

Patch feels awkward. He doesn't want to reveal to this new friend who has risked his life for him the terrible news that he has absolutely no chance whatsoever of going to heaven, for that glorious paradise is reserved strictly for Catholics, who alone belong to the one true Faith.

Fortunately, Captain Hughes now calls his men together and orders them to bivouac for the night.

'See you again, p'raps,' says Patch. *Thank-you* is too small a phrase to utter now.

'You never know.' The little man smiles broadly. 'Anything can happen on them battlefields.'

Rondebosch Number 3 Hospital, February

The basket which Sarah is carrying is overflowing with blue garlands. She feels as if she has reached up into the sky and pulled down a few handfuls of its brightness. The trails of plumbago will be draped over tables and bed-ends in the hospital tents, a job the lady volunteers would have loved, had they been allowed into this hospital by the chief medical officer. The Australian nurses had assembled a number of makeshift vases from broken milk jugs and glue pots before they left; it is Sarah's delightful task to fill these daily with fresh flowers.

Those men who can are pressing silver leaves from the mountain trees to send home as cards. How idyllic it all seems – on the face of it. Yesterday she and Louise had walked up the lower slopes of Devil's Peak to pick the leaves for the men. They gazed out over the long flat stretches of largely uninhabited land that ended in a ripple of misty mountains; then picked baskets full of the feathery silver leaves for the Tommies. Tiny purple flowers bloomed between the stones they walked on, and the bushes gleamed with yellow blossom. A dark fragrance rose from the mountain, intoxicating the two women with its potency. Even Louise was momentarily silenced by the power of the place, and murmured to Sarah, as they returned to their respective hospitals in Dr James' Cape cart, 'We must be the luckiest women in the world.' Though she felt she should query this comment, Sarah could think of nothing more apt to say, other than a sharp retort such as 'here for the unluckiest of reasons,' which would have spoilt the afternoon.

As she expertly arranges eight hibiscus heads in a tin basin, she hears the bugle call that announces Mail Day. No doubt there will be a patriotic letter from mama, and perhaps some news from Sophie, who now writes every week. She stands back and admires the effect of her floral arrangement which now resembles a pool of vivid red water lilies. The men are stirring hopefully, for Mail Day is for them a source of joy, a lifeline to their families who send such sackloads of misspelt love. Soon she will be reading and writing letters on behalf of those who cannot do so themselves. And here already is Corporal Harris with the post; the men watch him with ravenous eyes – thank God everyone gets at least one letter today and she does not have to bear any bitter disappointments.

She herself is handed a missive from her mother, the contents of which she can predict. Nevertheless it is always pleasant to receive news of home and conjure up the comforts of the family house in Hampstead. But there is no time to read her letter now; the Tommies who are either illiterate or too ill to read themselves are gazing at her in expectation. She pockets her mail, and goes to the bedside of Private Tomkins.

He is clutching a page of neat writing to his chest, and smiling in anticipation in spite of the agony etched on his features. Sweat pours down his cheeks; his body shudders with the torture of advanced gangrene.

'Is it the baby?' he gasps.

Sarah scans the letter. Her heart sinks. The news could not be worse. Mrs Tomkins died in childbirth three weeks ago, together with the baby. She looks at George Tomkins' anxious eyes. His facial skin is almost green. It is unlikely that he will survive the week.

Sarah makes a decision. She smiles delightedly. 'A bonny daughter!' she exclaims. 'Both doing well.' Congratulations! She touches his shoulder; her hand is shaking.

Private Tomkins sighs in relief. The furrows in his face

relax. 'Great news!' he whispers. They will probably be the last words he utters.

She moves on round the ward, fighting down her guilt. What if he should recover? But there is no chance of that. Look at him now, a happy man.

Though the other troopers' letters do not carry similar tragic news, they reveal to her the dire poverty in the homes left behind. It seems that the funds raised by *The Absent-Minded Beggar* are available only on production of the marriage certificate. This means that common-law wives or women who have lost their certificates cannot receive payments even though they are the families of men who are fighting the war for Britain, and they are starving.

After reading out three letters which refer to this bureaucratic injustice Sarah says to a trooper whose family has been refused support, 'We should write to Mr Kipling about this. That money was meant for families like yours.'

The trooper shakes his head. 'I don't want to sound ungrateful, nurse. Mr Kipling is the soldiers' friend. I wouldn't want to worry him.'

If he visits here I shall mention it, thinks Sarah; then attends to her mother's letter:

London,
1 February 1906

Darling Sarah,

A quick note to let you know that Marble has given birth to *seven* kittens, all ginger, except one pure black! As Marble is neither ginger nor black we wonder who on earth the father can be! And on a sadder note, our beloved Striker breathed his last two days ago. He had grown blind and deaf, as you know, and could no longer enjoy his walks on the heath – so though I shed many a tear (even Father was seen to wipe his eye), in the end his departure was a blessing. We are now looking at young golden Labrador pups, but will wait till the grieving period is over before we rush into anything.

We think of you every day, darling, but are relieved that there is no war in Cape Town and that you are actually enjoying yourself in the beauties of the Cape. You say you can understand the Dutch of the Friendly Boers – it is always agreeable to know the language of the country you visit (who would have thought our long sojourn in the Netherlands would have stood you in good stead in this way?)

What a contrast is your experience with those who are besieged in Mafeking and Ladysmith! We hear Col. Baden-Powell keeps up the spirits of the citizens of Mafeking wonderfully with all kinds of entertainments, but to starve in the midst of constant bombardment from Boer artillery must be agony indeed (I believe they are reduced to eating dogs and horses – I shudder to think of it). Of course, the pro-Boers here have no sympathy for the besieged and probably rejoice that both towns have been surrounded for over a hundred days!

Father sends his love and asks me to tell you that his study of The Exotic Tulip in a Puritan Society will be published in *Nature* before long. He hopes to create quite a storm!

All our love, darling,
Mother

Paardeberg, 27 February 1900

When the white flags had rippled above the trenches, four thousand (is that all?) Boer burghers had staggered out of them, looking like a nightmarish army of bedraggled tramps, with their unkempt beards, and their tattered trousers and waistcoats and moleskin jackets, not a sign of a uniform. Behind them trailed large numbers of unsmiling women and children, surprisingly clean considering they'd spent the last two weeks crouched in muddy caves; then hundreds of kaffir servants herding thousands of cattle and horses. On the procession went, and on, till finally out came Cronje himself, sluggish and plump as an uprooted queen ant, the reins of his not-so-white horse in one hand, the fingers of his frozen-faced wife entwined in the other. Amazing that so many had survived the pounding of the laager with shells and lyddite as ordered by Bobs when he eventually appeared on the scene.

Now Colonel Pretyman is leading Cronje and his off-white horse to the awaiting Bobs while the vanquished Boer commando is packed into ox wagons heading for the prisoner-of-war camp in Cape Town. Cronje is surprisingly small – no bigger than Bobs, whose height is only just five foot. Pretyman introduces the midget generals. Patch, watching with the troops, feels he could tuck one under each arm. Cronje's shoulders are slumped. His famed and feared *sjambok* dangles in his left hand. Roberts, erect and dapper, extends a firm arm. His turbaned sepoy hovers discreetly behind with folded arms. The two generals shake hands.

'You have fought a fine battle, sir,' barks little Bobs. 'Will you join me for breakfast?'

Cronje stares at him, baffled. He can't speak a word of English. He cannot comprehend his defeat. He does not appreciate the fine British breakfast laid before him on porcelain plates with solid silver cutlery. Through an interpreter he growls out a demand to keep his wife and servants with him. Bobs agrees. Harmless old git now. (In fact, two years after the war Cronje will horrify his people by re-enacting the Last Stand of Paardeberg at the St Louis World Fair, with a team of willing Boers and American acrobats. His remarriage to an American woman will complete his treachery.)

While the generals breakfast, a handful of men, Patch among them, are sent in to clear up the laager and retrieve the five Boer cannons.

Carcasses of one species or another are decomposing in the Modder River as the men wade through a shallow ford. Mud River: more like a swamp by now. On being disturbed, the putrid waters shove a fist of leper-stink down the men's throats, straight through the useless kerchiefs tied beneath their eyes. This stench is going into my body thinks Patch, in a panic as the putrid smell gnaws through his skin, into his blood, into his lungs, through his eardrums into his brain; his whole body is seething with stink, like the river. He feels nauseous; he must vomit his guts out into the bubbling Modder brew.

Yet by the time they reach the trenches their nostrils have hardened and their empty stomachs have settled again and the excrement and filth, buzzing with flies in the Boer hideouts, has lost its power to disgust. In fact, a stir of amazement runs through the men as they scrutinise the deep, narrow trenches in which a rifleman can crouch with a minimum of danger from shells. To think less than two hundred casualties emerged after ten days of bombardment, while the British dead and wounded numbered over a thousand – thanks to K of Chaos on the day Bobs caught a cold.

'If ever there is a lesson to be learned by the British Army, this is it!' cries an officer-engineer, pointing to the festering cesspits with undisguised admiration. 'Today it is the *defence* who have the advantage, not the attack.' And 'Hear! Hear!' murmur the men, thinking of Hannay and the others.

But no one is prepared for what lies beyond the trenches.

As the little group of men and officers move on towards the laager itself, a shadow of black gauze lifts up from it and billows towards them like some avenging Boer spirit. The shadow drops a skein of sound, a hum, a drone, such as the moan some peasants make for their dead. *Dear God*! screams a man.

Is this what the Bible means by Plague?

Now the shadow has become a net of black flies joyfully attaching themselves to all exposed faces and stinking clothes, and no amount of arm-waving or shouting will dislodge the crust of winged insects whose proboscës Patch can feel sucking at his skin. 'How can people live like this?' cries out the captain as they gaze at the putrefying bodies of oxen, mules, horses, black servants, all seething with a new and virulent parasite life. The covered wagons are now charred skeletons; faeces and rotting food everywhere, the heavy rainfall of a few days before having contrived to make a rich stew of rancid ingredients beneath their feet. They trample on the Boer flags and banners with their orange stripes and quotations from the Bible. Patch picks up an orange flag stained with shit. Shit'll wash out alright. He notices a tiny chain of orange words stitched in the flag's corner. *Die Heer is My Banier*. The Lord is my banner. He folds the flag into his pocket. He will give it to the Orangeman who saved his life.

No sign of the pom-poms, the dreaded ten-a-pennies the men have been sent to recover. They lie in the depths of the Modder, pushed there by the tattered burghers en route to surrender, and no-one's going to wade in there and drag them out, thank you, not even the kaffir servants.

By the time they get back, Cronje is having a celebratory champagne lunch with Bobs. The troopers are scandalised by Cronje's lack of gratitude. This fine lunch (where did they get the chicken and potatoes?), and Cronje just stuffs the food into his mouth like the peasant he is; not a word of thanks, or even conversation. He must know a few words of English, surely? Bobs looks thoughtfully into the middle distance, he's given up trying to be hospitable.

Then, once the prisoners have been packed off to Cape Town, the troops stagger on towards Bloemfontein. Patch is not feeling well. Since leaving Cronje's laager he cannot get the rotten smell of the place out of his nostrils, and by extension his throat and bowels. He wonders about the state of the latter and the new type of exhaustion that has overtaken him and all the others. Forty thousand men should be euphoric but most are thinking: what kind of a victory is this against a mere four thousand? The tropical floods have made a mud bath of the veldt and the carts get stuck all the time and the troopers haven't the energy to push them out. A trail of dead horses and oxen lie behind them, rotting in the heat.

Patch and Cartwright put up a blanket bivouac the first night – two blankets slung over a string – and lie in their greatcoats in the mud. At nine o'clock the lightning starts, with crashes of thunder worse than any they've heard on the battlefield, and then the rain comes down solid, like tea pouring out of a million gigantic teapots in the sky. The horses stampede and gallop about the camp over bivouacs, one nearly gouging its hoof into Patch's face. The blanket bivouacs are beaten flat by the rain in five minutes; in ten, the whole camp is flooded. Patch and Cartwright crawl out, swearing: not a dry spot to be seen.

'Up a tree is better than stuck in mud,' says Cartwright gloomily. The two of them wade to a bally old thorn tree on the edge of the camp and sit in its inhospitable branches till sunrise. Cartwright tries to keep his spirits up by telling khaki jokes while the rain streams down all over them. 'Did you hear about the Tommy running for his life in a shower of bullets?' He pulls their soaking wet blanket a bit closer.

'Clever chap,' murmurs Patch who has grown suddenly hot,

and that watery feeling has come on again. Sweat runs down his face with the raindrops.

'The officer shouts out, 'Dash you! What the dash are you running for? (Cartwright can imitate a toff's voice to perfection). Quick as a flash the Tommy shouts back " *'Cause I ain't got no bleedin' wings!*"'

This feat of repartee causes the thorn tree to shake helplessly with laughter for some minutes and for Patch's spirits to revive momentarily. 'Could do with a pair of bleeding wings right now,' he snorts.

The reveille sounds, a desolate cry in a wet wilderness. Men squelch out of the trees all round, or from under bushes or from out of the mud. No dry wood to boil the Modder water on. Only the old dry biscuit, probably best used as firewood.

Now it's marching along the river five miles a day. The men, being famished, can't walk any faster. Half rations of water make them drink the Modder neat. That's thanks to Bobs' mishandling of the transport. Next thing there's another battle at a place called Poplar Grove, with the rumour that President Kruger was there himself giving his men a pep talk. The cavalry are meant to charge with sabres drawn, the mighty *arme blanche*, but the whole thing fizzles out, with Bobs and his generals blaming each other for a lost opportunity.

The usual chaos has set in with men from all regiments wandering around foraging for food while generals try to decide what to do next. Patch catches a flash of orange hair in the back yard of a deserted farmhouse. He rummages in his rucksack. 'Bill!' he calls in a weakened voice.

Bill pulls his hand out of a clay bread oven. 'Thought there might be somethin' in there to eat,' he says in an aggrieved voice. 'You look terrible, man, what's up?'

'Gut ache. But never mind about that. I've got something better than stale old bread for you.' Out comes the flag. Patch unfurls it with as much drama as he can muster.

Bill gazes in rapture. 'An Orange flag!' he breathes, as if looking at a famous work of art like that Mona Lisa picture which has mysteriously turned up in Patch's rucksack. He takes the battle-stained cloth into his reverent hands. 'What does the stitching say, eh, Patch?'

'God is my banner. Didn't help them much in Paardeberg.'

Now Bill is refolding the Boer banner rapidly and burying it in his rucksack. When he raises his head, he has something else in his hands, something made of orange and purple satin with long fringes. He unfolds the fabric reverently. It reminds Patch of that scarf thing the Catholic priests wear round their necks when saying mass. But this garment is embroidered with single eyes, ladders, open bibles. Bill drapes it across his chest, over one shoulder, under the other. 'Very nice,' says Patch doubtfully. 'What is it?' 'It's me lodge sash,' says Bill. He is stroking the faded glossy fabric. 'Belonged to me grandpa. It's the most precious thing I have. I wanted you to see it. I'll be wearin' it on July the Twelfth, same as other Orangemen in the troops.' He takes off the sash and folds it up carefully. He looks troubled. 'You know, it's mighty difficult for one Orangeman to fight another. But thank you, Patch. I'm mighty grateful to you old chap for the flag.'

He looks thoughtful; plunges his hand in his pocket. 'Tell you what, you've given me somethin', now I'll give you somethin' too.'

'I can't take it,' says Patch, staring at the music box. 'It's your special thing.'

'Take it,' says Bill. 'You can give it back after this bloomin' war.'

'You've already given me something. My life. For instance.'

'Och, that's nothing. Keep this for me.'

Since the rosary, Patch hasn't received a gift. He is engulfed with gratitude. If only his legs would stand upright. He pockets the little box, swaying. 'Till after the war then.'

'Here, hang on, what's happenin' to ye?' Bill watches in astonishment as Patch sinks to the ground, uttering a moan that seems to be ripped out from the pit of his stomach.

Next thing, Patch is in one of those unsprung bullock carts that have replaced ambulances cut back by Bobs and K. He feels a sickening ache in his gut yet when it comes to it, hasn't been able to shit anything out. His brains burn in sympathy. The sun is beating down but the heat he now feels seems to be radiating out of the unbearable pain in his head – like a gigantic halo, it seems. Is this what saints feel like? Perhaps this time he really is going to die. He loses consciousness in the middle of an act of contrition.

Sarah's Diary

14 March 1900

I can scarcely write this, my hand is trembling so. Louise and I have been asked to pack our bags and leave *tonight* on a civilian train to help out in the hospitals of Bloemfontein! I'm afraid that I pulled a string to get Louise to come with me when I was told the news, knowing that the chief medical officer here has a soft spot for me; I could not bear to think of going to the Front alone.

Having never heard of this Boer capital city, I looked it up in my atlas immediately. It lies right in the centre of South Africa, hundreds of miles away from the oceans that border this country. Apparently it will take at least two days to get there. I now experience such conflicting emotions – real regret to be leaving majestic Cape Town (and in my case, the dear Frangipani Villa with its exotic blooms and pretty wrought iron decorations, to say nothing of dear toothless Sameela and Rushda), and excitement that we are at last moving north to the battlefields of the Orange Free State! I have planted a little frangipani bush at the bottom of the garden and wonder if I shall ever see it bloom.

Louise's Diary

14 March 1900

Well, really, this order from above to leave *tonight!!* for Bloemfontein – an extremely dull little town in the middle of a dreadful desert from all accounts – couldn't have come at a worse time. Apart from the fact that things are just starting to improve at the Number 3, I am now going to have to miss the banquet at the Mount Nelson on Saturday – how exasperating! I had planned to wear my khaki drill evening frock and cause a sensation! The last time David and I went there we had such a hilarious time with the officers who are so bored with having to stay in this stately home of the Cape . . .

Needless to say, selfless Sarah is terribly excited about going to the front, even though she loves it here – she certainly has perked up since entering the Southern Hemisphere. Someone should write a book about the power of sunlight to change one's mood.

I had better see how Dolly is getting on with my packing. I hope there is room on the train for my all suitcases.

Three

Extract: Letter from Lieutenant Ronald Charles to his mother

Royal Engineers, Cavalry Division,
Bloemfontein,
15 March 1900

. . . The town council came out in all their glory of white top hats &c about 10.30 a.m. on the 13th & solemnly handed over the keys of the capital to Lord Roberts, who promised to respect life & property & all the rest of it & the Advanced guard of the British Army marched into Bloemfontein in rather scattered detachments to the accompaniment of the ringing cheers of the inhabitants, black & white. I never heard such cheering, though doubtless many of them were cheering the Boers a week before we arrived. Everyone was wearing tricolour favours, brand new Union Jacks were being flown, people were singing God Save the Queen, Rule Britannia & other patriotic and marshal (*sic*)airs. I don't suppose we could be given a more hearty reception on returning home; & mind you we were entering the enemies' capital as victors not as a relieving force . . .

Bloemfontein, March 1900

Patch does not see much of Roberts' victorious march into Bloemfontein. Stacked among others in the bullock cart, he smells drifts of women's perfume and catches a glimpse of a Leghorn hat with fluttering green ribbons; hears the kaffirs chanting *thank you, thank you*, but by now spikes of agony are plunging and replunging into his head, agony intensified by the cough that has come from nowhere, so that smells, sights and sounds melt into his hallucinations . . . he floats in and out of the District: !Xolo the bushman dances on the pavement with his foot-rattles made from the ears of springboks, filled with karee seed; Fancy's red skirts flash briefly before transforming into a great gush of blood; Mr Feinstein counts his shoes and says reluctantly to Patch *I am sorry to say there are three pairs missing. Three pairs missing*! sing the Trusty Trio in unbearable harmonies to the tune of Three Blind Mice; then a violent coughing fit shakes him back to consciousness and the cheering crowds. Back to Cape Town, the Island this time, blundering through the fog, an English country garden and a woman at the gate gazing after him hopefully; Dr Simmonds angry because he has thrown away *David Copperfield*, but has he? Then he screams in agony as the cart begins to jolt into a rough road, and the men around him howl as well, grown men, all crying and whimpering as their bony bodies shake about – the reek of them is vile. And to think they should be in proper horse-drawn ambulances – even in his pain he feels another brief pain: indignation. He moans pitifully, then, through the whimpers, his body tells him the jolting has abruptly stopped.

An orderly crawls into the cart. 'How're you doin', me maties?' He presses a can of water to Patch's dry lips but the water slips over Patch's tongue, grown gigantic with thirst, and slides out as he retreats once more to the Island, a cauliflower from her garden in his hand; a cauliflower that decomposes into a man's brains that slither into a snake, coiled and hooded . . .

Now they are being hauled from the cart, the orderlies cursing away, their curses mere blooms on their language, not expressing anger. Carried by their arms and shoulders they find themselves somewhere that isn't a cart, that has a bed of some sort, into which Patch collapses, his broken boots removed by nimble fingers; then the utter darkness of an endless unlit tunnel, a faint light flickering at the end, towards which he is travelling at top speed.

Sarah's Diary

17 March 1900

It is now eight o'clock in the evening and in a few hours' time we shall arrive in Bloemfontein. I am writing this while travelling on a washed, scrubbed and scoured hospital train (perfumed with antiseptic) which we boarded after crossing the Orange River *on foot* (more of this later as I must try to achieve chronology). I must say these hospital trains, with their fading Red Crosses painted on the outer panels, are very well equipped and looked after: I can hear orderlies bustle about and bottles clink in the pharmacy as we clatter over the rails.

Travelling right into the heart of South Africa has been fascinating. We've lived and slept in our own little compartment and brought food supplies made by Rushda, and a spirit kettle so that we could make tea when we wanted to, and thank heaven for that. Because there has been so much sabotage by the Boers, every inch of the railway has been guarded by Tommies, poor things! They are so bored and lonely – many of them have not even seen a glimpse of the enemy, and they can't bear the solitude of the veldt. At every station they beg us for old newspapers or books – or a 'mouthful of human speech', as Mr Kipling puts it – just to relieve the tedium. They long for the excitement of battle, but have found that the reality of war is long, weary waiting and monotony.

I loved the barren Karoo land, and we were treated to a truly apocalyptic sunset. The beauties of this semi-desert were,

124

I'm afraid, rather lost on Louise, who quickly grew bored with the thorn bushes and anthills and kopjes (little flat-topped hills), and expressed the hope that a Boer Commando might swoop down and capture our train. To distract her I produced one of Rushda's seedcakes, which we sliced and enjoyed with a cup of our home-boiled tea.

After two days travelling, we were confronted by the awesome sight of the broad, calm Orange River, with a ruined bridge dangling over it. The army has built a pontoon bridge while the damage created by the Boers is being repaired. We were obliged to leave the train and walk across this in utter darkness (see above) while local kaffirs carried our belongings. Streams of wounded or sick soldiers on stretchers or hobbling with crutches poured over the bridge from a hospital train on the other side of the bridge in order to embark the train we had just left. They greeted us in delight, not having seen a woman for weeks. Louise cheered up immediately.

Apparently this train will gather a cargo of sick men from Bloemfontein for an epidemic of enteric is ravaging the triumphant army. We are told by officers on this train that many nurses have caught the dreaded disease in the course of their duties. I try not to feel apprehensive about this. It seems we have left the Paradise of the Cape to enter an Inferno of illness – not quite what the British Public expected, responding as powerfully as they did to the image of the *bandaged* Tommy.

From Lord Roberts to Queen Victoria, 15 March 1900
The Orange Free State south of Bloemfontein is rapidly
settling down. The proclamations of an amnesty I have
issued are having the desired effect, and men are daily
laying down their arms and returning to their usual
occupations. It seems unlikely that this State will give much
more trouble. The Transvaalers will probably hold out, but
their numbers must be greatly reduced, and I trust it will
not be long before the war will have been brought to a
satisfactory conclusion.

We are obliged to rest here for a short time to let men and
animals recover, and provide the former with new boots
and clothes.

Sarah's Diary

18 March 1900

Bloemfontein station, even at midnight, was so crowded with soldiers behaving officiously that Louise and I decided to return to our carriage and cower on the hard seats till daybreak. More and more sick men were being ferried on stretchers into the train so, as soon as the sky lightened, we plunged through the sea of khaki and managed to find a brougham of sorts outside the station. It was very surprising to us that the soldiers could not conduct themselves with more propriety towards two unescorted women who were clearly nurses. They expected *us* to stand back and make way for *them* as they rushed about, yet found time to demand, in a most unfriendly fashion, to see our papers, even though we were in full nursing uniform.

As our carriage drew out of the station, day had fully broken and we looked with interest out of the windows. We could see large numbers of Union Jacks hanging out of the windows of kaffir homes to celebrate the arrival of Bobs and his army just a few days ago. Apparently the kaffir population in this republic – which I suppose will soon be declared a British Colony – are absolutely overjoyed by the British victories; they see the British as their saviours and hope to be rewarded with their independence from the oppressive Boer once the war is over. They evidently expressed their joy by looting the shops of Bloemfontein and dancing in the streets, to annoy the Boers, I suppose. It was noteworthy that there were so many armed and uniformed kaffirs in the streets, confirming the Conciliation Committee's report that many black-skinned men are helping out in this white man's war. Apparently many of these black men in khaki drill act as scouts; knowing the lie of the land so well they can smell out where the Boer commandos are hiding, though not even they can detect a Boer in a trench six feet deep and barricaded with mimosa bushes.

We made our way through the little city's broad streets towards the school which has had to become a military hospital. The name Bloemfontein means 'flower-fountain', a sweetly innocent name, and there is something innocent about the layout of this place, its main streets all blooming with roses – in this heat! Obviously rose petals are far tougher than we have been led to believe in England. However, the poor little city has been entirely swamped by the army. The pavements are crowded with men in khaki, and on the surrounding hills hundreds – or perhaps thousands – of tents are stretched out in neat rows.

We found my ward to be a tin hut hastily built on to a girl's school to help accommodate the huge numbers of sick men. Louise is to nurse in a far grander building than my little tin hut: no less than the old Boer parliament, known as the Raadsaal. It seems that no public building still standing has not metamorphosed into a hospital. Everyone is awaiting the arrival of three tented general hospitals, arrived from Britain two weeks ago and so desperately needed here, but which sit in Cape Town waiting for permission from Roberts to be delivered. As ever, medical needs come last on the railway line. Louise and I have been given a bell tent which is to be our home, along with four other British nurses.

I have to say that the conditions on our tin hut ward are quite appalling: twenty men crammed in on stretchers, no beds as yet (they await delivery from Cape Town); very little fresh water as De Wet has captured the city's waterworks at Sannah's Post, and the water from Bloemfontein's old wells and streams is mostly bad – infected partly from the network of open trench latrines which are black with flies – as are the open-air hospital kitchens. We see the regimental water carts filled without protest at wayside pools that are almost certainly contaminated. It is incredible that men suffering from enteric have to drink infected water. I feel very sorry for the men in our hut, all at different stages of the disease; some with no chance of recovering, some listlessly emerging from the nightmare of illness, others able to walk around and smoke cigarettes and follow their special diet. They are all so thin and sallow; clearly, they were underfed and unable to resist the onslaught of the bacteria. One poor man died in terrible agony within an hour of my arrival. Yet the unfailing good humour of these emaciated creatures can only fill one with admiration.

20 March

If conditions in my tin hut are bad, the situation in the field hospitals is a hundred times worse. Today Louise and I were taken on a tour of these tents – I think to prove to us how much better off our wards are – and it was quite heartbreaking to see so many men in the worst stages of enteric fever packed into their tents with only a blanket and a thin waterproof sheet between their aching bodies and the hard ground (which can stream with water after a thunderstorm); no beds, stretchers or mattresses; no nurses; only three doctors to every three hundred patients. The fly situation is actually worse there than in our ward. The hands and faces of the desperately ill men are covered in droves of black flies, attracted by the nearby uncovered latrines, and the stench made us cover our noses and mouths with the edges of our pelisses. The problem is of course that field hospitals are supposed to be mobile, for use on the battlefield; men are not meant to spend more than three or four days in them before being transferred to the base hospitals or hospital trains, but this epidemic has taken the army by surprise. They are dying fifty a day in the city of flowers, and no one with real power seems to care. Reinforcements, horses, food, ammunition and – I'm sorry to say – officers' personal belongings arrive daily, but not a sign of the tents, beds, staff and equipment that would save so many lives.

When I came back from my tour I found two new patients had replaced the man who died yesterday. Both seem to be in the last stages of enteric. The orderlies (there are four of them in my hut) were already washing them, and moistening their lips with our ghastly contaminated water.

Rossetti Mansions, London, April 1900

Inside the reticule belonging to Miss Hobhouse there are three keys: the largest is for the gigantic front door that opens into the entrance hall of the red-bricked Rosetti Mansions; the smaller one opens the door of her flat, Number 33; the tiny one is for her letter box. It is her habit to stop at the ornamental cherry tree outside the front door and remove these three keys from her bag, in readiness. This evening she looks up at the tree and notices it is already sprouting buds of pink promise on its leafless twigs; by next week she will be able to look down from her sitting room window on to a cloud of pink blossom that confirms Spring has at last arrived.

She runs up the short flight of steps leading to the solid front door and turns the huge key in the great keyhole. She is feeling exhilarated. Today she has addressed the Oxford branch of the Women's Liberal Foundation on the disastrous implications of the annexation of the Orange Free State, now that Bloemfontein has fallen to General Roberts. Her address was sympathetically received; someone murmured that a protest meeting should be held; she visited Christ Church where her brother Leonard had tutored for so long; caught the train back to London, and arrived home before dark. And tonight the Courtneys, who live a few blocks away in Cheyne Walk, have invited her to a special dinner to celebrate her fortieth birthday. It is always good to have something to look forward to when one feels happy, she reflects as the front door swings open, so that a little more happiness is guaranteed and melancholy fits are kept at bay.

She allows the heavy door to slam behind her, the crash reverberating all over the building, and darts over to the bank of letter boxes in the entrance hall, her tiny key poised. Her box is overflowing, as usual, mostly with matters concerning the Concilation Committee, to which she will attend tomorrow in her capacity as the Women's Branch Secretary. Sophie will come and help tomorrow evening, as will Miss Griffen, if she has recovered from her bad attack of influenza.

Mrs Potter from Number 32 is majestically descending the stairs, dressed in starched black in sympathy with the forty years of mourning of the Queen, a similar expression of discontent etched on her bloated face. She nods coldly at Emily, whom she considers to be a traitor to her country. (Emily once caught her pulling letters out of her over-full box and examining the envelopes for evidence of treachery.) 'Good evening, Mrs Potter.' Emily's smile is friendly, but it does not crack the ice of her neighbour's displeasure; Mrs Potter sniffs a message of disapproval far stronger than any spoken word. She sweeps out of the front door, closing it with exaggerated quietness behind her. A whiff of camphor hangs in the air.

Emily pulls a wry face but, being by now accustomed to this kind of behaviour, continues to turn over the events of the day in her mind; the annexation issue, the earnest ladies of the Liberal Foundation, Christ Church, pleasant train journey, all running seamlessly into each other as she looks through her post. There are several birthday cards in among the circulars and committee letters. She gathers them all into a larger bag she had brought with her to Oxford and runs up the three flights of stairs that lead to her flat, nearly colliding with plump, pin-striped Mr Somerset-Glance of Number 43, the flat directly above her. 'Really, Miss Hobhouse, you must look where you are going!' he exclaims in a voice tight with disapproval. 'Oh dear, I am so sorry!' she cries. 'I try to do all the stairs in one go, you know, to get them over with quickly.'

She is a little breathless as she unlocks the door of her flat and throws herself down at the table by the window. Perhaps it is rather unladylike to rush up the stairs like that, but she always seems to be in a hurry, and to walk sedately anywhere is a trial at the best of times. She picks out her birthday cards from her mail, smiling with pleasure. Cards from all the family and most of the committee; one from dear Sophie, another from Griffy, posted before she went down with flu; and what is this one with an American stamp? Probably from one of the many friends she had made during the '95 temperance campaign in Virginia, soon after her father's death. A Chicago postmark; a typewritten address. She opens it with interest.

Many happy returns, from J.E. Jackson with love. (In brackets) *I think of you often.*

Her hands are already tearing the card to shreds. 'I am not allowing you to return!' she shouts. Her earlier exhilaration has vanished. Her body feels slack. With a wail of horror she makes her way to her bedroom to change, and catches sight of herself in the looking glass on the dressing table. She is unable to move her eyes from what she sees in the multiple mirrors. 'Forty years old,' she breathes. 'And still nothing achieved.'

Had she been a vain woman she would have consoled herself with the smoothness of her forty-year-old-skin and her open, appetising face, framed by waves of lustrous hair. But she can only stare at these genteel features in despair: four decades have passed and what is there to show? No great work. No husband. No children. Three gigantic craters of nothingness in her life. She has not pushed herself hard enough. The temperance campaign had lasted a mere nine months nearly four years ago, and whatever self-respect she might have gained then was utterly cancelled out by the folly that had ensued. At the mere thought of the Mexican disaster beads of sweat appear on her forehead; her hands begin to shake violently.

Thank heaven the chiming of the clock tells her it is time to leave for the Courtney's celebratory meal. Already she is relaxing at the thought of Kate's bright, intelligent eyes, and Leonard, smiling thoughtfully as he tugs at his little beard. The image of these two precious faces is doing its work: the butcher from Virginia with the ravishing eyes and the elegant moustache is fading from her mind. As she chooses the evening dress she will wear (black velvet with silver trim) she is thinking about an idea she had on the train – a public protest against the annexation of the defeated Boer republics.

She will be late if she doesn't leave at once, even though it takes only seven minutes to walk from Rossetti Mansions to the Courtneys' home.

She runs up the steps that lead to the Courtneys' front door. Protest, that was all one could do. Protest against the extinction by force of a state which clings as passionately to its separate nationality and its flag as Britain does to hers. A great protest, too great for the government to ignore.

And as she rings the Courtneys' door bell, already preparing her apologies for her seven minute lateness, she is seized by inspiration. She will organise a public protest against annexation composed entirely of women. It will be held in London's mighty Queen's Hall. Miss Griffen will move into her spare room and write a thousand personal invitations, vetted by herself. It will be held in eight weeks' time. If, of course, the Women's Committee agree.

Which, of course, they will.

Bloemfontein Hospital, April 1900

Patch has wet the bed again. At first the sensation is warm and comforting but soon it grows cold. Sister Madeleine says there is only one way to cure wetting-the-bed and that is via the shillelagh. Although Patrick is only four he understands the cause-and-effectness of this: if you wet the bed you get beaten, same as if you fall down you hurt yourself, or if you tell a joke someone will laugh.

Now he's really gone and done it. His whole body is wet, not just the bottom half. So as he curls up in the last hint of warmth in his soaked bed he feels the familiar onset of dread about the shillelagh. And on his bare bum which sometimes has boils on it. There was a time of sweetness a few weeks back when a young novice suggested rewarding him for *not* wetting the bed. The Sisters of Holy Charity were astounded. But, out of interest and a desire to prove her wrong, tried it out. For five days he woke up in a dry bed, knowing there would be an extra portion of porridge if the sheets didn't have to be ripped off and washed yet again by Sister Maria, who suffered from tuberculosis and kept all the orphans awake with her coughing. Then on the sixth they were wet again and Sister Madeleine triumphantly went back to beatings, no questions asked.

He feels the familiar terror gripping his gut. It is not so much the pain of the beating, though that is bad enough, but the fact that she who slashes the bamboo stick on to his thin buttocks is beautiful. Sister Madeleine has calm eyes, good cheekbones and a smiley mouth. But when she hits him, and the sleeves of her white habit flare out and the giant black rosary on her leather belt jingles, she becomes a she-devil, a demon in white who can enter the secret cavities of Patch's heart and fill them with dread. Later, when he no longer wets the sheets, she will find other reasons to beat him thus, and when he is ten years old and taller than she is, she whips his outstretched palms, sometimes with the bamboo cane, sometimes with a school ruler, sometimes with a broom handle or a splintered plank. For that is how you discipline boys: through fear. Yet Patch could not submit. In a frenzy Sister Madeleine might split the cane across his hands or snap the ruler, but Patch stubbornly remained himself. She might wipe the sweat from her brow, and pant from the exertion of punishment, but her victim would coolly slide back to his desk, apparently untouched by the onslaught on his hands. But inside his heart, what turmoil! What rage, what hatred. But only in his sleep does the anger seep out, poisoning his bloodstream, triggering panic. He wakes with a start, his body seething with revenge. In his mind he sees her face, calm, sweetly cruel, smiling at him in pity. If only he could fist his hand and shoot it into those eyes which mock . . .

Now she is sticking a thin cold cylinder under his tongue – a new weapon of torture? – and someone else is ripping off the sheets. 'Soaked through!' exclaims a voice. A male voice. Can it be Father McKewan who says Mass every morning and hears the boys' confessions? Something cool and soft and feathery has landed on his forehead. 'The fever's coming down,' murmurs a female voice. It is not Sister Madeleine's voice. 'He'll be very dehydrated after all that sweating.' He remembers in a flash that he is twenty years old, and has fought in a battle. He tries to shuffle his mouth into his daredevil half-smile, but discovers his lips have turned to splinters of solid wood. Just the attempt to smile has caused cracks of pain to split open the area where the lips once were. Now someone is sponging cold water over the cracks, washing the stabs of pain away and bringing the lips back, softening the wood.

'Come on, Private Donnelly.' His head is being raised and a beaker is inserted, gently, into his newlyrestored mouth. 'Sip.' His tongue recognises milk and instructs his throat to swallow. Patch has forgotten how you swallow. It amazes him that he ever knew. The milk lies in his throat, threatening to choke. 'You must swallow,' urges the female voice. The tip of a finger, soft as a kitten's paw, massages his Adam's Apple. In astonishment, a muscle in his throat contracts and a thick dry tunnel opens inside his neck and the milk slides own.

He slits open his eyes and looks through his lashes.

A nun is bending over him. Hang on a minute! Definitely not Sister Madeleine. As consciousness floods he remembers he has long ago left the orphanage – and fought heroically in a battle! His body feels jolted as if he's been tossed around inside a hard, unsprung cart. That swimming sensation in his head is familiar.

The nun – or is it a nurse? – is smiling serenely. 'Another sip,' she says. Through his eyelashes, he studies her perfect features. Her white cap flares in folds from her head. Her eyes are calm. He drinks in her cool composure.

Another book Dr Simmonds told him about was *Gulliver's Travels*. In one part Gulliver is a midget; in another, he is a giant. Patch feels as if he has grown into a giant; he can feel his feet sticking out the end of the bed. His arms have grown as long as the branches of trees. He can feel the bud of his penis blossoming joyously into a gigantic thing.

'And a little brandy,' whispers the nun-nurse. *Whooh!* His whole body comes shockingly alive as he swallows. He wants to grab her by the wrist and bring her down on top of him, and feels sweat burst from his forehead and neck. He allows his eyelids to close.

'I have an idea,' says the lovely female voice to someone. 'That music box we found in his pocket. Can you bring it here?'

Next thing his ears are full of song. He knows those sounds, but from where? They soothe him. His head throbs pleasantly with the delicate chimes. No place like home, they assure him.

Now rough male hands are rolling him over and pulling off his sodden clothes and tut-tutting about the state of things. Off come his pants and there is a gasp. 'Will you take a look at this then!' exclaims the voice. 'Well, there's nothing wrong with your manhood, my dear. Better cover you up before the sisters get excited too.'

But as clean pyjama pants are pulled on, a male hand lingers over his gorgeously erect prick and gives it a bit of a rub. Patch groans in pleasure as the come spurts out on to the helpful, knowing hands.

Then, miraculously, brandy-soaked sleep takes over.

Louise's Diary

28 March 1900

Who would have thought it possible that we could have such fun in this dreary little town? Bobs is determined to fraternise with the enemy and the enemy seems only too happy to oblige, with the result that we have an endless succession of parties and dinners designed to make us all friends. Rumour has it that the enemy simply run back to their farms and feed the commandos, then scurry back to the British banquets – well, who can blame them? I could almost have fallen in love with a couple of them for the Boer men are a handsome enough crowd with their sunburnt skin and humorous eyes . . . but there is a rather attractive senior medical officer, Dr Theodore Chappell, who is making a play for me. Why am I so susceptible to these medical men?

But I must now write in some detail of the extraordinary events of today. It all started this morning in, of all unlikely places, the Boer bread shop (I wouldn't grace it with the name 'bakery'). Who should be buying a packet of syrup-soaked sugar dumplings, which fat old Mrs van Reenen makes herself, but the creator of the great Sherlock Holmes, Sir Arthur Conan Doyle!! I had heard, with some disbelief, that he was working as a doctor, medicine being his original profession, in one of the privately funded hospitals here in Bloemfontein. I recognised him at once from the many portraits of him that have appeared in our newspapers and journals. 'Oh, Sir Arthur!' I exclaimed in excitement. 'I would so much like to tell you how much I enjoy your detective stories and how relieved I was when you brought Sherlock back to life – in fact, I was one of your many readers who wrote to you to assure us that he and Moriarty hadn't really fallen into that cataract (my mother cancelled her subscription to *Strand* magazine as a result), and I believe I suggested an explanation for his survival. And I am so pleased to hear that you are writing further stories in your spare time.' Conan Doyle clutched his dumplings to his breast as if I might snatch them away (which I was inclined to do, knowing the syrup would seep out and stain his spotless shirt.) 'Madam, may I inform you my work here has nothing to do with that – that loathsome amateur detective and his infatuated sidekick. I am here to serve my country only. And any writing I might do concerns the chronicling of this war, which I am pleased to see will soon be over, thanks to the brilliant strategies of General Roberts. Good day to you, madam.' 'Oh, but Sir Arthur (I placed a restraining hand on his arm) you cannot leave without giving me your autograph. I insist. Let me find some paper and a pen.' There followed a frantic scrabbling around by me in my overloaded reticule, but no paper could I find, though at least I could produce a rather fine fountain pen. He gave me what I can only describe as a venomous glare; then, turning to Mrs van Reenen, said to her in most familiar tones, 'Tannie, can you rescue me from this nurse and get me a piece of paper?' 'I have some in my newly built water closet, sir,' grinned the fat old monster. She shuffled off and returned with a square piece of paper, the proper function of which I did not care to determine. Sir Arthur thanked her, dashed off his signature, and fled from the bread shop, followed by me, my precious sheet of paper now safely in my reticule.

Back at the Raadsaal I was alarmed to discover that one of my nursing colleagues from Australia, Sister Hemmings, has fallen seriously ill, with all the symptoms of enteric. Once again, it is the orderlies who are actually *promoting* the spread of the disease rather than hindering it, with their unwashed hands and dirty habits. They are no different from the riff-raff I worked with in Wynberg. When I once again pointed out his lack of hygiene to Mr Watson, he had the cheek to rejoin, in his thick provincial accent, 'You're a fine one to criticise, with your swearin' and drinkin' and gallivantin' about with officers. You might be a grand lady, ma'am, but a kitchen girl's got better manners than you.' I was speechless with rage, of course, and thought to report him at once to Dr Chappell but decided against it in case Theodore (as he asks to be called by me) discovers that what the loathsome little orderly says is true.

At the end of the day Sarah and I generally meet for a cup of tea in the relaxed atmosphere of a little tearoom in the centre of town, unfrequented by the khaki that surges on the pavements everywhere. Today I had much to tell her, but needless to say she had had a less eventful day. Then, just as I was showing her Sir Arthur's sprawling signature, she signalled me with her eyes to look at the table across the room. There, leafing through a pile of newspapers, was none other than Mr Kipling, whom I have not yet quite forgiven for the bandage episode in Wynberg. 'Why don't you get his autograph too?' said Sarah, a naughty look in her eyes. 'On the same piece of paper – where *did* you get it from, dear?' 'Good idea!' I cried, and dashed over to Kipling's table. He, thank goodness, had no recollection of me and my scowls, but, observing my nurse's uniform, pointed to his newspapers and asked me if any of my patients had a poem or observation to contribute for he was about to bring out the last edition of this troopers' broadsheet before returning to England. I promised him I would check to see that my men had contributed what they could, then asked him for his autograph. Somewhat wearily he scribbled his name on the scrap of paper I laid before him. When he saw the other name he said in rueful tones, 'If only I had his talents. All writing strives to tell a detective story of sorts, and he does it best of all of us.'

At this, a man at a table near us leant over and asked, 'Is it possible that I have the honour to speak to the author of *The Absent-Minded Beggar*?' 'Yes,' replied Mr Kipling, quick as a flash. 'I have heard that piece played on the barrel organ and I would shoot the man who wrote it, if it would not be suicide.' I suspect he has said this many times before, it all came out too pat. The man laughed in rather a startled fashion and I quickly said, 'I do think Sir Arthur Sullivan could have done better with the music he wrote for your verses. You would not think the same man composed *The Gondoliers*.' 'At least it has raised the money needed,' said Kipling, turning back to his papers.

To my surprise, Sarah was suddenly at our table. In a strong, clear voice, quite unlike her usual low murmur, she *demanded*, rather than asked, 'Did you know, Mr Kipling, that the funds raised by your absent-minded beggar are not awarded to the common-law wives of troopers, nor to soldiers' wives who cannot for some reason present their marriage certificate? The forsaken families live in abject poverty in Britain while the breadwinner fights for his country.' Mr Kipling blinked his eyes rapidly behind his thick glasses. He opened his mouth to speak – and I could have sworn from the way he puffed himself that he was about to make some self-righteous pronouncement but thought better of it. He looked up at Sarah and seemed to warm to her. 'Thank you, Sister, I did not know about this. I shall look into the matter,' he said, frowning, then returned once more to his papers, this time with an air of finality that we could not ignore.

'Well really, Sarah Palmer,' I said to my companion as we returned to our table. Her cheeks were blazing crimson. 'Since when do you heckle great men, pray? I thought you were the shy retiring violet.'

'Oh, I am, I am,' stammered she. 'But this is a topic that has worried me for some time through reading out the soldiers' letters, and when I heard mention of the absent-minded beggar I seized the opportunity. I could never have done it if you had not gone over first.' Even though her chest was heaving, she had a determined look about her.

Quite a change has come over Sarah since arriving in South Africa, apart from the fact that she has cheered up so considerably. Is she turning into one of those rights-for-women campaigners who shout at powerful men at every opportunity? Next she will be shaking her fist and demanding the vote.

I have suggested to her that we hold a small tea party in our bell tent and invite a couple of medical officers from our wards, but she feels it would be too cramped (all to the good, in my opinion . . .) There is a firmness in her voice which somehow prevents me from arguing.

Telegram from Mr Chamberlain to Sir Alfred Milner
03/04/1900 The Queen regrets to observe the large number of ladies now visiting and remaining in South Africa, often without imperative reasons, and strongly disapproves of the hysterical spirit which seems to have influenced some of them to go where they are not wanted. I conclude their presence interferes with work of civil and military officers, and they must largely occupy best Hotel accommodation required for wounded and invalid officers.

Can you send telegram, with or without concurrence of Roberts, representing that number of lady visitors is now so considerable as to encroach materially on Hotel and Railway accommodation etc, and otherwise impede business, and suggesting that some notice might be issued here calling attention to inconvenience of this unusual number of ladies visiting seat of war.

This I would submit to the Queen and Her Majesty would instruct me to publish.

Sarah's Diary

8 April 1900

Ever since I recognised the desperately ill man in my ward I have been overwhelmed by a sense of destiny. That the man who stirred my heart to music three months ago should have arrived in *my* tin hut ward when there are so many improvised wards all over Bloemfontein suggests to me that there are greater forces at work than we poor mortals can ever understand. I feel that in some extraordinary way, beyond anyone's control, Patrick Donnelly has been delivered into my hands. Fate has decreed that we are to come together. He lay comatose in his bed for several days before I recognised him, so changed was his appearance. Gone altogether was that bronzed, flirtatious face: instead, his features were stamped with the greyness of a man tussling with death, like so many of the men here.

Even when he opened his eyes a little after his crisis was passed, I could see no Patrick Donnelly there, no flickering greenness that reminds me of English country lanes in the depths of summer; only that dull grey of a man who is drained of life but whose heart yet beats feebly. Can I still have feelings for such a man?

My mind has been in such a state of turmoil since my discovery that I have been unable to write coherently in this diary. Till today I wondered if he would survive – in which case, why had malignant fate brought us together? – but something has now happened which I think has helped him to take an important step forward: today Patch Donnelly received a letter.

At first I felt a stab of jealousy in case it was from a lover – though of course I have no right to feel any such thing – but soon realised from the markings on the envelope it was from another trooper. I knew it must be something special as, unlike the other troopers who receive several letters from home on every mail day, he receives no post at all. I showed it to him at once and he motioned to me, with the faintest nod of his head, that he would like me to open and read it.

I looked quickly at the name signed at the end of the letter. 'It's from a friend of yours called Bill,' I said. There was another sheet of paper attached. 'He's drawn you a picture.'

Patch's face lit up with joy. It was pathetic to see how his dry, cracked lips longed to stretch into a smile. Still, he managed to clench his lips together and somehow puff out the first letter of his friend's name, B. The effort of this exhausted him, so I placed the beaker of water against his lips and waited for him to swallow. 'Are you ready for the letter?' I asked cautiously. Once again, he gave the smallest nod of assent, but with a look of excited anticipation on his emaciated features:

17 March
To my dear Fenian friend, Patch, (I read).
As it is St Patrick's day I thought I would draw you a picture of the old boy driving the Protestant snakes out of Olde Ireland where you come from. Look at what he is holding – a four-leaved shamrock, to bring you good luck wherever you are.

I am grateful to you old chap for giving me that orange flag from Cronjay's laager. You didn't look too good when we parted but who did? My brigade is still in the Orange land. We have to stay here because so many of our men are down with enteric. I hope you have escaped this dreadful disease; so far I am all right.

Yours truly
    Bill
PS how is the music box?

Accompanying this strange missive was an extremely colourful and quite skilful representation of St Patrick, complete with a vicious-looking snake which the saint is prodding violently with his gilded crook.

'I'm sorry it has taken so long to get to you,' said I. 'St Patrick's day was a good three weeks ago. In any case, you'd have been in no condition to read it.'

He stared at me blankly. For the first time since his arrival I met his gaze – and went racing giddily down those green lanes and mossy paths that open up in his eyes. He opened his lips and I thought, joy of joys, he was about to speak – but no words came.

It was indeed hard to drag my eyes away, but at that moment Sergeant Watkins helped me by leaping out of bed and cavorting about like a maddened scarecrow. I have never seen anything like it: he performs a kind of Zulu war dance, then collapses to the ground. They say he has been eating the gunpowder in his bullets, and swallowing it down with brandy.

Bloemfontein Hospital, April

Patch keeps having visions. First, the nun who turned into a nurse gives him drinks and moistens his lips; next, St Patrick, surrounded by coils of snakes, hovers shakily before him. The nurse seems to be saying something about Bill, and next thing the little orange-haired Irishman is prancing around in his head as well. Like a leprechaun, perhaps. There are long passages of darkness too. When Patch emerges from them he is soaking wet and dizzy.

Then one day he wakes up and understands where he is and what's going on. His head feels astonishingly clear as if someone has scrubbed and dusted and polished his brain. He wants to leap out of bed and run cheering down the central aisle of the marquee. But when he tries to lift his legs he finds they aren't there. Dear God, he hasn't lost them, has he? Had them chopped off by an army surgeon because of gangrene, like that screaming soldier in Rondebosch?

So instead of trying to get out of bed he, less ambitiously, curls his toes. Yes, they are there, unless he's got that phantom limb thing where you lose an arm or leg but they still ache. Patch progresses through his whole leg, first one, then the other, foot upwards, clenching and unclenching batches of feeble muscles. The effort exhausts him, but his brain is still clear.

Or is it? Because here comes that nurse again, smiling dreamily. By the time she has reached his bedside he has recognised her – but cannot tell if she is another phantom. Patch attempts speech.

'Good morning, Sister,' he whispers. His vocal cords are covered in cobwebs but he manages to infuse a suggestive inflection into these neutral words. Normally he would accompany such an overture with a twitch of the eyebrows and the lopsided smile, but he can only do one thing at a time for now.

She stares at him with an odd expression on her face. She is listening to something. In fact, she is listening carefully to the three words he has spoken, sifting them through her brain until she pigeonholes them. She is definitely that Rondebosch nurse now, and he feels his heart stir with wonder.

'Say that again,' she says, to make sure.

Has she misunderstood him? He repeats his greeting, more clearly this time. He cannot take his eyes off her.

'So,' she says at length. 'I thought you were Irish.'

With some difficulty – at least the eyebrows are still there – Patch frowns. 'I am,' he croaks. What's she on about? He feels the familiar fatigue creeping into his limbs, his head, his eyes.

'You don't sound Irish, that's all,' she says. 'It doesn't matter. It's wonderful that you're talking. Tomorrow you'll be walking.'

She swings off with a briskness that suggests displeasure. His brain is too tired, too empty to work out what the problem is. He sinks back into the comfort of sleep.

The next day she tells him it is time to get out of bed and walk to a chair outside the marquee. It seems an impossible journey. He breaks out in a sweat at the mere thought of it, but she helps him swing his legs round the side of the bed so that he can put his feet on the floor. Meekly, he tries to stand up. His muscles liquefy. His knees collapse. But she stands on one side of him with that smelly orderly on the other and they hold him up, like a puppet, by his elbows. She pushes his bare foot forwards with her nurse's boot, and his legs remember how to walk. A cheer goes up from some of the bedridden patients as the three of them totter down the central aisle.

Outside, in the brimming sunlight, a row of wicker chairs has been arranged for convalescing troopers. He collapses into one of them, panting with exhaustion.

'Sit there for a while and get your strength back,' she says. The orderly has already returned to the tent, leaving a trail of old cigarette smoke behind him. The smell ignites a dormant desire.

'Some baccy,' he wheezes. 'Any chance of?'

'I'll bring you a block in a minute,' she says. 'I've something for you better than baccy.' She produces an opened envelope addressed to him. Then off she goes.

This is the first letter Patch has ever received. He trembles. There is St Patrick, drawn by Bill. He reads the words over and over. And there is his sainted namesake, cheerfully offering him a shamrock, above fleeing snakes. He feels better just looking at it. Good old Bill.

He becomes aware that the trooper in the chair next to him is speaking. 'Nice bit of arse there, I said.'

Patch glares at the poor botched-up trooper. 'Different class from the likes of you,' he growls, and folds away the sheets of paper.

'Oh, I'm sorry Mr High an' Mighty,' says the trooper. He begins to roll himself a cigarette.

Patch looks at the baccy longingly. 'The name's Patrick Donnelly. I need a smoke, man, that's my problem.'

And the trooper takes pity.

Rossetti Mansions, London, April 1900

'Hooray!' cried Emily as she replaced the telephone mouth-piece on its hook. 'Mrs Scott has agreed to propose at least one of the resolutions. That will give us even more credibility. When a woman of her stature agrees to address the meeting, Britain will recognise the seriousness of our intention. I think she should propose the *first* resolution, don't you, Griffy dear? Read it out to me, there's a love.'

Miss Griffen quivered. Though utterly prepared to do Emily's bidding in the realm of the written word, she did not care to read aloud important documents, being unable to pronounce her r's adequately, an impediment which tended to diminish the importance of what she was saying.

'Oh, let *me* do it, Miss Hobhouse,' intervened Sophie, who not only enjoyed reading aloud but had recently made some very rousing speeches in the village halls of Cumberland and Lancashire during a few days off from her nursing. 'Poor Miss Griffen still has a sore throat.'

'Very well then.' Miss Hobhouse ticked something off on a list, then looked up at the young nurse and smiled playfully. 'Stand up and pretend you're addressing thousands of females from the stage of the Queen's Hall.'

Sophie leapt to her feet, swinging her red pelisse round her shoulders. 'Resolution one!' she bellowed. 'That this meeting of women brought together from all parts of the United Kingdom condemns the unhappy war now raging in South Africa as mainly due to the bad policy of the Government, a policy which has already cost in killed, wounded and missing over twenty thousand of our bravest soldiers, and the expenditure of millions of money drawn from the savings and toil of our people, while to the two small States with whom we are at war, it is bringing utter ruin and desolation.'

'Oh vewy well done!' exclaimed Miss Griffen, clapping her hands in excitement. 'I hope Mrs Scott will do it as well as you.'

'I do think the word *sick* should be added to the list of epithets describing the twenty thousand soldiers,' said Sophie in her normal voice. 'Going by what my friend Sarah tells me most of the soldiers are ill or dying with enteric.'

'Yes, of course it must,' said Miss Hobhouse. 'What an interesting person your friend sounds, Sophie.' A furious thumping in the ceiling made her look up. 'Oh dear, there's Mr Somerset-Glance again – see what your oratory has done. Is it so very late?' She glanced at the grandfather clock which used to tick resonantly in the vicarage entrance hall. 'Good heavens, it's well after nine. We must eat at once. Let's clear these papers from the table and have a little cold mutton. I don't think there's much more than that.'

'Mrs Potter stopped me on the stairs this evening,' said Sophie as she helped clear the table of its load of paperwork. 'She asked, very severely, whether you had permission from the council to change your flat into an office for pro-Boer agitation. I told her once again that we were pro-Britain and anti-war, not pro-Boer. She growled and said it came to the same thing.'

'I can never see Mrs Potter without thinking of the housekeeper in *Bleak House*, I forget her name – the one who looks as if her stays are made from the family fire grate. I don't think I've ever seen her smile.' Emily spread a cloth over the table. 'Now, shall I make tea or coffee or both?'

'Just before we eat, dear,' said Miss Griffen sweetly, 'I'd like to raise a point about the resolutions.'

'Not the kaffirs again,' frowned Emily. When Griffy rolled her r's, one could expect obstinacy.

'I wondered if you'd read the account in the *Pall Mall* gazette yesterday about the starving Barolong people in Mafeking. It is really a heart-rending story and throws quite a different light on Baden-Powell.' Miss Griffen, a firm supporter of the Aboriginal Movement, looked hopefully at Emily.

'Ah, yes, the black-skinned inhabitants of Mafeking, made to fight the white man's war,' said Sophie. She had spoken about these very people in her most recent speech.

'Sophie's quite right, though other tribal people have moved there too. There are far more blacks than whites in Mafeking, you know.' So pleasant and light was Miss Griffen's voice she might have been giving a recipe for roly-poly pudding or telling a story about her darling nephew's new toy elephant on wheels. 'B-P got the Barolong to dig a four-mile trench all round Mafeking, and then armed three hundred of them to help defend the citadel, as it were – much to the annoyance of General Cronje of Paardeberg fame. He sent B-P a letter reminding him that it is supposed to be a white man's war, you know,' she added with a melancholy smile. Sophie's stomach rumbled. 'Now B-P is trying to stretch out the rations for the white citizens – the siege has been going on for six months as we are constantly reminded – so now there is to be no meat and veg for the Barolong, only oat husks. As a result they have resorted to digging up dead dogs and horses and eating them.' Griffy's eyes were as round as her little spectacles. 'It's all in the gazette. Have a look, dear.'

Emily took the journal reluctantly but was at once startled by a cartoon of ragged, dark skeletons standing in a queue before a pot of porridge. Baden-Powell, a wild-eyed, savage giant, loomed behind the pot, brandishing a small teaspoon. *Please, sir, can I have some more?* she read aloud, her voice shaking. Then: *Words could not describe the scene of misery; five or six hundred frameworks of both sexes and all ages dressed in tattered rags, standing in lines, each holding an old blackened can or beef tin, awaiting turn to crawl painfully up to the soup kitchen where the food was distributed.* She put down the gazette. 'This wicked war!' she exclaimed in distress. 'Why should innocent people have to starve for the sins of Whitehall?'

'But we can do something about it!' Miss Griffen's voice was tremulous. 'We can adopt a *fifth* resolution at the meeting that would express concern for the fate of the indigenous peoples of South Africa who are clearly being exploited and ill-treated by both the Boers and the British.'

A pause followed this outburst. Emily wiped away a tear that had grown cold on her cheek. 'I absolutely understand your concern,' she said gently. 'I feel it myself, you know that. But we cannot lose the focus of the meeting, which I need not remind you is the annexation of the Orange Free State to the British Empire. Some would regard annexation as actually giving upliftment to the natives, who have welcomed the British as their liberators. They are expecting to be granted a qualified franchise as a reward for their support, but we suspect – we *know* – otherwise, with good reason. Leonard is quite sure of this. But to raise the question of black exploitation and maltreatment, especially at the hands of the hero of the day, would not do our cause any good. You must bring the matter up with your Aboriginal Committee. They have a stronger voice than we do in these matters. Now let's see what I can find in the pantry.'

While Emily clattered in the kitchen Sophie whispered to Miss Griffen 'Good try, Griffy. But don't you think she's overdoing things – I mean, only allowing women she has personally invited to come to the meeting? It's taking forever and I don't see how we'll fill the hall at this rate. I know we've still got two months, but I'm worried.'

'But Emily is determined there will be no troublemakers or hecklers. The will of the women must be expwessed with dignity.' Griffy shot an anxious look towards the kitchen. 'No fish heads and wotten tomatoes, or women shouting insults.'

'Here we are.' Emily emerged with a tray of bread, meat and pickles. 'This will keep us going, don't you think?'

Miss Griffen tried not to think of the starving Barolong as she made herself a rather delicious mutton sandwich. Perhaps she should introduce a campaign of fasting in sympathy with those poor people; if only she had the energy and initiative of dear Miss Hobhouse.

Two hours later the helpers were asleep in the spare room. Emily, still fired with energy, searched for a newspaper report she had put aside a week or two ago. She really must get Griffy to help with the filing tomorrow; papers were lying in piles all over the place. Perhaps she should visit the market and buy a good second-hand filing cabinet. Now that her flat had become a campaign headquarters she might as well turn the sitting room into an office, specially as *Mrs Rouncewell* – that was the name – already believed the transformation had taken place.

Emily began to pick her way through copies of the *Manchester Guardian* which contained reports on South Africa by her brother. No luck. In the bottom drawer of her bedroom dressing table was another load of cuttings; probably the report she wanted had got mixed up with these. Kneeling on the carpet, she began going through the papers one by one. Then gasped. Her heart, which had been beating as steadily as the grandfather clock in the sitting room, suddenly broke into painful syncopated rhythms. Under the pile lay a yellowed cutting she thought she'd thrown away three years ago. 'Throw it away *now*' she ordered herself, as her heart lurched. But even as she withdrew the cutting from the drawer she was reading it again, although she knew the contents by heart.

Virginia News, 8 April 1897
Without a handshake or a parting word, Mayor Jackson stepped on to the Duluth and Iron Range train last Monday morning and as he watched our city recede from sight he soliloquised: 'Virginians, I leave you! The parting gives me

*pain, but if I tarry at thy threshold, methinks it would not
be wise, therefore I go. Adieu.'*

*His hasty departure has caused much comment, but we
are informed this was due to a telegram which he received
Saturday night requesting him to be in Chicago Tuesday
morning. There, it was said, he was to meet Miss Hobhouse.
A ceremony was to have followed which would make them
man and wife. They were to leave immediately for Mexico
where Mr Jackson has a position awaiting him.'*

Mexico! Her darkened flat filled up with dazzling sunshine
and the perfume of tropical flowers. She was in the Plaza del
Domino where raven-haired women in mantillas peered over
ivory fans as they clattered past in their carriages drawn by
Arab steeds; exquisitely dressed young men, avid for attention, reared up on their horses among fountains and arcades
. . . And now she was floating, in the company of three
thousand Mexican guests, up a flight of stairs carved from
marble, past balconies dripping with bougainvillea – and
there, on the banqueting terrace stood the president of Mexico
himself, with a thousand beautiful servants ready to distribute
champagne (not for me, thanks. A little lemonade, perhaps?).
She looked out on the snow-capped peaks surrounding the
city; inhaled the intoxicating scent of jasmine; heard the
sensual strum of guitars . . . What joy! And soon she would
be married. He had not met her train when she arrived with
bridesmaid and wedding dress – but the cake had been
ordered and the bridesmaid fitted. Day by day, day by endless
day, she awaited word from him in the post . . .

With a cry Miss Hobhouse slammed shut the drawer. She
crumpled the cutting in her hand. The embers of the fire still
glowed in the grate; the paper flared briefly, then collapsed
into ash as she watched. 'Gone forever!' she exclaimed out
loud.

And look, there was the *Manchester Guardian* with the
article about women's protest groups in the Cape Colony
peering out from under a cushion. She grasped it, and felt an

instant joyous union with those sisters in South Africa who fought for the same ideals as she. What wonderful women! Pray God she would meet them in the flesh some day. She would write a letter of support to Mrs Fourie immediately.

Bloemfontein Hospital, April

Every afternoon from two till four the female nurses are relieved of their duties so that the men can pollute the air with their manly language, unfit for women's ears. Patch chooses to totter to the wicker chair during this time (aided by Orderly Jones), and light up with his new friend.

One afternoon, a couple of weeks after his first journey, he finds himself more or less alone among the chairs, his friend having moved on to a rehabilitation centre on the other side of town. The hospital tents gleam in the afternoon sunshine. He stretches out his legs and rolls a cigarette. In the morning, Orderly Jones had given him a shave and, as the cutthroat blade had skimmed over his soapy skin, he had felt his health tentatively return. This is how your soul must feel after confession, all fresh and smooth and shiny, the sins all washed away by penance and contrition. Jones had fiddled longer than necessary round Patch's jaw when it came to the cleaning up and he'd outlined a handlebar with his index finger all round Patch's upper lip in an attempt to persuade him of the necessity of a moustache, but Patch preferred the clean-shaven look.

'This is the life,' he thinks, blowing a haze of smoke around his head. Then, in the middle of the haze, *she* appears, fixing him with those serious brown eyes.

'Do you mind if I sit next to you for a while, Private Donnelly. No, don't stand up.'

He is overcome with embarrassment. He cannot find the right words.

'You seemed very happy to receive your letter the other day.' She shakes her head and smiles shyly. 'May I ask you who Bill is?'

'Bill.' His face is shining. 'Bill saved my life. Even though I'm a Papist.' He manages a laugh. 'I'd be a goner but for him.'

'I could tell it was someone special. Was it on the battle-field?' It was. He tells her the whole story in a rush, Orange marches and all.

'It's amazing how fate brings people together,' she says. He nods, looking at her sideways, wondering what's coming next.

'There's something I want to ask you,' she adds, after a few moments' silence.

He panics. It's the phoney Irish brogue. She wants to know why he spoke to her with a Dublin accent when they first met in the Rondebosch hospital. How can he explain to her that his lowly origins are stamped on every word he says when he speaks normally? Her own voice is so upper class, just like the officers', but without sounding snooty.

'Go ahead,' he says nonchalantly. He blows a smoke ring.

'What was it like on Robben Island?' Her face is full of sympathetic interest. 'I believe you were working with the lepers there.'

He jumps, as if she has fired a bullet into his heart. She hears him gasp.

'I'm so sorry if I've upset you.' She backs away from him, her eyes registering distress. 'I'll go if you'd prefer.'

'No!' The word blares out. He looks at the tents on the hill, so perfectly drawn up in neat lines; up, down, across, zigzag, typical army discipline. Unexpectedly it calms him, and places a grid of order over his swirling thoughts.

He looks into her eyes and tells her everything. It is as if a plug has been pulled from a dam of emotion he scarcely knew existed. He starts from his earliest days: how he was dumped at the orphanage with only a rosary from his mother; the beatings; how he was never made an altar boy; right up to the Island. She regards him with profound seriousness throughout. She does not say a word, though at one point she fleetingly touches his hand, to soothe. After an hour he looks away and smiles. 'That's the lot.'

Phew, that was better than Confession any day, with an old priest behind a grid, not even listening properly. But her compassion has in some way absolved him of his past, as if a burden of mortal sins has melted away. He feels light-headed.

At this point the four o'clock bugle sounds. She cannot draw her eyes from his. 'I have to go back to the marquee. Thank you for telling me this. We must speak of it again.' Their eyes meet. 'My name is Sarah.'

She has presented him with a priceless gift. He swallows. 'Most people call me Patch.'

'Patch,' she murmurs. The intensity of eye contact can be more sensual than physical touch. 'Patch,' she says again. She puffs the word out from her lips. Then she turns and glides away, in that way of walking she has.

On her way back to her bell-tent where she plans to spend half an hour thinking about this exchange, she is stopped by Mrs Mopeli who is passing by. Mrs Mopeli takes in washing from the tin hut ward, and is able to speak good English, having been partly educated in an English missionary school. On occasion she adorns the lower half of her body with red, white and blue stripes, which cling to her backside like a patriotic spider.

Mrs Mopeli likes to talk about England, which she regards as a fabled land, the very heart of civilisation, where everyone lives in peace and harmony under the gracious reign of a benign monarch. She can sing 'God Save the Queen' perfectly, a skill which she now demonstrates to Sarah, even though an exceptionally large basket of laundry is balanced upon her head and a small baby is tied to her back by a blanket.

'Goodness me!' cries Sarah in admiration, for the rendition has been filled with a dramatic intensity which suggests that

God is receiving orders from a woman whose overflowing head basket has assumed the qualities of a gigantic crown. 'That is very impressive, Mrs Mopeli. I see that you have a great respect for the British race.'

'Britain, she will give back the land to our people,' replies the washerwoman who has learnt her admiration for the Empire at the missionary school. 'Those Boers do not treat us like human beings. They think we must jump off the pavements when they walk past. They think we are first cousin to the baboon. They whip us with their *sjamboks* if we displease them!' (Here, to Sarah's alarm, Mrs Mopeli's body writhes as if the leather thongs of the whip in question were already slashing across her back, yet the washing basket remains perfectly poised upon her head and the infant sleeps on.) 'But the British!' Mrs Mopeli's eyes grow misty. 'The British will give us our freedom. We burnt our passes when the British came.' She sighs with pleasure. 'Yes, when the British came to Bloemfontein we burnt our passes and we waved the Union Jack! And when this war is over our men can vote just like the white men.' Mrs Mopeli slaps her thighs in case her patriotic attire had not been noted by this representative of the Mother Country.

'I am so glad you think highly of us,' returns Sarah, who nevertheless feels a spasm of anxiety. 'The British certainly could not conduct this war without your help.'

And nodding pleasantly to the smiling washerwoman Sarah hurries on towards the bell tent, where she takes out her diary:

8 April 1900

I feel I have a whole *aviary* of songbirds in my heart; their trilling floods through my entire system and fills me with a happiness never known to me before.

Yet I am only too aware that none of this makes sense. I am reminded of *A Midsummer Night's Dream* – perhaps a Puck-like creature has poured a love potion into my eyes and madness has set in. *Lord, what fools these mortals be . . .*

And dare I tell Louise? I think for the moment that I'll savour these moments on my own. Nothing will come of them, in any case.

At the same time – how is it possible to experience such different emotions simultaneously – I am worried about the high expectations the black population here has of Britain's promise to give them equal rights with the white population if they help out in the war. From what Sophie has told me, this is extremely unlikely, as Milner's idea is to create a union of English and Dutch in which the black man plays no part. I fear the worst.

Louise's Diary

9 April

Our fancy-dress parties, concerts and tableaux continue in our efforts to assure the enemy we are all now friends – what a jolly time we are all having. So popular is our diminutive general that there is a move to re-christen the town 'Bobsfontein' – what an idea! And yesterday Dr Theodore Chappell proposed to me and I am seriously considering his offer. I realise it is rather sudden, but he seems in earnest, saying that my laughter had completely conquered him!

I told Sarah the news as we walked back to our bell tent in the afternoon. Instead of the excited congratulations I expected, and wanted, she looked at me with her head on one side and said, 'This is very soon, Louise. Are you sure he's not married?'

'Of course he's not!' I shouted at her. I felt like shaking her fragile little shoulders till she begged for mercy.

'Well – remember Dr James.'

As I've remarked before, there is a directness and confidence about Sarah now that seems to have come about as a result of her lift of spirits. Just as I was about to smile frigidly and march off, she burst into peals of laughter and squeezed my hand hard. 'Oh, Louise,' she cried. 'Falling in love is such a curious thing.'

'What can you mean?' I stared at her. She suddenly seemed to be glowing, her eyes, her cheeks, her whole body. She looked at the ground, avoiding my stern gaze. 'You haven't – fallen in love yourself?' I demanded suspiciously.

'It's not worth talking about,' she whispered. A gust of red sand blew up and threatened to wrench our veils from our heads. After it had died down, and we had stopped coughing from the dust that had whirled into our noses and mouths, she continued in the same unwilling tones, 'I'll tell you when – or if – it is. I hadn't meant to speak to you about it. It's nothing, really.'

'Well, you're the one!' I exploded. 'Fancy deliberately keeping it from me! Who is he?' I felt a twinge of anger – and sadness – that she had not told me.

She looked up at me in a rush. 'Darling Louise.' She squeezed my hand again and I realised she had been holding it all the time. 'There is honestly nothing to tell. Something's in the air, that's all. It'd be bad luck to talk about something so – insubstantial. Let's be happy for you and Theodore.'

She gave me her new radiant smile and I had to be satisfied with that. For the moment.

10 April

Though life in Bloemfontein is full of parties and romance, things are going badly wrong in the tents of the field hospitals. A British Member of Parliament, Mr William Burdett-Coutts, comes to report on the medical facilities provided by the army for the enteric-stricken Tommies. He walks about, his face livid with horror, as if he has just walked through the gates of hell. It is certainly time the British public are made aware that their troopers are not receiving the best medical treatment that money can provide, but just the opposite. Mr B-C blames the Medical Services for this, and of course the Medical Services blame the Military. Kitchener summed up the situation in his bullish way to the Royal Army Medical Corps who have dared complain to him about lack of supplies: *You want pills and I want bullets, and bullets come first.* I wonder if he still has his pet flying fish.

Sadly, Sister Hemmings passed away last night after a

sudden decline – just when we thought she was over the worst. Even the orderlies were upset as she was a great favourite with them. She had such high ideals, perhaps unrealistically high, but that doesn't mean she deserved to die. We nurses take such a risk here – I am not sure that I want to breathe my last in Bloemfontein.

11 April

At last the tents of three General Military Hospitals, numbers seven, eight and nine, which have been waiting for weeks in the Cape Town docks, have arrived, together with sixty-two truckloads of hospital and medical supplies. It seems that in a supreme effort of determination, the Royal Engineers have repaired all the broken bridges and culverts. Of course, it does not help that there is only a single track railway which means one train can't go up while another is going down. I hope the arrival of these hospitals doesn't mean I'll have to move from the spacious Raadsaal where my patients and I are very comfortable. I am growing very worried about the state of my skin. All the unguents and emollients I brought over from England are quite useless in the violent South African sun, and not only am I growing as bronzed as a Boer, flakes of dry skin are peeling off my nose and forehead. No wonder the Boer women wear those monstrous flapping sunhats which completely conceal their faces, like nuns' wimples. Some of them are made out of layer upon layer of lace and frills and look as if they have been concocted from my old petticoats. I think on reflection I'd rather have sunburnt skin than one of those ghastly things on my head.

I noticed that a similar thing is happening to Sarah's skin. She asked me if she could borrow one of my unguents the other day, which is unlike her. Something is definitely on the go in her life. Why can she not tell me about it? How different we are.

28 April

The new hospitals have been erected and thank heaven it has been decided my officers and I can stay in the Raadsaal. Theodore is relieved as it is hell in the marquees. Sarah has been moved from her tin hut, with her patients, into hospital number nine where she found that all 520 beds are already taken, so twelve more beds had to be moved in for them. The next day two hundred wounded men arrived. They have to lie in their filthy bloodstained uniforms because there isn't enough hospital linen to go round in spite of the sixty-two truckloads, which turned out to have equipment only for the officers – linen, not cotton, sheets, and so on. Sarah says the marquee is filled with an appalling stench as the night stools aren't regularly removed. Thank God we have working lavatories in the Raadsaal.

Mr Burdett-Coutts holds a perfumed handkerchief over his nose and mouth as he creeps about the tents and marquees, shaking his bald head in disbelief. Apparently his despatch to *The Times* has shocked the British nation.

29 April

Today Lady Roberts arrived here with great pomp and ceremony. She is twice the size of her little husband, who obeys her every word. I'm told that she personally stitched the silken Union Jack that flutters in the Market Square where the Highland Brigade now play their bagpipes every evening. The gossip is that she has managed to convey eight large personal trunks from Cape Town to Bloemfontein. A fatigue party has been sent to the station to fetch the eight trunks, and mutters are being heard about the 'plague of women'. Somehow a crowd of those lady amateurs who pestered us so in Cape Town have now arrived in poor little Bloemfontein. They spend most of their time squabbling over officers or tittering at parties; they fill the hotels and barge into the wards, offering to read novels to the Tommies or comb their hair with pomade. I give them short shrift when I am on duty in my ward. I recognise a couple from the *Dunottar* once again. They are thoroughly enjoying this war.

Theodore has obtained a phonograph from Cape Town and plans to hold a musical evening in his villa soon. I have decided to accept his offer of marriage in spite of Sarah's lukewarm response to the news.

30 April

Seven of Lady Bobs' trunks turn out to be filled with comforts to be distributed among the Tommies. All is suddenly forgiven. She has managed to smuggle in several hundredweight of tobacco, chocolate etc for the men. Only one small trunk contained her kit. Or so they say . . .

3 May

Roberts has given the orders to advance to Pretoria! The men threw their helmets into the air; then began to dismantle the field hospitals which of course must be taken with them. This means that all the sick men inside them are now pouring into the hospitals which remain: in the space of twenty-four hours there are a thousand patients in tents meant for little more than half that number. Even the Raadsaal is filling up with rank and file.

At least we all have fun with the 'garglers'. It is hilarious to watch the daily ritual of convalescent rank-and-file Tommies gargling their antiseptic together with their commanding officers. They all pull agonised faces as they throw back their heads and gargle, each man on a different musical note – what hilarious discord – but are not allowed to spit out the foul-tasting stuff till the nurses are satisfied that the antiseptic has done its job.

I must say I do enjoy working with entirely male patients. It is hard not to tease them and make them laugh. I think Theodore grows jealous of the fun we have.

Sarah's Diary

6 May 1900

I hardly know if I dare describe what happened yesterday. Yet though I am utterly exhausted now, I simply must record what I suppose I can call a *romantic encounter*.

During the afternoon I had an idea that some hospital linen might have been left in the abandoned tin hut. It was the time of day when the men are left to themselves to smoke and swear while the female nurses grab a couple of hours sleep, or go shopping in the little Boer stores nearby.

The sky was purple with storm clouds as I hurried towards the school to which the hut is attached, and as I unlocked the door sheets of lightning flared up over the open veldt which lay just beyond. It is always a dramatic moment when the elements run wild. The huge, distorted shadows of a troop of Lancers passed the window, each holding erect his lance with its triangular pennant a-flutter, as if preparing for battle in some celestial Valhallah; the thunder exploded overhead, and the music of the Ride of the Valkyries began to pound in my head at once.

To bring me back to the twentieth century (as it has been for over four months now), hail and rain began to clatter down like bullets from a thousand Maxim guns; the hailstones grew larger and larger, some of them the size of a small fowl's egg. I could see the tethered English horses rearing and prancing in terror: many broke their halters and tore away. Although I have experienced numerous thunderstorms over the past few weeks, this one was certainly the fiercest, and I began to feel slightly anxious as I threw open the doors of the linen chest, for buildings and animals and humans are often struck by lightning in these parts. However, I was delighted to see that a large pile of cotton sheets and pyjamas had indeed been forgotten by the orderlies in the rush of the move, and I began to pile them into the basket I had brought with me. The touch and smell of their homely fabrics soothed me in the violence of the storm, and I stopped a moment, relishing the howl of the elements from within the safety of the hut. Just as I braced myself to return to the Number 9, the door flew open before a particularly furious gust, and wind and rain whirled into the ward. On turning round, imagine my amazement when I saw the bent figure of a trooper staggering in with the elements!

'Goodness me!' I exclaimed. 'What are you doing here, Patch?'

A range of expressions which I could not interpret passed over his face. He walked towards me. 'You are always too busy to speak to me now,' he said.

'Have you followed me here?' I asked in alarm.

'Why do you not speak to me?' he asked. I could see he was in an emotional state, and had indeed followed me.

'It is not intentional,' I replied as calmly as I could. 'You must know how busy I have been with the move and the new intake of patients. We no longer have free time during the day. Don't think I've forgotten what you told me. The only time I have to myself is at night and I cannot see you then.'

At this the hut seemed to burst apart as a thunderous explosion rocked its fragile walls. I think both of us thought for a moment that it was a shell from the Boer artillery. He took a step towards me as if to protect me. But when it became apparent that our assault was no more than a particularly ear-splitting thunderbolt hurled by Jove rather than De Wet, we looked at each other in relief and smiled shakily.

He was so close to me that I could inhale his scent of warm tobacco and sweat, and though I am not normally fond of either of these smells, their combination on his body aroused in me an overwhelming desire to be touched by him.

'Sarah,' he whispered. 'There is something I would like you to do.'

'And what is that?' If only my voice did not grow tremulous.

'I would like you to take off your veil.'

I said nothing, nor did I move.

'I would love to see your hair.'

I lifted my hands as if mesmerised by his request, and began to withdraw the pins that held my headdress in place. Who would ever have thought that unpinning one's nursing veil, usually a brisk, everyday deed, could turn into an act of surrender – for in obeying his request I knew I was already giving him some mysterious part of myself. One by one the pins went into my pocket until I could lift the square white fabric and reveal my brown hair, tied back tightly into a knot.

'And now,' he said in a low voice, 'will you undo your hair?'

My fingers were already removing the grips that held my knot in place. It is not often that I allow my hair to fall about my shoulders in public, but now I felt as if some convolution within myself was unwinding as the skeins of hair swung down, almost reaching my waist.

To my astonishment Patch fell on his knees before me and flung his arms round my lower body, his fingers winding my hair between them. Outside the wind continued to hurl itself at our hut, as if trying to wrench it apart. I felt my back arch as his embrace grew stronger. 'Patch!' I cried out, frightened of the sensations running through my body. 'I must return to the hospital!'

At this he leapt to his feet, an expression of acute embarrassment on his face. 'Forgive me,' he mumbled. 'Forgive me.' Then he closed his eyes and stammered, 'But you are the most beautiful woman I have ever seen.' He smiled his strange half-grin which I think is designed to be irresistible to women, and spoke with his Irish brogue. 'Sure, when I first saw you I thought you were the Blessed Virgin herself!'

'Well, that's a compliment coming from a Catholic,' I said, not knowing if I cared for that analogy much. My heart was beating rapidly, making me want to dance around for joy. I began to wind my hair back into its accustomed knot, thankful to have something sensible to do with my hands, for I longed to lay them on his shoulders. 'But I must get back.'

He pulled himself up to his full figure, as if on parade inspection. 'Message understood, ma'am!' And gave me a very smart salute that made me laugh – rather too fulsomely, I suspect.

'How strange: the wind has dropped altogether,' I remarked as I re-pinned my veil to my head (even though it is quite normal for the wind to drop after a storm). I peered out of the window. 'The clouds have vanished. The sky is clearing. The light has returned.' I started to pack the sheets and pyjamas into the basket I'd brought with me.

'Let me carry the linen for you.'

'We can each take a handle.'

The sun was blazing down as we left the hut, no hint of fiery battles in the sky. It was hard to believe that we had sustained such an assault from the heavens. Had I imagined *everything* that had just happened?

In the distance a line of English cavalry seemed to be floating two feet above the ground: a phenomenon caused by the sudden rising of condensed air, I'm told, which always looks so ghostly, reducing solid substance to slippery fragments.

I felt that I too was floating two feet above the ground, and could have believed that the solid substance of my body had melted into a mirage. I was glad of the weight of the linen basket or else I might have soared upwards into the clear blue heavens.

Louise's Diary

14 May 1900

If things were good while Roberts was here, now that he has left with the bulk of his men they have grown even better. Bloemfontein positively bubbles with new life. There is an outbreak of fancy dress parties, musical evenings, afternoon teas, games, dances, plays and concerts! I have had to get Dolly to take in all my evening dresses as I have lost a huge amount of weight here (joy of joys) – the heat reduces the appetite, and there is only one word for the food provided for nurses: *filthy*. Potatoes and rice are served on the same plate with a lot of sweetened carrots and a lump of meat. *Horribilis*! My stomach heaves at the sight of it. Things are of course very different in the officers' bungalows: legs of mutton, whole capons, sides of beef, fresh green vegetables, trifles, fruit puddings, and an endless supply of claret and champagne.

15 May

Last night Dr Phillips held a fancy dress party and I went as the Absent-Minded Beggar, Sarah's little outburst in March having reminded me of his existence. Theodore managed to get hold of a trooper's khaki uniform complete with pith helmet for me to wear, and I paid a local carpenter to carve me a wooden replica of a Lee Enfield rifle. I bound my khaki arm with bandages (unbloodied, I'm afraid), and begged Sarah to come as the cowering Boer for the *tableaux vivants* afterwards but she declared the idea to be in bad taste and wore the kimono she uses for a dressing gown and drew lines slanting up from her eyes with a kohl pencil in an effort to look Japanese. Halfway through the evening I was startled to see a scarecrow peering through the window. I recognised him as one of the troopers Sarah has nursed back to health. He was gazing hungrily at what I at first thought was the piles of food on the tables, but what I then realised was none other than Sarah herself. As usual, she was surrounded by admirers, so he couldn't have seen much of her. I was about to report him to one of the officers, for surely rank and file can't just wander about whenever or wherever they wish, but when I looked again he had disappeared. A handsome man he must once have been, before the ravages of enteric.

16 May

Today Sarah and I have managed to get a pass which allows us to ride a couple of wild little Basuto ponies out on to the veldt beyond Bloemfontein and towards the no-longer-besieged Kimberley. The ponies are in their element here, being the same breed as those used by the Boers and loving the freedom of the broad, flat plains; quite different from Missy Mare at home, who knows only obedience. We race each other like the wind in this empty landscape. I don't know which is emptier – the land or the sky. Certainly the sky is vaster, there being no hills or mountains or even trees to encroach on its space. You can almost understand why Kruger believes the earth to be flat.

We came across a group of officers sitting smoking on the great red anthills that stud the landscape, their horses grazing nearby. These anthills make convenient seats for the army, it seems. The men made us stop and show our passes – in case we were Boer spies, I suppose.

'You have heard of ants in the pants, I expect,' I said sarcastically, for nothing would induce *me* to sit on a mud hillock full of termites, dead or alive. Sarah blushed, for she finds such talk too risqué.

'You know what De Wet does to those who disobey?' laughed one of the officers.

'I should hate to think!' exclaimed I.

'Ties 'em over a live anthill for a couple of hours!' exclaimed the officer. 'And lets the ants do the punishing. We're thinking of adopting the same tactics for those who show no respect . . .'

'Would you care for a wee dram, ladies?' offered another young officer who already seemed the worse for wear. 'A new consignment's just arrived. Ah, Scotland!' and he held up his glass to the blazing sun. 'To your hills and glens, to your rain and mist, to your pheasant and partridge – I salute you!'

I was all for climbing down and joining them, but Sarah urged me away, reminding me that our passes expired within the hour – and that I was about to become an engaged woman . . .

On our way back as we trotted side by side, she said in a reproachful voice, 'How do you think Theodore would feel if he knew you were drinking whisky out in the veldt with tipsy officers? Can you really love him, Louise, if you can flirt behind his back?'

I flinched at this, having had similar thoughts of my own, but nevertheless defended myself gamely. 'Well, really, Sarah, I don't think you have any understanding of the word 'flirt' nor how necessary flirting is to women like me who don't have your natural attractions.' There! Might as well put the knife in and let her have it. Trying to keep the bitterness out of my voice I continued, 'We less well endowed women have to work harder at gaining the attention and admiration of men. For you it is effortless. Perhaps you should try to put yourself in my place.' I could feel tears dangerously near.

'But Louise!' Sarah cried in a choked voice. 'It is *you* who attract and amuse men, not I. Surely you know how I envy your – *jeu d'esprit* – your joyousness your humour. I am merely your shadow.'

I drew in my pony and she was forced to stop as well. Taking a deep breath I said, 'You may think me joyous, Sarah, but I can assure you that my happiness depends entirely on the approval of men. Without that, as you must know, I am in despair.'

'So one man's love is not enough for you?'

'Yes, it is, of course it is, but I must constantly reassure myself that others admire me too.' She was staring at me in amazement. 'You take that admiration for granted. In fact, you aren't even aware of it, as far as I can see.'

She was silent for a minute. Then she said quietly, 'I am aware of the admiration of one man.'

I felt all my self-pity evaporate at once, so strong is my curiosity about the state of Sarah's heart. Was she at last about to confess to me her secret passion?

'May I ask who he is?'

'Someone you would despise,' she said simply.

'Not a Tommy, surely?' I exclaimed.

'He belongs to a colonial brigade but he was born in this country.'

'An officer?'

'No.'

'Are you going to tell me more?' I tried not to sound horrified.

'There is still nothing to tell, dear Louise.' She looked away and I felt she was lying.

'I think you are very unwise to consort with someone of a lower class than your own, Sarah. Even I would not do that.'

'I'm hardly consorting with him,' she said in a small voice.

I felt myself losing interest. 'Well, all I can say is, be very careful. Whatever would your parents think?'

She laughed a little shrilly. 'You're a fine one to ask me that. Have you ever cared what your parents think?'

I tapped my pony's flank with my whip, not caring to reply to that question. 'Well I never,' I exclaimed in rural Oxfordshire accents. 'I can 'ardly believe my hears!'

And we both burst into slightly hysterical giggles as our

ponies bounded forward, relieved to get away from the intensity of our exchange.

I arrived at the Raadsaal to hear wild rumours circulating: Mafeking is about to be relieved! The siege has been going on for so long it will be strange to live without it.

Rossetti Mansions, London, 17 May 1900

'That can't be Mrs Potter!' exclaims Miss Griffen, peering out of the window of Number 33.

Emily leans over her shoulder, unable to resist the mayhem that has suddenly broken out on the street, though it is well past nine p.m. 'She's evidently thrown off her fire-grate,' she says sardonically, for that august lady is now running up and down Rossetti Street faster than Emily ever did, her hat awry, her hair falling over her shoulders as she tickles the faces of the passers-by with a peacock feather, and doubles up with laughter.

'I don't believe I've ever seen her smile let alone laugh,' says Emily, about to close the curtains. Then, snorting with sudden laughter herself, she points at the cherry tree beneath the window. 'Just look at that, Griffy!'

Brilliantly lit by the street lamp beside the tree, a pair of pin-striped buttocks bulges out from the mass of blossom. The owner of the trousers is delivering a tuneless rendering of the national anthem, while attaching a chain of miniature Union Jacks to the cherry tree twigs. He turns his face in purple triumph and grins fearfully down at the cheering crowd below.

'Mr Somerset-Glance!' cry Emily and Miss Griffen simultaneously; then collapse in cruel mirth as they watch the plump little man gingerly lower one spatted foot below the next, clinging to the trunk of the tree like a child to its mother while a band of delirious men, women and children leap round the corner, banging on tin pots and dustbin lids, chanting out two names in a fever of celebration: *Baden-Powell (clash-clash boom!) Mafeking (bang-bang crash!)*.

'You'd think we'd defeated Napoleon,' says Emily sourly. 'I assume Mafeking has been relieved.' The sky begins to blaze with fireworks. She closes the curtains with a briskness that is final. 'Let's hope all this xenophobia isn't going to affect our bookings.'

The bookings, in fact, are going well. The women-only protest meeting against the annexation of the defeated Orange Free State is only a few weeks away, but tonight the entire nation appears to have suffered a personality change and succumbed to hysterical rejoicing at the relief of a little railway siding on the edge of South Africa. Who would have thought that the sober people of Britain were capable of such communal bliss? What if the stolid British people metamorphosed into the unfettered spirits found on the shores of the Mediterranean; if they continued to dance in the streets; if *mafficking* became a way of life? But Emily has more important things to think about, for Kate Courtney has persuaded the great poet William Watson to write a sonnet about the patriotism of anti-war women, and Madame San Carlo has agreed to declaim it from the stage of the Queen's Hall.

'I think we should have a thousand copies printed and distributed to the audience as they arrive,' says Emily. 'Good heavens, what on earth is that racket?' She pulls a face.

Miss Griffen peeks through the curtains. 'Now Mrs Potter is leading a band of men and women beating biscuit tins and buckets with knives and forks. She is waving her feather in the air in time to the music! Oh do come and have a look, Emily dear.'

'I can imagine it well enough,' says Emily. She runs her finger down a list.

'Oh, goodness, there's poor Sophie twying to beat a path through the crowds. They keep pulling at her cloak and waving Union Jacks in her face. She looks wather iwwitated, I'm afraid.'

'At least she's escaped being tickled by Mrs Rouncewell,' says Emily. She is poker-faced but Griffy can detect humour in the twitch of her lips.

Tonight will go down in history as the greatest spontaneous expression of joy ever demonstrated by Britain (greater even, it is whispered, than those spectacular celebrations held for the Queen's Diamond Jubilee, less than three years earlier). But Emily remains firmly in her flat, with Miss Griffen and Sophie, where they draw up a seating plan for the meeting on 17 June. Mr Courtney has expressed a longing to be smuggled into this exclusively female gathering, but Emily decides to allow him no further than the corridor, where he must be content to listen behind the red velvet curtains and not show his face.

Bloemfontein, 17 May

There it is again. The strains of music float out from Dr Chappell's bungalow. Patch recognises some of the songs and can sing them himself 'She Was Only A Bird In A Gilded Cage'; 'Come Into The Garden, Maud' 'Drink To Me Only' . . . He can hear Louise tittering, then teasing a group of officers who laugh uproariously. He can hear the clink of glasses, and the low voice of Sarah woven into the tissue of sound that billows in and out of the night air. Dr Chappell rewinds the phonograph. There is a scratch, a hiss, then a whole orchestra waltzes into the shocked Bloemfontein night.

He'd get into trouble if they caught him here. But tomorrow he is leaving with his column: next week he'll be marching north, scouring the land for treacherous Boer guerrillas. He must touch her before he leaves. He moves towards the roomy back stoep, lit up by lanterns and candles and lamps, all hung at different heights.

How golden it all looks; how beautiful the ladies' evening gowns; how smart the officers' uniforms. Dr Chappell is winding up the phonograph again.

Patch stands behind the huge blue gum tree in the back garden. While the music plays his body is molten. He can see her smiling dreamily at an attentive officer. She shakes her head. The officer moves to another seated woman and bends down to ask her something. She rises; they extend their arms as if for flight. Soon they are all dancing – waltzing, he thinks – to the gush of music. Only Sarah does not dance. She moves to one of the big concrete pillars that hold up the tin roof of the stoep and gazes out into the night. Dr Chappell rushes over to wind up the phonograph as the music begins to sag.

Patch tilts his head from behind the tree and wills Sarah to look at him. But the darkness in the garden is dense. She is not going to see him unless he moves into the light thrown from the stoep. And then he will be seen, reported, disciplined . . .

He thinks. A soft but clear sound will attract her attention. A small pebble? A whistle? Neither seems appropriate for attracting the attention of a Blessed Virgin.

At once he remembers. He has the perfect sound. As long as Dr Chappell keeps the music going.

Sarah wishes she hadn't come. She had thought there was to be a concert, a string trio made up of medical officers. She would have been uplifted by the lightness and delicacy of the strings performing Haydn and Beethoven. Instead it turned out that Dr Chappell had just received a set of new phonograph records from a store in Cape Town, together with some other luxuries to which officers are entitled, and wanted everyone to hear them. The string trio could put aside their instruments and wait.

Now there is dancing. She does not want to dance. She has never wanted to dance. She wants to go back to the bell tent. She wants to think about Patch and enjoy the sensations that such thoughts arouse.

Dr Chappell is mercilessly replaying that Strauss waltz on his phonograph. The brilliance of Vienna ravishes the darkness of Bloemfontein. The stoep has become a ballroom. She hums the familiar tune. The beautiful not-so-blue Danube. The beautiful typhoid-infected Modder. The sick troopers have described it to her: fringed with African willows and fever trees; haunted by mynah birds and sacred ibis. This was never meant to be a battleground.

Unexpectedly, a wave of nostalgia stirs deep inside her. Why is she suddenly overcome by homesickness for the grey skies of Hampstead; for the comfort of her soft bed; for the fire burning in the hearth and finely sliced sandwiches? Can those be tears pricking her eyes? A lump in her throat? Why is she thinking of Home when her heart is in Africa? She has not given the gloom of England a second thought for months.

Her ears give her the answer. From out of the darkness a silvery tinkle is wafting across to her. The music could be spun from sugar – so sweet, so light, so delicious. It sings of home. Sweet Home. She is not humming the Blue Danube after all.

The dancers, swirling energetically in the confines of the stoep, do not notice her departure. She moves out into the garden, following the Hansel-and-Gretel trail of sugary sound.

Bill would be pleased to see to what use Patch is putting his musical snuff box now. The blessed virgin Sarah is answering its call, gliding across the long dry lawn, caught in its sticky sweetness. To encourage her further, he sings softly:

> *An exile from Home, Splendour dazzles in vain*
> *Oh! Give me my lowly thatch'd Cottage again!*

He can feel her smile drift towards him in the dark. And gradually her form materialises out of the shadows of the night.

Her shoulders gleam white in a haze of tulle. The music box falters, then stops. She is standing before him, saying nothing. She is an angel, cracked out of her stiff uniform. His eye travels down her evening frock, the colour of the palest sky. A beaded V-pattern in darker blue plunges down to a point below her waist, her waist is naturally slender, he can see that; not misshapen by stays. One hand holds up the hem of her froth of skirt to make walking easier. The waves of her hair are piled on top of her head – so much hair, twisted and tangled into loops and curls; he longs to pull out the combs that hold it up just to watch it tumble over her shoulders, but forces his hands to hang still.

183

'I thought it might be you,' she says softly.

The Blue Danube has stopped flowing. A little laughing chatter replaces it.

'You are beautiful,' he whispers.

Then a new music rises out of the phonograph. A violin is sobbing out a tender melody, an avowal of love, for sure. A piano picks out some jewel-like chords. Sarah begins to sway to the music.

'*Salut d'amour*,' she says.

He steps towards her. That perfume rising from her body is almost too delicate for his nostrils, used to stronger stuff. Yet it is overwhelming him with its fragile power. He gazes down at her and lowers his face, his eyes and lips moving towards hers. He gathers her up against him, his mouth in her hair. He melts into her movements, so that they rock together, as fused as the violin with the piano, fused into a single sensation . . .

'Sarah!' Was it an hour or a minute later that Louise's sharp call split them apart?

'*Where are you, Sarah?*' A torrent of noise is sweeping down from the stoep – shouting, cheering, handclapping.

'Oh my God, where is she?' An Australian nurse takes up the cry. Dr Chappell is no longer winding up the phonograph. Three cheers! Hip-hip-*hoorah*! And again *hoorah*!

Sarah is laughing softly. Patch can feel her laughter flowing over him like warm scented water. Now that they are separated he wants to pull her to him and tear the tulle from her shoulder and bury his face in her flesh.

'I must go,' she apologises, with that broad smile he does not recognise. She steps towards him and pulls his face down to hers. It is she who is kissing him; he is being kissed by the Virgin's soft lips. She pulls herself laughingly away just as he begins to slip his tongue into her mouth; he takes a deep breath.

'I'm leaving tomorrow, Sarah. I came to say goodbye. I'm going north with my column. To join Bobs.'

She blinks, trying to make sense of what he has said.

'The war is nearly over. They say we'll be back in a month.'

From the stoep: 'Sarah! We're going to send out a search party!'

'I don't want to go, you know that.' He fears she will weep. Instead she encloses him in her arms. Her fingers run down his thin body, sliding along his skeletal ribs, cupping his hipbones, and then, to his astonishment, brushing against his excited cock. Louise is shouting something that causes another 'hoorah' to break out, but now Sarah lifts her face and he kisses her again; her lips are warm and parted a little this time, suggestive enough to make him weak with desire.

'*Sarah!*'

There Louise stands beside the rose bushes, hands on hips, panting a little. She gazes at them, the excitement in her eyes slowly converting to surprise. Then pain. She does not move as they look up at her.

'So that's—' The two words have an accusing ring, but delicacy prevents her from going on.

Sarah detaches herself from Patch. She flits over to Louise and lays a hand on her friend's arm.

'This is Patrick Donnelly, the man I told you about. Patch, this is my friend Louise. She nurses in the Raadsaal.' She looks pleadingly at both of them.

Louise's mouth drops open. For a moment Sarah thinks she is about to scream. Instead she says in a shaky voice, 'Mafeking has been relieved.' And before either of them can respond she wheels round and runs back to the villa.

'I'll have to follow her.' Sarah is shivering suddenly. 'I must join the celebrations.'

'Don't go.'

'I have to go.'

'Will you wait for me Sarah?'

'Of course.' She pauses. 'But only if you'll write to me.'

'I'm no great letter writer.' He laughs nervously. 'But if you write to me I'll reply – but don't expect much from me.' Spelling has never been his strong point.

'I will write to you.' She begins to drift away. 'Goodbye, Patch.' She glides back to the lamps and candles, her gauzy skirt held out like two pale moth wings.

A rocket screeches up into the sky and explodes into falling stars. The whole of Bloemfontein seems to be singing the British national anthem as a thousand champagne corks punctuate the night air. 'To Colonel Baden-Powell, hero of Mafeking!' calls out Theodore Chappell as Louise clings to his arm and raises an unsteady glass.

Cape Town, May 1900

Dear Patrick,
I told you I would not write to you and I would not but now I have something to tell you. You are going to be a father, Patch. The baby is due in October (add up the months if you like). They say the war will be over by then. If it is a girl I want her to be called Fancy. If it is a boy you can choose the name. Write and tell me which name you want. Love from your Fancy fionsay!!!

Telegram from Mr Chamberlain to Sir Alfred Milner
08/06/1900 In view of possible early annexation of the
South African Republic what are your suggestions as to the
name? I should like if possible to associate future name
with Her Majesty. What do you think of Queen's Colony?

London, 13 June 1900

The Queen's Hall is filling up with women. The balconies are in danger of overflowing as mothers, grandmothers, aunts, sisters, nieces and cousins, greet each other and exchange stories about their long journeys from all over Britain. The circle is already crowded. A long, entirely female queue curls out into Upper Regent Street and into a neighbouring square. The women are conversing animatedly. The accents of Yorkshire, Scotland, Wales, Cumberland, amaze the Cockney tradesmen and stall holders who have never seen so many ladies in one place nor heard the entire country so represented on their streets. Miss Griffen and Sophie are distributing leaflets; Miss Hobhouse stands beside one of the great doorways, exultant. The three of them glance at each other now and again, barely able to believe what they have achieved. Members of the press hover in the street, affecting world-weariness. Only female reporters will be allowed in. There will be no heckling, only the dignified protest of resolute women.

And then the entire hall is full. Some of the women remove their hats, splendid milliners' concoctions – a flare of ostrich feathers here, a cluster of brilliant cherries there, froths of net foaming within wide brims tilted at an angle. Emily is tall, poised; very fine in her feathered hat and intricately striped skirt. She has a feeling for fashion which in itself uplifts the atmosphere of the hall. Now she strides up the stairs with the guest speakers to the stage door, her practical, powerful gait suggesting a woman with a clear head and abundant vitality.

The hall is thundering with patriotic themes played by Mrs Holloway on the great, ornate organ, whose massive pipes occupy an entire wall. It is fitting that this historic meeting takes place in a hall built for queens; and, as they wait, the audience acquires a certain majestic authority. The strains of a Pomp and Circumstance march fade, and the organ blower (the only male allowed in) retires. The speakers, including Emily, take their positions on the stage. Then Madame San Carlo appears on the platform, a formidable figure in black lace and flashing jewellery. She begins her recitation of the verses written by Mr Watson for the occasion:

> *Yet being brave, being women, you will speak*
> *The thought that must be spoken without fear . . .*

Madame's arms shoot out, her hands spread beseechingly, palms upwards. Her voice is a trumpet of defiance; with each new line she takes a step forward and assumes a new, more dramatic stance, so that it is possible to be mesmerised by the theatre of her delivery and to forget to listen to the words.

Now it is time for the resolutions and the speeches. Before she proposes the first resolution Mrs Scott, dressed in tastefully muted colours and possessing a gravity of demeanour that at once quietens the excited audience, lifts her chin and says, 'You will be aware that on 24 May Lord Roberts annexed the Orange Free State and renamed it the Orange River Colony. We can expect annexation of the South African Republic before long. But do not think this meeting is therefore in vain. Even if we can achieve nothing practical, we, the women of Great Britain, are coming together to express our combined protest against injustice. The two former republics will know that we have publicly expressed our outrage, and take some comfort from this.' She pauses. 'History will prove us right, of that I have no doubt.' In the stillness of the hall she says, 'I now propose resolution number one.'

Her quiet voice carries easily: the acoustics of the hall, only five years old, are said to be the finest in the world. One by one the women on the stage rise to read out their resolutions; one by one the resolutions are unanimously passed. Emily will be the last to speak, when she proposes the fourth resolution. Her heart is racing as she hears Lady Symington, a small, animated aristocrat, delivering the third resolution which protests against the annexation of the Boer republics 'whose inhabitants, allied to us by blood and religion, cling as passionately to their separate nationality and flag as we in this country do to ours.'

It is Emily's turn to speak. She rises and looks at two thousand female faces gazing back at her, faces old and young, expressing interest, intelligence, indignation. She has attended several of the new Promenade concerts and sat on the stage seats looking down at the mixed audience, smiling with pleasure as the young Henry Wood conducted his 'lollipop' favourites, but this is utterly different. She has never spoken to so many people at once.

At the end of the long central aisle, just beyond the curtained doors, she can see the dome of Leonard Courtney's head against the *portière*. The sight of the familiar head protruding above the curtain rim agitates her. He is her pillar of strength. Without him none of this could have happened. Yet, perhaps he will sit in judgement. He is such a distinguished statesman and she – she is nothing by comparison.

Emily Hobhouse draws a deep breath and reads out in a solemn voice:

'Resolution Four: That this meeting desires to express its sympathy with the women of the Transvaal and Orange Free State, and begs them to remember that thousands of English women are filled with profound sorrow at the thought of their sufferings, and with deep regret for the action of their own Government.'

She looks up from her paper with its strong words written by herself. 'Please raise your hands if you agree to pass these resolutions.' The hall blossoms with uplifted hands, some gloved, some calloused, some smooth and white, some holding programmes. Unanimously passed. 'God save the Queen!' cries Emily.

The women stand to sing out the national anthem. For this is no pro-Boer meeting, whatever the journalists might think, but an affirmation of Britain's Honour which must not be marred by an unjust and unworthy act. Emily, singing, stares up at the great rafts of dignified women, and her heart swells with the music.

'This is a magnificent assemblage, nothing less,' she thinks as she sings the thrilling words of the anthem. 'We women have spoken without fear and our message of support will reach the women of South Africa and give them heart. And there have been no fish-heads or rotten eggs thrown. Only decorum and courage. It has been worth all those hours of work.'

The women leave the hall, elated. Outside, Leonard Courtney is being guided through the throngs by his wife. Emily lays an anxious hand on his shoulder. 'Well?'

He beams. The brass buttons on his blue frock coat twinkle as brilliantly as his sightless eyes. Kate Courtney is laughing. 'Wonderful Emily!' he cries. 'An historic occasion! Congratulations is too pale a word. Perhaps we should have more meetings without gentlemen.' Miss Griffen and Sophie hover. 'Griffy! Sophie!' Emily throws an arm round the shoulders of each woman. 'Without the two of you none of this would have been possible. And now—' she exclaims in triumph, 'we can begin preparing for the meeting in Liskeard next month. My home town in Cornwall. *That* should be a challenge!'

Telegram from General Roberts to General Kitchener 14/06/1900: Let it be known all over the country that in the event of damage being done to the railway or telegraph the nearest farm will be burnt to the ground. A few examples only will be necessary, and let us begin with De Wet's farm.

Louise's Diary

15 June 1900

Ever since I caught Sarah in the arms of that scarecrow, things have been different between us. She didn't even show much interest in the Mafeking celebrations, refusing a glass of champagne as we toasted B-P. (I was very sorry not to have been in London that night – apparently the whole city went wild and a new word 'mafficking' was coined.)

I must confess I didn't really know how to react to Sarah's treachery; *horror* that she could be in love with someone so far beneath her socially, though I could see at a glance that he is a remarkably good-looking man, in spite of the ravages of enteric; *anger* that she had not brought herself to tell me how far her relationship with him had advanced; *misery* – why? *jealousy?* – perhaps. Although Theodore and I are now officially engaged and I wear his ring, I have to admit he is no Adonis. I have already had to tell him to lose a little weight round his midriff. Yet if the most handsome Tommy in the world made eyes at me I know I would turn my nose up at him, so why do I envy her?

I suppose I have got so used to Sarah's *not* falling in love that it is quite difficult for me now that she clearly has at last been pierced by Cupid's arrow. Would it have been any easier for me had she fallen for one of the many good-looking officers who admire her? She keeps sending me little notes suggesting we meet up at the Railway Hotel and talk things over, but so far I have not responded. We no longer share our bell tent. I asked for a private room in the Raadsaal and because I am now the ward sister, and Theo's fiancée, the request was granted. Now she asks me in her notes why I am punishing her. I cannot answer that question yet. There are too many answers.

Orange River Colony, June

After a week of tramping round the northern reaches of the Orange River Colony with his column, Patch receives another letter. Two months have passed since he heard from Fancy; he has thrust her news to the back of his mind and has not been able to bring himself to write a reply to her.

He recognises at once Johan's exquisite copperplate handwriting:

> *Dear Patch,*
> *Fancy is now very pregnant and you are the father. She waits to get a letter from you, man.*
> *I had a accident with Luthando's hair. I try to die it red white and blue stripes which he asked for but it come out green and orange, then he got a rash, then it all fall out. Sies, man, he make such a fuss, after that no one wants to come to my salon no more. Then I see a sign in the Gateway to Africa window asking for someone with good handwriting for a clerical job on the south arm of the docks. So now I am busy there recording how much hay comes in from all over the world for the war horses. Yeerah, there's a lot of hay here. The docks is full of haystacks.*
> *So us coloureds have our uses in the white man's war.*
> *Yours sincerely,*
> *Johan*

Patch feels a sudden nostalgia for the District. For a few minutes he savours the unique District aroma of horse manure and rotting fish and curry spices and sweet syrups; hears the call of the imam curling over the city like audible smoke; kicks at a couple of rats; treads among the children absorbed in their pavement games . . . Of the first two lines of the letter he will not allow himself to think.

His column had returned to base in some Boer village when the mail arrived; he was beginning to dread the post, what with Sarah writing to him all the time and dropping hints about wanting a letter back. But how *can* he write back when every day he helps to set fire to farmsteads, now that Bobs is taking sterner measures with the Boers. She will not understand that this is the only way to stop the Boers fighting for their land, because they don't understand that the war was won by Britain when Roberts took their capital, Pretoria, and Kruger fled. If the Boer guerrillas don't have their homes to return to for food and fresh horses and stocks of rifles and bullets hidden under floorboards or in holes out on the veldt, then they won't be able to continue fighting, it's as simple as that. He could explain all this to Sarah, so logical, but she has sentimental feelings for homeless women and children and he had as well to begin with but the lieutenant said if the women refused to aid the enemy they wouldn't lose their homes, it was the women who were keeping the war going, that was his argument and Bobs', but Sarah wouldn't see the larger picture.

The next day the column arrives at a farmhouse near a damaged railway bridge. There is a pattern now: burn all the crops, either stored in barns or growing in the fields; slaughter the cattle, pigs, horses, sheep and chickens, or herd them off to the nearest army base; chop down the orchards – before finally setting fire to the house. Patch is sent to demolish the orange groves.

It is a long time since he has chopped down a tree, let alone an orchard, but his body feels the better for it. The axed tree trunks, their branches laden with ripe oranges, lie on the ground, a sudden sweet-smelling undergrowth that he enjoys wading through after the emptiness of the veldt. The oranges glow like little suns and moons among the dark leaves. They remind him of Christmas decorations in the orphanage, hanging from a pine tree donated by the Cape Town Catholics. What a hero he will be when he returns to the men, his pockets bulging with the sweet juicy fruit! The troopers will be getting plenty of fresh meat from the farmstead: the abundance of livestock and crops in this desolate interior continues to amaze them every time. Cartwright was once a butcher's boy and hooted with joy at the sight of all this live meat. He'd grabbed Patch's axe and split a piglet in two then and there. The sleepy mother pig had stumbled to her trotters but she'll be pork chops by now. Even though Patch certainly enjoys a pork chop he knows he would rather hack down trees than animals.

He feels a sweet well of saliva spring up under his tongue. All this food, meant to sustain the Boer commandos, not the likes of him. He has put on some weight at last, in spite of roaming across miles of veldt every day with his column, in search of guilty farmsteads. He swallows the last lukewarm drop of water in his bottle and hopes the men haven't done anything stupid to the well, like piss in it so the Boers can't drink it. You can go too far with this scorched earth business.

He is hungry now and strides back to the farmhouse to get bread and fruit. Tonight they'll burn up some furniture or a few fence posts and roast a mountain of meat. Maybe there'll be bread fresh from the clay oven in the yard. Chickens all over the place so there's bound to be eggs. Then tomorrow they'll burn down the farmhouse. They've given a lot of time to the women and old people to pack their things in the ox wagon, not like yesterday when they had to do six houses in one day.

There's something disturbing about the women: they wear these frilly sun bonnets called 'kappies' which make them look like the nuns at the orphanage. They move about in the same quiet way, as if praying and singing hymns is what the body should really be doing. Do they have normal emotions? He thinks he might make a fuss if he was turned out of his home, but as he has never had a home except for the orphanage he doesn't know for sure. The Boer children cling to their mother's skirts, he can understand that. Sometimes the grandmothers get emotional, shouting and weeping, but the mothers tend to remain grim-faced and silent.

Last night the children had stood motionless in their big cotton hats, gazing as the fire burst out of their bedroom windows with a loud roaring, and black volumes of smoke rolled overhead. 'That's a sight they'll remember till the end of their lives,' said the captain. The women clasped their young ones to their breasts or hid their faces in each others' laps. An old hag screamed at them in English, 'Yes, you've made a mighty fine blaze now, but nothing like the blaze you'll burn in hereafter!' Well, it's her fault they're having to do this dirty work.

He hopes the women and children have finished moving their bedding and sticks of furniture out of the house and on to the ox wagon. There are plenty of farm kaffirs to help, all screeching and howling because they too are losing their homes. The kaffir scouts who accompany the columns like to be cheeky to the Boer women: 'We are the bosses now!' they laugh as they pat their rifles. 'Soon we will have your farms.' The captain doesn't really like what he has to do. 'Madam, I regret to tell you we must burn your house down.' The woman draws herself up and stares over his shoulder. 'We've done nothing wrong. My husband has signed . . .' The captain explains about the railway, the wrecked bridges, the buckled girders. Within ten miles is the rule. Are there Republican flags in the house?

The captain sometimes tries to reason with them: 'If your men stopped their pointless fighting we wouldn't have to do this, you know.'

The women look at him in surprise. 'We won't stop fighting. It is an honour to suffer for our land.'

'But how long can you suffer like this?' He points to a group of Tommies setting fire to a barn full of grain.

'Oh, as long as may be necessary. Till you go away. The Lord is our shield. He has saved us many times before.'

'At this rate your race faces extinction,' mumbles the captain, who has no faith in the Lord's shield. He gives the order for the men to storm the house.

The troopers tear the place apart like wild barbarians, looking for flags but helping themselves to violins, sewing machines, perambulators, cutlery, trinkets, jewellery, it's all the same to them. The women look on with eyes of freezing disdain. Then – up in flames go their carpets, furniture, paintings, ornaments. Patch wants to hang his head in shame but he has found a beautiful silver bracelet with a turquoise stone in the trinket box of a silent woman. With what contempt did she gaze at him as he shoved it into his pocket just as she came into her room to fetch her clothes. He couldn't really explain to her it was for Sarah and expect sympathy.

Cartwright has developed a routine: he likes to pull the piano out (strange, how many houses have them) and get a Boer girl to play on it while the flames roar behind. '*Sing!*' he shouts, and the family gather round and bellow out their doleful hymns as if the hand of God might come down from heaven and put the fire out. In the meantime the Tommies fling stones at the poultry and throw themselves prostrate on terrified chickens and squawking ducks as the hymns thump out. Further off, other troopers collect cows and sheep and horses and drive them off, or slaughter them then and there while, on top of the nearest high ground, a party of men, rifles in hand, stand guard against a surprise attack from the enemy, a few of whom can often be seen in the distance, watching the destruction of their homes.

Then, as the family is bundled on to the ox wagons, Cartwright raises his axe high into the air and smashes it down into the guts of the piano and chops it up as if it was a log of wood. What hair-raising dissonances thunder from the strings and metal frame! The echoes ring through the farmyard for hours, or so it feels. Everyone says pianos make the best firewood but, though Patch enjoys the barbecued meat afterwards, he often fancies he can hear a mournful music rising from the charred cinders of the upright Bechstein or Broadwood.

Now, his mouth sweetened by oranges, Patch keeps his eyes on the hard red earth. Captain Cooper has ordered them to look out for buried ammunition, or treasure, come to that. When the Boer women hear you are coming they bury the Mausers and bandoliers belonging to their men, or the family china and jewellery. Yesterday they'd uncovered a whole cache of rifles which all turned out to be Lee Enfields, looted from the Imperial troops, with the barrels exposed to make them lighter. Cheek! Mind, he'd like to lay his hands on a Mauser if he could get one. You could load five cartridges simultaneously, unlike his own Lee Metfield where the cartridges have to be loaded one after another, giving the Boers more time. Only trouble, they were running out of Mauser bullets. So if he did manage to loot a Mauser he wouldn't be able to shoot with it.

He is getting closer to the farmhouse now. He hopes there will be water to wash in, piss-free water, that is. He can smell his own sweat, a dark perfume drifting from his armpits in that dry air. Some plant on the mountain in Cape Town smells like that. What wouldn't he do to be there now. Can that twinge in his heart, like the string of a fiddle twanging out of tune, can that be homesickness in someone who never had a home?

He begins to run in case they've decided to burn down the house now instead of tomorrow. He's running through the field of mielie-corn and then out across the vegetable garden. Not much there now. A squawking chicken flutters up. There are strange things hanging on the tree, thongs of leather waiting to be turned into God knows what. Reminds him of the blessed martyr's flagellation kit, a bit creepy, really. The Catholic religion is so lush with blood and grief and pain, we're brought up on the Queen of Sorrows with her legs wide open and the whipped son like an unstrung puppet across her knees. With a Requiem Mass in the background, plain chant, or resounding with trumpets and drums and triangles, enough to shoot you up to heaven like a rocket, or a bit of dynamited Boer thatch. But in this land there are no *pietas*, just thin lips and muttered prayers under the kappies, and God has a larger purpose, it's all in the family Bible, the Old Testament specially.

It is at this point in his tumbling reflections, which so often tilt back to the Catholic church these days, that Patch spies newly dug soil. And stops his running. He begins to dig with his bare hands.

Liskeard, Cornwall, July 1900

A riot has broken out in Liskeard Town Hall. Though the members of the audience who sit in the front rows look up seriously at the speakers on the stage (Emily recognises the cook, the gardener and the maidservant from The Rectory), the members at the back are waving flags and whistling patriotic airs. The chairman of the meeting, Mr A. Quiller-Couch, is a famous Cornish novelist and poet, but the youthful brigade at the back of the hall are impressed neither by his literary status nor his introductory words. So little do they accord respect where it is due that they have succeeded in shouting him down every time he tries to speak.

To Emily, sitting behind the platform table and preparing to deliver her speech, the worst moment (and there are to be many very bad moments) comes with the public betrayal of that most honourable of politicians and her closest friend and mentor, Mr Leonard Courtney. She can scarcely believe what she is hearing.

'Mr Courtney has served you well,' says Mr Quiller-Couch. 'He is a man whom you have trusted long—' *No more! No more!* yells the mob. 'He has brought honour on your constituency,' continues the famous author nevertheless. 'You have been proud to have such a man to represent you in Parliament.' (Groans and hisses.) 'But now, because he advocates conciliation between the white races of South Africa you have turned your backs on him and chosen another candidate for the next election.' *Quite right! Hooray!* And the mob, most of whom have been helped out of some scrape in previous years by Leonard Courtney, break into cheers and clapping at the back of the hall.

'I am merely a private citizen whose judgement refuses to approve of the war,' declares Mr Quiller-Couch. The hissing that fills the hall at this announcement drowns his next words. 'But our speakers have higher credentials than I. Despising popularity they have come to speak the truth as they see it.' This information is greeted by catcalls and an impromptu march around the back of the hall to 'Soldiers of the Queen'. The Cornish Bard raises his voice. 'May I remind you that the war you support so vociferously costs us over one hundred men and about £750,000 per day?' Someone blows a voluntary on a tin trumpet. This is the signal for a prominent citizen of Liskeard, with an equally prominent belly decked in buttons and chains, to mount a chair and raise a Union Jack. The mob bursts spontaneously into the National Anthem and the prominent gentleman conducts this melodious expression of patriotism with a baton of red, white and blue. The more timid ladies in the audience flee to the ante-rooms for safety.

Emily breathes deeply. 'Calm and composed,' she reminds herself. Leonard Courtney's advice. She stands up. The crowd that stares back at her is hostile. Even as she tries to project composure, a familiar throb of hot anger overwhelms her. She entirely forgets her official opening words. 'I think you will agree with me that if Her Gracious Majesty the Queen, whom you are so anxious to *save*, if she were present now she would be heartily ashamed of her Cornish subjects!' She is shouting. There is uproar. 'I have addressed meetings lately all over England – in Leicester, London, Leeds, Bradford, Liverpool and Manchester – but it has remained for me to come to Cornwall, my home county, to see the worst behaviour of all!'

This is not a good start and both Emily and the audience know it. But nothing can stop her now. 'One wonders how the people of an old respected town like Liskeard should endure a handful of thoughtless boys to upset their meeting.' Her voice brims with contempt. The handful of thoughtless boys wave a forest of miniature Union Jacks and burst into 'Soldiers of the Queen' again, thumping their feet on the floor in time to the marching rhythms.

Once the din has subsided a little she draws herself up and cries out: 'No one in this hall can be more patriotic than I. And let me assure you that there is no one at this table who is a pro-Boer. We are all pro-Englanders, every one of us. We are firstly concerned about our own country and whether or not she is acting upon the highest principles of justice and humanity'

At this the handful of boys, whose numbers seem to be swelling to a hall-full, spring to their feet and sing 'Rule Britannia!' with great energy, as far as they know the words, and Emily loses her last vestige of self-control. 'And do you know what our beloved Britannia is doing to the women and children of South Africa?' she yells. Even her hair loses its control as several strands fly from her coiled coiffure and spring over her eyes. Mr Quiller-Couch rolls his eyes at the Quaker organisers. 'I'll tell you if you don't. The soldiers of the Queen you admire so much are marching through the Boer Republics—' '*Ex*-Boer republics!' calls someone from the middle of the hall. '—setting fire to farmsteads and private homes, and leaving innocent women and children and old people to wander homeless about the veldt in the middle of winter. And I have letters to prove it.' From her opened reticule she whips out a pile of papers.

'Here is one from Captain March Phillips. I'll read you a paragraph.' The uproar abates suddenly. The entire audience leans forward to hear. Emily's voice has grown even stronger – perhaps there is a touch of Madame San Carlo in her delivery. '*The worst moment*' she reads – then pauses to savour the intensity of the silence in the hall – '*the worst moment is when you first come to the house. The people thought we had called for refreshments, and one of the women went to get milk. Then we had to tell them we had come to burn the place down. I simply didn't know where to look.* And here's another, from Private Percy Day: *We were only there*

for a few minutes but we did do a little damage in a short time.
I put the butt of my rifle through a large looking-glass over the
mantelpiece and put my foot through a sideboard with glass
doors. One of the others smashed up a piano and an organ.
The women didn't half scream. I thought they would go for
us, but it was an awful sight. I should not have thought that I
could have done such a thing, but when you get in with the
regular soldiers and have a good gallop we get a bit excited
and don't care what comes next.'

Emily puts down her bundle. For a moment the audience
stares back at her, stunned. Then, from the back of the hall –
'Forgeries! Fakes! Lies!' and even 'Serves 'em right!' The
entire audience seems to erupt and Emily steps back. The
handful of flag-bearing boys leap from their seats, march up
the side hall, sweep up the stairs and surge upon the platform,
bellowing, singing and cheering all the way. One tries to turn
over the speakers' table; the others seize a number of chairs
and pile them in a heap across the middle of the platform. In
the ensuing chaos Emily distributes Conciliation leaflets
among the audience – and to her horror she sees several
local councillors and farmers tear them to pieces and throw
them in the air. The cook and the gardener crumple her
leaflets contemptuously and hurl them on to the stage, though
the kitchen maid merely chews her knuckle – how humiliating
to see one's servants trample over one's attempts to convert
them.

Now another speaker, Mr Lloyd George, the Radical
member for Carnavon, who has not yet uttered a single word,
moves to the platform centre with a view to dismantling the
barricade of chairs. At once the mob rushes at the chairs and
begins flinging them in all directions, at which point the police
arrive on the platform and the conflict abruptly ceases.

Emily's cheeks are burning scarlet as she and the other
speakers leave the stage in exasperation. She pins up the
undisciplined curls and blots away the beads of perspiration
that have gathered on her forehead. As the singing and
horseplay continue (someone has just fallen off the stage with

a crash, causing much hilarity) she exclaims, 'And to think this is a non-political meeting.'

The Quaker organisers raise their eyebrows but not their voices. 'A little mafficking goes a long way,' says Mr Quiller-Couch. He accepts a cup of rather milky tea. 'It's time the British public calmed down and became more objective. One sugar, thank you.'

'Women and children in distress,' said Emily bitterly. 'You don't have to be objective to recognise that what's happening to the Boer people is a crime against humanity.'

A rescue plan is already formulating in her head.

Orange River Colony, June

When Patch had started digging up the loose earth with his bare hands, his imagination came up with all sorts of wild ideas about what lay down there: rifles, tea sets, jewels, gold, diamonds. Something he could give Sarah to impress her, along with the turquoise bracelet. Maybe even something for the woman on the island.

Now his fingers scrabbled through the red earth and, sure enough, struck something hard. A box. He felt a surge of pride, of achievement. The satisfaction of discovery, possibly even leading to promotion. He brushed away the layer of earth covering the lid, planks of cheap wood nailed hurriedly together from the look of it. He lifted the lid in a state of some excitement, as if opening a Christmas box. Inside it, a shape was wrapped up in a piece of cloth. A shawl. The soft fabric was embroidered with Dutch biblical texts.

A cold shadow of fear dropped over him. The hope that the shawl would contain fine china or the family jewels vanished, the knowledge of what was really in there made his skin crawl with an army of flies, as bad as Cronje's laager . . .

The baby boy's eyes were shut. His skin was not quite waxen. He bore the mark of illness.

Patch heard a terrible sound, like a cow giving birth, or a train howling in the wilderness. It was only when he began to vomit that the sound stopped. He pushed the earth back on to the box. Still on his knees, he began to pray, his face in his dusty hands:

Out of the depths I have cried to thee O Lord
Lord hear my voice.
  O Lord hear my prayer

The oranges were lying all around, spilt on to the red earth.
He gathered them on to the burial place and arranged them
into a crucifix of bright fruit. As he prayed, he lifted and held
them, one after the other, as if their radiance might enter his
darkness.

  And let my cry come unto thee.
  And let my cry come unto thee, O Lord.

But the image of the dead baby in the biblical shawl kept
bobbing about in his head, like a discarded box on a slippery
sea . . .

Sarah's Diary

13 July 1900

Why is Louise doing this to me? Nearly two months have passed since she found me with Patch – surely by now she should have forgiven me. For what, though?

The pain of waiting to hear from her combined with the agony of waiting to receive a letter from Patch is beginning to wear me down. Never did I think Mail Days would be so painful for *me*. Now I understand so much better my poor patients' suffering when nothing arrived for them, week after week.

At least I have heard from Sophie. She writes of the wonderful Queen's Hall all-women meeting – how inspiring – I should love to have been there. How sad that both the Boer republics have been annexed in spite of this magnificent protest, but at least the women can feel they have made their voices heard about the iniquity of war. Sophie asks me if there is any evidence that their message of support has reached the women of South Africa who are so much in this war, specially those who have had their homes razed to the ground. (It is so dreadful to hear that this is happening round here, and the hideous thought occurs to me that Patch may be involved in this wicked farm-burning policy.) I must approach the Loyal Ladies' League here in Bloemfontein and find out whether they are aware of the great Queen's Hall message. I believe they are non-partisan. Perhaps I can join their League and make a contribution towards Conciliation through them. At the very least it would take my mind off my waiting.

15 July

Yesterday I paid a visit to a Mrs Stuart of the Loyal Ladies' League. She made it quite plain that the League accepts only loyal daughters of the British Empire who will throw their womanhood's loving gentle influence on the right side. After a short conversation with her I realised that my contact with the Conciliation Committee immediately disqualified me for membership of this august League. The fact that the women at the Queen's Hall had sent a message of support to suffering Boer women made it clear that they were all pro-Boer; she was surprised the meeting had been allowed. The Loyal Ladies felt no sympathy with the Boer women, who deserved to have their houses burnt down.

I left her house feeling a very *disloyal* daughter of Empire, and not a little entertained by Mrs Stuart's views. If only I could talk to Louise about this – what fun we would have!

Still no word from Patch. I never thought one could grow so weary through waiting.

Louise's Diary

24 July 1900

Today, during our time off in the afternoon, I heard a light tapping on my fine Raadsaal bedroom door. On opening it, I was greeted with the sight of tear-stained Sarah, who broke down in sobs the minute she saw me. Though my first impulse was to slam the door in her face, on speedy reflection I decided I had punished her long enough, and she must be coming to apologise for – for all those misdeeds concerning the Papist scarecrow.

'Darling!' I exclaimed, and opened my arms. She flung herself against my upholstered breast, wept copious tears all over my apron-bib, then snivelled, without looking up at me, 'Oh, Louise, I have just heard such a terrible thing.'

'And what is that, Sarah? There, there, it can't be as bad as all that.' (I have no hesitation about using the most blatant of clichés, as often this is exactly what unhappy people want to hear.)

In between horrid gulps and snorts she whispered: 'I have just heard that Patch's column burns down six farmhouses a day, at least. Oh, Louise, can it be true?'

Though this was not at all what I'd expected her to say, I felt obliged to answer wisely. 'Oh yes, indeed it is. All Roberts' idea. He did the same thing in Afghanistan, you know.'

At this, Sarah raised her stricken face to mine and said in a voice, fierce in its intensity, 'But we must stop it, Louise. It is a vile wicked thing. How can a British general order his men to behave like this? We must protest, we must—'

212

'Stop!' I commanded. 'You are growing hysterical. Come and sit in my nice armchair and I shall sit on my bed and persuade you that there is no way a few nurses are going to stop Roberts in his tracks.' She obeyed me without resistance, and I seated myself on my soft mattress. 'I'm sorry to say that your Patch is probably rather enjoying himself right now. The troopers all start off feeling sorry for the women and children; then they start getting a thrill from their extraordinary power – you know, building the fire, lighting it, watching the house go up in flames while the family pours out . . .'

'Don't!' cried Sarah. But she blew her nose and appeared to compose herself. 'And to think we sailed to South Africa on the same ship as Roberts. He seemed such a gentleman then, such a hero. Little did we know.'

'I know something rather unheroic about Roberts,' I said mysteriously. 'I promised him I would tell no one. I can't breathe a word until you promise me you will keep it completely to yourself.' In fact, I had told Theodore, but we are engaged after all. Normally Sarah would be too high-minded to listen to gossip, but this time she merely accepted a second clean handkerchief, blew her nose, wiped her eyes, and settled down to listen. I plunged into my story of how, about six weeks ago, the Raadsaal Hospital prepared itself for a formal visit from Lord Roberts in which he would shake hands with the patients, distribute tobacco and other delicacies, no doubt from the trunks of his redoubtable Norah, and raise the morale of the bedridden, that sort of thing.

He arrived without too much pomp and ceremony, then requested to use a water closet before visiting the men (probably has a prostate problem). Well, we all waited for him to re-emerge; the minutes accumulated, and after half an hour a medical officer was asked to tap delicately on the WC door. No sign of Bobs. Perhaps he had decided to visit the patients without us – but no. A search was ordered. Had he been captured by a Boer ambush inside the hospital, which, after all, was the one-time Boer parliament? We branched out in all directions. I was sent to the little offices and washrooms that adjoin the WC area. As I prowled about, not really expecting to find anything of interest, I heard a whimper coming from the private study of ex-President Steyn. In fact, a series of whimpers, uttered by a male person. I marched into the study, a gloomy place with portraits of extremely ugly Boer men, including Kruger with his quadruple under-eye bags (strange, as all the Boer men I've met have been very attractive . . .) and odd bits of heavy mahogany furniture.

To my utter astonishment, I found Bobs cowering in the corner, uttering the very whimpers I had heard from the corridor. 'Your Lordship!' cried I. 'Are you ill?' he seemed quite unable to speak, staring at me with huge, frightened eyes. 'Can I help you?' I asked anxiously. He at last began nodding his head and rolled his eyes in the direction of a large leather armchair near the door. In it reclined our beloved mouser, Katie, the tortoiseshell cat. 'Hello darling,' I greeted her fondly, and ran my hand over her silky back. A flurry of purrs broke out beneath my fingers and Katie began licking a paw rather ostentatiously. In the midst of all this, I became aware that Bobs was trying to speak to me. 'N-nurse!' he croaked. 'Yes, your Lordship?' said I, now tickling Katie under the chin. 'C-can you remove that monster from this room, please?' 'Katie?' replied I, in astonishment. He straightened himself up to his full five foot. 'I have what I believe is called a phobia about cats.' He stared straight ahead as he delivered this information, not meeting my eye. 'Oh, of course.' I oozed as much sympathy out of these three words as I could manage; then picked up an indignant Katie and carried her, hissing and spitting, to an outside door.

Once she was safely seen scratching herself on the Raadsaal lawn, Roberts strode out of the study, a stern look upon his weathered face. 'I would ask you not to repeat this incident to anyone.' he snapped. 'I hope I can trust you, Sister.' And gave me a very severe look that was meant to suggest ruthless punishment should I repeat the story. Then off he strutted, the very image of a fearless general, which of course he is – as long as there is no cat near him.

At the end of this story, which I had related with all the appropriate sound effects, dialogue accents and facial expressions, Sarah rewarded me with a tremulous giggle. She laid her pale, pretty hand on mine and said, 'We *are* friends again, aren't we, Louise?'

Her voice and eyes were so beseeching that I mumbled, 'Why, of course, my dear. Whenever weren't we?'

Her face visibly flooded with relief. For good measure, I added, 'And have you heard from your Patch?'

The light went from her eyes as I had expected and, biting her lip, she shook her head. She could not bring herself to speak.

'Well?' I prompted.

She gazed at me in her soulful way. 'Perhaps I have made a mistake,' she whispered.

'Perhaps you have,' I said softly. 'But there are many more fish in the sea, as well you know.'

I am so glad to speak to you again.' Her voice was still faint as she stood up. 'It has made all the difference in the world to me.'

And yes, I too am pleased to have her as a friend again, as long as that bag of bones keeps away.

Orange River Colony, July

Cartwright was getting worried about Patch. Ever since that day a few weeks back when he'd gone off to chop down some orange trees while the rest of them had rounded up cattle and such, Patch had begun acting strange. He'd come back from the orchard looking a bit pale and smelling of vomit, but hadn't said anything. Cartwright was pulling the piano out of the house with some of the lads at the time so he didn't get a chance to ask his pal if he was all right.

But later, when they sat round the camp fire munching fresh pork and chicken (the Boer woman even baked some bread for them in the big clay oven outside the kitchen), Patch seemed to be in another world. Normally he'd've been capering about, trying to flirt with the sombre Dutch girls, singing his favourite ditties, and enjoying the lovely pile of smoky meat. That night he'd excused himself from the celebrations and gone back to their tent early, claiming exhaustion. Yet when Cartwright had himself reeled back into the tent hours later (one of the lads had found fifty demijohns of home-made peach brandy in the farmhouse cellar), Patch was lying on his back with his eyes wide open, his hands clenched behind his head.

'You look like you've seen a ghost, old chum,' said Cartwright.

Patch shifted his gaze to his friend. But he didn't look *at* him, he looked *through* him which made Cartwright feel a bit creepy. 'Tell you what,' he said in a jovial sort of voice, 'I'm going to get you some of Mynheer Boer's peach brandy. That'll sort you out.' Because the way Patch looked was beginning to remind him of the way some of the troopers had looked after the Tugela disaster, as if they no longer belonged to this world and were faintly puzzled to find themselves fighting a war in a foreign land. Some of them started acting really weird – couldn't walk straight and talked to themselves out loud – but it was generally felt that they were trying to get out of the army by pretending to be mad.

On the way back to the farmhouse he nearly collided with Captain Smithers, a decent chap though a bit squeamish about the house burning. He kept his eye on the well-being of his men too.

'Oh, Cartwright – stand at ease, man – how is Private Donnelly? Is he sickening for something, do you know?'

'Wouldn't be surprised if he ate too many oranges, he didn't even bring any back,' said Cartwright who had formed this opinion to explain the vomit. 'I'm just getting him a little pick-me-up, sir.'

'That should do the trick.' The captain didn't look too well himself. A mummy's boy at heart, Cartwright thought, from some la-di-dah family, like all them officers. Posh. A different world.

Patch had a posh sweetheart now, that stuck-up Nurse Palmer who looked at Cartwright as if he was something she'd scraped off her dainty little shoe. You'd think she'd have gone for an officer and a gentleman, being upper class and a bit prim and proper, but she'd fallen for Patch's good looks and humour, just like all the girls did. Cartwright thought he had seen that give-away look in her eyes even before Patch confirmed his suspicions.

When he returned with a mug of brandy he found his friend pacing about outside the tent. 'Here's your medicine,' grinned Cartwright and handed over the mug.

Patch gave the brandy that weird, unseeing look then said, in a slow, heavy voice as though he were trying to remember how to speak, 'Have you ever seen a dead baby, Fred?'

217

Well, as a matter of fact, Cartwright *had* seen a dead baby, or a dead foetus, more like. He'd found it wrapped in a brown paper bag addressed to him. A little boy, not much bigger than your hand. THIS IS YOURS, said the note in shaky capitals. Well, he'd disposed of it pretty quickly down the docks and though old Mrs September upstairs had asked him what was in his parcel, her wizened old face alight with malicious curiosity, he'd just laughed and said wouldn't you like to know.

But now, as Patch fixed him with that strange look, he decided he wouldn't admit to that particular episode and said in an encouraging voice, 'Well, I've seen a dead baby *seal*, old chap, but that's probably not what you mean!'

Patch's face darkened; this was the wrong answer, clearly.

'Drink up, my friend,' urged Cartwright.

Patch did as he was told but the brandy didn't seem to help him much. From the look of him the next day he hadn't slept a wink, purple circles round his green eyes. He looked a sight, really.

Yet as the days progressed there was a change. For nine consecutive evenings he was seen on his knees behind a karee tree or a thorn bush, praying. From a slender twig of tree or bush hung his miraculous medal.

For Patch had remembered from his orphanage days a guaranteed method of getting what you wanted from God: he was making a Novena for the soul of the Boer baby boy, who would have no chance of entering heaven otherwise, not having the necessary Papist qualifications. Now his own soul could be at peace.

Telegram from Colonel Kelly-Kenny to General Roberts
08/09/1900 General MacDonald refers to me for a definition of the expression lay waste. I suggest the following answer. Gather all food, wagons, Cape carts, sheep, oxen, goats, cows, calves, horses, mares, foals, forage, poultry. Destroy what you cannot eat or remove . . . Burn all houses and explain reason is that they have harboured enemy and not reported to British authorities as required. The questions of how to treat women and children and what amount of food and transport to leave them will arise. As regards the first part, they have forfeited all right to consideration and must now suffer for their persistently ignoring warnings against harbouring and assisting the enemy. As regards the second give them the bare amount to reach Winburg and there confiscate all transport. The object is to destroy or remove everything which may help the enemy or his horses or oxen to move or live.

General Roberts to Colonel Kelly-Kenny in reply
Fully approved. I think you should add that kaffirs who are reasonably suspected of having assisted the enemy should also be made prisoners.
The more difficulty the people experience about food the sooner will the war be ended.

Chelsea, London, September 1900

Leonard and Kate Courtney have not yet risen from the breakfast table when Emily arrives, breathless. 'I'm so sorry to barge in like this,' she cries, handing her coat to the maid. 'I've been up for hours and forgot that sensible people are still eating their breakfasts at this time.'

'We finished eating some time ago,' says Kate, in some trepidation for Emily's cheeks are flushed and her eyes blazing. 'We like to go through the post at table, as you can see. But perhaps you'd like a kipper? Cook can grill you one in a minute.'

Emily feels the familiar order and warmth that the Courtney household always emanates, even in times of great crisis. She sinks down on to the chair which Leonard smilingly pats, and refuses the kipper.

'You don't mind if we finish reading these letters,' says Kate. 'We'll be finished in a minute. We get so many letters of support from Leonard's old Liskeard constituency.' Emily pulls a sardonic face. Kate notes this and adds, 'I'm sure you'll be pleased to hear that Liskeard isn't entirely composed of rabble-rousers and warmongers.' Both Courtneys laugh tolerantly.

In the soothing ambience of the breakfast room, Emily feels the fierce beating of her heart begin to slow down: she fingers her pulse to verify that she is now calm. After exclaiming in delight at the expressions of loyalty in the letters which Kate reads briskly to her blind husband, Emily opens her reticule. 'I too have some letters,' she says.

Emily's eyes shine with a warning intensity, and the Court-neys wonder if they are about to be presented with a *fait accompli* or a *fait about-to-be-accompli*.

'I have to tell you,' says Emily, 'I now have a new idea. But I must be sure of your support before I go any further. These letters here' – she slaps a bundle of them on to the table so that blind Leonard can hear how very many there are – 'express horror at the farm burnings in the ex-Boer republics, and at the distress of the women and children who are left behind. Many of them send money to feed, clothe and shelter these burnt-out people.'

'Roberts will be returning to England soon,' frowns Leonard. 'And Kitchener will become Commander in Chief. He will of course continue with Roberts' scorched earth policy.'

'So what is it you want to do, Emily dear?' enquires Kate Courtney.

'I want to open a public fund for those burnt-out women and children who are the shame of England!' says Emily in the fervent tones the Courtneys have come to recognise. 'People have already sent me donations without my asking. Others like these (she taps the pile meaningfully) write to ask to whom they can send their contributions.'

Leonard rises from his chair and begins to pace the length of the room in silence. The autumn sun catches his waistcoat buttons; his unseeing eyes gleam; he tugs at his little Abraham Lincoln beard, always a sign of intense concentration. Kate pours Emily another cup of coffee while they patiently await the verdict. Emily is watching a tiny wren flutter among the pansies, pecking at invisible insects inside the yellow and black petals. The little creature's rapid movements reflect the dartings of her own brain, pecking at this, fluttering at that – then, suddenly, swooping like an eagle on its prey.

Finally Leonard speaks. 'I agree in principle, of course.' His voice is gentle, friendly. 'But there are a myriad practical implications. For instance, how much information do you have about these burnt-out women and children? Where are they going once their homes have been destroyed? Are they left to wander round the veldt, or do they go to relations in the Cape Colony?'

'Oh, I am now in touch with many of the loyal Dutch families in the Cape,' exclaims Emily. 'Some of the dispossessed families come to the Cape and tell their terrible stories. It is rumoured that a refugee camp is being established for less fortunate women and children in the city of Bloemfontein.'

'And what is happening to the black servants and farm labourers?' demands Leonard sharply. 'When the farms burn, it is not only the Boers who suffer.'

It is on the tip of Emily's tongue to say, 'When I get there I'll find out' but for the moment she withholds this plan. At this point it is crucial for her to form a distress committee to receive and distribute funds to Boer families. 'I will make enquiries,' she says. 'You know that I have always been concerned with the plight of the native peoples of South Africa.'

For an hour Leonard raises objections to Emily's scheme: how much does she hope to collect? No more than ten thousand pounds most probably, and what use could such a small sum be? And would the Military allow such a fund? Emily has anticipated all these objections and can reply with a fluency which she can see is impressing her mentor. As she swallows her third cup of coffee – and how quickly her heart now beats! – she feels she has convinced him. She knows she has Kate's full attention and sympathy, but cannot hope for her active support now that her husband is so dependent on her energies.

Finally, in a voice made shaky by caffeine she asks, 'So, do I have your blessing?'

He pauses. And taps the window panes one by one as if somehow the contact of his finger tip with glass gives him an insight into the little garden beyond. 'Yes, Emily, I support your movement.' A tame squirrel runs up from the garden thinking the tapping might be an invitation to a plate of nuts. 'But not without trepidation. It is an enormous undertaking, an enormous responsibility. But being those things makes it all the more attractive to you.' He turns away from the window, leaving the squirrel in a beseeching, upright position. 'I can think of no one else I could trust to undertake such a mission. But I am not convinced that it will be successful.'

'That is all I want!' cries Emily. 'That you do not *oppose* my plan.'

'You will need to get your aunt to obtain official sanction for your fund. She can consult with Mr Chamberlain and Lord Lansdowne about guarantees for distribution.'

'And what do you propose to call your fund, Emily?' enquires Kate. Her eyes shine with the warmth of her affection. Whoever would believe that this is the broken woman who had returned from Mexico only four years ago?

'I'll leave that to my committee-to-be,' says Emily earnestly. Then smiles broadly. 'But my favoured name would be The South African Women and Children Distress Fund.'

She leaves the Courtney's home in a frenzy of optimism. The Walls of Jericho have collapsed at the trumpet of Leonard Courtney's assent: now she can start working in earnest to set up a committee. And as she strides down the pavements that lead back to her flat, she is already formulating the aims of the fund in her head. Mrs Potter, the fire-grate now fully restored, frowns at her as she runs up the stairs. Emily hardly registers the venomous glare. By the time she has unlocked her front door the wording is complete: *To feed, clothe, shelter and rescue women and children, Boer, British, or others who have been rendered destitute and homeless by the destruction of property, deportation, or other incidents of the military operations.*

Four

Bloemfontein, September 1900

'Return to Cape Town,' advises Louise. 'Join me at the convalescent camp by the sea. Theodore says there is a ladies' swimming club.' She looks closely at Sarah's face. 'You must take more care of your skin, my dear. It is coming out in little heat blisters. What a shame there is nothing left of my skin emollient.'

The two women have ridden their ponies up the iron-ribbed little kopje just outside Bloemfontein and are resting at its flat table-top. September: the end of winter. Scarcely credible. The landscape seems little changed from its aspect at the height of summer, though films of green now shimmer in the dry grasses. Even the trees round the scattered farmsteads have not lost their leaves. By British standards it is a hot summer's day. Only the faint crispness in the atmosphere – which seems actually to sparkle when drawn into the nostrils and lungs – reminds one that the nights are icy and hot-water bottles are necessary.

The enteric is abating; the general hospitals are moving on. Only last night the little nurses' house in Rondebosch had appeared again in Sarah's dreams, the frangipani she had planted at the bottom of the garden miraculously bursting into starry bloom in the space of a few months; Rushda and Sameela waving at the gate.

'He won't come back,' Louise assures her friend. 'It's been at least four months since he left. Roberts is determined to reduce the ex-republics to cinders and that will take some time. Besides,' and here her voice sharpened, 'you're wasting yourself on him, my dear. Let's be frank. He comes from nowhere and he's going nowhere. Your family would be mortified. Don't look at me like that, Sarah. I can understand a flutter, you know me; but to *mope* over that – scarecrow – this is absurd.' And here Louise blows out a long stream of knowing cigarette smoke which Sarah fans away with her hand.

'I promised to wait,' she says calmly. There is a radiance about her today that has been lacking for many weeks. Louise wonders if she is adding rouge beneath the blisters.

'You're impossible!' exclaims Louise. 'There are at least half-a-dozen medical officers madly in love with you, all from the best families with town houses and country residences, and who do you choose? A common, yes, common-as-dirt young man with no family at all and certainly no fortune. Come to your senses, my dear.'

Sarah smiles and inhales deeply. 'I often think that breathing in this air – this *common-as-dirt* air – is like drinking a very fine chilled hock, don't you, Louise? It quite goes to my head.'

'You haven't received even a line from him since you left. Don't think I don't see your face on mail days.'

'As a matter of fact,' Sarah gropes in her pocket, 'I heard from him just yesterday. He sent me this.'

She had not meant to show anyone; to keep his gift entirely to herself; to savour the joy of it alone but, provoked, she changes her mind.

'A rosary!' Louise looks at the gleaming beads with distaste. '*His* rosary.'

'Is he trying to convert you?'

'Who knows?' Sarah squeezes the mother-of-pearl beads in her fisted hand. The sensation is thrilling, as if the rosary might be the beginning of a chain that ends in Patch's hand.

Louise laughs. 'I'd forgotten he is a Papist on top of everything else. A Papist and a pauper. Your parents *will* be pleased!'

But Sarah is staring down at the base of the kopje. A few neat rows of bell tents have appeared on its slopes and a number of ox wagons are being unloaded by some black servants. Some Tommies wander about.

'Lend me your field-glasses, Louise. Something very odd is going on down there.'

With the aid of magnifying lenses Sarah is able to make out a few bustling Boer women, their faces hidden in the folds of their great sunbonnets. A black man is chasing after a small herd of cattle; chickens scratch in the dry soil. Clay ovens already stand before some of the tents. A few Tommies are digging a pit some distance off. A Boer burgher, instantly recognisable by his heavy beard and waistcoat, carries a mattress into a tent. Another burgher seated at a table energetically grinds coffee.

'Good heavens, who are those people?'

Louise glances at the scene. 'Oh, those are the refugees. You know, the hands-uppers – the Boers who've signed the oath of allegiance and handed in their firearms. They are loathed and detested by their brethren. They're being brought in here next to the military camp for their own safety, to save them from their bitter-end brothers who'd probably execute them for their treachery. An act of mercy on behalf of the British army, you could say.'

'How do you know all this, Louise?

'Oh, I know Captain Nelson of the Imperial Yeomanry quite well. He's a friend of Theodore's. We play bridge together often. He's been put in charge of the camp.'

'They look a sullen lot. I suppose they don't want to leave their homes and live in tents.'

'They should have thought of that before declaring war against us,' says Louise airily. 'Now, Theodore says we can use the army tennis courts and he'll lend us racquets. It'd be such fun to biff a ball about.'

Since their earlier estrangement a certain coolness had settled between the two women. Louise could not see Sarah without the shadow of that penniless trooper lurking over her, and though they had returned to their former outings, and tea-drinking at the Railway Hotel, they no longer shared intimacies. In any case, Louise's impending marriage in Cape Town absorbed much of her energies. A date had not yet been set, but her parents were planning to come to the wedding and Sarah had agreed to be bridesmaid, along with two Australian nurses. Sarah herself was resigned to the new relationship, and happy that at least something of the old friendship remained. Once Louise leaves for Cape Town she will be alone again. She touches the rosary in her pocket.

On arriving back at the hospital she finds a problem has developed. Mrs Mopeli is refusing to wash the sick soldiers' dirty linen. Her smiling face has turned to stone. She no longer envelops her haunches in her multi-striped Union Jack. Once again a small bundle is tied by a blanket on to her back.

'*Passes!*' It is a good word to spit out and Mrs Mopeli allows a great deal of saliva to fly out of her mouth as she exclaims in disgust.

Sarah wipes her cheek. 'I'm so sorry, Mrs Mopeli. There must be a good reason. The war . . .' They have bumped into each other outside the Boer woman's bread shop.

'We African people have chosen to help the British, Nurse Palmer. We expect the British to help us. Now they have brought the Pass back worse than the Boers. My husband, he received five lashes because he could not show his Pass. My husband, he is born in this town. He works for the Imperial Railway. That is very terrible, Nurse Palmer.'

'Oh I agree, I agree!' cries Sarah. 'Your husband, a respectable man – but we all have to carry passes these days, Mrs Mopeli.'

The washerwoman looks at the young nurse with such contempt that Sarah cringes. 'A white person's pass is a very different thing, Nurse Palmer, very different.'

'But at the end of the war Britain will not let you down, that I can promise you.' Sarah does not care for her role as envoy for the British Government and cannot quite meet Mrs Mopeli's eye.

A shrill mew rises from the bundle in the blanket. The washerwoman jogs her body. then points to the great pot on her head. 'This is what the British Army is doing, Nurse Palmer.'

'What is in there, Mrs Mopeli?'

'In there is mielie-pap, which I take now to my people by the railway station.'

'The refugees?'

'The black servants who also lost their home when the Boers' farms are burnt. Where must they live? They must build their own shelters by the railway, and find their own food. The British do not think of them when they burn the Boer homes. My very own aunties and uncles live down there now with nothing.'

The bundle on her back emits a small complaint. She hums a brief lullaby. 'We are very very disappointed, Nurse Palmer. We want respect. We expect respect.'

And she sails off, her head high.

Sarah stares after her in dismay. So this is the messy aftermath, neither contemplated nor intended, of a war that is by no means over; devastation and homelessness for those very people who had expected just the opposite from the invading forces. She makes a quick decision: she will visit the kaffir refugee camp from time to time during her afternoons off, for sickness is sure to break out in such makeshift quarters.

Extract: Letter from Sir Alfred Milner to Lady Edward Cecil, 29 September 1900

Kitchener! It is fortunate that I admire him in many ways so much, and admiring, am prepared to stand a lot and never take offence . . . I am determined to get on with him . . . but shall I be able to manage this strong, self-willed man 'in a hurry' (for he is dying to be off in time to take India), and to turn his enormous power into the right channel?

Extract: Letter from Sir Alfred Milner to Lord Kitchener, 30 September 1900

. . . I should take all the houses I could lay my hands upon, but I should *burn no houses*, except for definite acts of treachery, nor should I attempt to clear the district of food-stuff or of population. Instead of rounding up the cattle, I should turn my attention to chivvying the marauders, and in that enterprise I believe it would be possible gradually to associate some of the inhabitants with us . . . In any district once cleared of the enemy, garrisoned and policed, I think we should be fully entitled to call the war over . . . I believe that if we were to devastate all South Africa – an impossible task anyway – we should only find that we had a greater number of roving blackguards to deal with than ever.

Hard Choices, October 1900

Louise has returned to Cape Town. Though their parting was warm enough with a few tears shed, Sarah has not yet received a letter from her friend. She herself has written twice to the convalescent hospital where Louise has been posted, mentioning her visits to the black refugee camp. Perhaps Louise does not care to read about the suffering of the kaffir people, driven from their homes to live in shacks on the edge of the city. She would consider it to be another humanitarian act by the British Army, rescuing homeless people, for how can anyone survive upon a scorched earth? Sophie, on the other hand, will be horrified to hear about this development and Sarah has sent her several pages of description of the camp with its lack of medical facilities and outbreaks of measles epidemics among well over a thousand forcibly removed and distraught farm workers. Perhaps Miss Hobhouse could be informed.

Riding in her free time is a source of delight that offers warm contact with her beloved little pony as well as the calm lines of the local landscape. There is a limit to how far she may go but the veldt is vast and though occasional columns of soldiers go by, sweating copiously beneath their rigid pith helmets, she is seldom required to show her pass.

In the distance the railway line to the Cape Colony glints among the dusty thorn bushes. An armoured train, packed with armaments and troops, thunders slowly northwards. It is only when its iron-clad carriages have finally lumbered from sight, smudging the skyline with a trail of black smoke, that she notices the cattle trucks in the siding. A couple of Tommies lounge nearby, their rifles in their hands. Louise has given her a pair of field glasses as a farewell gift, and Sarah raises these to her eyes to see what manner of cattle need military protection.

Inside the trucks are not cows, but people. Women and children are neatly packed together, standing upright to save space. There are a number of very old men and women wedged between them. She can hear the dismal, hopeless howls of a baby. It is two o'clock in the afternoon and the mild spring air has suddenly grown furnace-hot. She cannot read the expression on the faces of the women. They are enduring an emotion which she does not know.

Where are these burnt-out families going? Something too appalling for her to understand is about to happen, something worse even than the burning of homes, that much she can tell. A wave of nausea overcomes her. She digs her heels into her pony's flanks and gallops away.

The land is shimmering: the salt lakes in the distance rise into the air and hang there, gleaming fantasy-lakes. She rides towards them, the hooves of her pony drumming out any thoughts that attempt to form in her head. Her mouth is dry.

She passes a farmhouse, nestled among bushy African willows and karee trees. Black men are picking oranges from the adjoining orchard; a windmill spurts water into a round corrugated iron reservoir. A warm wind laps at her body, converting the heat into streams that flow into the folds of her garments and over her flesh. A thorn bush sails through the sky. She sees a crowd of meerkats sitting on their haunches, erect and alert, their dark eyes watching her movements anxiously.

Sarah trots up to the farm, scattering ducks and chickens on the way. A flurry of snow-white bantams bursts out of the crimson hibiscus tree on the lawn, crowing raucously. Pumpkins of all shapes and sizes ripen on a flat roof. Some children are playing on the great shady stoep that extends across the front of the house. She greets them in Dutch. 'Good day,

234

children. Can I have a little water, please?' She has addressed them in Dutch, but is very conscious of her English accent. The children stare at her as if she is a poisonous snake risen from beneath the thorn bushes.

A woman emerges from the house. She wears a kappie even though she is not in the sun. She wipes her floury hands on her apron and smiles a welcome. '*Kom binnen, kom binnen.* You must be thirsty in this heat.' She peers at Sarah's sunburnt face. 'My dear, you are letting the sun hurt your beautiful English skin – peaches and cream, is it not? Come in, come in.'

The woman's friendliness envelops Sarah like a gust of sweet, unexpected music. 'I have a special cream that will heal your broken skin, my dear, made from the wild flowers of the veldt,' she continues. Her face shines with kindly concern. 'And you know what it also has in it?' Sarah shakes her head. 'Something very precious from our own beehives – buchu honey – you will be surprised at the result!'

The completeness of the welcome is something she has not experienced before. She has heard it said that Boer women are well-known for their hospitality, their generosity, but this has a dimension beyond welcome. She does not remember that Dutch women welcome so extravagantly so it can't be inherited from the forefathers. Perhaps the phenomenon is a result of living so far apart – twenty or thirty miles at least – and seeing so few visitors. But she succumbs gratefully to the woman's warmth, and steps over the threshold of the farmhouse.

The interior of the house is dark and cool. They pass through the sitting room with its sparkling furniture, its scrubbed floor boards, its embroidered biblical texts hanging on the wall. There is a smell of polish and soap, and other mysterious cleansing odours which seem to clear Sarah's brain as she breathes them in. A large upright piano is centrally placed with a hymn book open on its stand. The gigantic family Bible rests on a table nearby. 'Excuse the mess in my house.' The woman laughs apologetically. Although the wind is raging now, stirring the dry earth into clouds of crimson,

Sarah can see no mess or untidiness in this spotless room, unless one considers that someone's jacket hanging on the back of a chair creates disorder.

In the kitchen the farmer's wife offers her milk from a stone storage container. Spirals of tangerine skin dangle in the window to dry. A black woman is chopping up a pumpkin; she smiles and greets Sarah. Two of her children romp with a small Boer child beneath the table. Strips of dried meat studded with spices hang from the ceiling.

As the farmer's wife stands by the window, pouring the milk, Sarah experiences a *déjà vu*. For a sudden moment she is a child in an Amsterdam museum, staring at a painting of a woman in a kappie pouring milk. *She is pouring light into the bowl, not milk* says her governess, a Miss Pieters. Sarah drinks gratefully, though she would have preferred water. Through the small window she sees the farmer out in the yard giving orders to a group of black labourers. He points a finger at the orange orchard and his voice rises in anger. The workers eye the plaited sjambok which dangles in his other hand.

The farmer's wife is concerned for Sarah's safety. 'You shouldn't ride alone, my dear.' Her Dutch has seventeenth-century words and constructions as well as other vocabulary that Sarah does not recognise. 'The Kaffirs think they can do what they like now. They think the British are going to give them our farms and that makes them cheeky. You must watch out. Here, my dear, have a slice of seedcake with your milk. I am going to get you the cream I told you about.' She bustles into the enormous pantry.

Just outside the kitchen door the smell of baking bread drifts from a clay oven. Sarah enjoys the comforting fumes. Surely, where bread is still baked things must be well. The smell mingles headily with the powerful scent of the oranges which topple from great wooden crates as the workers load them on to a wagon.

The woman reappears with a stone jar in her hand. 'Please take this. You will be surprised how quickly our Boer remedy' – she emphasises the two words – 'will heal your skin.' For the first time Sarah detects a hint of resentment, for Boer remedies are held up to ridicule by the British medical officers. 'And take some oranges with you to keep away the thirst,' urges the woman, as if to make up for her moment of quiet bitterness.

'Thank you – *dank u*. After all your kindness, I don't even know your name.'

'Theron. Eva Theron. That is my husband, Dawie.'

Dawie Theron nods from across the yard. He does not smile.

'My name is Sarah Palmer. I appreciate your kindness, especially as you can surely tell from my accent that I am English.' Sarah stumbles through all this Dutch, but Eva Theron smiles forgivingly.

'Your Dutch is much better than my English, I can assure you. And it is a pleasure to hear the enemy speak our language.'

'I don't feel I am your enemy,' says Sarah quietly.

'Of course you are not yourself my enemy,' says the Boer woman. Her face suddenly flushes. 'But your people have taken our land for which our forefathers shed their blood. How can this land now be British?' And she waves her hands at the vistas of yellow grass which bake like her bread in the warmth of the sun. 'God gave us this land, my dear, and now for our sins He has deserted us.'

'Your bread is burning, Mrs Theron.' For the smell of smoke now overwhelms the pleasant farm aromas, and a pall hangs above the farmhouse.

The woman's eyes harden. 'That is what the British do to our farmhouses when we do not sign the oath of allegiance. This wind carries the smoke for many miles.'

'What can I say?' whispers Sarah. Her heart lurches painfully as the forbidden thought comes rushing in: does Patch do these things? But it is no longer a question. She has long known the truth about his column but querying that truth makes it easier to bear.

'Last night a command led by De Wet tried to blow up the Kimberley railway line. So the farms near the line are blown up instead.'

'And you?' Flakes of ash settle on Sarah's riding habit and Mrs Theron's apron.

'We are protected by British troops,' says the woman simply. 'We have signed, and for that we pay a terrible price.' She swallows. 'We are known as the *hands-uppers*, a horrible, insulting word. We are hated by those who will not sign, who will fight to the bitter end.' She stares at Sarah in confusion. 'To tell the truth we never wanted this war. But now we have the choice between the hatred of our brethren or the burning of our farm. Have we made the wrong choice?'

Sarah rides away. It would have been so much easier to return to Cape Town, where none of this horror would impinge on her life. She would pick flowers and drink tea at Dix's. She would live in a lovely villa, not a battered bell tent. Has she too made the wrong choice?

Bloemfontein, November 1900

The streets of Bloemfontein, the Fountain of Flowers, are bearing a new kind of traffic. From Kimberley in the West, from Kroonstad in the North, from Koffiefontein in the South, from Sanna's Pos in the East, from the burnt-out farms of the new Crown Colony trundle the endless lines of open ox wagons and mule carts and Scotch carts. They are laden, not with sacks of mielies or boxes of peaches or new blades for the windmill, but with mothers. Pretty young mothers, grim-faced old mothers, silent mothers, sulky mothers, panic-stricken mothers, tear-stained mothers, rich mothers, poor mothers, mothers large and small; mothers of mothers; mothers of children, who cling to a doll or a top or a favourite book with one hand and to a mother's skirt with the other; mothers of children whose cheeks have burnt fiery red on the long journey in the summer sun; mothers of small, still bundles that lie in their arms and will not move again. Every mother and daughter wears a sun bonnet of a different style; some are plain white linen, some are adorned with a floral pattern; others are a concoction of frill upon frill, a wedding-cake of a hat, in contrast with the simple frocks that are mostly worn.

Herded alongside the wagons are more mothers. They are the servants of the mothers in the carts. Their homes too have been burned down, they too have nowhere to live. Their husbands and their brothers and sons now work for the British Army, helping them win the war against the Boers.

These mothers and their children merge with the herds of cattle and goats that mounted black soldiers drive before the wagons. Oh how the cattle and the oxen bellow in hunger: they cry out for the comfort of their kraals. Their journey has been long; they have not had time to rest and graze; some of them collapse on the very streets of Bloemfontein.

British soldiers on horseback mill among the creaking wagons, the running servants, the staggering cattle, the wailing mothers, the ailing children. They have a job to do. They must keep the mothers and the livestock in order. They must drive their charges through the streets of this city, past the roses blooming so prettily to welcome them, past the willows dipping their leaves into the little stream, past the looted shops slowly recovering from the first arrival of the British, and into the fields beyond where preparations have been made.

The mothers disturb Sarah profoundly. She has written to tell Sophie of the endless processions through the streets of this little town. Already Sophie has responded angrily about the black camps and urged Sarah to approach the Loyal Ladies' League for help. They can surely throw their womanly gentleness in the direction of these suffering black people? Sarah doubts this very much but will try.

Now, as she watches these cartloads of angry women creaking up the street she feels a sudden fury flare up. 'So, are these families prisoners of war?' she shouts up at a young officer prancing on his charger beside the wagons. He grins at the pretty nurse. 'We are providing homes for the homeless, Sister. A humanitarian act of the British Army.' 'Homeless because you have set fire to their homes!' she retorts. 'All's fair in love and war, m'dear,' he smirks at her, then shouts at a trooper who has allowed a cow to stray into the Boer bakery and incurred the wrath of Mrs van Reenen, her hands coated in flour as she shoos the intruder away.

Where are all these women being taken? Sarah rides out towards the hands-uppers' camp; reins in her pony at the top of the kopje – and sees what she had feared.

A vast grid of white triangles now enmeshes the hill. Oh,

how exact is their symmetry – whichever way you look the tents stretch out in the straightest of lines, some parallel, some diagonal, each one equally spaced from the next with awesome precision. And in the epicentre of this geometrical perfection stand some corrugated iron huts and three marquees which look like hospitals, and on the edge, a number of crude country stores have erupted, suggesting that this mathematical masterpiece might serve a human purpose.

Sarah lifts her field glasses and follows the women and children's movements. Some are standing in a long queue with buckets in their hands; others are jostling in even longer queues with plates and bags to receive food from a shouting corporal. Some carry bundles of washing; others are trying to light fires in the clay ovens with the green bushes their children have chopped down. A group of old people is singing hymns outside a tent round an enormous family Bible.

There are too many people in the tents, Sarah can see that. A whole family plus servants must fit into a bell tent meant for six, and often there are ten or more people squeezed under the canvas and between the possessions they have brought with them on their journey. These possessions spill out of the tent flaps for there is no room for basins and pots and pails and plates and spoons and coffee mills and pestles and mortars.

Where are the cattle of these farming people? Where are their sheep? Where are their crops, shining in the fields, ready for the harvest? Where are their pumpkins and gourds, ripening on the roofs? Where are their tapestries, their sofas with embroidered cushions, their jars of spiced peaches, their vases from the East, their babies' cradles, their pianos?

Ask the troopers, who stroll among the tents keeping an eye on things. They can tell you what they have done with the cattle and the crops and the embroidered cushions and the pianos with their hymn books. They have *laid them waste*. They have obeyed the orders of Field-Marshal Lord Roberts. That's what soldiers are trained to do, no matter what they might personally feel.

Sarah sits on her friendly pony and watches the horror

unfold beneath her. Her instinct once again is to flee to Cape Town and forget she has ever seen this. She knows now that if she stays she cannot turn her back on this devastation.

She rides back to the Raadsaal, where evening meals are now held. On the notice board she sees an advertisement written in large letters: URGENT. WANTED: DUTCH-SPEAKING NURSE TO WORK IN BLOEMFONTEIN CONCENTRATION CAMPS.

She stares at this request for several minutes, then copies down the application details.

Orange River Colony, November 1900

Patch is feeling better. Since making his novena to Our Lady for the dead baby's soul he has banished the recurring image of the infant in the soil, for now he knows that the little Protestant boy will be frolicking, diving among the sunlit clouds, juggling with the stars – for Mary, being the Mother of everyone, will certainly have agreed to his nine-day plea to ask her Son to allow the little Boer fellow into the Heaven designed for Catholics only. But with the disappearance of his torment, indifference has set in. His emotions feel as if they are coated in concrete.

Now he stacks furniture into a huge pile in the middle of the farmhouse sitting room. Outside the men are slitting the throats of cows and pigs. The air is full of the screaming of animals. The Boer children and the Kaffir servants are pulling sacks of corn and bits of furniture out of the farmhouse and piling them up on the ox wagon. The old people carry out the family Bible and the hymn books. The farmer's wife clasps a baby's cradle. She is pregnant.

Captain Smithers has explained about the railway attacks and Roberts' regulations. It is as if he is attempting to impose a grid of order upon the mayhem he has created. The Boer himself is there but appears to be dying from an infected bullet wound. He too is carried out.

'Why don't the Boers give in?' the captain asks the woman as she places the cradle in the wagon. 'You would have been spared all this misery.'

The woman draws herself up and with flashing eyes replies, 'For the very same reason for which our men began this war.'

'You are right, they began the war and fired the first shot.'

'And who provoked the war?' demands the woman in her guttural but fluent English. 'And were the Boers to sit with folded arms while gold and diamond grabbers come in swarms to snatch the inheritance of our children from under us? It is our *misfortune* and not our *fault* that Providence has placed stores of gold and diamonds beneath our soil as an inheritance for our children, which is now taken away from us.'

'I don't think your people realise to what extent they are outnumbered,' says the captain. He means well; he does not like to be the Goliath, but would prefer an enemy equal in might. 'For every Boer burgher there are seven or eight British soldiers.'

'Including the kaffirs you have armed!' she exclaims angrily.

'Now why do you say kaffir? We do not use coloured people against you.'

'Look at Mafeking,' she retorts. 'And look at the armed kaffirs continually passing between these wagons.'

'They are only used as guards,' replies he.

'As if there are not Tommies enough to do this sort of work. What respect will these kaffirs have for white women after the war, over whose head they have stood with loaded rifles? Is that not degradation enough?'

'The war must end soon enough now,' he says, not angered by her inflammatory words. Indeed, he sounds almost melancholy. 'We are laying the entire country waste. Your commandos will be starved out.'

She climbs into the cart and soothes her weeping children.

The troopers tear down curtains from the windows and stuff them in between the legs of the chairs. Patch himself throws paraffin over the pile and Cartwright applies a light. The men run around helping themselves to things before it is too late: china plates, bushbuck skins on the floor, a text on the wall with a tapestry or roses round it: *God is mijne rots, ik sal of hem vetrouwen.* God is my rock, I shall trust him.

The room is full of smoke. Cartwright is enjoying himself: he picks up a sewing machine and throws it *wallop!* through the works of the piano. Flames are crackling but the men scrabble through a chest of linen they have just found. Patch feels himself choking and runs outside where the kaffirs and Boers have gathered in their separate carts. He looks at the pile of household goods thrown into a box in the back of the ox wagon. There is nothing that interests him: kettle, sausage maker, coffee grinder, pestle and mortar, mincing machine, bowls, spoons. The sun is setting in its extravagant way, throwing ribbons of red and yellow and purple into the radiant sky. He runs his fingers among the implements to check for flags or guns. Then feels his concrete heart crack open with shock.

There it lies, underneath the kitchen implements, in all its orange and purple glory, a bit of the sunset fallen into the wagon. Every hair on his head stands on end individually, as if God is counting them. And look how his hand is shaking as he plunges it into the higgledy-piggledy mess and pulls out the sash. He pulls out the Orange sash and stares at it. He does not know what to do.

His hands pull the Orange sash across his breast. They reach into his top pocket. Slowly he winds up the music box and places it on the still-warm bread oven. The sweetness of home floods the purple air.

Then, out of the blazing house, bursts Cartwright with a crowd of troopers. They have thrown off their helmets and slouch hats and pulled on the womens' bonnets instead. They have tied pantomime bows beneath their chins. They are delighted to hear the music playing on the bread oven, which acts as a vast clay loud-speaker. The bonneted men grab partners and caper round the oven in pairs. Their kappies flutter and flounce as they dance. They bow and curtsey to each other, shaking their heads, and smiling comically.

There's no place, oh there's no, oh there's no place like home! sing the laughing men.

'That's enough now, men!' calls Captain Smithers. 'Show respect!'

Reluctantly the dancers begin to remove their bonnets. Cartwright pretends he can't undo the bow under his chin. They are still laughing when the shot splits through the merriment, like the ring of an axe.

Now Cartwright is doing a kaffir war dance – leaping into the air with his arms and legs all over the place, as if trying to swim.

His white kappie has sprouted a red flower.

Patch runs over to his friend, who has collapsed on the ground and is still. Blood trickles out of his mouth. Cartwright is trying to smile. 'Take the bonnet off my head, there's a good fellow,' he croaks. 'Can't die wearing a lady's hat.' Patch unties the bow under his friend's chin and removes the sticky headdress with gentle fingers. Cartwright is looking at him hopefully as if Patch is about to reveal to him whether he will go to heaven or hell. Does he want a prayer? Patch can't remember what prayers you say for dying people. It is too late for a novena. For a moment he wishes he had his rosary to wind through his friend's fingers.

'I'll get the bastard,' he says instead.

Cartwright's eyes are fluttering. He chokes. Patch lowers his ears. 'A good fuck,' wheezes Cartwright. 'That's all that matters. In the end. Remember that, old chum.'

'I will,' promises Patch, though wondering briefly if this is true. 'I will, my friend.' And folds Cartwright's hands across his chest. At least it is death by the bullet rather than the bacillus.

As he stands up he realises his body has become a different thing now; he feels the hot surge of a new emotion, which sweeps away any other feeling. The word *revenge!* springs into his head. To kill the killers, that is all that matters now. There is a sweetness to this new emotion.

'Find the sniper!' roars Captain Smithers.

The men run off into the darkening veldt, their eyes dazzled by the setting of the sun. But who is there to shoot? Patch is desperate to kill, to kill a Boer, any Boer. He kneels motionless behind a rock. The Sash still crosses his chest, its fringes ruffling in the soft wind. He perches the barrel of his gun on the rock.

A bullet whines past his head, then another. They might just as well be mosquitoes. There is an explosion – mortar, perhaps. It seems to shatter in his leg. Yet there is no pain. He places his hand on his leg to check. And passes out as his hand slides into a stew of blood and flesh that has replaced the muscles of his thigh.

Rossetti Mansions, London, November 1900

'Another seven refusals, I'm afwaid.' Miss Griffen places seven letters on a rather large pile marked NO.

'*Humph!* Who are the cowards?' Emily looks up from the begging letter she is writing to the Rowntree family.

'The Reverend Hugh Price-Hughes, the Reverend A.H. Stanton – who, by the way, says that to keep Boer women alive might pwolong the war. The Reverend Price-Hughes, on the other hand, feels his support of our committee might cast a reflection on the honour of the British soldiers, whom he knows to be gentlemen because Lord Woberts has told us so.'

Emily puts down her pen. 'And to think these are clergymen. Well, Griffy, we are receiving quite an education in the lack of imagination in the saintly, and the fear of those with influence in case their big reputations be marred.'

'But let us not forget the support of your committee – such wonderful people, also with big weputations – Herbert Spencer, Sir Edward Fwy, Sir Thomas Acland, the Marchioness of Wipon, your own dear aunt and uncle . . .' says Miss Griffen before Emily can become too bitter.

'I shall never forget them, dear Mary. But I find it quite extraordinary that so many important people are too frightened to voice their support of a committee whose aim is to feed and clothe destitute women and children. I shall not forget *them* either.'

'Well, at least Lady Hobhouse has secured the approval of Lord Lansdowne and Mr Chamberlain – pwovided, of course, the food and clothing don't reach the enemy in the field. And several donations have arrived today. I have already witten to thank them. Just think – we now have something like three hundred pounds in the Fund!' Miss Griffen's eyes shine behind her spectacles.

'Yet England's contribution to those destitute families is far lower than that of other countries.' The new batch of refusals has annoyed Emily: she turns her mind to more positive developments. 'Of course, as one might expect, the Society of Friends has done such wonderful work I could almost turn Quaker myself, so much do I admire their breed, to say nothing of the Women's Congress in the Cape Colony. I have received such a vivid account of their great open-air gathering in Cape Town from a Miss Molteno. She describes how the women stood in the blazing sun beneath the oak trees and solemnly protested against the burning of private property by the military—'

'In contwavention of the wesolutions of the Hague Peace Conference, I know!' interrupts Miss Griffen, who has heard the contents of Miss Molteno's letter several times. 'I wonder if the forty-one cases of clothing the Women's Congress despatched to Bloemfontein ever reached the burnt-out families.' She takes a deep breath. 'To say nothing of the burnt-out *native* families. Sophie is quite horrified by what is going on. Her friend Sarah sends her graphic accounts of the conditions in their camp. I have urged the Aboriginal Committee to look into this.'

Emily narrows her eyes. 'What nobody really knows,' she says in a low, intense voice, 'is *where* or *how* the families, whatever their skin colour, are being held, apart from those in Bloemfontein. This worries me a great deal.' She pauses. Miss Griffen can feel something coming. 'I am learning to speak Dutch, Griffy.'

'I want to go to South Africa as soon as possible to see for myself what is happening to the families whose homes have been destroyed by our army.' Emily speaks so quickly now that her friend can scarcely hear what she is saying. 'We are receiving money and the donors wish to know who will actually convey relief to these families. I should like to be able to tell them that I myself will do the conveying.'

'But Emily – would you be allowed into the war zone, as I suppose it still must be called?' Miss Griffen looks alarmed.

'My aunt is a friend of Sir Alfred Milner, as you know. If she supports my plan, she will write a letter of introduction for me. Of course, I cannot go without my aunt and uncle's permission.' She takes a deep breath. 'I plan to ask them this afternoon. I must take with me all those letters from the Cape expressing hope and support, and the English letters asking how the funds could best be spent.'

'I shall put them together for you now,' says Griffy at once. 'Thank heaven for the new filing cabinet.'

Five

Bloemfontein Concentration Camp, November 1900

Sarah is holding a sheet of paper covered in triangles. Before she studies it, she watches the mothers gliding in their long aprons and kappies among the bell tents and the tumult of livestock, Tommies, bread ovens, kaffir servants, crockery, bits of furniture. You cannot see their faces. Many wear black.

She closes her eyes. How is it possible that these blameless slopes have become a pestilence-ridden camp where children die daily of simple diseases and women covered in filth queue for rotten meat and adulterated coffee? Can a hill like this ever recover its innocence? And how many other hills like this pollute the air of Africa?

At this stage of the day she still has the energy to think of such things. But now there is a disturbance in the temporary mortuary tent where the children's bodies are laid out in preparation for burial in the town centre. A mother has begun screaming in the tent. A pig rushes out from beneath the tent flaps, followed closely by the screaming woman; then lumbers off, its jaws moving. Now the mother is wrenching out fistfuls of her hair from beneath her dark kappie, and howling out to the Lord: *That a pig should eat the hand of my dead son! Have mercy on us O Lord, have mercy!*

Sarah feels she might be sick. But instead she looks at the map of triangles in her hand. Some of the triangles are marked in red. The bell tents have not been numbered, the streets have not been named. Today's visit will be harder because of the heavy downpour last night. Now the ground beneath the tents will be quagmires in which whole families have been obliged to sleep overnight. Rain water had rushed through her own tent which she now has entirely to herself, but at least her mattress lies upon a raised bedstead, and the canvas is lined. The camp bakes in the early morning sun, releasing vapours that smell of human excrement and unwashed bodies. Sarah treads carefully among the busy flies.

'*Goeden morgen*, Mevrouw de Klerk.' Sarah's Dutch has progressed over the past month, though it is not quite the Dutch she had learnt in the Netherlands. Sometimes her throat feels quite ragged with all the guttural aspirations the language demands, and she can never hope to achieve the volume of delivery apparently essential for communication among Boer families. Nevertheless, the women applaud her efforts; at least she is able to understand their complaints and discuss the symptoms of illness, even if her own pronunciations raise a titter among some.

Mrs de Klerk is grinding what smells like roasted acorns and chicory outside her tent, while the little kaffir girl, Katie, who wears a mere scrap of cloth around her hips, tries to get a fire going in the mud. Blankets and underwear hang out to dry on a makeshift line. The single mattress, occupied by five sick children on one end and a grandfather with a long white beard on the other end, is soaked through. Mrs de Klerk and Katie had slept directly on the ground, with the result that both are caked with the red mud that squelches beneath Sarah's feet.

'*Goeden morgen*, my dear, my goodness but your accent is improving! Will you have a cup of coffee with us perhaps?'

'*Nie dankie*, Mevrouw, I've just had some.' Sarah tries not to stare at the trousers which Mrs de Klerk is wearing. In London, such attire would suggest an allegiance with the Bohemian underworld in which women smoke cigars and drink absinthe at all hours of the day, but Sarah recognises the trousers as belonging to Oupa de Klerk who has no use for them now, having taken to his end of the mattress with an air of finality. 'And how are the children today?' She braces herself for the reply.

The Boer woman throws up her hands. 'Ah, never did I think a civilised nation like England could treat women and children so! Many a time have I cried Ah! Why must we mothers suffer more than the men, for here we sit helpless with our handfuls of children who we have to clothe; and when they are a-hungered they cry to us; and if the little things are barefooted, where are we to get shoes? Must we then entrust all our little ones to earth? What will the future bring us? How shall we struggle through the dark nights of watching and fear? Surely against me is the Lord turned; he turneth his hand against me all the day. My flesh and my skin hath he made old; he hath broken my bones.'

Sarah pauses. The first time she heard this lamentation she had been moved to tears; but just as one's patience eventually wears thin with friends who passionately tell and retell the same tragic tale, each time as if for the first time, so Sarah has learnt to disengage herself from this recital of woe. For Mrs de Klerk has elevated the act of complaining to a work of art. Her tirade has become a magnificent edifice which must remain intact, any practical appeasement serving only to undermine the mighty monolith by now cast in metaphorical stone. On the other hand, Mrs de Klerk is no hands-upper: she will support her husband through to the bitter end.

'May I take the children's temperatures? I have brought some milk for them – the real thing, not condensed milk or water.'

The bottom flaps of the tent have been drawn up to allow a little circulation of air, but the heat in the tent is almost solid. For a moment Sarah fancies it radiates from the flushed little bodies that lie under the blanket of the sole mattress. The children snort and wheeze as if some terrible obstruction has entered their breathing passages.

'They all have the fever now,' she murmurs. More than the fever, she suspects. Gently pressing on the lower lip of one of the children so that the mouth swings open, she peers into the child's throat, covered, as she expected, in a leathery film.

'This little one has diptheria, Mevrouw de Klerk. Her life

can only be saved if she goes to the hospital.' Sarah has learnt to be blunt. 'In the hospital they have anti-toxins which will kill off the diptheria poison in the first few days. If you leave it longer it will be too late.'

'Oh my dear father in heaven!' wails Mrs de Klerk, 'is it not true that our children go alive into the camp hospital and come out in a coffin? In the camp hospital will they lie and take condensed milk every two hours instead of the fresh milk and raw carrot juice which we their mothers would give them? Then will they surely die straight away. Ah, the Lord hath set us in dark places; he hath made my chain heavy.'

'There is very little fresh milk and no raw carrot juice,' begins Sarah. 'And your—'

'Ah, but General Liebenberg did ask leave of the British to send in here a number of wagons loaded with vegetables and fruit and meat for the women and children, but the major only swore at him and so it did not come to pass.'

'Mrs de Klerk, I have fifty tents to visit this morning. If you take your little girl to the hospital *now*, she will live. Now I must look at the other children.' It is difficult not to sound impatient.

'But Sister, my *Huis Apothek* has always cured us of our illness. On the farm if my child or my husband or my servant has a chill or a sore throat then there are infusions from *Katte krui* or *Wijnruit* or *Wilde als* sweetened with a little sugar which banish the illness within hours. Why now can I not use the remedies of my forefathers, Sister?'

'Because you no longer live miles apart from your neighbour, Mevrouw. Now your children are catching illnesses which your home remedies cannot cure. They are not immune, like city children who mix together all the time.' She removes her thermometer from under the tongue of one of the flushed little bodies. 'Still no soap?'

'No soap and no water! The Tommies think we can wash in mud. And when I think of my sparkling kitchen floor and the scrubbed faces of my children . . . Oh, the Lord is harsh in his ways. He hath bent his bow and set me as a mark for his arrow! He hath also broken my teeth with gravel stones, he hath—'

'Mrs de Klerk, all your children have high temperatures. I am going to have to report the diptheria to the hospital. It will spread to the children in the surrounding tents.' Sarah sways.

'Poor little nursie. Shame, you are so pale, so thin. Katie, pour the nursie some coffee, it will help you, my dear. Shame, poor girlie' And the mother forces a tin mug of the evil-smelling potion into Sarah's hand.

'I am exhausted already,' thinks Sarah. 'How will I manage another forty-nine tents?' But the sweet drink gives her a sudden lurch of energy and, thanking Mrs de Klerk, she moves on to the next tent on her diagram.

She wipes her feet on the tin cans wedged deep into the ground to be used as foot scrapers before the tent opening. Here, a woman is panting in the heat, just sickening for her confinement. Her nightdress is stained with mud; there are no gowns for her baby. She sips unclean looking water from a tin. Her mother stands by, grim-faced, accusing. Sarah feels the woman's swollen belly and notes that the head of the baby has dropped into place. 'Has your husband received your letter yet?' she asks as her fingers explore the outline of the baby.

'His ship has not yet reached Bermuda,' gasps the woman.

The mother speaks. 'That a father should be separated from his child in this way. That a Boer should be torn from his land and sent on a ship to a faraway country in the East. The Lord will take revenge.' Her voice is a growl. Sarah has no reply. She moves on between the cluttered lanes. Many of the children have contracted measles and cry out in the heat of their tents. With the correct diet and hygienic living conditions they would recover normally, but here the disease blossoms into pneumonia and the children die in their hundreds. Sarah remembers enduring measles as a child and is thankful that she is now immune to the disease.

Someone is running behind her. A young girl from one of the tents hurries up to her. 'Sister! Sister!' she calls out in Dutch. She has an open, pretty face shaded by her white kappie, covered in frills which shiver in the breeze she has caused.

Sarah stops. Has she left something behind? 'Yes, my dear?'

'I would like to be a nurse, Sister.'

Sarah smiles patiently. 'You'll have to wait for the war to end, my dear. Then you can go to a nurse's training hospital.'

'No, Sister. I want to help in the camp hospital. It will make the mothers feel better to see one of their kind looking after the children in the wards. I can learn on the ward. I would ask not for payment.'

Sarah thinks quickly. The refugee nurses who work in the children's hospital were forced to flee from Johannesburg and are full of loathing for all Boers. 'What is your name, my child?'

'Poppie Naudé, sister.'

'And what does your mother think?'

'That is not my mother in the tent. I know not where my mother is. When our house was burnt down we were put in the trucks. They would not let me go with my mother.'

'And your father?'

'My father is a sick man. He is in another camp, in Norval's Pont. He wrote me a letter.'

Poppie looks sad. But Sarah can see that this young woman is strong and energetic. The children on her own ward would love her toothy smile and lively nature.

'I work on the wards in the afternoons,' she says. 'I'll speak to the deputy matron and see what she thinks. Meet me outside the children's ward tomorrow. I see you have your own apron. Bring it with you. We have nothing to spare on the ward.'

'I am so happy,' says the girl simply. 'My people need me and I can do something to help – if your matron says yes. Thank you, Sister.' Poppie gives a little curtsey.

Sarah moves on, feeling briefly cheered by this encounter. But as she takes temperatures, makes notes of the sick, applies remedies, she grows more aware of the hopelessness of it all, grows more tired until she herself feels not unlike the apathetic, fatigued children whose limbs seem weighted with stones. She has not heard from Patch for so long that she has stopped thinking about him. It saddens her that Louise has still not written for weeks from Cape Town – how she would enjoy a lively letter filled with gossip and confessions, making her laugh at her acid observations. Why has Louise fallen silent? Surely their long friendship cannot be over?

In the meantime she has one solace. She has found a Catholic priest in Bloemfontein and is receiving instruction. She plans to convert. It is a comfort to say the rosary every night, even though, as she is still only an Anglican, perhaps Our Lady does not listen.

Sophie writes to say Miss Hobhouse has formed a Distress Fund, and will visit South Africa soon. Perhaps they can meet? Sarah is too exhausted to write back. At the end of the day she washes in her sail-cloth bath with her tiny sliver of soap, and falls asleep immediately.

Army Circular
The General-Commander-in-Chief is desirous that all possible means shall be taken to stop the present guerrilla warfare. Of the various measures suggested for the accomplishment of this object, one which has been strongly recommended, and has lately been successfully tried on a small scale, is the removal of all men, women and children and natives from the districts which the enemy's bands persistently occupy.

This course has been pointed out by surrendered burghers, who are anxious to finish the war, as the most effective method of limiting the endurance of the guerrillas, as the men and women left on the farms, if disloyal, willingly supply burghers; if loyal, dare not refuse to do so.

The women and children brought in should be camped near the railway for supply purposes, and should be divided into two categories: 1st: Refugees, and the families of neutrals, non-combatants and surrendered burghers. 2nd: Those whose husbands, fathers and sons are on commando. The preference in accommodation etc should of course be given to the first class.

Kitchener
21 December 1900

Orange River Colony, November 1900

While he is recovering from his thigh wound at the field hospital in a remote part of the newly christened colony, Patch once again feels the familiar icy cloak of despair drop round his heart. This time there is an air of finality about it. He can't very well make another novena asking the Blessed Virgin to intercede for dead but disqualified people: in any case would Bill, so proudly Protestant, want to spend eternity with millions of Catholics all milling about in clouds of incense and singing hymns to Our Lady? Wouldn't Cartwright the atheist be mortified to find himself welcomed at the gates of Paradise by a smug archangel? Perhaps he should just pray for his own poor soul. *I'm a Papist!* he spits at the Anglican curate who wants to convert him to that wishy-washy version of Catholicism.

He spends a lot of time staring at the blank, yellow face of the veldt. The flatness of it all adds to his self-pity. If only there was a hillock or a little mountain to break the perfectly circular rim of the horizon – if you are born among mountains the absence of them is like losing a limb you didn't know you had. His eyes long to look upwards at the earth's struggle to caress the sky, or pierce it; for the rugged crags and rearing cliffs, or even the smooth swell of rounded hills, can lift the spirit as well. As for that fine flush of revenge he had experienced after Cartwright's death – where is that now? How can you track down snipers and act the daredevil when your leg is massively bandaged and a bunch of orderlies won't let you out of bed? If he is honest, his desire to kill a Boer has evaporated. Instead, he continues to gaze through the open tent-flap at – nothing.

The field surgeon who removed the bullet is delighted with the healing of the wound. 'Nothing goes septic here!' he exclaims every time he visits Patch's bedside. 'It's this wonderful dry air that does our work for us. Aren't you a lucky fellow to have been shot in Africa ha-ha-ha?'

'Very lucky,' says Patch sourly, as is part of the routine.

'You know what your problem is?' says the surgeon looking at the vacant eyes of the young trooper. 'You're bored. Haven't you got letters to write like everyone else – or a book to read?'

At the mention of letters Patch flinches (Fancy and Johan have gone silent, thank heaven) but the word *book* suddenly flicks open a memory that had been long closed. That heavy load, wrapped in brown paper, right at the bottom of his rucksack, which Dr Simmonds had given him as a parting present and which he had so nearly discarded while trying to lighten poor Olga's load . . . '*David Copperfield*!' he exclaims in surprise.

'Ah, now there's a good read.' The doctor's eyes light up. 'Got it on you then? That'll take your mind off your troubles. Now I'm going to leave off this bandage; you'll be walking round before long.'

Patch retrieves the parcel from his haversack and removes the brown paper. As he opens the soft vellum cover he can smell the sea and hear the waves hiss on the spiked shore of the Island. There is the first line that he never got beyond. *Whether I shall turn out to be the hero of my own life* . . . He looks up at the blank landscape and feels his heart sink. How pathetically far away he is from being a hero, further than ever before. Nevertheless, he reads on.

Three hours later he has filled the tent with Peggoty, Uriah Heep, Barkis-is-willing, Mr and Mrs Micawber, all of whose lives have become immeasurably more important to him than any real person he knows – for the moment anyway. That had happened on the island, he remembers, with Dr Simmonds urging him to enjoy yet more fictitious characters and enter their worlds. But how real their sufferings and joys are now; how he longs for success on their behalf, how passionately he hates the villains; how his heart aches on behalf of David, as painfully as it has ever ached for himself.

'Private Donnelly.' Patch looks up at the orderly, a pale snivelly fellow with gigantic black-rimmed spectacles. 'You're going to walk to your supper tonight – doctor's orders. Now put that book down. Too much reading is bad for your eyes. And in this light.' The little beast actually extracts the volume from Patch's grasp.

Three weeks later, on Christmas Eve, when, to his sorrow, he has reached the end of volume two, he finds that two fine sheets of writing paper have been inserted between the pages of the last chapter. He recognises Dr Simmonds' handwriting:

Dear Patrick,

Reached the end, have you? Good. Now I have something to tell you: something that not even Dickens could have dreamed up in his final chapter.

Your mother – for Mary Donnelly is your mother, as you suspected – will have the operation you spoke of, on condition that she can live with you when she returns to the mainland. She would have had it earlier but had no one to whom she could return. I think you do not have a home in Cape Town. We can discuss this later.

I knew your mother in Cape Town when she was a vibrant Irish Catholic girl who emigrated here after the devastating famine of her homeland. She became a kitchen maid in the home of my brother and within a year they were married. Yes, Patrick, I am your uncle. How do you feel about that? To continue: your father converted to Catholicism, so that you and your five brothers – now all over thirty years of age and all Catholic priests in Ireland – were born and baptised Catholics. Unfortunately, the affairs of your family did not proceed well. At first they lived in a pretty two-storey house in the District, with wrought iron balcony and sweeping flight of stairs, but my brother, though initially a successful business man, sadly became addicted to the demon drink, as did your mother after the first five sons were born. The house became uncared for; disreputable tenants moved in; and I regret to say you were born in conditions of squalor such as Mr Dickens has so vividly brought to our attention.

Your father died of alcohol poisoning at the same time your mother began to exhibit the first signs of leprosy – numbness in the face and extremities, scaliness of the skin, swelling of the nose, lips and lobes of the ears – while she carried you, her 'late lamb' as they say here. It is to my lasting shame that I, a doctor, was unable to recognise these symptoms, not that the medical world has yet any cure for this dreaded disease. These marks grew quickly, and by the time you were born, you had to be removed from her by law, and she herself was taken by force to the Island. You were delivered to the orphanage run by the Sisters of Mercy, to whom I paid a certain sum every year for your upkeep.

Despite the enormity of her problems, your mother was anxious not to stain the name of her five sons who were studying for the priesthood. Consequently, she requested that the newborn innocent bearer of the stain be known not as Simmonds but as Donnelly – her maiden name.

Had I a wife, I should gladly have accepted you into 'our' home, but being an entrenched bachelor and not especially fond of children, I felt unable to accept this responsibility.

My horror at my sister-in-law's fate grew as time passed. I did not expect her to survive long, her health being broken by alcohol even before the leprosy revealed itself, yet, after five years on the Island, she was allowed to move from the wards to the makeshift house which you have visited. A vacancy occurred for a medical officer to work with the surgeon of the lazaretto; I applied for the position and was accepted, and have lived there ever since. I visit your mother in her hut regularly, and much enjoy the roughness and isolation of the place.

When I met you in the gloom of the Gateway to Africa I was startled out of my wits even though I knew very well who you were to me, for burning in the shadows across the table were my dead brother's green eyes. And, for that matter, the eyes of my father and his father and his grandfather. Green eyes of extraordinary intensity, lit from behind by an inner radiance, run in the male line of our family, though not every male gets them – you probably don't remember the nondescript colour of _my_ eyes. (Grey, whispers Patch).

You will think it too much of a coincidence that you came unknowingly to the Island where lived your uncle and mother. However, the explanation is quite simple; even banal. My contact with the Sisters of Mercy continued after you had somewhat abruptly left their orphanage. They expressed themselves disappointed with how you had turned out; in spite of their arduous discipline you had still turned out 'slippery' – the curious word Sister Madeleine chose to describe you. They informed me that you were living with the Witbooi family in the District, and that for a while you had worked as a shoeshine boy and then as a shoe salesman for Feinsteins Fabulous Footwear, a position which you lost on account of the disappearance of three pairs of soft-shuffle shoes, even though they re-appeared, somewhat soiled, after the annual Tivoli Talent Contest in which you and your singing and dancing friends were awarded first prize.

You were therefore without employment. I thought it was time for you to meet your mother, if only indirectly. I visited Mrs Witbooi and asked her to tell you that your application for the post of leper guard would be favourably considered. She agreed to encourage you in this, without demanding to know why she should do so. You know the rest.

Shortly after, war broke out. I feared you might volunteer but you assured me nothing could be further from your

*thoughts. I am not sure what made you change your mind –
perhaps the suspicion of the identity of your mother, somewhat sooner than I had planned. I had intended to reveal
her to you on your twenty-first birthday, an event which
will shortly occur.*

*I would hope that by the time you read this – if you read
this, for I have left it to your perseverance in reading the
novel as to whether my letter falls into your hands – the
necrosed bone will have been removed, and your mother will
be ready to return to the mainland, on your own return,
which I hope will be as soon as this wretched war has ended.*

Your affectionate Uncle,
Jack Simmonds

'Seen a ghost?' enquires the bespectacled orderly. 'You're as
white as a sheet, man.'

Indeed, there are many ghosts clustered round Patch at that
moment. David Copperfield is dancing with his mother, who
has miraculously regained her features; Pegotty with Dr
Simmonds; Barkis embraces Patch; Uriah hovers, a hopeful
shadow. And there are Johan and Cartwright and Bill frolicking about with Fancy and Sarah. What larks! He himself is
repeating four-word phrases to himself. They rush through his
system, flooding out every stale and bitter thought, ripping off
that cloak of desolation. *I have a father. I have a mother. I
have an uncle. I have five brothers.* The chain of words
encircles him like an amulet. As they spin round, a new,
enchanted idea is born. *I must go back to the Island.* He
remembers the ring of ecstatic dolphins. And then: *but first
Bloemfontein – and Sarah.*

Captain Smithers, who is not much older than Patch and
suffering from homesickness, is sympathetic. Farm-burning
has ceased over Christmas, but will continue after Boxing
Day, so there will be new homeless families to be taken to the
shelter of the Bloemfontein concentration camp. Normally, at

this distance, the wagon loads of Boer mothers, children and servants would be offloaded at the nearest railway station to board convenient cattle trucks for their transport, but the trains are unreliable during the festive season. A convoy over the veldt would be practical.

The Captain gives Patch a note for the commanding officer at the Bloemfontein barracks. In it he asks for the young man to be put on duty in the camp. 'I believe there is a need for guards there,' he says. 'Apparently some of the women have grown troublesome.' And gives the handsome young trooper a sad, knowing smile.

Voyage, December 1900

Emily has never travelled second class anywhere before, but on the steamer which will carry her to Cape Town she shares a cabin with a cook, a lady's maid and a milliner. Though wary of the gentry, these women who are emigrating to the Colony in the hope of a better life, soon relax in Emily's cheerful company. She makes no attempt to preach at them about burnt-out mothers and children, and spends much of her time studying Dutch in the small cabin. It is wintry outside, with the occasional blizzard, and the sodden decks are not conducive to learning a foreign language. By coincidence, Mr and Mrs Joshua Rowntree are travelling first class to Cape Town on the same boat, and Emily often meets these gentle Quakers at their dining table, where they discuss the relief missions upon which they have separately embarked.

Never has she felt so certain that she is doing the right thing. Her brother Leonard had raised several objections to her project: she might catch the enteric so prevalent in the ex-republics; she will be vilified in England for this blatant support of the enemy; it would be better for her to go at a more opportune political moment – all of which misgivings she had swept away with not a moment's hesitation. For the feeling is that she *must go*, in response to a *strong call*. Her path is as clear as that of an arrow speeding to its target. The hugeness of her task beats through her brain incessantly. It is a relief to sit in her cramped bunk and force herself to memorise the Dutch words for *Hello, thank you, I am delighted to meet you, I am sorry, I am so very sorry.*

Without warning it is summer. The sunshine and warmth of the Canary Islands take her by surprise. She accompanies the Rowntrees on a tour of volcanic Tenerife. The red hibiscus and purple bougainvillea at first fill her heart with painful joy, for the last time she saw these tropical blooms was in Mexico where one evening she had woven garlands of crimson flowers through her hair in preparation for . . . But now she regards the heat with a practical eye: will her Leghorn hat and cotton parasol guard her from the ravages of the South African sun? A stall offers unguents to protect ladies' skins. The stall keeper speaks in dramatic Spanish about the efficacy of his products. Every word he utters tries to prise open the slammed door in her heart, until she feels agitated. Suddenly, urgently, she must return to the ship in the harbour, and feigns tiredness: the unexpected heat. The Rowntrees remind her that it is necessary to be rowed to the steamer, and he-who-rows-the-boat will do so only when his boat is at least half full of passengers. Fortunately she sees the lady's maid, the cook and the milliner, their cheeks aflame, their foreheads wet with perspiration. They too wish to return to the relative cool and calm of the ship, empty of passengers. Emily introduces them to the Rowntrees; they grow saucer-eyed.

'Be he the Mr Rowntree who makes the chocolate?' enquires the cook as their rowing boat splashes across the halcyon sea to the steamer ahead.

'And the fruit drops?'

'And who built a whole town in Yorkshire for his factory workers with pensions and a library?' The milliner has a sister who works in such a factory.

He is closely related, Emily assures them. And once a member of Parliament. They look at her in admiration. On the strength of this she ventures, 'He is a Quaker, as are all the chocolate makers. The Quakers disapprove of the war in South Africa.' A gull squawks a warning but she plunges on, 'As do I. We place our consciences before the law of the land, you see.'

Three pairs of eyes gaze at her disbelievingly. Even the oarsman scowls, though perhaps that is because he is facing the sun. Will they throw her out of the boat, to be rescued by boys diving for pennies? She feels the familiar rush of fury, but does not change the sweet expression on her face.

'An eddicated lady like you should know better,' mumbles the milliner.

'They's pro-Boers!' snarls the cook.

'Too scared to fight in the war, case they get shot.'

Cowards. Traitors. Namby-pambies.

'Well,' says Emily brightly, 'they provided nearly four hundred thousand tins of chocolate for the British troopers at the New Year. And just think, without those traitors and sissies we wouldn't have Rowntree's Fruit Gums or Chocolate Drops or Jelly Babies. Now who's going to climb up the rope ladder first?'

Bloemfontein Concentration Camp, December 1900

One day Sarah calls at the tent of the newly arrived Van Zyl family to visit seven-year-old Lizzie. The little girl had reached the camp in a fragile condition, her pale skin the evidence of many weeks indoors – so unlike the deeply tanned skins of other Boer children, no matter how ill they might be. Lizzie had a skeletal thinness, dangly limbs like flower stalks, and a violet stain around her pale blue eyes. Yet within this frailty she possessed a sweetness that burst forth in her frequent smile. Just to be in her company was a treat, for the child always had some whimsical remark to make, even after a prolonged coughing fit or a bout of retching. *It is the feather of the bokmakierie that makes me cough* or *A star from the sky fell into my throat last night and now it tries to escape.*

Today she seems to have lapsed into a coma. There is no sign of her mother. Her sisters are trying to feed the unconscious child with mashed pumpkin, a rare luxury which has to be bought at an inflated price from the camp store. 'Our mommy saved her money and bought this pumpkin and now Lizzie will eat it not. She wants only to sleep,' says the eldest sister.

'Perhaps she will eat not because there is no cinnamon and butter with the pumpkin,' suggests a smaller sister.

'Where is your mommy now?'

'She is at the dam washing people's clothes. Then she can earn money to make Lizzie better.'

The dam is a good half-mile away. Sarah looks at Lizzie,

unconscious on her mother's makeshift bed. The child's flesh seems to have melted away, revealing joints and bones and cartilage just beneath her skin. Her fine silvery hair is thinning so that patches of her scalp are visible; flies have gathered over traces of rejected pumpkin round her mouth. 'I think Lizzie needs to come to the hospital,' she says gently.

A jingle of reins and a familiar whistle just outside the tent makes the sisters sit up suddenly. 'That is the doctor!' they cry. The grizzled face of Dr Phillips, leaning down from his mount, appears at the opening. 'Anyone sick?' He continues whistling almost immediately his sardonic personal choice 'A Wandering Minstrel, I'. Though the Boer families do not on the whole know Gilbert and Sullivan's operettas, they know the tune of this carefree little song painfully well.

Sarah slips out of the tent. 'I can't wake the little girl up,' she says. 'I don't know what's causing her to be so ill.' Sarah dislikes this doctor intensely. He shows his superiority to his Boer patients by remaining, whenever possible, on horseback while diagnosing their illnesses.

'Oh, I think I've got a pretty good idea,' smirks the doctor. He climbs down from his saddle without showing any desire to enter the tent. 'I've been keeping an eye on that mother. Of course, that's exactly what she wants.' He stands too close to Sarah, who winces at his fleshy red face and fat white fingers.

'Whatever do you mean?'

'She wants to keep us medicals hopping in attention. In my view, and others', she's deliberately starving her child.' Dr Phillips' booming voice can surely be heard inside the tent; Sarah hopes the girls inside cannot understand his English.

'How can you say that? She loves Lizzie to distraction.' She moves away from him as she feels his breath on her face.

'Oh, they all do, they all do.' Now he is striding past her into the tent. 'Good morning, my dears.'

'Goot morning, Mynheer Doctor,' the girls sing back.

He glances at Lizzie's inert form. 'Yes, starving to death. Nothing else wrong with her. Made to look like anorexia but imposed by the mother, no doubt about it. I'll get a couple of bearers to take her to the hospital. We won't allow the mother to visit, of course. The child will almost certainly begin to thrive.'

'But this is appalling!' cries Sarah. Her temper suddenly flares. 'How dare you say these – *libellous* things? That mother slaves away doing other people's washing in that filthy dam just so that she can earn enough money to buy fresh vegetables for her children!' She can feel her blood throb violently in her throat; she has a reckless desire to slap the doctor's face before the watchful children.

'You wait and see, Sister Palmer.' He is on his way out already. 'And I'd be careful about my choice of words, if I were you. Libellous, eh?' And, after swinging himself into his saddle, the wand'ring whistling minstrel continues on his way.

Within minutes bearers arrive for the child. 'We cannot take her away without the permission of her mother,' cries Sarah. 'Doctor's orders,' reply the bearers, expertly sliding the inert child on to their stretcher. Sarah briefly considers barring their way, but clearly that will achieve nothing. 'Explain to your mother,' she murmurs, and moves on to the next tent, shaking with indignation.

Two days later it is mail day. Sarah receives a letter:

Dear Sarah,

I am writing this in a rush to make sure you get it in time. Great news! Miss Hobhouse sails to Cape Town tomorrow and will arrive at the end of the month. She is coming to see for herself what has happened to the devastated families. She very much hopes to be able to meet you in Bloemfontein, if she is allowed to go there. Perhaps you could introduce her to some of the children in the hospital. She will bring clothing and foodstuffs with her to dispense to the needy. She also has a bag of toys donated by well-wishers!

Yrs in haste,
Sophie

She reads these words several times. In the exhausted head-ache behind her eyes she feels a faint flicker of something hopeful. What a privilege if this strong woman should turn to her for help and guidance. She remembers Emily's face from the Bruton Street meeting: the intensity of her gaze, her quiet beauty, the passion with which she spoke. Yes, her presence in the camp would draw energy out of fatigue, like forceful breath on a dying flame; she would create order out of utter chaos. But which children would be most appropriate for her to see?

Lizzie would certainly charm her. Yesterday Sarah had visited the hospital where Poppie now helped with the children. The little girl had woken up and called out for her mother in piteous tones, much to the irritation of the two refugee nurses from the Transvaal. Poppie had at once appeared with a piece of paper and a pencil and the two of them were composing a letter to Mother when Sarah arrived. For a moment the scene resembled that of any children's hospital where nurses comfort and divert grief-stricken children. She smiled. Yes, Miss Hobhouse must meet Poppie.

Six

To Leonard Hobhouse

Kenilworth, Cape Town,
30 December 1900

Dear Leonard,

I must write something by this mail, but it will be rather vague and muddly for I am rather like a sponge continually sopping up new ideas and impressions, and am reduced to a state of mental indigestion, having had no time to think it over and sort it out. The beauty of the scenery impresses one all the time, and makes the background for everything, together with brilliant weather, light bracing air and gorgeous flowers.

The day of my arrival was a very full one – we came to anchor in Table Bay at four a.m. and shortly after that hour I was nearly knocked down by the overpowering magnificence of Table Mountain with its attendant Devil's Peak and Lion's Head, seen by sunrise. They are magnificent.

By five p.m. I was eating figs and apricots on a stoep and nursing an African meerkat as if I had known it always. The interval was spent in landing, myself and the Rowntrees, and trying to fit them into rooms – a very hard business for every hotel is choked. The docks are too full for the ships to get in, so we had to come off in tugs. After two and a half days I succeeded in getting my luggage, having lost all at the docks.

The first realisation of war comes on landing. The congested docks piled with forage etc – the long lines of military trucks in the streets of Cape Town – the swarms of Khaki people everywhere, sprinkled thick – the pavements crowded with idle people – prices of everything very high.

My welcome has been very warm – everyone seems to know me. Mrs Murray is a dear, but far from strong. The Harry Curreys, Sauers, Charles Moltenos and Merrimans have asked me to stay with them and I go on Thursday to the Merrimans at their farm near Stellenbosch. There are many people there whom I am told I must see. In fact, they are all anxious to keep me here till I have seen and known all of them, and seen such women here and there who have strayed from the Republics

Whether I can get up there or not, who can tell! Since we sailed so much has altered for the worse that it will be very difficult.

Your loving
Emily

Letter to Lady Hobhouse

Cape Town,
31 December 1900

Dear Aunt Mary,

There is so much to say I hardly know where to begin. As to my chance of getting north, it is far worse than when I left England, but I do not despair . . . All the best heads here from Sir Henry de Villiers downwards think, and I think myself, that my best plan is to go straight to Sir Alfred Milner with your note and tell him what I want to do. Meantime there is much for me to learn here.

Mr Schultz, who has all along been secretary to the committees here, tells me his latest news from Johannesburg, speaks of four thousand women and children in some sort of camp prisons up there. A good deal is learnt from officers who come to the Cape. One told a friend of mine this week that he himself helped in the burning of six hundred farms, hating and loathing it.

Mr Schultz has succeeded in getting one truck of clothing through to Bloemfontein but it is fraught with difficulty . . . I am told there are fifty-seven boy prisoners at Green Point prison-of-war camp, from seventeen down to nine years. The committee tried to get these freed to send them to school but only succeeded with one. He is eight years old.

Your loving niece
Emily

Orange River Colony, December 1900

The journey with the burnt-out families down to Bloemfontein takes four days and by the end of it Patch's euphoria has ebbed a little. There is something humiliating about herding women and children in ox wagons to a concentration camp; it is not heroic work but someone has to do it. These women and children are sullen and unfriendly. 'Daily our cup is more bitter,' the grandmothers moan. 'You Tommies are starving us. Where are our eggs and bread, our milk and butter?' cry the mothers. And the children scornfully throw the rationed biscuits at targets in the veldt instead of eating them as the British Army has done. 'We can't eat stones!' they shout as they hurl the *klinkers*, as they call them, with deadly accuracy at anthills or meerkats or a low-flying ha-de-dah flapping its prehistoric wings.

The black servants are no better, weeping and howling in their own language, keeping everyone awake, and setting off the oxen and cattle till the bellows of hungry livestock drown those of the women and children. Patch tries to adopt an indifferent pose, and in fact feels sorrier for himself than for his cargo – they've brought it on themselves anyway – for now that his thigh wound has healed he is left with a slight limp, invisible to most eyes, but one that interrupts his fluid saunter and makes him walk carefully. He hopes it will not detract from his appeal to Sarah. Most probably she will love him all the more, being a nursing sister. To cheer himself up he visualises their joyous reunion in Bloemfontein, which is followed by a five hundred mile ride to Cape Town on the back of a black charger, Sarah astride the saddle with him, across the Great Karoo desert and the purple mountain ranges all the way, and thence to the Island. His mother and uncle stand waiting for him at the jetty which is at last finished. Thank heaven he won't have to be carried on a grinning convict's back. But what will happen as he steps off the ferry and they walk, arms entwined, towards him? Will he kiss his mother on her self-cured cheek? Will Sarah be at his side? He shakes his head and frowns at the blank horizon.

When finally the flat earth begins to undulate and redden, he knows the Fountain of Flowers is near. The kaffir drivers crack their whips more energetically across the long teams of weary oxen; the mothers fall silent. Smoke hovers over a hill. The railway glints nearby. A chain of artillery, ammunition and ambulance wagons grind out from the hills: his cargo is forced to leave the road and crash among the bushes and anthills until they reach the outlying hills of the little city.

First the kaffir families must be dropped off at their camp, a collection of hastily made shacks near the railway, already overcrowded with refugees from their employers' farms, and sticky with flies. The servants screech in sorrow; they would rather go with their mistresses into the unknown. A few young black girls are allowed to remain.

And suddenly they are in the heart of Bloemfontein, creaking and rumbling up the central main road lined with roses. His heart is in his mouth as he scans the face of every woman who passes by on the busy pavement, but none of them bears the features of Sarah. There are plenty of ghosts about though, and the tin hut he can see just over the road is inhabited not only by the phantoms of Sarah and himself but also by his long illness, and the other sick troopers, and that orderly who liked to touch him. The hospital tents and marquees have all gone: the appalling thought occurs to him for the first time: *what if Sarah has left?* He hasn't heard from her for a couple of months (quite a relief in a way) but the passion of her letters had convinced him that she would be there waiting for him.

They pass the army barracks in Tempe and then come to the hillside where thousands of women and children swarm among ragged bell tents. It is not his job to find homes for the families, thank goodness, so he leaves the scowling women, good riddance, and rides back to the barracks.

'Ah!' exclaims the superintendent as he reads the note from Captain Smithers. 'We've just the job for you. Hope you like birds.'

Bird Cage, December 1900

He quickly learns that the Bloemfontein 'Bird Cage' is the penal area for 'undesirables', fenced in by barbed wire and crammed with those too headstrong to be allowed to remain in the main body of the camp: but 'Tiger Cage' would be more like it. Some of the women bare their teeth at him and hiss when he walks by, then laugh contemptuously. He feels as trapped as they are, for the bird cage is some distance from the main camp, and his sentry duty hours are long.

The ringleader of the headstrong women is Mrs Roos, sent here for provoking a demonstration against the meat rations. Tall and angular, with piercing blue eyes, she looks nothing like the average Boer woman Patch has come across. For a start, she never wears a kappie, choosing to adorn her head with an English-style sun hat laden with silken roses. The two garments she possesses indicate an interest in fashion, her erect posture creating a graceful flow to the fabric not often seen even in clothes unstained by filth. She speaks perfect English.

'Private Donnelly,' she sneers, or so it seems to him, 'can't something be done about the state of our tents? There are eight of us living in an unlined tent full of holes. When it rained last night we were all drenched. My children have to lie in mud. I myself spent the night in a river. *Pray*,' and she lingers on this word for a second, extending it into a cruelly melodious reminder of his inferior social status, 'find us a tent that wasn't used during the Crimean War.'

'There are none.' Patch delivers these three monosyllables with a heaviness designed to crush further mockery. The humour submerged in her sarcasm is lost on him, he feels diminished.

'I think you are mistaken,' replies she, raising her perfectly arched eyebrows, 'for my boys on their way to the camp school yesterday saw a wagon-load of tents being off-loaded at the ration house, and that is why I ask immediately for fear of being late.'

'I shall not let you have another tent. They are for women who obey the camp rules.' Patch cannot meet her eye but his voice is masterful. He wants to add, 'And who speak respectfully to the sentries,' but knows this will only release a stream of more unfathomable insults.

Mrs Roos bestows upon him a look of pity, then sails off. Next thing the whole fence is covered with wet blankets drying in the sun when the rules state, quite clearly, *Nothing to be hung on the wires*. A tent from the ration house arrives in the bird cage that afternoon. Patch looks away as Mrs Roos thanks him softly. He is beginning to realise that he has seen her somewhere before.

Then there is the problem with Mrs Potgieter. She had been sent from the main camp because she had bitten the arm of a British trooper! Scarcely credible that a respectable mother of seven who made the best *melktert* in the ex-republic should become a wildcat only a few weeks after arriving at the concentration camp. The reason why she had behaved so uncharacteristically lay in the latrine system which had been installed on the outskirts of the camp, far from the tents. No less than eight trench latrines with ninety-one seats next to each other had been installed for the use of the twelve hundred inhabitants. But the ungrateful inhabitants preferred to relieve themselves in the ditch even further away, many of them never having heard of the sophistications of the latrine system. The real reason, though, was the nauseating stench which emanated from the trenches as the slop buckets, which should have been removed by the town council by eleven a.m., sat festering in the sun all day discharging their unmistakeable odour. You had to fight your way through swarms of flies to get to the seats. On top of this serious deterrent to emptying your bowels or bladder, there were no separate facilities for men and women.

One day, Mrs Potgieter, who had summoned up her courage and braved her way into the latrines, was surprised by a visit from a British trooper just as she was raising her skirts and sitting down. 'Kindly leave the latrine while I am here,' she called to him in her best English. Ignoring this command, the Tommy proceeded to undo his flies. So outraged was she by this unseemly behaviour that she leapt up, grabbed his arm, and dug her teeth into it as hard as she could. For this reason she is now imprisoned in the bird cage, where there are no latrines at all. The women must improvise. They have no option but to use their cooking pots and pans or empty coffee or golden syrup tins, and leave them outside the tents to be collected – by Patch himself, who has to empty the contents into buckets which he must then place outside the barbed wire gate. So disgusting does he find this task that he often finds reason not to perform it, much to the indignation of the inmates.

When one night Mrs Potgieter's daughter is ill with diarrhoea, the desperate mother has no option but to throw the endlessly recurring slops through the wire into the main camp. Some of the child's watery faeces have spilt on the ground of the penal enclosure, a pathetic pathway to the wire fence. Patch finds the mother trying to clear up the mess the next day. He has had a bad night, dreaming that Sarah has married dead Cartwright, whose ghost taunts him with lewd barrack-room ditties. He is not in the mood for trails of excrement, nor for impertinent women.

'Good God, woman, what are you doing?' he finds himself exclaiming in horror. 'Do you Boers have no pride? This time I will report this to the commandant.'

'Good!' she replies. 'That is exactly what I want. I should like the commandant to know how we are situated here. I have asked you often enough for a sanitary bucket.'

In fact, Patch had several times requested sanitary buckets, as much for his own convenience as for that of the inmates, but to no avail. Perhaps if he brings in the commandant this shrew will force him to do something about it.

She does not let him down.

On the arrival of Captain Nelson, Mrs Potgieter is holding an elegant bone china cup in one hand.

'Good morning, madam. Now what seems to be the problem?'

'Good morning, Commandant. I'm afraid this teacup,' and she points at the pretty thing with her free hand, 'is the problem.'

The captain blinks. He can see it is a fine piece of china. The pattern of pink roses suggests it is probably from the kilns of Wedgwood in the Black Country from whence, as it happens, the captain hails. 'In what way, madam?' he enquires, testily.

'Commandant, I regret to say that I am unable to empty my bladder into this charming vessel. It is not quite large enough. As we are not allowed latrines in this – this *cage*, perhaps you would prefer me to use the floor of my tent. Do I have your permission, sir?'

A slow blush spreads over the Englishman's face. He opens his mouth to speak; closes it again; shakes his head; clears his throat. These outspoken Boer women are too much for his English reticence.

'Perhaps a sanitary bucket is the solution, sir,' murmurs Patch, feeling sorry for the chap.

Captain Nelson is torn between disciplining his subordinate for speaking out of turn; barking a refusal to the woman who has so embarrassed him; or giving in to her request. He is due on the golf course in ten minutes' time. He draws himself up even straighter than his normal erect military bearing and snaps, 'I shall order a bucket for each tent in this enclosure.' He turns to Patch. 'Kindly see that the buckets are removed and emptied every morning by the Native servants. It is, after all, a *penal* camp, not a *holiday* camp, you know, ha ha.' And rushes off.

After he has left Mrs Potgieter erupts with suppressed mirth. Patch cannot resist a chortle as well. Their eyes meet: they explode with laughter. 'I must say I don't think I'll ever feel the same about this poor old teacup again,' she gasps.

Patch has to admit there is a certain liveliness about the bird cage which appears to be absent from the larger camp. But where is Sarah? In the little free time he has he wanders through the small military hospital that remains, his eyes on the alert for her crimson pelisse. There is an entirely new staff in the hospital; no one has heard of her. Most of the Army Reserve nurses have returned to Cape Town or gone back to England, he is told. The turquoise bracelet is in his pocket. If he holds it tightly enough she might appear. Coming here is beginning to seem a mistake. Perhaps he should have requested to be sent to Cape Town and have done with it.

At least there are some attractive young women in the bird cage, many of them here for consorting with soldiers in an immoral way in the main camp. Among them is a high-spirited creature who makes a point of catching his eye as he does his rounds. Although covered in mud from sleeping on the wet ground in the tent, her waist is nevertheless nipped in by stays and her breasts thrust upwards so that inviting little mounds of pink flesh rise above the low neckline of her dress. One day she beckons to Patch to enter her tent as if to point out some defect within it, as is usually the way. Once he passes through the open flaps of the tent, he finds her standing before him, her hands pertly held over her swaying hips. 'Yes?' Patch demands. 'I need your help,' she murmurs in broken English. And in a flash she raises her skirt above her head and reveals the naked lower half of her body. Patch tries to avert his eyes but finds himself unable to stop staring at the great bush of black curls that springs from between her legs. As he stands frozen before her she places her hand on her bush and begins to rub it with a slow circular motion. 'I very much need your help,' she says again, her eyes filming over with desire. Patch forces himself to turn his head; he fears he might ejaculate with excitement all over his khaki then and there if he tries to speak. He leaves the tent shaking all over. He has not had a woman for nearly a year.

A few days later the same woman is unrecognisable. A sort of scurvy has broken out among the camp people: it attacks their mouths, which become covered with sores; their gums bleed and, in some cases, perfectly healthy teeth fall out. The women complain it is the diet, since no vegetables are allowed, even from the expensive stores of the main camp. No matter how often Patch tells them that their daily supply (courtesy of Her Majesty's Army) of meat, coffee, flour, condensed milk, salt and sugar far exceeds any ration he, as a mere trooper, had ever received on the great flank march, the women continue to insist it is not good enough. For a start, they say, raw meat, flour and coffee have to be cooked, and where is the fuel? The green bushes on the hillside have long ago been used up. In any case, axes aren't allowed. Sometimes a little coal arrives but you can't light coal without firewood. The bird-cage women grow frantic trying to get a fire going in their braziers cut from old paraffin tins; they are not allowed the clay ovens of the larger camp. Mrs Roos has organised the hollowing-out of a couple of convenient ant-hills in which batches of bread can be baked for the penal community, and this comforting kitchen smell mingles oddly with the general camp stench.

But the children of the bird cage are fading away, in spite of the women's best efforts at feeding them. They grow scabby and spotty, their noses always oozing something green. They walk around sometimes wearing only a vest, not even pants. Only their blonde hair distinguishes them from kaffir children as their skins are burnt deep ochre by the sun, and then there is a crust of dirt over that. Patch has had to witness the deaths of three children, who are taken to the mortuary tent at once. The mothers make head-stones for their sons and daughters out of slate or wood, and inscribe with their own hands the dates of their children's deaths.

Mrs Roos begins to complain of fits. She has grown alarmingly thin, and her sapphire eyes gleam even more fearfully than ever in their dark sockets. It is the custom for the whistling doctor to call around at each tent every morning on his horse. Leaning down from his horse he shouts out: 'Anyone sick?' 'Yes, doctor,' comes the answer from those who do not fear being taken to the camp hospital from whence, in their opinion, there is no return. 'Well (still on his horse), what's the matter?' 'So-and-so-and-so, doctor.' 'All right, I'll send you some medicine,' and off he rides to the next tent.

Needless to say Mrs Roos isn't putting up with this. She doesn't like the medicine he has prescribed her. He tries to slip past her tent and begin talking to the neighbouring occupants. She pops her head out of the tent flap. For once, her hair is in some disarray. 'Excuse me for interrupting you, doctor . . .' Even in illness her voice can't lose that sardonic ring, or is he imagining it? 'That medicine you sent me doesn't agree with me. I cannot even retain it. You will greatly oblige me by changing it.'

Doctor Phillips has no time for women who complain. From the great height of his horse he shouts down at her angrily. 'It is all nonsense! You Boers want to live on nothing but medicine. You are not ill at all, it is only a sham!'

'If I were not sick I would not trouble you,' says she quietly.

'You are not sick, it is all fancy. You've probably been drinking jackal's blood or lying in baboon's dung – then you come to us to pick up the pieces.'

'Thank you, doctor, if that is your opinion of the case I suppose I must believe it.' Mistaking her irony for humility, the good doctor whips his horse and canters off, well pleased with the success of his scolding. Next thing, the woman really is ill, her sons whimpering around her,

'Lieutenant Donnelly,' she whispers (this is her little joke – she has promoted him for good behaviour over the sanitary buckets, which are now cleaned daily, and for slipping her the odd piece of fruit which she immediately gives to her children), 'could you send for the doctor?'

Patch is startled by her pallor. 'D-Doctor Phillips?' he stutters.

'Not the wandering minstrel, please. Could you perhaps send for Doctor Pern who works at the Tempe hospital? He is not due to do his rounds till tomorrow, and that may be—' she looks around at her frightened children '—too late.'

'I will send a scout to call Dr Pern,' says Patch though he does not really have this authority.

Mrs Roos smiles weakly. 'Thank you, Lieutenant. I always knew you had a good heart underneath all that khaki.'

He watches the sweat trickle down her forehead into her eyes. What will become of her children if she dies? He knows she has relatives in the Cape who will take them in, but permission has not been granted.

After a few hours Dr Pern arrives. He spends a long time in Mrs Roos' tent. Patch hovers nearby, pretending to examine the fraying edges of the tent canvas. Finally the doctor emerges. He looks alarmed.

'This woman must be taken to the camp hospital immediately. She's dying of starvation, or maybe something more serious.' He frowns at Patch. 'Hasn't she been receiving rations?'

'Yes, sir. Same as everyone else. She probably gives her portions to her children.'

Dr Pern wrinkles his nose. 'Terrible smell here. It's actually worse than the main camp. And these flies – I'd like to throw a vat of disinfectant over everything in sight.' He pauses to apply a cologne-scented handkerchief to his nostrils. 'Can you get her carried on a stretcher? She'll need to go to the central hut.' He tucks his kerchief into his top pocket and scribbles something on a notepad. 'Take this.'

'Yes, sir.'

Dr Pern mounts his horse briskly. 'There's some good nursing in that hospital,' he says. 'There's also some bloody awful nursing. Try to get Sister Palmer for her.'

'Yes, sir. Sister Palmer, did you say, sir?'

'She used to work in the enteric wards at the height of the epidemic. Got offered the chance to return to Cape Town once things had died down, but applied to work here in the camp hospital. Speaks Dutch, would you believe?'

Patch wonders if his knees will buckle under him. 'Sister *Sarah* Palmer, would that be, sir?'

'Yes, I believe that's her name. Friend of yours?' The doctor looks sceptical.

'You could say that, sir.' Patch can hear he is smirking so straightens out his voice and says more soberly, 'She nursed me through the enteric. I would have died otherwise.'

'She's a good woman,' says the doctor. Patch's sharp ears pick up a hint of regret. 'Needs to look after herself though. She works too hard.'

'Thank you, sir.'

Behind him, the whore who lifted her skirts is gathering the children and murmuring to them breathily as their mother is lifted on to a stretcher by a couple of bearers.

'I'm coming with you,' says Patch to Mrs Roos. He attempts a smile. 'I may need your help.' He has recognised her at last.

Cape Town, January 1901

Sir Alfred Milner has a weak spot for witty women. He prefers elegance to beauty and claims to know a woman by her posture.

The woman who now fixes him with a steady gaze and speaks about farm burning and the Honour of England is not elegant, nor is she witty, but her demeanour is composed, unlike other 'screamers' he has met. Miss Hobhouse's face is clear as a mountain pool. It is not just that she is past the first flush of youth; it is clear at once that this potentially good-looking woman has *no mystery*. She hides nothing. But in spite of these disadvantages Sir Alfred thinks he detects a hint of irony in her speech, perhaps encouraged by the lugubrious roll of eyeball he has cultivated for accompanying the utterance of the word *Kitchener*.

'Miss Hobhouse, I can do nothing but refer your request to Lord Kitchener. I may be High Commissioner but he is Commander-in-Chief now that Lord Roberts has returned to England. He is in charge of this war, not I.'

It is a tribute to the intelligence in her face that he has permitted the eyeball indiscretion, usually reserved for close friends, of whom there are few enough, God knows, in this African backwater.

Miss Hobhouse allows a flicker of a smile to soften her lips before replying. 'I should have thought, Sir Alfred, that a woman-hater like Lord Kitchener would *welcome* my intercession, if only to relieve him of the necessity of dealing with difficulties he has created for thousands of angry women, both Boer and native.'

The High Commissioner's opinion of Emily rises at once. He even begins to think she has a certain feel for style, though clearly she has made no effort with her face or hair. But then, you didn't expect glamour from feminist do-gooders. The only reason why he'd consented to see her was that her aunt, Lady Hobhouse, had asked him to, and you could not refuse the Hobhouses – several notches above himself in the hierarchy of the Upper Classes, pro-Boer though they may be. When she'd arrived at Government House for luncheon, his heart had sunk. Her pale gaze was too direct. He likes a woman whose eyes glint with dark secrets and look upon him with suggestive drollery. He'd get rid of her immediately after the obligatory meal to which he had invited her. He'd asked seven military gentlemen to come along as well and steamroller her for him, but she'd slipped through the net by imploring him beforehand (and, by God, those eyes could implore) to speak with her about the burnt-out women *after*, not *during*, luncheon. He pleaded press of work; she pleaded her mission was part of his work; in the end he promised fifteen minutes, *not more*.

Now, sitting beside her on the low couch in the cool spaciousness of the great drawing room of Government House, with the windows opening on to the green lawns and grand old oaks planted by Simon van der Stel a hundred years or more ago, he finds that over an hour has passed seamlessly. He has succumbed to his own charm, which Miss Hobhouse has subtly encouraged. If only they could have been gossiping about the gruesome behaviour of certain MPs, or the recent death of his friend Oscar Wilde, he would have positively enjoyed himself, for Emily has a generous smile which lights up the drawing room, and generations of well-bred forefathers have assured her manners are impeccable.

Unfortunately, she is there to tackle the refugee situation and gain his permission to travel to the camps. Ever since he had seen for himself open truck-loads of women and children roasting in the African sun, he has felt that Kitchener, damn him, had made a ghastly mistake. Miss Hobhouse was right when she asked him how he thought he was going to govern thousands of Joan of Arcs, exulting in the thought of martyrdom.

Although it was Roberts who had started the whole scorched-earth policy months before, as long ago as October Milner had written to Chamberlain objecting to the indiscriminate burning which he considered both barbarous and ineffectual. Now here is this unflirtatious woman – an Old Maid, really, a proper spinster – asking for permission to visit these Joans of Arc in their refugee camps; though hardly 'refugee', more like prisoner-of-war, he has to agree. He doesn't want to hear about the conditions in the camps: the mere thought makes his sensitive stomach turn. When he'd met Kruger at the conference on Bloemfontein railway station, a few months before the outbreak of war, he'd simply planned to take over the South African Republic, complete with gold mines: a brief war between two nations of white gentlemen which would clear the air and settle the mining problems. A token war, really, over by Christmas. The whole of South Africa, with her unsuspected heart of gold, part of the Empire! Everyone speaking English in a few years' time! Wonderful! Now, buried in the most secret recesses of his heart is the terrifying thought: he'd got it wrong! Not that, of course, he'd have got it wrong if he'd been allowed to direct the war himself (his comment to Miss Hobhouse had a bitter resonance), but he had misjudged the military: bunglers, every one of them. No idea of the repercussions of their simplistic strategies.

Now he has to live with the vision of thousands of women and children in cattle trucks on their way to concentration camps, as they were now being called, after the Cuban *concentrados*. They think that setting fire to the enemy's house is as simple as burning an unwanted letter. Even if the women in the trucks weren't the type he'd care to mix with socially, they and their children were living evidence of a flagrant breach of gentlemanly conduct by the British, and the thought of it made his long dry body break into a cold sweat.

Miss Hobhouse is gazing at him with her compassionate eyes, her head tilted solicitously to one side. He has to resist an urge to pour out his heart in order to be comforted. She speaks calmly, lucidly, about the uneasiness of the English conscience over these very women and children who have been trooping through his nightmares. On behalf of her Distress Committee she wants to take two trucks up to the camps, one with clothing, the other with provisions; she wants a Dutch lady to accompany her. She would appease the situation; she would appease his pain. He would grant her anything. But only, he repeats, with Kitchener's permission.

'Even a woman-hater like Kitchener would not want to exterminate the entire female Boer population, but that is what he will do, Sir Alfred, unless something is done immediately to ameliorate the situation.' Yes, he can imagine her on a platform addressing thousands of like-minded women, or retorting to hecklers at local meetings. Would she lose that calmness under pressure?

He narrows his eyes into hawkish hoods, then decides to risk a little digression. 'Lord Horatio Kitchener is not a man to be moved by the deaths of women and children if it means winning the war. But the death of a *starling* – that is a different thing altogether!'

There! He has startled her! She blinks rapidly several times and shakes her head. A small frown appears between her well-spaced eyebrows. 'Did I hear correctly?' And yes, her lips have a mischievous curl to them. Nothing can stop him now.

'He is completely besotted with a baby starling that fell down his bedroom chimney at GHQ. Keeps it in a cage and gets his staff to look after it. Feeds it earthworms he dug up himself and tries to teach it to whistle Irish reels.'

Milner is not entirely sure he has Miss Hobhouse's full interest. She is listening intently to what he is saying, but does not snigger or raise her brows as he would have hoped. He can tell that the focus of her attention is not on his story, but that her perfect breeding would not permit her to steer him swiftly back to the reason why she has come. 'One day,' he continues nevertheless, 'while its master was on a visit to some far-flung troops, the bird escaped. Consternation!' (Come on, woman, at least round your eyes.) 'A telegram was sent to inform our Commander-in-Chief of the tragedy. On his return he organised a small army to hunt down the starling.' Milner pauses.

'And?' Her voice is patient.

'I'm pleased to inform you that it was found in the early hours of the evening in a neighbour's chimney. The chief himself emerged from the expedition covered in mud from tripping over in flowerbeds. But with his equanimity restored.'

As she does not snort with derisive laughter he waits for her to return to the concentration camps. Instead she says, 'I often think we must look to the childhoods of people like Kitchener to discover the roots of their instability. And his iron will. I gather he had an oppressive father.'

Did he see a shadow flit across her face as she said this? 'My cousin tells me of the punishments inflicted on the young Horatio by his father,' she continues. 'Did you know that if he disobeyed his father in any way he was spread out on the front lawn and his limbs pinned down with croquet hoops?'

'Good heavens!' Milner tries not to smile at the image. At the same time he can see Miss Hobhouse is troubled.

'Yes, fathers have a lot to answer for,' she says at last. 'Thank heavens for mothers – unless they die young.' There is undeniable pain in her eyes.

He quells a sudden longing to tell her of his own mother, the widow of a feckless German student half her age; now dead and unable to witness his great achievements. He guides her swiftly back to her Mission. 'To return to the mothers of whom we were speaking. As I have said, I can do no more than urge Kitchener to allow you to go to the camps, if only on the practical ground that they need to be properly organised. I fear the military men in charge of them have not had much experience in running their own households, let alone an entire refugee camp.' He grimaces. 'And they are likely to exist not for weeks but for months, if not years.'

Miss Hobhouse stands up, perhaps because she knows the interview is drawing to a close, but perhaps so that she might gain in stature. 'I would be grateful if you would stress to Kitchener the necessity of a Dutch female companion to guide me and translate for me. I have learnt a little Dutch but not enough to make myself understood.'

'I shall do my best, Miss Hobhouse,' says Milner smoothly. 'But remember that, even though the Boers of the Cape Colony are loyal, they are not to be trusted once they meet up with their oppressed brethren. Don't expect too much in the way of charity from the military.'

'A little kindness from the military might lead the Boers anywhere,' replies Miss Hobhouse. She gazes at him with the full force of her good sense. 'I know I can rely on you, Sir Alfred.'

'Do please remember me to Lady Hobhouse when you write to her.'

'She will be pleased to hear that we – got on so well!' Now a full smile breaks out on Emily's face and for a moment he is dazzled.

He stands at the great windows watching her brisk departure into the blazing Cape Town afternoon. Up shoots her parasol. Womanly wisdom. Calm efficiency. That's what the camps need. His conscience will be salved.

He calls his secretary and begins to dictate.

Bloemfontein Concentration Camp, January 1901

'You wish to speak to me?' says Nurse McKillen with an air of haughtiness. This young nurse from England must remember who is in charge here. Nurse McKillen came from England as well. She and her husband had emigrated to Johannesburg a few years back where they'd been regarded as 'uitlanders' – foreigners – by the native Boers. When these Boers expected Mr McKillen to join their ranks in their hostilities against Great Britain, husband and wife had joined the fleeing uitlanders, and become refugees in Bloemfontein. Mrs McKillen was lucky to find work in this camp hospital.

'It is possible that a lady from England will be visiting the camp.' Sarah feels faint in the stifling heat of the children's ward. Nurse McKillen frowns. 'I would like to bring her to visit the children here.'

'As long as she doesn't interfere and tell us how to do our work. We don't need busybodies here,' snorts the senior nurse. There is a sour beery smell on her breath. She gives Sarah a suspicious look. 'What's she want to come here for?'

'She's bringing clothes and comforts for the children,' says Sarah. 'How's little Lizzie?' she asks quickly to divert the inevitable tirade against 'pro-Boers'.

'See for yourself.' Nurse McKillen nods at a bed near a window. 'Putting on weight, as you'd expect.'

Lizzie lies, still as death, her eyes wide open, staring at the busy flies on the ceiling. There is more flesh on her arms which lie limply on the unwashed bed cover. Her face has filled out a little.

'Good morning, Lizzie. How are you, my dear? Sarah greets the child in her now confident Dutch.

A suggestion of a smile appears on the child's bluish lips. 'Good morning, nursie. Where is my mother?'

'I tell you what, Lizzie: will you sing for me?'

The child thinks a moment; then obligingly sings, in a thin whispering voice, the first verse of a Boer hymn, *De Here is Mijn Gehulp* (The Lord is My Help)

'That's all we need now,' mutters Nurse McKillen. 'A whole lot of Dutch dirges.'

Poppie comes bustling by, all freckles and smiles, in the whitest apron Sarah has seen for a year. 'Time for the bedpans!' she sings, clearly enjoying herself in spite of the malevolent glare directed at her by Nurse McKillen. 'Are you ready, Jan Pierewit?'

A grey-faced little boy giggles and hides beneath his grey sheet. 'No, nursie!' comes a muffled voice.

Poppie leans over his bed and tickles the little heap of bones beneath the blanket. 'Here comes the bedpan bird!' she cries, swooping the urine receptacle above the sheets and imitating the raucous cry of the ha-de-hah.

Nurse McKillen sniffs. 'She's as bad as the children. As if we haven't got enough on our hands.'

'That's all we need,' agrees her refugee colleague, Nurse Nicholson.

Outside the ward entrance, someone is waiting.

'Mrs Mopeli!' cries Sarah. She can tell at once that the ex-washerwoman to the troops is in a state of repressed anguish. No longer either jolly or bitter, she now looks like so many women in the camp: helpless and frightened. 'What is it?' for Mrs Mopeli seems incapable of speech.

'Nurse Palmer, will you come with me to the Native Refugee Camp?' she says in a strained voice. Her eyes have lost their lustre, but she does not appear to be ill. 'It is my sister's daughter.'

Sarah wavers. It is the end of a long weary day among the tents and in the ward, and she longs for the secret luxury of her sail-cloth bath. Just lately she has been too exhausted to visit the native camp after her day's work with the children, and has felt guilty about this.

'Of course.'

The two women walk quickly through the Flower Fountain city. 'Isn't it amazing,' remarks Sarah, who cannot bear the silence of her companion, 'how the roses bloom so beautifully at the height of an African summer.' She glances nervously at Mrs Mopeli, who shows no interest in the Barronne Prevost Hybrid Perpetuals, their salmon pink faces turned towards her as if in preparation for praise.

'This war,' says Mrs Mopeli, pushing her way through the soldiers who crowd the pavements and make no effort to stand aside for the two women, 'is a bad bad bad thing. Now everyone is dying. Children are dying. We thought the British Army came to help us; to give us back our land; to put our people into the government. Now *we* help the British Army and they kill our children. They even kill the children of the Boer people.'

'Well, not intentionally,' says Sarah, though without much conviction.

'Is it not intentional when they burn down our kraals and villages, saying that we feed the Boer commandos? Is it not intentional when they steal our cattle and sheep and set fire to our crops? Is it not intentional when they force the women and children and old people away from the homes of their ancestors, into camps which they must build themselves out of rubble? You know that there is not one hospital, not one ward, not one doctor, not one nurse in the native refugee camp, Nurse Palmer. The children are sick. They are hungry, They are dying. You will see when you get there.'

'I'll do what I can to help your sister's child,' gasps Sarah. The thorns of a pale cream *Souvenir de la Malmaison* cling to her skirt and she wrenches it free. 'I am a nurse, not a doctor.'

'You can help her.' Mrs Mopeli sails through the rose

garden, untouched by thorns. 'You must not let her die, Nurse Palmer.'

The sprightly cadence of bugles and drums precedes a brisk regimental parade; a non-commissioned officer stops the two women. 'Your passes, please.' His voice is accusing, as if they have already broken some law. Both women produce their documents with an air of indifference; the young man examines them with exaggerated mistrust. 'It'll be curfew shortly,' he says. 'Don't let me catch you out of bounds later on.'

Sarah can smell the camp before she sees it. The air is suddenly alive with flies and stinging insects. Beyond a row of armed native pickets stands what seems to be a squatter camp made up of precarious-looking shacks. A woman wrapped in a blanket is attempting to light a fire in a tin brazier; naked black children are tumbling about in the mud. The familiar stench of human faeces hangs over the camp.

'There are still no latrines here,' said Mrs Mopeli emotionlessly. 'Our people have to go up the hill. Some people cannot wait. They are not used to living like this.'

'Still no tents?'

Mrs Mopeli looks around at the dwellings built out of scraps of corrugated iron and bits of wood and canvas, and pulls a disgusted face. 'It is the wish of the British Army. This is my sister's shack, Nurse Palmer. Her name is Namzuma. She doesn't speak English.'

Inside the shack a group of white-haired old people in blankets sit listlessly on the earth floor. There is the smell of hunger: Sarah can see none of the basic rations evident in the Boer bell tents. 'This is my sister. She comes from the village of Mapele.' They moved towards a blanket-clad woman whose features Sarah can only just distinguish in the gloom. Namzuma makes as if to curtsey, but is holding a small baby against her naked breast. Sarah lays a restraining hand on her shoulder, then drops it to feel the child.

'What is your baby's name?' Mrs Mopeli translates.

'Nyanga, madam,' says the mother, averting her eyes in the way of country Africans.

'And what is the matter with Nyanga?' Sarah feels she is choking with the smell in the shack. Flies cake the baby's face. They attempt to gather round her own mouth as she speaks. 'Her skin feels hot and dry.'

Nyanga has chronic diarrhoea. She will eat nothing. According to her mother, who speaks languidly, she defecates a transparent mucus, though this morning her faeces look like fragments of overstewed meat. The baby passes wind as her mother continues with her catalogue, then shrieks in pain. 'Many many children have this sickness,' translates Mrs Mopeli. 'And the old people too. Some have died already.' She addresses the white-haired people in rapid Sotho. They chorus a reply, holding their stomachs and moaning in imaginary agony. Some of them begin to hiccough. Others pretend to vomit. Sarah can see they are all dehydrated, as is the baby.

'Do you have salt here? These people are suffering from dysentery. It comes from these flies sitting on food. They must drink a lot of water with salt in it. They mustn't even try to eat. As for Nyanga, if Namzuma will allow it, I shall take her to the hospital. She is very ill. Perhaps they can save her there.'

Mrs Mopeli speaks in an authoritative voice to her sister. Namzuma moans and rocks Nyanga; then allows Mrs Mopeli to lift up the child. In one deft movement the baby is tied to her aunt's broad back: 'Let us go together. You are very tired. You are not strong enough to carry the child.'

Namzuma murmurs something in a choked voice.

'She says that children die in the hospital,' translates her sister.

'Only if they come too late.' How often has she uttered these words? 'We will take her to the ward for contagious illness. They will drip saline water into her arm. If it is not too late, that will save her life.'

*　　*　　*

303

As Patch, Mrs Roos and the two stretcher bearers draw closer to the central hospital hut, weaving their way through lanes between tents cluttered with kettles, chickens, chairs, children, coffee grinders, slop buckets, flies, clay ovens, guards, pigs, pots, pails and pestles, Patch becomes aware of the beating of drums. Perhaps it is thunder he hears, though the evening sky is clear and the web of southern stars is already flickering into life. The Tommies say the night sky is different 'back home', when they can see it through the clouds and smog, that is, but 'out here' – they shake their heads and wonder if that starry net might swoop them up into the heavens if they don't look out.

He is wondering if he should confess to Mrs Roos that it is her turquoise bracelet that he carries in his pocket, and which now has a leaden feel to it. But then he would have to return it to her and then what would he give Sarah? If Mrs Roos dies things would be easier, but there would still be a sin attached, perhaps only venial . . . They enter the hospital.

At the door Mrs Roos murmurs from her stretcher, 'God help me!' For the drumming has become a-hammering as hobnailed boots and heavy-heeled shoes pound across the bare planks of the hospital floor, set three feet above the ground; a-hammering that the corrugated walls and roof magnify into a-booming; and into that warp of boom is woven the shrieking of nurses, the shouting of soldiers, the moaning of mothers, the wailing of children, all combining together in one giant cacophony that charges out at you like a savage animal, unleashed as you open the hospital door. And with it the twin beast of heat and stench as the unshaded metal hut slowly roasts the patients who lie within its walls. So violent is the attack on his senses that Patch for a moment wants to faint: he feels sweat break out and run in rivers all over his body. Mrs Roos, on the other hand, seems to have died. She has closed her eyes. The flies make a rush for her face; she does not attempt to brush them away.

Once he has got his breath back, the sight is familiar to Patch. But there is a difference here, a profound difference between his enteric marquee and this corrugated iron ward. For here is a panorama of the dying – from the anguished infant, through the pallid mothers, to the grey grandparents dissolving with age and illness beneath their dirty blankets. They are not unattended; never has Patch seen a ward so full of scrubbing, sweeping kaffirs, and uniformed soldiers who stride around with documents in their hands, and impatient nurses shouting in English at uncomprehending patients and thrusting thermometers under their tongues.

He catches the attention of one of these nurses who has just finished berating a flimsy old man who has wet his bed.

'I'm looking for Sister Palmer.'

'She don't work here,' snaps the young woman. 'She's in the tents.'

'What's she doing in the tents?'

'Getting the sick babies off their mothers,' replies the nurse, evidently irritated by his question. 'Dunno why she bothers. Who's this then?' And she glances at the inert form on the stretcher.

As Mrs Roos is moved on to an empty bed, Patch tries not to look at the children in the corner of the ward. Since leaving the orphanage he hasn't had to witness large numbers of children crying for their mothers. But his fleeting glimpse of the drumming thrumming rumbling ward shows him that things are worse here for these children than they ever had been in the frigid silence of the orphanage dormitories. One infant actually tumbles out of bed while droning the syllables *ma-ma-ma-ma-ma-ma* as his contribution to the cacophony, and Patch cannot prevent himself from watching the emaciated little body being strapped to the bed by his wrists and ankles with strips of linen so that the inconvenience of picking him up would not be repeated.

Mrs Roos now lies under a dirty blanket like everyone else. Her eyes flutter open and Patch is amazed that they still blaze blue, for every bit of colour has drained from her face which now seems to have been fashioned from wax. She is trying to say something. Patch leans over and places his ear near her mouth.

'Don't let my children come here,' she gasps, those brilliant orbs rolling back in her head, defeated at last.

'I won't,' says Patch. His voice sounds wobbly.

The nurse bustles up with a cup of milk. 'Off you go then,' she orders Patch. 'We'll soon have her up and about. No Boer remedies in this hospital.' She pulls Mrs Roos' inert torso upwards and thrusts the cup against her lips. Mrs Roos begins to retch.

He turns away from her so as not to embarrass; then addresses the young nurse. 'Sister Palmer,' muses Patch. 'Which part of the camp does she visit?'

'Don't ask me!' exclaims the nurse, wiping her soiled apron. 'Come on, madam, drink up.' She gazes round the ward, following a handsome young medical officer with her hopeful eyes. Suddenly she gives a snort. 'Well, you're the lucky one! Here comes Sarah through the door. With another sick baby of course.' The look on the nurse's face is slowly rearranging itself. 'Am I seeing right,' she whispers, 'or is that baby *black*? And who is that kaffir woman with them?'

Patch hardly dares to look. However, he has his techniques. Turning his head away, he slides his eyes with lowered lids in Sarah's direction.

Oh Mary Mother of God, can that be the woman I love?

The turquoise bracelet which belongs to Mrs Roos is in his pocket. But does he want to give it to this exhausted-looking woman who has aged twenty years since he last saw her? Where is her luminous beauty, her angelic composure? Her face is grey, her shoulders slumped. Disappointment rather than pity wells treacherously in his heart. Sarah does not see him. He turns away quickly and walks back to the bird cage, his head in turmoil.

Dear Aunt Mary,

I arrived at Bloemfontein, the only woman, and began to learn from that moment what it is to be dominated by the Military. All the railway officials sink into nobodies and soldiers rule the station. You can't stir without their sanction. The whole town is full of soldiers – and the little hotels and the post office and a great ring of camps all round and picquets continually demanding your pass. It is a perfect terror, and I feel inclined to kick all day long.

The splendid truck given me at Cape Town, a large double one, was capable of holding 12 ton. Colonel Cowie had sent word I was to have the largest they had available. My humiliation was that I was not able to fill it. £200 worth of food, groceries, etc. barely filled half, and all the clothing I could muster left much space in the other half. And it was such an opportunity missed for it travelled up gratis. It left Cape Town the day before I did and was hitched on to my train at De Aar and so arrived when I did.

The first thing I did next day was to go down to the goods station, claim the truck and arrange for its unloading. Mr. Arthur Fichardt, the son of my hostess here, has most kindly put a row of vacant rooms at my disposal and this morning I have spent arranging all my stores – unpacking and sorting them. It is very hot work. I think the essence of delightful work is when you quite forget you have a body, but here the heat keeps you in constant recollection that you are still in the flesh, and it is a great hindrance.

But I must pass on to tell you about the women's camp which, after all, is the central point of interest. General Pretyman gave me his blessing over it and a permanent pass and introduced me to Captain Nelson who, until recently, has been in charge of it. The Authorities are at their wits' end and have no more idea how to cope with the one difficulty of providing clothes for the people than the man in the moon. Crass male ignorance, stupidity, helplessness and muddling. I rub as much salt into the sore places of their minds as I possibly can, because it is so good for them; but I can't help melting a little when they are very humble and confess that the whole thing is a grievous and gigantic blunder and presents an almost insoluble problem, and they don't know how to face it.

I explained that I was not going to do what the Military ought to do, but really, when looked into, what they are able to do is so little that I feel that donors would wish that the suffering of the women and above all the tiny children should be the chief thing taken into account. Major Cray, now in charge not only of this camp but of everyone in the once Free State, told me how he was curtailed – no money, no trucks in sufficient quantity, no power to do what he would like to have done. He begs me to go to all the camps – the wild demand for clothing at places like Rhenoster drives him to despair and he and I together are going to concoct a letter to Kitchener to obtain leave for me to go up north. I hope he will.

The camp is about two miles from this town, dumped down on the southern slope of a kopje right out on the bare brown veldt. Not the vestige of a tree in any direction, nor shade of any description. It was about four o'clock of a scorching afternoon when I set foot in the camp and I can't tell you what I felt like, so I won't try.

I began by finding a woman whose sister I had met in Cape Town. It is such a puzzle to find your way in a village of bell tents with no street or names or numbers. There are nearly 2,000 people in this one camp of which some few are men – they call them 'hands-up men' – and over 900 children. Imagine the heat inside the tents and the suffocation! We sat on their khaki blankets rolled up inside Mrs. Botha's tent and the sun blazed through the single canvas and the flies lay thick and black on everything – no chair, no table, nor any room for such, only a deal box standing on its end served as a wee pantry. In this tent lived Mrs. Botha, five children (three quite grown up) and a little Kaffir servant girl. Many tents have more occupants.

Mrs Pienaar came in and Mrs. Raal, Mrs. Roux and others, and they told me their stories and we cried together and even laughed together and chatted bad Dutch and bad English all the afternoon. Wet nights, the water streams down through the canvas and comes flowing in (as it knows how to in this country) under the flap of the tent and wets their blankets as they lie on the ground.

While we sat there a snake came in. They said it was a night adder and very poisonous. So they all ran out to make room and I attacked the creature with my parasol. (Afterwards I was told it was a puff-adder.) I could not bear to think the thing should be at large in a community mostly sleeping on the ground. After a struggle I wounded it and then a man came with a mallet and finished it off . . .

Bloemfontein Concentration Camp, January 1901

Sarah, drawn from her tent-rounds by the shrieks of fear and merriment from the Bothas' tent, stands apart and watches. It seems she has witnessed an apparition such as she is learning about in her Catechism lessons from the Catholic priest. Light streams from the eyes of the woman who stands alone in the tent, the tip of her parasol thrust into the body of the puff-adder. The woman's face is exultant. Her clothes are clean and crisp. A stylishly striped skirt reveals the shapeliness of her hips and waist. Her hair is golden. No such woman has ventured into the bell tents: can Sarah, in her exhaustion, be hallucinating?

'If only Eve had had a parasol we'd all still be in the garden of Eden!' calls out the apparition cheerily.

The entire Botha family, the kaffir servant girl, and all the other women who have evacuated the tent burst into hysterical laughter, clapping their hands, wiping their eyes with their aprons. They call out in wonder; Sarah hears the Dutch word *Engelse* – English – and translates it as *angel*, without thinking.

Now a black soldier in khaki runs up and removes the dead snake from the parasol tip. If he eats the liver of the creature he need fear the puffadder no longer. The apparition thanks him delightedly, except that Sarah now recognises this angelic presence as Miss Hobhouse, who was wearing the same striped skirt at the Bruton Street meeting.

Now the Boer women return to the tent and order the kaffir

girl to light a fire while Mrs Botha's daughter grinds the coffee beans, mixed with acorns and dried roots, so that they can celebrate.

As if mesmerised, Sarah finds herself moving, floating, towards that tent. Like her, the women clustered round Miss Hobhouse are utterly captivated; they do not notice the silent approach of Sarah, who feels she may have become transparent. Mrs Pienaar, heavy with child, sits meekly beside the visitor while Mrs Botha explains how the pregnant mother has to sleep on the bare ground till she is stiff and sore. 'She has not a thing to sit upon, but must squat upon a rolled-up blanket, as in this tent,' continues Mrs Botha angrily. 'She had not time to collect her belongings, not even her baby linen, when the Tommies came.'

The sympathy which now brims in Emily's eyes clutches at Sarah's own heart: will this Englishwoman be strong enough to endure the mass suffering of the camp? It is not possible to bear the pain of two thousand women and children without somehow creating a distance between yourself and them.

'I have brought with me a truckload of equipment donated by the Distress Fund for the camp,' says Miss Hobhouse. Her merriment has vanished. 'Would you accept a mattress from us, Mrs Pienaar?'

The mother-to-be is overcome. She shakes her head while the tears roll down her dusty cheeks. As she leans over to squeeze the weeping woman's hand, Mrs Botha sees Sarah just outside the tent. 'Come in, Sister Palmer!' she calls. 'We have a visitor here from your country!'

Sarah hesitates. But Miss Hobhouse, who is scribbling notes in a pad, lifts her head when she hears the word *Palmer*. She stands up immediately, a brilliant smile of welcome replacing the sombre look that had settled on her features. The pale nurse who is swaying at the entrance of the tent is not what she expected, but her smile does not diminish. 'How wonderful! You must be Sophie Harris' friend. I have heard so much about you, how do you do, Sister Palmer.'

'And this is Miss Emily Hobhouse,' adds Mrs Botha, truncating the introduction she had planned.

Sarah feels her knees buckling. 'How do you do,' she whispers. And staggers forward.

Miss Hobhouse peers at her suspiciously as if alcohol might be the cause of this unsteadiness, then her gaze softens. She lays a gentle hand on Sarah's shoulder. 'But you are worn out,' she says with concern. 'Come and sit in our tent and have a cup of acorn coffee.'

The mothers in the tent are also concerned. They seat Sarah in their only chair. They remove her boots and prop her aching feet on a sewing machine. 'We love Nursie Palmer,' says Mevrouw Botha. 'She speaks our language. Boil again the kettle now up, Katjie, and find another tin cup for the nursie.'

Sarah is now seated among the women. She closes her eyes and enjoys the grateful throb of her resting body. She can hear Miss Hobhouse speaking with authority.

'This young lady must spend the day in bed.' Startled, Sarah opens her eyes. 'I don't need to tell you that you will wear yourself out if you don't give yourself a break from your work – and then you'll be no good to anyone at all,' continues Miss Hobhouse. 'I can tell you from my own experience that a day's rest is far more effective than any pill or tonic.'

'But the mothers . . .' Sarah protests faintly. She waves away the flies that settle on the rim of her cup.

'Don't you worry about us, my dear. You must look after yourself – haven't we always said so?' croon the mothers.

'And then perhaps you'll be strong enough tomorrow to do me a favour,' smiles Emily Hobhouse.

'A favour?'

'Could you take me to the camp hospital? I should be so interested to see how Britain has provided for the relief of her victims.' The sarcastic inflection goes unnoticed.

Sarah rises to her feet. 'We are already expecting you, Miss Hobhouse,' she says simply.

*   *   *

When she returns to her tent there is an unexpected letter:

Cape Town
17 January 1901

Dear Sarah,
   You will be surprised to hear from me after so long a silence – I have received your letters and longed to reply but felt not quite ready to do so – for reasons which will soon become clear.
   I may as well tell you immediately, but only on condition, dear Sarah, that you will tell no one else. The truth is I have married a Boer! This may be scarcely credible to you, knowing my original anti-Boer feelings, and I beg you to try to understand.
   You will remember that I planned to work in the convalescent hospital in Cape Town. Instead, I found myself sent to the Boer prisoner-of-war camp and hospital in Simonstown – where Mary Kingsley met her untimely death, in fact.
   Yes, you will be thinking 'but she was engaged to Theodore. They were planning to marry in Cape Town.' I'm sorry to tell you that poor Theodore contracted enteric from one of his patients, no doubt due to the filthy habits of the orderlies. I was at his side when he died. My heart was broken, yet within a few days – and I would confess this to no one else but you and I know you will not repeat it – I felt a certain relief that I was not to be Mrs Chappell. He was a fine man, full of fun, as you know, but in the end I have to confess that I felt very little physical attraction for him. The dear man didn't deserve to die.
   I threw myself into my work on the Boer wards with a new seriousness. I discovered among my patients a masculinity, a frankness, an earthy humour which was very refreshing to me, almost healing, you might say. In this environment I found myself to be a different person, more subdued yet appreciative of the friendliness of the men. I cannot describe to you the

horror of the Palace Barracks which made our Bloemfontein hospitals seem like paradise by comparison. Can you believe that? I set about introducing hygiene on a ferocious level; the orderlies had to scrub the walls as well as the floors and I was not happy till the wards in my charge positively glittered with cleanliness and smelt of soap and lavender.

Fransjohan, who is from the Transvaal, was recovering from a broken leg. A perfect gentleman, he never expressed any animosity towards the English in my presence. To begin with I hardly noticed him, as he could not move around and sat reading volumes of Dutch poetry, or writing it himself. One day he presented me with a set of verses which he had translated into English – and, Sarah, they were written in praise of *me*! You, who have always attracted the love and admiration of desirable men will never understand the pure wonder of this moment for me. I felt I had been floating about aimlessly all my life, drifting wherever the wind blew, and now, suddenly, I felt anchored in the love of a good man. I wish I could adequately describe to you the great wave of joy that crashed through my heart and washed away my silly past.

We were married last week by the camp chaplain, and the very next day Fransjohan was deported to Ceylon. For my husband is a *bittereinder* which means he will not take the oath of allegiance and admit defeat, therefore he must be banished. Yet he loves me, a woman who is as English as it is possible to be. How strange life is.

You can imagine how I am feeling. I ache with longing for him in every part of my being. But at least there is no war in Ceylon, and I do not fear he will be shot at by a Lee Enfield. I know this war cannot last too much longer; even he knows that. It is the moral principle of the thing that prevents him from surrendering.

I hope you are not too shocked by this revelation. I have not yet written to tell my parents what has happened. I do not quite have the courage. I often wonder what has happened about your 'Patch' – I remember advising you to give him up, but now I understand the nature of the attraction of opposites better.

By the way, I notice that little villa in Rondebosch you loved so much is up for sale – let me know if there is anything I can do to get it for you.

With love from your newly-Boer friend (I am learning to speak the language and love it.)

Louise van der Walt

Bloemfontein
25 January 1901

My dearest Louise,

What a wonderful surprise – and relief – to receive your letter – and your news. I am full of joy for you. Forgive me if I do not write at length now as my energies have drained away. You know I work in the Boer women's concentration camp here; it is not easy.

Today I met a wonderful woman who I think will help the situation here.

Of Patch there has been no word for months, not since his rosary arrived . . . do you remember?

And yes, how wonderful if you could get Frangipani Villa for me. Please let me know what I need to do.

We shall meet again after this war when I look forward to meeting your husband with you (whatever made you think I would be shocked at your marriage?)

Your affectionate friend
Sarah

Bloemfontein Concentration Camp, January

Patch approaches the bell tent to which he has been directed. His thigh wound is hurting even though it healed long ago; he is conscious of his slight limp. In the darkness, her tent glows yellow. So, she is not asleep.

He feels himself drawn to the candlelight as foolishly as any moth. That person he had seen yesterday was some sallow haggard other masquerading as Sarah the Madonna. But still, he must see her, if only to decide what to do next. He calls her name softly outside the drawn tent flap. No reply. He tries again. He can see the flickering candle flame through the canvas; the outline of a bed, and a few bits of furniture.

Something is taking over inside him, for his instinct is to turn away and have done with it. But he undoes the tent flap as easily as if it were his own, and enters.

The figure on the bed is so still that at first Patch thinks the tent is empty. He pauses when a slight movement of her hand indicates her presence. Woven between her fingers is his rosary. She looks as if she is dying.

Patch finds himself at the foot of her bed. The candlelight makes his shadow loom. She is not dying; she is exhausted. Although he has moved silently some disturbance of the air causes her to open her eyes. Her stare causes him to gasp and fall to his knees at her feet.

Now he is bending over her boots which she has not removed before collapsing on the bed. The leather is caked in mud, the soles worn nearly through. He pulls at the knotted lace, as if opening a gift. The lace undone, he begins to ease the boot off her foot. He cups the foot in his hands. With his thumbs he strokes the ankle. He is holding the most precious thing in his life, and rivers of awe run through his body. There is no longer any indecision for him.

He lowers his head and presses his lips against her stockinged foot. He inhales the lovely human smell of it. Through the odour of leather, mud and sweat he can detect that rare and wondrous perfume, the smell of soap. He hears her sigh.

As if in a trance he unlaces the other boot. It peels away so easily, as if it is the skin of some exotic fruit. He covers the fruit-foot in kisses, then clasps both feet to his breast. He can feel his heart pounding into the soles of her feet.

'Patch!' she murmurs.

His hands slide up beyond her ankles. The contours of her calves fit precisely into his palms. He fingers her knees, then the firmness of her thighs. Her feet are still on his chest: she is pushing against him, but not pushing him away.

A delicious fatigue overcomes him. He wants to stay on his knees holding this woman's legs for the rest of his life.

'Patch!' she says again. 'Come to me.'

Patch releases his grip. He stands up. The stab of pain in his thigh means nothing now. He moves over to the side of bed. Her white hand still dangles, the rosary beads laced between her fingers. Her eyes are closed.

He lifts her hand and unwinds the mother-of-pearl beads he sent her all those months ago. Her finger nails are not quite clean.

That music that sometimes plays on his heartstrings when he thinks of her begins to break through his body. The golden running arpeggios pour from his heart-harp into the tent and though he can't hear them he is held by their vibrations. Maybe one of the angels of heaven is hovering overhead invisibly with his great wings, playing his great harp, inaudibly. When David played his harp, the horses danced to it; he can understand that.

There is dirt between her fingers. With all the tenderness he did not know he had, he kneels down and begins to kiss her hands. Then he fits each finger into his mouth and sucks it gently. He smoothes out her hand on the grey army blanket. From his pocket he withdraws the turquoise bracelet. He slips it on to her wrist. She does not raise her head to look.

Now, disobeying the urgent instructions of his groin, he leans over her and gazes at her pale face. Her lips, once so full and rosy, are set in a straight line. He bends his head downwards and places his mouth on hers. How often has he dreamed of this moment. Yet she does not respond to his soft kiss; she is quite passive.

Patch slides his lips beyond her mouth and up to her cheekbone. Then he kisses each of her closed eyelids.

She stirs. She opens her eyes reluctantly and turns her gaze upon him. 'Am I dreaming? After all this time?' Her voice is faint.

He lifts her arm up to show her the bracelet. 'If this is still on your wrist tomorrow morning it will prove you are not dreaming.'

'It is lovely.' She stares at the bracelet. 'But where—?'

'I bought it for you.'

'Ah!' She sighs. Then takes a deep breath. He can feel that a question is coming, the answer to which might determine his future.

'Did you – did you – burn –?' She does not look at him.

'Sometimes,' he says gently. 'I didn't like doing it.' She winces. 'I had to obey orders, you know.' Well, there was no point going in1to why it was necessary now.

'So terrible.' She turns her head.

'I'll go now. You must sleep.' He is whispering into her ear. A tendril of her hair catches in his lips. 'War is a terrible thing, Sarah.'

She is beautiful. He adores her. He kisses her lightly on her mouth. 'I have so much to tell you.'

She must come with him to the Island.

*   *   *

318

'My dear Sister Palmer, you look so much better. There is colour in your cheeks. Your eyes sparkle. See what good your rest has done you.' But Miss Hobhouse is having trouble with her hat which is about to blow off in the fierce wind that has arisen. The tents billow and flap, the children scatter.

Sarah colours prettily. 'Good afternoon, Miss Hobhouse.' A blast of red sand intensifies her blush. Miss Hobhouse begins to cough, but soon regains her composure.

'I've heard such warm reports from Sophie – and the mothers – about the good work you're doing with the camp children. More than can be said for the refugee nurses, I'm afraid.'

'There is not much choice, ma'am. Nurses don't want to work in these camps.' Sarah cannot quite meet Miss Hobhouse's eye. She feels contained in a cocoon of joy. Her body is transformed, like a colourless bud that has blossomed, after many months, into a brilliant, tropical flower. She can feel Patch's presence, as if he were physically holding her at this moment. 'Shall we go into the ward and get out of the wind? This ward is for children who are failing to thrive. The other wards are for children and adults with infectious or contagious diseases.'

Unfortunately the two refugee nurses are having an argument across the children's beds just as Sarah and Emily enter the overheated ward. Carpets have been nailed across the floorboards to block out drafts and keep down the volume of noise, but the disagreement between the nurses gusts through the ward more raucously than the gale outside and makes the children shiver in their sheets. The issue is over whether mothers should be allowed to spend longer with their bed-ridden children than the hospital rules of one hour every second day allow. Nurse Nicholson, from Benoni on the Witwatersrand and undoubtedly the softer-hearted of the two, is in favour of the mothers being allowed to visit the ward at any time every day, while Nurse McKillen wants them banned altogether.

'These women just get in the way, Nurse Nicholson, you

must realise that. They waste our time trying to smuggle in their Boer remedies and so on. They would bring in dead animals to split open and place on their children's chests if they could. They listen to their children's complaints and try to tell us how to do our job. They're not satisfied that Britain has to look after the results of their filthy living habits, free of charge.'

'Free of charge,' echoes Nurse Nicholson who has a tendency to repeat the ends of other people's sentences. 'But it's understandable that the children are homesick and their mothers want their sons and daughters back home.'

'If they go back into the tents they'll die and then we'll get it in the ear,' says Nurse McKillen, tying an emaciated child back into her cot. 'At least they're properly looked after here. Stop that grizzling, Maria. Good afternoon, Sister Palmer.' She looks mistrustfully at Sarah's companion who is gazing round the ward, horror and compassion etched on her expressive face.

'Nurse Nicholson, Nurse McKillen, this is Miss Emily Hobhouse from England,' says Sarah. 'She is the lady I told you about.'

'Humph!' This grunt expresses Nurse McKillen's low opinion of lady amateurs from across the waters who think they know better than anyone.

Emily smiles frigidly. She is forcing back tears. It is a relief to bend over and undo the bundle she has brought with her. 'My Distress Fund has sent over some bits and pieces for sick children,' she murmurs.

'Well, I don't know—' begins Nurse MacKillen, but Emily interrupts in a piercing voice, suddenly resonant with the self assurance of the headmistress of a large girls' public school or the matron of a famous hospital.

'Sir Alfred Milner and Lord Kitchener' – she could be announcing their names at the school prizegiving – 'have given our project their blessing.' Nurse McKillen flushes and retreats, muttering under her breath to Nurse Nicholson who is trembling.

The nearest bed is occupied by a small boy whose head peers out above the grey sheets. Emily leans over the child and brushes away the flies. '*E wat is je naam?*' she enquires pleasantly.

'Piet,' whispers the boy. His skin is yellow as old writing paper.

'That's funny,' says Emily, digging into her bundle. 'I've got a Piet in here.' She pulls out a home-made golliwog which Nora had donated to the Distress Fund, golliwogs being all the rage after the success of the eponymous poems from America. 'Can I put him in the bed next to you? He's a friendly little chap.'

The boy's eyes widen. Somewhere in their blank depths a puzzled interest stirs. Slowly – what an effort it seems – he nods his head. Some of the pallid children in the beds nearby turn equally slow heads. Emily lifts his sheet, and gasps out loud. The boy's thin body is clad in rags. Quickly she tucks the golly beside him on the pillow. Then she turns to Sarah. 'Aren't the children supplied with bedclothes?' she asks in an undertone.

Sarah shakes her head. 'There just aren't enough to go round.' Her right hand is twisting the bracelet on her left wrist, beneath the long sleeve of her uniform.

'I have some little nightdresses in my bundle, but looking round this ward I suspect every child here needs one.' Emily sighs and groans simultaneously. 'To say nothing of every child in this camp. To say nothing of all the children in all the camps.'

'To say nothing of the native children in their camps,' adds Sarah. She has still to visit the central hospital to find out the progress of Namzuma's child. 'If you think this is bad, you should see the native camp. They don't even have a doctor. They've just been dumped there to look after themselves.'

'I must have a look at them too.' Miss Hobhouse sounds dismal.

'Let me introduce you to some of the children,' says Sarah. 'Lizzie over there writes letters to everyone in the ward. Most of the patients can't read but they love getting post from Lizzie. Ah, Poppie!' The young Boer girl in a very white apron curtsies shyly. 'This is Miss Hobhouse from England. Poppie is one of our trainee nurses, Miss Hobhouse. Her father is in the camp at Norval's Pont but she is staying in one of the tents here because they got separated during their – deportation. Poppie says she would like to become a nurse. She comes round the tents with me sometimes, and helps out in the ward.' She smiles affectionately at Poppie. 'She's also Lizzie's postman!'

'I will be going to Norval's Pont soon!' exclaims Emily. 'Poppie, perhaps you would like to come with me and we will find your father. Could you translate for me, Sister Palmer? I'm afraid my Dutch isn't up to that yet.'

Poppie lowers her eyes and performs a half-curtsey. 'I am sorry, Sister, but I love my work here, and I think the children need me.'

Dr Pern, who has just entered the ward, calls out, 'We can't do without Poppie!'

Miss Hobhouse looks at the young woman with approval. 'You are right, my dear. They cannot do without you. How do you do, Doctor.'

'This is Dr Pern – Miss Hobhouse.' Sarah wants to say 'the *good* doctor' but checks herself in time. 'She has come from England to help the children and their mothers.'

'Just what we need.' Dr Pern smiles a welcome, then feels the forehead of a small boy.

As the two women move round the ward, greeting the ill and possibly dying children, Emily's heart sinks. Can the word *distress* explain what she sees before her? The children look as if they belong to some other species: skinned monkeys, or albino frogs. Their mouths are slits. Their black-ringed eyes glowing in ashen faces remind her of the adorable meerkat she had met in Cape Town. This is too painful; too distressing. How is it possible to separate oneself from the suffering of children? But no doubt Miss Nightingale had felt the same while walking round the unhygienic wards of Scutari and look what she had achieved, single-handed almost. 'There *is* something you can do,' she urges herself as she cheerfully tucks dollies into little girls' beds, and rattles bags of glass marbles at the boys. But where to start? The ghost of Miss Nightingale (who has not yet died but has retired from public life for so long that most people assume she has) whispers: *soap and clean water. Nothing can change until people can clean themselves.*

'And this is Lizzie!' exclaims Sarah. A waif-like child with a halo of bright hair gazes with fascination at Emily's clothes: her straw hat with its English-country-garden accessories; the leg-of-mutton sleeves of her cream blouse; her neat waist; the elegantly striped skirt. The child smiles. 'Auntie is pretty,' she croaks.

'And so are you, Lizzie!' cries Emily in delight. 'And I hear you are a great letter-writer.'

'Shall I perhaps write Auntie a letter too?' enquires the child hopefully.

'I'd like nothing better,' replies Emily. Her cloud of anxiety begins to lift. 'And I promise you I'll write back to you because I'm a great letter-writer too.'

Nurse McKillen scurries over. 'It is our policy not to excite the children,' she says in hostile tones. 'I must ask you to leave now that you've seen our ward. There are other wards for you to visit.'

'Thank you so much for letting me see your little patients,' says Emily in her headmistress voice, smiling and waving to the children who are watching her closely. 'I can see that you care for them deeply.' She gives a dismissive nod.

Outside the ward, the air seems fresh by comparison. Miss Hobhouse inhales, holds her breath, sighs profoundly. Then bites her lip. 'It is a terrible thing to see children lying around in that collapsed state,' she whispers. 'They are just exactly like faded flowers thrown away.' For a moment it seems she may weep, but she looks fiercely at Sarah instead. 'And I do so hate to stand and look on at such misery and be unable to do something.'

'Oh, please don't say that, Miss Hobhouse!' cries Sarah. 'Please don't lose heart, we depend on you to stop the misery.' She gazes at her with admiring eyes.

Emily is clearly embarrassed by the young woman's vehemence. 'My dear, do not expect too much of me. I am ashamed of the inadequacy of my truckload. All I can give them now are comforts and extras. I had absolutely no idea when gathering gifts that a truckload of *soap* was what was really needed. Absolute basics.' She pauses. Sarah can see from the narrowing of her eyes and twitching of her mouth that Miss Hobhouse's thoughts are racing. Finally she says in a low, rapid voice, 'I need to awaken the conscience of England. That will do more for the mothers and their children than anything I can get out of my truckload.' She frowns at the lines of bell tents fanning out from the hospital. 'I have contacts in high places, Sister Palmer. My aunt has the ear of the prime minister. That counts for a lot if you want to get things done.'

'You don't intend to return to England already?' asks Sarah in alarm.

'I plan to gather facts, Sister Palmer, and when I have an armoury of information – and photographs to back it up – I shall return to Britain and wage my own war. But in the meantime I will do my best to enlighten the idiotic men who run this camp; get them to boil the water for a start. And impress upon them the necessity for soap. Really, you'd think they'd understand these absolute basics of hygiene.'

They walk along the cluttered lanes running between the tents. 'Extraordinary what these women have brought with them,' muses Emily. 'Look over there.' A marble bust of Shakespeare lies in the mud, gazing thoughtfully at a hairbrush, two umbrellas, a candlestick, a sewing machine, and a child's tin drum. She smiles. 'Do you not find the Boer women here among the most charming you have ever met? How do they manage to exude such warmth and hospitality in the most iniquitously deprived of circumstances? And so brave. The magnitude of their suffering has lifted them beyond tears.' She shakes her head at a three-legged cooking pot in which is stored a variety of crockery and cutlery, some of it very fine. 'I am indeed privileged to be among them. And it is women like you, Sister Palmer, who will help to redeem the besmirched name of England.'

Sarah feels a stir of pride. She will do whatever Miss Hobhouse asks of her.

Dear Aunt Mary,

. . . it is such wholesale cruelty and one of which England must be ashamed. It can never be wiped out of the memories of people here. And it presses hardest on the children. They droop in the terrible heat and with the insufficient, unsuitable food.

Will you try somehow to make the British Public understand the position and force it to ask itself what is going to be done with these people? There must be already 50,000 of them and I should not wonder if there were more. Some few have means, but most are ruined and have not a present penny. In one of two ways the British Public must support them; either through the Military or else through voluntary charity . . . Dear Aunt Mary, couldn't you write such a letter about it to *The Times* as should make people listen and believe and understand – which would touch their conscience? Is England afraid of losing her prestige? . . . To keep these camps going is *murder to the children*.

Today is Sunday and all the morning your unregenerate and unsabbatarian niece has been toiling and moiling over the bales of clothes, unpacking and sorting and putting up bundles. We were so glad of such *odd* things . . . such as a little boy's braces. I found some baby linen for Mrs Pienaar. We have much typhoid and are dreading a great outbreak, so I am directing my energies to getting water from the Modder River boiled. As well swallow typhoid germs whole as drink that water. Yet they cannot boil it all; for first, fuel is very scarce. That which is supplied weekly would not cook a meal a day, and they have to search the bare kopjes for a supply. Secondly, they have no utensil to hold the water when it is boiled.

30 January

Captain Hume, Dr Pern and I sat in council yesterday, and the doctor supported me loyally. I suggested a big railway boiler to boil every drop of water before it is served out. This will economise fuel and be cheaper in the end.

Do not worry about me at all. I am perfectly well in body, only desperate in mind, and I understand now how wise it was in Bible days to send people out two by two when there was something difficult to be done . . .

Your loving niece,
Emily

Cape Town, 10 February 1901

Siyabulele Tamara looks out over Table Bay and yawns. The overspill of ships from Cape Town docks bob peacefully in the long purple shadow of the mountains, for the sun is just rising from behind the mountains, a signal to Siyabulele that his night shift is nearly over. Further along the lawns of Green Point, next to the docks, reveille has not yet sounded among the military tents that line the beachfront. It is hard to believe there is a cruel war waging in the north, so calm is the city in the early morning. Siyabulele takes a final swig of the home-brewed beer that helped him get through the long night; puffs on the long pipe he has brought with him from the Eastern Cape; then frowns. From behind the great stacks of tarpaulin-covered military supplies which he guards every night, he can hear a pattering sound, as if rain has begun to fall. A glance upward reveals a clear dawn sky with a crescent of white moon above the mountain. The pattering sound quickly grows into the swift rush of river which now, to the terror of the drowsy night watchman, seethes before his eyes, streaming over the common towards the houses on the other side of the road.

Siyabulele drops his mug of beer. Sweat breaks out over his entire body in ice-cold bubbles. For the river does not foam and splash with water; this river leaps and skips with creatures that Siyabulele knows only too well from his home in the District: rats. In their panic-stricken thousands they race from the nearby South Arm of the docks where forage for the military horses is unloaded and stored.

'*Aikona!*' screams Siyabulele. He stands up and finds his legs are shaking so much that he has to sit down again. There is only one thing to do, something he has in fact always longed to do. Siyabulele lifts his rifle, a Lee Enfield, the same model that is issued to the soldiers of the British Army, and fires a shot into the air. The startled rats slide into a thousand rivulets. At the same time Captain Philips from the Green Point camp comes running towards the night watchman in his embroidered silk dressing gown, shaving foam still on his jaw.

Though Siyabulele knows very little English he does know the word *rats*. Has not the chief sanitary inspector paid regular visits to Horstley Street in the District, where the African labourers live in shifts of twenty to a room? And has he not examined the men for illnesses on several occasions? Luthando Gobelo, who speaks good English, explained to the bewildered men that the Sanitary and Health Committee of the Cape Town City Council felt that the kaffirs' overcrowded and unhygienic living conditions could be a breeding ground for disease. The inspector had been quite astonished at the number of rats that tumbled through the houses and across the streets and had said to Luthando, who seemed to have become the spokesperson for the Horstley Street occupants, that only someone called a Pied Piper could get rid of such vast numbers of *rattus rattus*. Strangely, the inspector found that there were fewer cases of infectious disease among the kaffirs than among the same number of other racial groups in the District.

Now Captain Philips looks at the khaki-clad young guard, shivering and gibbering in kaffir language, and smells the sweet fumes of kaffir beer. In spite of the fact that the word *rets* featured prominently in Siyabulele's outburst, Captain Philips has him arrested immediately, for of the *rattus rattus* there is not a sign, and we can't have blacks firing off rifles just for the fun of it.

The same day Johan Witbooi finds a swelling in his left armpit. As he lists the huge stocks of grain and forage conveyed to the South Arm of the docks from Argentinian ships, he finds his hand has developed a tendency to shake. Nevertheless, he continues filling in his columns: a hundred tons of hay to various parts of the Orange River Colony where tens of thousands of military horses are dropping dead of starvation; twenty tons of corn to the Transvaal for the same reason. Suddenly he feels overcome by nausea and is obliged to rush to the toilet area at the back of the army ordnance stores. While vomiting horribly into the portable lavatory, he wonders whether he might have caught something unpleasant when, a few days ago, after an appalling smell had refused to go away, the floors of the storage shed next to his office had been lifted to reveal hundreds of dead or dying rats under the floorboards. Many of the creatures had been so dazed that you could have caught them with your hand (had you been so unwise). Some of them staggered out among the horrified troopers as if they were tame family pets. And at least two hundred dead rats were discovered when the haystack in the next shed was taken down. The anxiety among the authorities was not so much over the huge number of rats but the fact that most of them were dead or dying. And all of them were covered in giant fleas that leapt gladly up the legs and arms of their human saviours, for a dead rodent is a useless host to a flea infected with a bubonic bacillus.

By the time Johan returns to his desk the ache in his back is excruciating and his head is gripped in a vice of pain. Lieutenant Jones, who had spent time in Calcutta, diagnoses the young clerk's condition immediately.

By 15 February, foreign powers are notified that Cape Town is a port infected with bubonic plague. Johan dies horribly in the plague camp hospital hastily erected near Maitland; Siyabulele gains both an acquittal and an apology on the same day; Cape Town, which has escaped the horrific epidemics of the war up north, is thrown into a state of panic. Extreme measures must be taken immediately, starting with the rat-infested District.

The City Health Department moves swiftly. The Witbooi family – including a three-month-old baby with blazing green eyes – are evacuated to the plague camp in Maitland, where they are isolated, inoculated and disinfected. The house is cleaned, fumigated and whitewashed by a team of masked men largely composed of foreigners and convicts. Even so, it is too late for Fancy, whose groin and armpits began to swell the day after her brother died. As she is swept off to the isolation hospital, she cries out to her mother: 'Tell Patch he must look after his son!' Her red skirt drips over the edge of the stretcher; even in her dying throes her hair shines blue-black and her eyes are fierce. Sunflowers and lilies lie in her arms, sent in great bunches by the Parade flower-sellers, and are thrown with her body into the mass grave for victims of the plague a few days later.

In the meantime, doors all over the District are sealed up for fumigation and daubed with yellow. A leaflet, accusing in tone, is distributed by a self-righteous Health Department: *For cleanly people in cleanly homes which are free from rats there is practically no danger of getting the plague ... DIRT, OVERCROWDING, WANT OF VENTILATION AND THE PRESENCE OF RATS encourage the presence of Plague in any home or locality. Old, dilapidated, dark, un-sanitary, and overcrowded houses infected by rats are parti-cularly dangerous as filth associated with darkness and dampness is peculiarly favourable to the growth of the mi-crobe. Rats and house vermin often carry the infection from dirty into clean houses.*

Mrs Witbooi, even in her grief, is outraged. Didn't she scrub, clean and polish her house from morn till night? Didn't the plague start in the docks through careless administration? Isn't the local council to blame for not getting rid of the rats? She holds Fancy's gurgling son in her arms and rocks him angrily.

It is time the father of the motherless baby is told the news.

Bird Cage, February 1901

There is a stir among the inmates of the Bird Cage: a new undesirable is arriving. She is being shepherded by two Tommies across the barren land that lies between the penal area and the main concentration camp. Thin and pale, she has nevertheless a regal air about her which even the hardened troopers feel; one of them extends his hand to help when she stumbles, the other is carrying her bag of belongings.

Patch looks up from the cleansed sanitary buckets he is inspecting. His thoughts are on the Island, his uncle, his mother, Sarah. In his mind they are all sitting round a table in his mother's garden, surrounded by hollyhocks and roses and contentedly humming bees. The lawn beneath their feet is green and smooth. Sarah is pouring out the tea. 'Three sugars, please,' says his mother in her husky Irish voice. Bill and Cartwright drift about diaphanously, unburnt by the fires of hell.

'Private Donnelly!' calls out one of the whores. 'She is returning!'

Now that she is closer to the barbed wire, the approaching woman is suddenly recognisable. *Mrs Roos!* The women clap their hands and wave. Her name rustles among them; her children cry out in delight.

Patch too is glad. He has seen so much death and suffering that he has hardened himself against her inevitable terminal decline, so he welcomes her unexpected reappearance. He grins with pleasure as he unlocks the bird cage gate. The lopsided smile has long ago disappeared.

Mrs Roos sails in, her sharp eyes searching for her children among the gathered inmates. They run up to her, shouting with joy as she embraces them one by one.

'We have already lit a fire for coffee!' exclaims the mother who has looked after these children. 'Though we use the last of our firewood, we cannot celebrate your return without coffee.'

There is laughter all round, even though everyone knows that there is precious little coffee in the beverage they will drink. Even Patch laughs.

Mrs Roos looks at him. 'You are a happier man,' she pronounces. 'It must be the company you keep here.'

Now he understands she is teasing him, and pulls an agonised face at the whores. In fact, these women have been doing him a favour recently. Like every other Tommy, Patch's uniform is crawling with lice. A million nits are embedded in the seams of his jacket and trousers. The whores, who originally laughed at his agonised scratching, have taken pity on him and boil his trousers once a week. This does not entirely eliminate the problem but keeps it under control, for which Patch is grateful.

He has a sudden longing to tell Mrs Roos about Sarah, and the unexpected problem he is encountering with her. He has managed to waylay her on her tent rounds so as to discuss their return to Cape Town, but to his irritation she tells him about the wonderful Englishwoman who is transforming the camp with her energy and efficiency – preparations are being made to boil the camp water; a consignment of soap has been ordered; fifty milch cows have arrived. Although she looks at him with delight and clearly enjoys his physical presence, Patch can tell her mind is often focused on the measles epidemic or the sewing-machine project rather than his own personal yearnings and needs.

Now he eavesdrops on Mrs Roos and her friends. She is telling them of her stay in the hospital; how a black child had been admitted with dysentery and under-nourishment, but is now miraculously thriving; how the doctors discuss with the

nurses whether the plague in Cape Town will reach Bloemfontein, and how the kaffirs in that unhealthy place called the
District would soon be moved out forcibly because it was
thought that the plague had started in their squalid rooms.

Patch's ears prick up at this, and a nameless anxiety flows
through his veins. It is nameless because he does not dare to
say the names of those concerned to himself. He diverts his
dread by frenziedly digging a deep refuse hole at the back of
the bird cage, as the kaffir workers look on in surprise

Bloemfontein Concentration Camp, February

On her way to the Thursday afternoon tent committee meeting, Sarah passes the original 'hands-uppers' camp. She does not usually walk this way but the meeting is to be held this week in Mrs Malan's tent, which is close to the surrendered burghers' slightly superior accommodation. Just lately she has been feeling strangely exhilarated. Her exhaustion has vanished; she feels the blood beating pleasantly in her cheeks as she speeds from one task to the next. Suddenly, her life is presenting her with two very clear directions: Miss Hobhouse beckoning her to follow down the humanitarian road, Patch taking it for granted she will come with him down the tempting road of physical love. If only she could choose both; the dual attractions revolve in her head as she hurries along.

'Sister Palmer!'

Her name floats towards her from the direction of the hands-uppers' camp. A woman is smiling at her from behind the barbed wire fence which separates the two camps. 'You do not recognise me, I think?'

Sarah approaches the fence, frowning a little. She has nothing against these people herself but has heard them maligned so often by the mothers that she tends to think of them as traitors and cowards. As she focuses on the woman's face, enclosed in the great frills of her sunbonnet, the gentle face of the kitchen maid and her milk jug in the old Amsterdam portrait stares out. She closes her eyes and remembers. 'Mrs Theron! I am so sorry to see you here.'

'It is for our protection,' says the woman in her sweetly reasonable voice. 'At least our farm has not been destroyed. A troop of Tommies has been billeted there, we are told.'

'But your lovely farm!' cries Sarah. She knows what Tommies do to their temporary barracks.

'Everyone's lovely farms are paying the price for this war of the farmers,' says Mrs Theron quietly. 'But your skin, Sister Palmer, how much better it is looking. Have you been using my honey emollient?'

'Oh, I have, I have, and it is quite wonderful. The dryness has all gone.'

'Sister Palmer, may I ask you something?'

'Of course.'

'I know the children in the bitter-enders' camp suffer from a deficient diet. Things are a little better on this side of the fence. I even have a small vegetable patch outside my tent. It would make me very happy if I could supply some needy children with the carrots and sweet potatoes that are so much a part of our Boer diet.'

'That would be very helpful, Mrs Theron. I can think at once of which children would most benefit. Their mothers would be grateful.'

Mrs Theron shakes her head vigorously. 'No, they would not, Sister Palmer. You must not tell them the vegetables come from me. They think we are spies and informers over here. They hate us for signing the oath of neutrality and trying to stop this terrible war by any means. There is no chance at all that the Boer commandos can outdo the British army, yet they persist in believing that the Lord will save His people.' She has grown agitated. 'On no account must you tell them the vegetables have come from me.'

'But surely . . . if it is for the good of their children?'

'You know what these bitter-end women are like. The bitter, bitter end means even their children will be sacrificed rather than give in to the enemy. And they hate us hands-uppers more than the British!'

'Mrs Theron, I have a meeting to attend now. But tomorrow I will come and fetch the vegetables.' Smiling politely, Sarah hurries off, and after a minute turns round to wave at the woman who clings to the fence with white-knuckled fingers. No longer is she the placid milk maid: her face is now swollen and distorted with shadows, for all the world like a Rembrandt self-portrait in old age.

Today the tent committee is discussing how to provide new clean clothes for the camp inmates most desperately in need. The seven mothers who make up the committee have priori-tised: sick children first, exhausted mothers next; then the old bewildered grandparents whose only clothes are so caked with mud and sweat that they could stand upright without the owners inside them.

Those mothers who own them have brought their sewing machines to the tent, for Miss Hobhouse has bought fabric, scissors and thread in the Bloemfontein shops with the re-mains of the funds from England. As Sarah draws near the meeting place, still shaken by her encounter at the fence, the whirring of these machines, accompanied by womanly chat-ter, spreads out from the tent. She pauses a moment to savour these homely sounds. Emily's voice erupts into laughter now and then as she speaks a humorous mixture of Dutch and English; the machines hum busily, as if sewing together the tattered fragments of camp life and repairing the rifts that have fractured lives. She enters the tent; the women greet her warmly. She has brought a list of the neediest children with her – if only she could mention Mrs Theron's offer. What would Miss Hobhouse think of this? Surely she would accept nutritious food for the children even if offered by the devil himself?

But Emily is looking distressed. 'Scissors!' she exclaims as Sarah approaches her with the list. 'There is an utter famine of cotton and scissors. I have been to every shop in Bloemfontein and found precisely one pair of scissors and a few reels of thread. Our sewing programme can only go so far and no further if we cannot cut the fabric. Colonel Goold-Adams says he'll raise the money to pay for this project and we are still waiting. Oh, Sarah, I sometimes think cleaning the Augean stables was an easier task than cleaning up this camp.'

Something has happened to Emily's face. She now has the dark rings of exhaustion that encircle the eyes of everyone in the camp. Her complexion is no longer a confection of peaches and cream, but has roughened into a reddish-gold that may darken into a duskiness dreaded by most white women. Sarah considers offering her the honey emollient. Miss Hobhouse has worn delightful sunhats and carried a parasol, but nevertheless the sun has caught her hair as well and bleached it into tawny stripes so that as she sits, erect and energetic in the stifling tent, she radiates colour: even her grey eyes have turned blue in their new setting of bronzed facial skin. The women gaze at her adoringly. So what if there is only one pair of scissors: this Englishwoman has cut through more than cotton fabric – she has miraculously snipped through the bureaucratic red tape which has prevented improvement in camp conditions, and for this they will always love her.

At the end of the meeting, as Miss Hobhouse packs her notebooks and needles into her basket, she lifts her head and says in a rush, 'There is one other matter I'd like to mention.'

'And what is that, Miss Hobhouse?' enquires Mrs Botha.

Emily blinks rapidly. 'The virtue of the camp, Mrs Botha. There are so many impressionable girls here in these tents, innocent daughters who do not have the firmness of their fathers to instil discipline. The camp seethes with Tommies of the most uncultivated kind, many of whom smell – *stink* – of alcohol. Perhaps the members of this committee could report any suspicion of immoral behaviour.'

Sarah hopes her flaming cheeks are not noticed by the committee members. Strangely, Miss Hobhouse's words have the opposite effect to which they were intended upon her body: a wave of sudden desire floods between her legs and up into her belly and breasts. However, Mrs Botha is clearly not having the same reaction as she replies sombrely, 'And we still have none of our Dutch Reformed ministers, who could take the place of the fathers who are on commando and advise the young girls of their morals.'

Afterwards, while walking away from the meeting and back towards the central hospital, Sarah finds Miss Hobhouse's remarks on camp morality beating guiltily in her head. For the first time she begins to wonder about the sinfulness of her desire for Patch. Where *exactly* is the line between sin and purity drawn? Though her spiritual advisor from the Church of the Holy Rosary in Bloemfontein has made it clear to her that impure thoughts and sexual intercourse before marriage would deny you heavenly access (should you be so unfortunate as to die before confessing these sins), the boundaries of these sinful activities are blurred. Of course, actual penetration is out of the question, but kissing? She is too embarrassed to ask her spiritual adviser, a ruddy-faced Irishman suffering from emphysema, whether the entrance of the lover's tongue into one's mouth – being a form of penetration – means instant damnation, or whether it might fall into the venial sin category. There is other fondling too, involving sacred parts of the body . . . surely this is permitted if you plan to marry the lover?

She steps over a pile of frying pans, bread tins, coffee pots, butter dishes and a framed portrait of President Kruger. Mrs Pienaar calls a greeting from her new mattress where she lies, surrounded by neighbours, waiting for the contractions. Two small girls in enormous kappies stagger past carrying a drum of water which splashes a dark trail over the dust behind him. They sing out good wishes for the afternoon.

But does she plan to marry Patch? To go to the Island and meet his mother? Or will she continue to be swept by the flow of Emily's dedication and willpower? Miss Hobhouse, by all accounts, had once been infatuated by an inappropriate man. Would she have abandoned her humanitarian principles for love of this man? Yet some women could have the love of a man together with their charitable work: look at Lord and Lady Hobhouse, Beatrice and Sidney Webb, Leonard and Kate Courtney; who together, man and wife, had achieved so much for the improvement of mankind. But Patch is not exactly a Sidney Webb or a Leonard Courtney; he shows no interest in high moral causes, yet she is in love with him: it is all too complex for her to try to sort out at this moment.

By now she has reached the enteric ward. Mrs Mopeli's niece will be ready to return to her mother: she must try to arrange for bearers to take her to the black camp. As she moves towards her little cot, she sees Poppie moistening the lips of a feverish woman patient; a week ago the young Boer girl had been moved to this ward to gain further nursing experience. Poppie has privately complained to Sarah about the careless way the ward is run; enteric sheets are not boiled, but washed in cold water with other sheets and clothes; blankets are filthy; the pails from the enteric latrines are not disinfected; milk for the whole camp is often left on the window sills of the ward.

'The little kaffir girl has completely recovered – isn't that wonderful!' she cries out. 'You brought her just in time, Nurse Palmer.' She stands up, pats the hand of the feverish woman, and begins to walk across to Sarah. Halfway across the ward she gasps, grips at her belly, and doubles over.

'Poppie, what's the matter?' Sarah runs towards her in alarm.

The girl straightens up and smiles bravely. For the first time since she started this work, she looks tired; older, sallow. 'Agh, it's something I ate last night.' She lowers her voice. 'They say there is ground-up glass in our sugar rations and barbs in our bully beef. Some of it has got into my stomach, I think.'

'There are rumours about everything,' says Sarah gravely. 'But I would like you to see Dr Pern to check on the state of your health generally.' She turns to the little cot. 'Oh look! She's laughing. What an adorable child!'

Dear Aunt Mary,

I just want to say while it is on my mind that the blouses
sent from England and supposed to be full-grown are only
useful here for girls of 12 to 14 or so. Much too small for the
well-developed Boer maiden who really is a fine creature.
Could any out-out sizes be procured? And for camp life, dark
colours are best; it's hard to keep clean and soap is a luxury –
water not super-abundant. You would realise the scarcity and
poverty a little had you seen me doling out needles and pins by
twos and threes and dividing cotton and bits of rag for
patching. A few combs I brought up from Cape Town were
caught at with joy.

With regard to the vexed question of differing nationalities,
is it generally known and realised at home that there are many
large Native (coloured) camps dotted about? In my opinion
these need looking into badly. I understand the death rate in
the one in Bloemfontein to be very high and so also in other
places – but I cannot possibly pay any attention to them
myself. Why shouldn't the Society of Friends send someone if
this War goes on, or the Aborigines Protection? In my camps
there are many kinds of nationalities . . . Often there are little
Kaffir servant girls whipped up and carried off with their
mistresses, and those too need clothing. Decency demands

341

that all should be provided and though it is the business of the Government, which has either burnt or left behind their own clothes, yet that Government is so slow and uncertain and so poverty-stricken that it is on the cards the camp will be disbanded before it provides material!

Though the camps are called refugee, there are in reality very few of these people . . . It is easy to tell them because they are put in the best marquees and have time given to them to bring furniture and clothes. Very few, if any, of them, are in want.

As ever,
   Your loving niece,
    Emily

Bloemfontein Concentration Camp, 17 March 1901

On St Patrick's Day, the letter Patch has been dreading arrives. He recognises Mrs Witbooi's handwriting at once; solid, round, like her own comfortable shape. *Fancy. Johan.* Each name is a blow aimed at his head. Mrs Witbooi offers no consolation. Her grief and anger are embedded in her silence. At the end of this death knell a short sentence ripples accusingly: *Your son is waiting for you.*

'All right, Private Donnelly?' enquires Mrs Roos. It appears he has been sitting on the anthill oven for some time, staring into space. His mouth tries to articulate a reply but succeeds only in opening and shutting like a gasping fish.

'Bad news?'

'I have lost . . .' A swelling has mushroomed in his throat; his voice comes out high-pitched, squeaky, like a child's. He dare not speak further.

She looks at the envelope he is holding and sees it comes from Cape Town. 'You have lost someone dear to you in the plague?' she suggests gently.

He nods, bewildered.

'You have told me –' She hesitates. 'About your friend here. You must go to her. Tonight. And Private Donelly,' she adds as he stands up, 'I'm very happy that she is wearing my beautiful bracelet.' Her eyes gleam with ironic amusement but her smile is friendly. Patch feels a wave of hot shame. He has no reply.

* * *

Patch is walking among the rows of tents filled with sleeping women and children, grandparents and kaffir maids; tripping over stacks of plates, bookshelves, buckets of water, a mincing machine, a copper kettle, and a small portable organ that wheezes out a reproving chord as his boot crashes on to its ivory keys. He slips on something soft that gives off a foul smell; later he sees a dark shape nosing through the detritus – could it be a hyena? A baboon? One of the camp guards shot a lioness the other night.

He is walking towards her tent. It lies just beyond the camp, a little apart from the other tents. He has not visited her there since the first time; such visits are forbidden and could result in expulsion. Once again he feels drawn to the glowing canvas, careless of any punishment.

He can hear the slapping sound of water in her tent. The smell of warmly scented soap floats into the unappetising night air.

'Sarah?' The water stops splashing.

'I'm bathing.' Her voice drifts out with the soapy aroma.

'I'll wait here.'

The water splashes, then subsides. 'No, come in.'

'But . . .' He glances around. It is past ten o'clock and the other tents are in darkness. He swiftly unties the strings of the tent entrance and passes inside. Where he cries out in delight. She is seated in a little sail-cloth bath, her knees nearly touching her chin, blocking his view of her breasts. The light from the lamp gleams on her wet skin. He moves over to the bath.

She looks up at him, smiling. Her hair, normally so neat and hidden, is piled up carelessly, with many fronds hanging loose and wet. She is the cleanest, sweetest-smelling creature he has seen for months. She stops smiling and says, 'What's wrong, Patch?'

He licks his lips and tries to remember how to form a sentence. 'Friend. Dead. Plague.' What a struggle to release these words.

'Oh, Patch!' She stands up briefly in the flimsy bath. Her

body is exactly as he has imagined it would be, right down to the dark bush between her legs. The Virgin Mary, unclothed at last. 'Is it Johan?' She knows all about Johan and Cartwright, the Trusty Trio.

He nods, struck dumb by the beauty of her wet body.

'Can you pass me my towel?'

It is almost a relief to see her limbs and breasts disappear as she wraps herself in the worn cloth. 'This is a terrible war.' She rubs her body briefly. 'I am so sorry.'

To his horror, a tear has escaped his left eye. It runs down his left cheek like a bead of blood.

'Come here,' she commands.

Then her smooth arms are round him and her perfume is intoxicating him and making his knees weak. She rocks him and hums something tender. He bends his head to reach her lips.

He finds her little breasts under the towel as he kisses her. Oh, the silkiness of them, the roundness. And the soft pointy nipples becoming firm beneath his fingers His tears run down her body as he sobs out his sorrow into the warmth of her embrace.

Bloemfontein Concentration Camp,
April 1901

On her way to the tent committee meeting, shortly after returning from a visit to the concentration camps of Kimberley and Mafeking, Miss Hobhouse has an accident. The lanes between the tents seethe with khaki; normally she does not deign to cast a glance in their direction. For their part, the troopers too ignore the women and children, other than to check no trouble is brewing or to shout at an insolent Boer child. Miss Hobhouse's head is full of mattresses at the time: the tent committee has agreed to employ camp women to make at least one mattress per tent, once the superintendent has provided the forage for stuffing as well as the fabric. Emily, who has a good head for figures, has calculated the cost for nearly two thousand tents, but weeks have gone by, and still nothing has arrived. How frustrating! Still, if De Wet *will* go on blowing up the railways . . . Now she will have to inform the committee that the mattress project cannot go ahead for the moment, though a number of camp women are expecting to begin sewing next week; they are also expecting to be paid for doing so. At the same time the number of burnt-out women and children has doubled during her visits to other camps so that means her calculations are out-of-date. If a spasm of despair overtakes her as she walks between the tents, she shakes it off with a brisk twitch of the shoulders and vigorous inhalation of breath deep into her diaphragm, as her doctor had suggested.

The night before, stair-rods of rain had lashed down, which

means that once again the earth is sodden both inside and outside the tents. Emily has to watch her feet as she picks her way among the tin buckets and trunks; the Shakespeare bust; the mounted antelope horns; the piles of pots and pans, lifting her skirts to avoid the slippery mud. Every now and then a child cries out *Hello, Auntie!* and Emily smiles and lifts a hand to wave; or a woman runs up to her with some tale of misfortune, which Emily respectfully records in the notebook she carries round with her; so it isn't altogether surprising that in between waving and scribbling she is sometimes unable to watch her feet – which suddenly slither down the sloping lane to crack against a three-legged iron pot, much favoured as a cooking utensil by Boer and Black alike, though now home to a stuffed Sacred Ibis and a portrait of President Kruger. Although not given to screaming, a surprised cry escapes her lips, and she finds herself toppling over on to a passing Tommy with such force that they both tumble into the mud, one on top of the other, to the high embarrassment of both of them.

The young trooper is on his feet first – he is not, after all, encumbered by voluminous skirts – and naturally holds out his hand to help the lady up.

'I'm so sorry!' she finds herself gasping, for the collision is indeed her fault. 'It's this wretched mud! It's lethal!'

She then lifts her head to meet the apologetic eyes of the trooper – and, in a moment is back in her Mexican hacienda, pouring tea for her fiancé, a guitar strumming in the servants' quarters, the smell of cinnamon in the air. There sits Mr Jackson, grinning sardonically at her, the same emerald eyes flickering with treachery. How is it possible for two men to have the same impossibly green orbs, the same lean body supple as syrup, the suggestive slipperiness of the limbs – though this trooper has no moustache, unlike her fiancé whose heavy handlebar of hair outlined the self-deprecating downward pull of the mouth. For a moment her head swims with delirium; then she shrinks from the young man who has knocked her into the mud, rapidly withdrawing her outstretched hand as well as her unhappy gaze.

Now the mothers and children are flocking out of their tents to attend to their muddy angel, producing boxes of illegal Boer remedies to apply to her bruised shins.

Miss Hobhouse declines offers of sweet tea and acacia poultices. She thanks the mothers for their assistance, shoos them back into their tents, and continues on her way, light-headed with shock. Now, as she treads carefully along the muddy paths, Emily sees once again the fashionable Plaza del Domingo; once again she climbs the flight of graciously curved marble stairs and moves among the gigantic pillars that hold up a ceiling adorned with vast panoramas of Spanish victories . . . But where is Mr Jackson? Why isn't she leaning proudly on his arm, fanning herself in the delicious heat? Now Emily feels that aching loss which could not be consoled by the discreet fountains and tumbling foliage of the hacienda-style ranch she had bought as her home, where Mr Jackson would manage the cattle and horses for the rodeo . . . the ache of longing, far worse than any physical pain she has experienced; an ache that turns to despair, and results in telegrams to Virginia and a suggestion to meet in Chicago to become man and wife; her family's shocked silence; the wedding postponed. Emily finds she has walked right past Mrs Botha's tent as these frantic thoughts surface, released from the cage of her memory, but look! Once again paradise seems to shimmer above the snow-capped peaks and dizzying cataracts of the mountains; and in the ranch bedroom wardrobe now hangs a foaming white frock: just look at the beadwork on the bodice; smell the perfume of heady jasmine; look at the sunset slithering like blood down the white slopes of the mountains where human sacrifices were once performed by a circle of Aztec priests . . .

And as she abandons herself to her grief, the beloved faces of her brother, her aunt, her uncle, loom from behind the mountains of the Aztecs; they are watching her with hard eyes, they have made a decision – and in a sudden bolt of illumination she understands everything: *They paid him off! They gave him money not to marry her!*

She reels over, flimsy, insubstantial with shock. Perhaps she will allow herself to drift down into the mire, and lie there like a heap of discarded clothes . . .

'Miss Hobhouse!'

Someone is running after her and calling her name laughingly. She pulls herself upright; she expels the moan that has broken from her lips and fills her lungs with foetid air; her concentration is ferocious. She drives back Mr Jackson, the fountains, the forbidding faces of her relations, the unworn wedding dress; her body stiffens in triumph.

Sarah reaches Emily at last. Why is Miss Hobhouse staring into space like that, her hands fisted, her skirt and jacket smeared with mud? 'Goodness, Miss Hobhouse, you're miles away!' she exclaims.

Emily turns to her, at first without recognition. She appears not to know where she is. Then a faint smile breaks across her face; her eyes dimly register the face of the young nurse who stares at her with such anxiety.

'You can see I have taken a tumble.' Miss Hobhouse's voice is shrill but strong. She brushes her fingers over the fast-drying sludge on her skirt. 'We really must get Captain Hume to do something about this mud, it's lethal. I'm so sorry to keep the committee waiting. Have you ever eaten anything actually cooked in these three-legged pots? They seem to be used as dustbins or buckets or obstacles for silly women like me to trip over. Thank you so much for finding me. Perhaps the sun has gone to my head after all, just as some less charitable citizens of Bloemfontein have suggested.'

Yet in the midst of her frantic chatter her brain is calm. Now that she understands the mystery of his disappearance she can despise him fully. The last vestige of physical longing for him lies in the mud, shed from her heart like a snakeskin which will never grow again. A delicious feeling of relief unfolds through her body, warm as sunshine. She places her arm round the young nurse's shoulder and, to Sarah's astonishment, murmurs, 'Sister Palmer, I hope you will marry a man who deserves you.'

Bloemfontein Concentration Camp, 21 April

Lizzie has been returned to her mother for several weeks now. Things have not gone well; once again the child has drastically lost weight and displayed symptoms of her former mysterious illnesses. In this she is no different from a thousand children in the camp, but the suspicions of Dr Phillips and the children's nurses have grown to accusations, and it is rumoured that Mrs van Zyl will be criminally charged for the deliberate starvation of her child.

Yesterday Miss Hobhouse had arranged for photographs to be taken of skeletal children, which she plans to display to the British Public to make them realise where the brunt of war is most heavily falling. During the session with Lizzie, Mrs van Zyl is once again at the washing-dam, but her two other daughters try to arrange Lizzie's hair and nightdress so that the little girl, whose body has been reduced to skeleton and skin, will look pretty in her photograph. The child's life seems actually to be ebbing away before the camera lens. While the appalled photographer buries himself in his black cloth, the familiar wandering minstrel whistle and the thud of hooves announce the arrival of Dr Phillips himself. Miss Hobhouse silences him as he peers into the tent, an expression of deep cynicism engraved on his ruddy features. When the photographic session is over and Lizzie's flower-stalk limbs are wrapped up in the little blanket provided by Emily from the Fund, the doctor calls out in a mocking voice, 'Miss Hobhouse, may I have a word with you outside, please?'

Emily flashes him a contemptuous look. 'I happen to be speaking to Lizzie,' she says dismissively. 'Or rather' – her voice softens as she smiles – 'Lizzie is speaking to me.'

A drift of cigar smoke enters the tent. 'That's all right,' says Dr Phillips. He whistles another bar to show he has plenty of time. 'I'll wait out here.'

Lizzie is indeed speaking to Emily, though it is astonishing that her frail body can produce the energy required for speech. In her arms lies the little rag doll Emily had given her a few weeks before 'Auntie gave me this dolly,' she whispers, her huge eyes appearing to double in size as she speaks. 'Now auntie must give the other children dollies too.'

Emily strokes the little girl's thin hair while her sisters cluster round. 'Does your dolly have a name?' she enquires in her careful Dutch.

A smile trembles on the child's dark lips. 'I call her Miss Emily!' she exclaims, then breaks into a fit of choking.

'I'll leave now.' Miss Hobhouse touches the arm of a sister who is clutching Lizzie's hand. 'I think you should call your mother.'

Dr Phillips is waiting outside the tent, a cigar in one hand, the reins of his horse in the other. 'Seeing you plan to unleash photographs of dying children on the innocent British public, I thought you might like to know the true details of this case.' His horse tosses its head impatiently.

Miss Hobhouse lifts her chin and stretches her neck. 'Dr Phillips, do you speak Dutch?' She might have been the late queen speaking to her footman, thinks the doctor, wincing.

'I don't believe English people are expected to know that language,' he says coolly. 'There is no reason.'

'I think there is every reason for English people to speak Dutch,' replies Her Majesty. 'Specially for English doctors in Boer concentration camps, so that they may understand the symptoms of their patients.'

'I don't need to speak Dutch to understand what I can see with my eyes: filth, sloth, indolence, superstition!' In spite of his resolutions to remain languidly cynical he feels his temper rise. 'And in this case, deliberate cruelty inflicted by a mother!'

'On what grounds' – oh, how the ice in her voice would make a lesser man shiver – 'do you adopt this opinion?'

'The neighbours. They speak English.' The doctor shrugs. 'They say so. They've heard the child cry out for food. The mother did nothing. The child was in a filthy state. The mother did nothing. But worse than that—'

'I have heard enough from you, Dr Phillips, to believe that you are breaking your Hippocratic oath.' Emily's voice cuts through the bell tents. 'May I inform you that I have very considerable connections within the government of Great Britain, and I will not hesitate to report your libellous opinions if I hear them expressed again.' She adopts a different tone. 'You know perfectly well that malnutrition and disease are the causes of Lizzie's present condition.'

'Worse than that,' splutters the doctor, inserting his foot into the stirrup and swinging himself into his saddle, 'she's been seen to feed the child on her own faeces! Is that good enough for you, Miss High and Mighty Hobhouse? Go and tell *that* to the government of Great Britain!' And digging his heels into the horse's flanks he canters off towards the army camp, trailing behind him a defiant minstrel-whistle song to disguise his fury.

It is at this point that Sarah arrives with a basketful of carrots and spinach, and a bowl of fresh eggs. She runs towards Emily, having heard something of this exchange as she approached. Miss Hobhouse is trembling. Her back straighter than ever, her jaw clenched, she is magnificent in her outrage. 'How *dare* he!' Her voice has sunk a whole octave. 'How *dare* he!'

'What has happened?' cries Sarah.

'That doctor —' begins Emily, but now Mrs Botha is running up to them, her solid features distorted by anguish.

'*It's Poppie! Poppie is dead*! She caught the enteric and died within days!'

'No!' shouts Sarah. 'It can't be true!' Only last week she had seen Poppie, not well, admittedly, but with a clear bill of health from Dr Phillips. And pushing the vegetables into the hands of the Van Zyl sisters, she rushes to the enteric ward, with Emily not far behind.

Dear Aunt Mary,

   . . . Yesterday I had lunch with Colonel Goold-Adams and
he was, as always, very agreeable. But he tells me that more
and more are coming in. A new sweeping movement has
begun, resulting in hundreds and thousands of these unfortunate people either crowding into already crowded camps or
else being dumped down to form a new one where nothing is at
hand to shelter them. Colonel Adams says, what can he do?
The General wires 'Expect 500 or 1000 at such a place' – and
he has nothing to send there to provide for them. He being
wholly out of tents, has sent to Port Elizabeth and had thirty
shelters made of sorts, and there they lie, he can't even get them
up. And I told him I wasn't surprised for I don't believe all his
power as a Deputy Administrator (and that is not much) would
get things sent up unless he went and stood in the goods yards
himself and saw the trucks packed, as I found necessary in
Cape Town or I should never have got a garment north.

   About food too – the Superintendent of a camp is getting in
rations for such and such a number and suddenly 500 more
mouths are thrust upon him and things won't go round. No
wonder sickness abounds. There have been sixty-two deaths
in the camp [in six weeks] and the doctor himself is down with
enteric.

Two of the Boer girls we trained as nurses and who were doing good work are dead too. One of them, Poppie Naudé, was a universal favourite. She did not know where her mother was. Her father was in Norvals Pont and there had been some talk of my taking her to join him; but in the end she thought she was doing useful work where she was, earning two shillings a day, and had better stay and nurse the people in the Bloemfontein Camp . . . The doctor, the nurse and all had said, 'We can't spare Poppie'.

The Government clothing about which they made so much noise has hitherto come to nothing. I formed, as agreed, the committees; the camp was divided into sections, the minimum required was noted down and the total requisitioned for. There it has come to a full stop. Thus had it not been for our clothing, things would have been bad indeed.

Your loving E.H.

Bloemfontein Concentration Camp, April 1901

On the night of 30 April, Miss Hobhouse receives news that a berth has been found for her in a first class cabin on RMS *Saxon* which is due to leave in a few days' time. What is more, the *Saxon* will carry Sir Alfred Milner back to Southampton, where he will be met in full splendour by the new King – who refuses to be crowned till the war is over. Sir Alfred is to receive a peerage in return for his role in the war: he will assume the title Lord Milner of St James and of Cape Town, and will have even more power over the Colonial and War Offices. (The citizens of Cape Town are bemused; St James is a small seaside resort much beloved by children and entirely lacking in gravitas.) In her mind, Emily has already cornered Sir Alfred on the upper deck and made him promise to speak to the Colonial Office about the sweeping changes needed to save children's lives in the camps . . . but first she must arrange a train to Cape Town as quickly as possible – tomorrow, if she can pull the right strings. She has warned everyone of her imminent departure but that evening will suddenly be her last and she must, at the very least, say good-bye to the tent committee members.

She makes her way towards Mrs Botha's tent, taking care not to trip over three-legged pots. She is received lovingly; she assures everyone she is leaving only so that she might arouse the sympathy and support of public opinion; she will show the photographs of Lizzie and others to the newspapers so that a committee of women – including herself, preferably – might be sent out by the Colonial Office to formally investigate camp conditions so that the lives of tens of thousands of Boer and Black women and children might be saved; that she will return in October, whatever happens. Mrs Botha embraces her; uninhibited tears run down the Boer woman's cheeks, already deeply furrowed.

Then Emily races across the camp to the staff living quarters. It is dark by now, but at least the aisles between the tents are clear. Nevertheless she is careful, the collision with the young trooper suddenly thrusting itself into her mind as she hastens on. She stops to ask a passing Red Cross nurse for directions.

An almost maternal love for Nurse Palmer has slowly bloomed in her heart, unnoticed at first, but nurtured and warmed by the young nurse's steadfast devotion. This is the daughter Miss Hobhouse would love to have produced for mankind: selfless, gentle, loyal and – if possible – beautiful. When she returns to South Africa in a few months' time, Sarah will be there for her, of this she has no doubt, but her daughter-disciple must not make the near-fatal mistake she herself had made: she must never jettison her life's work for the sake of an undeserving man. No doubt she will succumb to marriage, but perhaps Emily can help her choose a worthy husband.

These thoughts and plans spin through her mind as she makes her way towards Sarah's tent. She looks forward to the warmth of their farewell: perhaps they might embrace and shed a few tears, but if the young nurse is asleep she must not be woken, not even to say a final goodbye. Nurse Palmer must conserve her energies for the great task she has set herself . . .

Kitchener to Roberts, 19 July 1901
I see a number of ladies are coming out, I hope it will calm the agitators in England. I doubt there being much for them to do here as the camps are very well looked after.

Cape Town, October 1901

On the evening of Sunday, 31 October, three orderlies are called from the Green Point military hospital to make up a stretcher party. It has become necessary to carry an hysterical Englishwoman from the *Avondale Castle*, anchored in Table Bay, to the hospital ship *Roslin*, about to return to Southampton.

Orderly Patrick Donnelly is annoyed. His uncle, Jack Simmonds, is over from the Island to help prepare for his mother's arrival next week – and for his wedding. The taciturn doctor had clearly resolved to help his sister and nephew to the very best of his ability; he had, for example, recently bought Frangipani Villa, which was large enough for everyone, even Sarah's madcap friend Louise, now in an advanced state of pregnancy. The two women had moved into the house only last week, and tonight he would have enjoyed a celebratory meal. But he is still on parole after the tent episode in Bloemfontein, and has no option but to obey the sudden, inconvenient orders.

Nearly six months have passed since their expulsion from Bloemfontein. Sarah still weeps every day over the shocking loss of Miss Hobhouse, as she has no doubt that the Englishwoman had reported their love-making to Goold-Adams – at least two women had seen her on her way to Sarah's tent on the night before she left for Cape Town. Patch himself has long since got over the disgrace of being demoted to orderly, and as the weeks have passed, has found himself actually enjoying the work: having spent so much time in hospitals as the passive patient, he takes some satisfaction in assuming a busy active role in administering to the needs of sick and wounded troopers. Perhaps he might even train to be a doctor one day, if he can get the educational qualifications – he certainly knows more than most about enteric and dysentery.

Occasionally he sees his green-eyed son who, for the time being, is living with his grandmother in the District. At first Mrs Witbooi had been resentful, but has softened since meeting Sarah. Sometimes he plays the music box for the child, and croons the melancholy words, *there's no place like home* – and you're a lucky boy to be getting a home, as well as a new mother and granny. The child sways blissfully to the music. He is learning to walk, and Patch can already sense his own easy saunter in his son's toddling. Not that there is much of the saunter left in himself. His thigh wound aches in the damp Cape winter, causing him to walk warily. To him, one leg feels shorter than the other, though to everyone else only the slightest limp is visible. Yet even Sarah had to admit that some of the jauntiness was gone; now there was no slithering of the hips or shoulders, such as first drew her to him. In fact, she has become aware that a certain ponderousness is beginning to prevail, perhaps as his confrontations with death and dying begin to take their toll mentally. She had had to gently interrupt as he told the story of Cronje's laager yet again: his conversation is weighted down with war.

As for the wedding, Sarah was determined to be married in the church of Our Lady of Mercy, with the nuns dancing around in delight; even Sister Madeleine, who seemed to have forgotten about the beatings and punishments and now declared him to be a fine young man. How longingly she gazed at the froth of Sarah's wedding dress, as if trying to imagine how she herself would look in trails of white lace and tulle. Well, Patch has a surprise lined up for them for the actual ceremony: across the black frock coat, which Uncle Jack has bought him for the occasion, an orange and purple sash will be draped, with all its Presbyterian eyes and ladders and open Bibles on full display, right in the heart of the Papist church. In this way Bill would be his Best Man, for he was the best man Patch had ever met, in spite of the Orange marches and kick-the-Pope bands. Most probably Sarah, newly converted, will be shocked, but not as shocked as those so-called Sisters of Mercy, who might have to call in an exorcist or someone to decontaminate the church afterwards.

On his first day off he had taken his bride-to-be to the Island. Uncle Jack and he shook hands solemnly then set off for the English Country Garden. How often had his mind feasted on this square of brilliance in the midst of desolation. Now, to see the real thing was an agonised joy but a mismatch with his fantasy. The garden was not as well-kept as he had imagined: there were bare patches, dry leaves; a certain carelessness about the place that he didn't remember. The lawn at least was thriving, and the vegetable plot had been carefully tended – just look at the size of that cauliflower!

Uncle Jack had prepared Mary Donnelly for their visit but there was no sign of her. Sarah, lovely as a flower herself, pressed Patch's hand. He opened the gate, which still meowed like a sick cat. To think that it still meowed after all he had been through – battles, illness, scorched earth, deaths, concentration camp; how utterly his life had changed, yet the gate still meowed as if nothing but his mother's simple life and the bad island weather had happened in the last two years. And, for a moment, that plaintive sound deleted all those tragedies and he felt himself transform into his boyish self of two years ago, with all the innocence that had since evaporated.

He tried to hold the lightness of that feeling as they entered the garden and moved slowly down its central path. Sarah exclaimed in delight at the roses and lavender, which exhaled perfumes soothing to her hidden agitation. For her, too, the occasion was momentous – a preparation for the bridal journey up the aisle, strewn with petals. In the roar of the wind lurked exultant organ chords, but also those strange words of Miss Hobhouse: *I hope you marry a man who deserves you.* What on earth had made her say that out of the blue, after tripping over a three-legged pot? Quickly Sarah dismissed thoughts of Miss Hobhouse before her heart sank with sorrow, and tried to focus on the meeting that lay ahead.

At the ramshackle front door – the house was no more than a hut, after all – attempts had been made to disguise the deficiency of paint and woodwork by the bright petals of a climbing rose. *Souvenir de la Malmaison!* cried Sarah in delight. Patch, bending his head beneath the tangle of blooms, knocked on the closed front door. 'It's always been open before,' he murmured fretfully.

It seemed there was no one there. The silence inside the hut was thick as mud. 'I told her you were coming.' Even Uncle Jack sounded querulous.

On impulse, Sarah slipped round the side of the little dwelling. The garden was everywhere, miraculously crowded with blooms that belonged to conflicting seasons: hollyhocks, snapdragons, white arum lilies, purple irises, obeying their own impulses and those of their gardener. In the far distance, over the high hedge, the trio of mainland mountains shimmered misty blue, like the pale silk of her evening gown.

A woman was sitting on a bench behind the house, flowers growing rampant all around her. She wore a loose crimson robe, her grey hair was tied up. In her lap lay a bouquet of roses. She did not move. From where Sarah stood a *tromp l'oeil* occurred as medieval portraits sprang to mind: the mountains appeared to be draped over the woman's shoulders. She was smoking a cigarette with the remaining fingers of one hand, inhaling abruptly. Sarah froze, then jumped as an arm encircled her waist. Patch pulled her close and she could feel his warmth and the shape of his body even through their thick clothes.

'Mother!' he called. The woman did not turn her head. 'Mother, I have brought you a daughter.'

Mrs Donnelly dropped her cigarette and ground it into the soil with her shoe. She rose from the bench, brushing ash from her robe, the roses a medley of brilliant colours in the crook of her arm. 'These are for you,' she said in her hoarse voice.

And it was the daughter, not the son, who stepped forward and kissed the leper mother's cheeks. Then Patch soundlessly enclosed the two women in his arms; they remained so entwined till Uncle Jack came to find them.

Now the months had passed and Sarah and Louise were preparing a room in Frangipani Villa for the arrival of his mother next week. Uncle Jack would bring her to the house and they'd have a welcome-home meal which everyone loved: Irish Stew with rice; a treat, because mutton was hard to come by these days. There was an argument about whether carrots were allowed but Mrs Donnelly, being the only one who had actually lived in Ireland, had the final say: there are no carrots in Irish Stew.

Patch would eventually be living in a house full of females, what with Louise there as well, but at least she'd calmed down a bit and joined a group of women who made comforts for the exiled Boers in Ceylon. Sarah was carrying on in bossy Miss Hobhouse's footsteps in spite of the old maid's treachery. (He felt a personal distaste for the woman, not that he'd ever met her, or even seen her, as far as he knew.) Sarah had continued to show an interest in the fate of the Boer women, and had formed a friendship with Mrs Roos after that formidable woman and her sons were allowed to join her sister in Cape Town. When the Ladies' Commission led by Mrs Fawcett arrived to inspect the camps, Sarah had been puzzled and disappointed that Miss Hobhouse was not among them. She made an appointment to speak to Dr Jane Waterston, a member of the commission who had very firm views about the 'hysterical whining', as she put it, which was going on among the pro-Boers in England. Sarah was anxious to tell this woman doctor about her own experiences in the Bloemfontein camp and the crucial role played by Miss Hobhouse, but Dr Waterston was interested only in voicing her own opinions. 'This war has been remarkable for two things,' she said. 'First, the small regard that the Boers from the highest to the lowest have had for their womenkind, and secondly, the great care and consideration the British have had for the same, very often ungrateful, women.'

Sarah stared at her in disbelief. 'But I was there,' she said. 'I *saw* what was happening.'

'You fell under the spell of that Hobhouse woman!' snapped Dr Waterston. 'She could make one believe black was white if she wanted. She told those Boer women they were being treated badly and although they knew how well they were being cared for, they believed her of course.'

'The presence of the concentration camps has in every way violated the articles of the Hague Convention,' said Sarah coldly. She could even quote chapter and verse. 'Good day to you, Dr Waterston. It is a pity that you cannot feel as strongly about the suffering of the inmates of the camps as you do about their hygiene,' she finished, and went straight out and joined the Cape Conciliation Committee. She and Mrs Roos seemed to spend most of their time collecting clothes for the camp women and children, and going to meetings. Though this was not quite what he expected from his wife-to-be, Patch felt sure this phase would pass – especially when she started producing his children. That was what women were meant to be: mothers, not political firebrands.

Milner's Journal, August 1901, after the inspection visit of the Ladies' Commission

In considering the steps necessary for improving the health of the camps, we now have the benefit of the experience of the Ladies' Committee . . . They have furnished notes on the condition of the great majority of the camps, and it is evident that they have subjected them to a most careful investigation. Their suggestions must, I think, strike everyone as both thorough and practical and we have much cause to be grateful to them for the reasonable spirit in which they have approached their task. I think a very grave responsibility would rest upon us if any one of these suggestions were not acted upon, except there was some insuperable physical obstacle to carrying it out.

Cape Town, 31 October 1901

Once aboard the *Avondale Castle*, Patch and the other members of the stretcher party drained their faces of any expression as they took up their positions on either side of the saloon door – to prevent escape of the mad woman, presumably? The Colonel came stamping through, fit to explode. Without altering their gazes they listened to him exclaim, in splintered tones, to the person hidden in the sofa: 'Now, Miss Hobhouse, you have had the scene you wanted. I am now obliged to arrest you forcibly under martial law.'

Miss Hobhouse! Patch felt his face flush violently. Was she going to follow him everywhere? Well, he might have guessed that the old harridan would stir up this sort of trouble. Best not to tell Sarah about it or she'd get even more tearful about things.

A weak but authoritative voice answered (sending shivers down Patch's rigidly straightened vertebrae), 'They may take my baggage but they will not take me.'

To which Colonel Williamson replied coldly, 'I am not here to argue. I cannot listen. I will touch you on the shoulder – that will be sufficient for the purpose. Will you yield of your own free will? Otherwise I have soldiers ready.' But already he sounded uneasy.

At this Patch darted a look in the direction of the sofa, expecting at the very least to see a plume of smoke rise from it.

'I will not go one step voluntarily towards the *Roslin Castle*. I am ill and need rest. I beg you to leave me.' This request was uttered in tones that were either haughty or filled with pathos, Patch could not decide which.

'Madam,' beseeched the Colonel, 'surely you do not wish to be taken like a *lunatic*?' The word burst from his mouth as if it had been hiding there for years and had finally escaped.

'Sir,' replied she, ready for this, 'the lunacy is on your side and with those who obey.' Her voice became infused with poisonous mockery. 'If, in addition to being an officer you also happen to be a gentleman, you will go and leave me alone.'

Colonel Williamson's voice turned cold as steel. 'Madam,' he intoned, 'I therefore have no option but to call over the soldiers.'

At a signal Patch and Perkins moved over to the sofa upon which Miss Hobhouse was draped, a shawl covering her lower half. Although she was no more than a pale invalid whose exhaustion threatened to seep into his own young limbs, Patch felt a stir of recognition – almost as if he had once experienced some form of intimacy with her. It was hard to believe she had once radiated fearsome energy and efficiency in the Orange River Colony camps; she looked as if she couldn't harm a fly right now!

The two orderlies stood uncertainly over her, awaiting a further signal from the Colonel. Patch had been reading a book about a convict and a small boy who met an old lady in an ancient wedding dress all covered in cobwebs, and there was something of that Miss Someone in the wraith-like Miss Hobhouse.

'Take her,' said the Colonel wearily.

The men bent over. Miss Hobhouse's body electrified with screams. 'You will not do this thing! You would not treat your mothers or wives or sisters so! There is a Higher Law – you cannot, you *dare* not, obey these orders!'

We dare not *not* obey, thought Patch grimly, though it was true he would not have treated his mother so (now that he *had* a mother) but now they were lifting her in her shawl from her resting place. Her screams turned to shrieks.

'You are disgracing your uniform by obeying such an order! A Higher Law forbids you! The laws of God and Humanity forbid you! Colonel Williamson, you will rue this to your dying day, you will all rue it . . . *you brutes, you dare touch me!*'

The invalid had surprising strength as they lifted her, and almost immediately struggled out of their grasp and planted her feet on the cabin floor. But they were prepared for this and, grabbing her shawl, wound it about her arms so that she could not struggle. 'Be careful, be careful, don't hurt the lady!' called the Colonel, sounding anxious, but he came to help them lift her off her feet until she lay all her length like a swaddled baby, helpless in their arms.

At this humiliation she gave out a terrible cry, quite unlike her previous screams. *Christ on the cross*, thought Patch, his heart contracting. *Father, oh Father, why hast thou forsaken me?* Now they placed her, still struggling and sobbing, into a Madeira chair on the deck and carried her, straitjacketed in her own shawl, down the steps into the waiting launch.

Emily Hobhouse stopped screaming. As if awakening from a nightmare, she sat suddenly upright in her chair and stared ahead in silence, the panic in her eyes gradually metamorphosing into dull sorrow. The launch wove its way in silence among the waiting boats. Wavelets threatened to explode on its deck. There was nothing for anyone to say – they could have been strangers bobbing in the middle of the ocean, each numbed by the aftermath of panic.

Low growls greeted them as they disembarked, for a crowd of rough-looking men had gathered to enjoy the spectacle. Patch and Perkins carried their load through hooting and hissing men all the way to the carriage which awaited them. '*Canting old hypocrite! Serves her right! Sousing in salt water would do her good!*' Miss Hobhouse seemed to have entered another world. She was beginning to collapse, Patch could see that, her head lolling to one side, her face empty of any expression.

Two colonial nurses stood ready at the carriage door, their faces contorted with disgust. Without greeting the men, whom they clearly held responsible for this maltreatment, they bundled Miss Hobhouse in to the vehicle, murmuring in sympathy as they tried to undo the knot in her shawl, but it was too tightly tied. Patch curved the top part of his long body into the carriage interior and gently unwound the shawl. Once again he had that curious sense of intimacy, as if he was actually undressing this trembling old spinster. Miss Hobhouse's impassive gaze passed across his young face. Then returned to hover. From a great distance a light began to burn in the dullness of her eyes.

'You – I – we . . .' She seemed to have forgotten how to speak.

'Yes, ma'am?'

'You – you have grown a moustache,' she whispered. The astonished words toppled out of her mouth

Patch's finger flew to the new growth above his lip. He frowned uncertainly.

'You know the lady then?' snapped one of the nurses.

'Mind your own business,' he snapped back. Miss Hobhouse was staring at him as if he was her long lost someone.

'What are you doing here?' The chain of words was so faint he had to bend his ear right over her mouth.

A thousand replies, not all of them courteous, swam into Patch's head. From the range of possibilities he picked out the one which might most interest her. 'I am about to get married, ma'am.' It was like speaking to someone on their deathbed.

'Ah!' She smiled timidly. 'Is she – is she someone I know?'

'Miss Sarah Palmer, ma'am. Formerly *Sister* Palmer,' he added sternly, to let her know.

Miss Hobhouse closed her eyes. Her face grew soft. 'This is wonderful news,' she murmured. Her voice was suddenly melodious. 'Dear Sister Palmer. I had so hoped to see her now.' A long pause followed as she constructed a new sentence in her swimming head. Then: 'Will you give her a message from me?'

'Yes, ma'am.' Where was Colonel Williamson? He'd get into trouble if he was caught taking messages from a prisoner.

'Tell her I shall be back. When this dreadful war has ended.' She fell silent as the image of Lizzie loomed. With a sudden burst of energy she added, 'There will be so much to do when the women return to their burnt-out homes.'

'That's enough now, Miss Hobhouse,' exclaimed one of the nurses, who had no sympathy with burnt-out homes. 'We have to go now. The *Roslin* will be leaving any minute and we're all going with her.'

Patch ignored this outburst. His lips were still near the ear of Miss Hobhouse, a pretty ear, untouched by age. 'I will give her your message,' he said. He almost wanted to apologise for the improvised straitjacket.

Footsteps ran up to the carriage. 'What, still here?' Colonel Williamson's voice cried out. 'You'll miss the boat, the launch won't wait any longer! Get out of the carriage, Orderly Donnelly.'

'Goodbye,' mouthed Miss Hobhouse as Patch slid away. The driver cracked his whip. And as the nurses slammed the carriage doors, it seemed as if the phantom of that waiting woman was drifting upwards, her crumbling wedding cake and cobwebbed marriage robes melting and diminishing into the darkness of the night.

'What was that all about?' sniggered Perkins. 'Got the hots for her, have you, Patch? Saw her frillies, did you?'

'Shut your mouth!' Patch flushed. 'The woman's a lady, not that you'd know one if she spoke to you.'

Miss Hobhouse's perfume had settled in his nostrils. Its musky fragrance smelt of foreign lands, and remained with him for some time.

Bloemfontein Concentration Camp, November 1901

Dr Phillips whistles his minstrel melody more penetratingly than usual as he rides through the Bloemfontein concentration camp, or *internment* camp, as some would now have it. He is experiencing the pleasant sensation of double-revenge. Both revenges concern toffee-nosed women who thought they knew better than he about Lizzie van Zyl.

He has heard of the disgrace of Miss Hobhouse's deportation and he rejoices. That'll show her, that do-gooding, pro-Boer busybody, speaking to him as if he were no more than her lackey. He chuckles as he remembers the furore over Lizzie when the child eventually died in May. The scandal had even reached the British House of Commons and Mr Chamberlain had made a speech denying that the child was emaciated as a result of life in the camp: she had looked emaciated when she'd arrived from the farm! Chamberlain had also claimed that a British doctor had taken the photograph as evidence in the criminal trial of the child's mother, and Conan Doyle had supported this view in a leaflet he'd written about it all. That'll teach Miss Emily Hobhouse to go round showing photographs of dying children to the British Public in the hope of stirring up pro-Boer feelings! And now, glory of glories, she'd been dragged kicking and screaming from one boat and taken by force on to another, so unwanted was she in the Cape. Dr Phillips briefly relives the shiver that Miss Hoity-Toity had caused to ripple through his flesh with her disdainful dismissal of his opinions. Never mind that she is idolised by the Boer women, she's got what she deserves now – ignominy!

As for that other woman, that high and mighty nurse who shrunk away when he came near her, she got what was coming to her as well – accusing him of libel in that well-bred voice. He'd kept his ears and eyes open since that day outside the Van Zyl tent, and during the course of his wanderings over the next few weeks he'd seen the wench in blushing conversation with that tall, green-eyed, limping trooper and sent his spies out. His industry had been rewarded. On the same night that the Hobhouse hag had left Bloemfontein, he'd received word from an orderly that something was going on; something worth following up . . .

Dr Phillips does not whistle his minstrel song as he harnesses his horse some distance away and creeps to the golden glow of the tent. And sure enough, on application of his eye to one of the holes in the canvas, raw licentiousness is revealed! Dr Phillips' eye stays longer at the canvas hole than is necessary for mere identification; it is with reluctance that he withdraws and makes his way to Colonel Goold-Adams. Together they return to the tent, where the couple are discovered in the fullness of *flagrante*, just as he'd reported. To his disappointment Goold-Adams decides not to disturb them then and there, but the following morning both are summoned to his office and expelled from the camp.

Goold-Adams is flustered about the affair, specially when he realises the pretty nurse is a favourite of Miss Hobhouse. How extraordinary that this demure young woman, the model of propriety – even saintliness, given the demanding nature of her work – should descend to the behaviour of a prostitute. Miss Hobhouse need never know. It is not the sort of thing one discusses with women, in any case. But he has no doubt she would agree with him that, at all costs, immorality must be rooted out of a concentration camp designed to protect women and children.

Mrs Mopeli is waiting outside the children's ward in the centre of the white people's camp. Strapped to her back is her little niece, Nyanga; in her hand she has a gift for Sister Palmer, a bangle of beadwork made by the child's mother, her sister.

She waits, but Sarah does not emerge from the hot pounding ward. Mrs Mopeli hums. She is used to waiting.

The child on her back whimpers. She begins to chant a husky lullaby, then turns away and strolls back to her camp, still crooning softly.

Epilogue

Lord Milner to Mr Chamberlain, 7 December 1901
. . . The black spot – the one very black spot – in the picture is the frightful mortality in the Concentration Camps. I entirely agree with you in thinking that while a hundred explanations may be offered and a hundred excuses made, they do not really amount to an adequate defence. I should much prefer to say at once, as far as the Civil authorities are concerned, that we were suddenly confronted with a problem not of our making, with which it was beyond our power properly to grapple. And no doubt its vastness was not realised soon enough . . . The whole thing, I think now, has been a mistake.

Afterword

448,435 white soldiers and 30,000 blacks fought on the side of the British

75,000 men fought on the side of the Boers

27,927 white men, women and children died in the concentration camps

22,074 were children under the age of 16

4,177 were women over the age of 16

Probably 20,000 blacks died in the concentration camps, of whom 81 percent were children

Ten percent of the Boer population of the two republics died during the war

A NOTE ON THE AUTHOR

Ann Harries was born and educated in Cape Town, where she worked in township schools and community centres. On moving to England she became active in the anti-apartheid movement. The author of the acclaimed *Manly Pursuits*, she divides her time between the Cotswolds and South Africa.

Also Available by Ann Harries

Manly Pursuits

'Outstanding . . . Funny, well observed and beautifully written' *Sunday Times*

Cape Town, 1899. Diamond tycoon Cecil Rhodes believes that he has only months to live, and that the only thing that can save him is the sound of English birdsong. He recruits Francis Wills to transport 200 birds to Cape Town, but on arrival the birds refuse to sing. This is but the first obstacle for Wills, who finds himself irresistibly drawn to intrigue, in a country on the brink of war.

'History is ingeniously rewritten in this witty and engaging novel' J. M. Coetzee

'I haven't turned any pages faster this year than I turned these' *Spectator*

'Both an entertaining read and a richly evocative portrait of an era' *Observer*

Buy this book at www.bloomsbury.com/annharries